WATCHER'S WEB

RETURN OF THE AGHYRIANS BOOK 1

PATTY JANSEN

CAPRICORNICA PUBLICATIONS

GET FREE EBOOKS

DID YOU KNOW?

Watcher's Web is also available in audio. Visit pattyjansen.com to find out more

1

WHEREVER JESSICA went, people watched her. Like those two teenage boys leaning on the fence, Akubra hats pulled down to shade their eyes. One of them dangled a cigarette in careless fingers; the other swigged beer from a stubby. Neither was watching her now, but she hadn't missed their gawking, nor their voices barely elevated over the noise of bellowing cattle, shouts and truck engines.

Wow! See that really tall one?

Bloody hell, yeah.

How'd you reckon she kisses a guy? On her knees?

They laughed and, when she came closer, faced the yard to watch the cattle as if they had said nothing.

Jessica walked past them to the gate, glaring at their straw-covered backs. *Well, I bloody heard you.* She was used to it, anyway.

It hadn't been the worst thing people said about her. They hadn't said the words ugly, or creepy, or *freak*, but she was used to hearing those words, too.

They went into a little hard spot inside her where she scrunched up the hurt and forgot it. She might look like a freak, but when she helped John Braithwaite and his mates from the Rivervale Stud Farm at a cattle show and Angus went into one of his fits, they still needed her to get him into the truck without spooking him. No one else could do that. No one knew how she did it, and no one should ever know. Because no one was crazy enough to get into a pen with a stroppy bull, right?

Well, we'll see about that.

She grasped the top of the gate with both hands, stepped onto the middle bar and swung her foot over. Jumped. Landed in sun-baked mud churned with cloven hoof prints and cow pats.

At least when Angus looked at her he didn't hide his dislike. He rolled a beady eye and blew a gust of hay-scented air from his nostrils. He stiffened, all fifteen-hundred-odd kilograms of Brahman bull-flesh of him. Then lowered his head, horns poised.

Someone yelled, "Watch it!"

No, he wasn't going to charge. He'd charge at the boys, he'd even charge at his well-heeled owner, but never at her. Call her arrogant, but she knew that; and how she knew it would remain a secret, too, thank you very much.

She stopped a few paces inside the pen and crossed her arms over her chest. Well, bugger that. She had a bloody audience. About twenty people, mostly men, sitting on the fence, with cynical hey-look-at-this-mate expressions plastered on their faces.

Beef cattle farmers, their lackeys and other hangers-on, those clowns who had partied in the pavilion last night, those who owned the bulls that had occupied the pens next to Angus'. All their animals were already in the trucks, ready to be taken home from the Pymberton show. None of them with a "best of show" ribbon, like Angus, and none with a diva mentality.

It looked like the boys had been trying to get Angus to move for a while. The gate on the opposite side of the pen was open, the ramp in place. Brendan held the door to the truck, ready to slam it. Everything about his expression said, *rather you than me*. The coward.

"Come on, Angus, in you go."

Men sniggered, including the two teenage boys. The one with the cigarette flicked ash into the pen and said something about a whip.

Now who was more stupid? Them or the bull? You did *not* frighten such a prize animal if you could help it. He might bolt and injure himself. An unsightly gash would take him off the show circuit for months. Sheesh!

Jessica reached through the fence into the bucket she had dumped there. Her hand came away black and sticky with molasses. Angus loved it.

She inched closer, holding out her hand *Come on, look me in the eye, if you dare.*

Angus blew out another snort, as if he knew what was coming. Backed into the fence. Met her eyes.

Jessica exhaled. Her breath seeped from her in tendrils of sparkle-filled mist, which sought out Angus' fur and crept over his grey-mottled back, a bit like glitter-glue, but *alive*.

Jessica lunged for the rope that dangled from Angus' collar. She couldn't quite reach it, and while Angus backed further away from her, scraping along the fence, he planted his hoof on the end of the rope, squashing it neatly in a fresh pile of dung. Just her luck.

A bit closer.

She pulled the mist tighter around him, so his coat sparkled and glittered with lights. His outline became fuzzy. She didn't know what to call it, and had learned not to talk about it to anyone. It wasn't that she could communicate with him, but she could tell him what to do. Sort of. In a weird way she couldn't explain in words. The mist soaked up emotions, as far as bulls have emotions, and dampened them, and she could override them with her own. If it worked.

Her audience had stopped talking. Anyone who watched always did that, even though they couldn't see the mist and didn't realise it influenced them, although not as much as it affected the animal. That was just as well, because she was making an idiot of herself. Angus was being bloody stubborn, his head still lowered, trampling the rope further into the shit. Something must have spooked him badly. Maybe it was the yapping from the dog pavilion. Well, she and Angus seemed to have something in common—she didn't like lap dogs either.

But he was going to get into that bloody truck, preferably before she missed her flight back to Sydney. All kinds of hell would break loose if she wasn't at the school basketball team meeting that night.

Jessica focused on Angus' beady eye and let out another deep breath. More sparkling vapour flowed. Pinpricks of light soaked into Angus' mottled fur. Angus relaxed, stuck out his head to nuzzle her molasses-covered hand.

But then . . .

The threads solidified and the mist spun into tightly-coiled cords, which wove into a formation like a spider's web.

What the hell. . . ?

She froze, staring at the writhing construction. It looked like someone had cast a living net over the bull, one made of sparkling mist that yanked and stretched of its own volition, or . . . as if something pulled at the other end. There were shadows in a nebulous space over Angus' back, and a male voice, just outside the edge of hearing, calling out to someone. The web vibrated and strained.

A tug of war between herself and . . . Who was pulling the other end?

In her panic, she broke loose from the construction. The shadows at the other end of the web faded. The strands dissolved into mist once more.

A wet nose touched her palm and Angus' rasping tongue curled around her wrist. The molasses was clean licked-off, but he probably liked the salt of her sweat, because her arms glistened with it. She hoped no one noticed.

Her legs still trembling, Jessica pulled the rope and inched towards the gate. Angus followed her meekly, up the ramp, into the truck, where one of the boys was ready to tie him up.

The onlookers applauded.

Jessica leaned against the truck, forcing herself to grin at her audience.

"Can anyone give me a lift to the airport?"

2

THE UTE CAME to a screeching halt, scattering gravel and dust in a cloud that wafted past the open windows.

Brendan grinned. "There you are, Jess."

Across the fence, beyond a section of desiccated grass, the tarmac spread out; a grey expanse of asphalt with white painted lines. On it waited a single-engine plane. A man in blue uniform sat on the folded-out stairs.

"Is that it?" asked Brendan.

Jessica glanced at the dashboard clock. Ten minutes late, if the thing could be trusted. "Bloody hell, I hope so."

She grabbed her bag and opened the car door, stepping into the dust and late afternoon heat. "Thanks for the lift."

"No worries." He tipped his hand to the rim of his hat. A broad grin split his face, and his eyes betrayed that he still held hope for the date he'd asked her on a few weeks back. As far as John Braithwaite's farm hands went, Brendan wasn't that bad, but after that business with Luke, she wasn't getting involved with any of them again.

She slammed the door and ran. The man in the blue uniform—the pilot, she now realised—pushed himself off the steps.

She called out, still running, "Is this Westways flight 265 for Sydney?"

"Sure. You're Jessica Moore?"

"Yes." She stopped, panting. They'd waited for her. How . . . good of them; how . . . totally embarrassing. Stupid bloody bull.

Jessica handed her bag to the pilot, took off her hat and clambered up the stairs.

A man in a grey suit looked up from his computer, his expression vacant. What would he be seeing? An exceedingly tall girl with lanky black hair, in a dusty shirt and jeans, smelling of cattle shit. Wonderful.

"I'm sorry."

He grimaced and went back to his machine. OK, so he was annoyed. Missed a meeting, an important deadline. *I bloody said I was sorry.*

He looked up again, meeting her eyes. A slight frown.

The other passenger paid her no attention. Also a man, perhaps in his forties, he wore faded jeans and a black leather jacket that had seen better days. He had tied his greying blond hair in a ponytail, the end of which disappeared under the collar of his jacket. He looked, for all she could think, like an ageing hippie escaped from a commune up the north coast somewhere. One of those with no pesticides, no poisons and no bloody crops either. He held a book on his lap and didn't even look up when Jessica excused herself to squeeze between the seats. She slid sideways into the back, bumping her head on the ceiling. Her phone beeped in her pocket.

She pulled it out. The screen displayed a message, *please return my call when you can,* from an unknown number.

The businessman glared over his shoulder.

Yeah, yeah, I'm turning it off.

She pressed the off button down and the screen went blank. Her mind churned. Who could that be? The only people she knew who would write in full sentences were her parents and John Braithwaite. Their numbers she knew off by heart, especially her mother's, because she sent messages every day to check on her well-being. Sending their shy, weird, traumatised and vulnerable daughter off to boarding school in the city hadn't been easy on her mother, but after the events at Pymberton High when Jessica was fourteen, there had been little alternative.

Jessica stared at the blank screen, pushing down memories of receiving vile messages she used to receive daily at that time. Apparently some people in town bought phones just so that they could harass her anonymously.

She shivered.

That crap wasn't about to start again, was it? Nothing had happened for over three years.

She settled on the back seat, wriggled to find the seat belt while the pilot slammed shut the luggage compartment and climbed into the cabin, pulling up the stairs behind him.

A few flicks on the instrument panel and the propeller rattled into life.

Bloody noisy, it was. It was only that John Braithwaite paid for her ticket, because otherwise she preferred the train.

But she had made it.

Stupid bull. Stupid . . . whatever had happened.

That should teach her not to play with this strange ability anymore. Every time she thought she understood it, some shit like this happened.

The pilot threw off the brakes and the plane jolted into action. He had put on headphones and was talking to air traffic control, his voice barely audible over the rattling propeller. Outside the window, wing flaps moved up and down and back into their normal position. Jessica knew the motions; she had been through this before. She still didn't like it.

The plane turned onto the runway and gathered speed. Engine noise exploded; a weight settled on her chest. The rumbling of the wheels stopped and the plane rose sharply until the cockpit window showed only merciless blue sky.

Jessica looked to her right. Down there was the main road, the Henderson orange farm and the place of those city folk who'd come to town a few years back to breed emus. A bunch of the silly birds clustered around a feed trough. She'd heard the owners were doing quite well. In the distance, farmland merged into wooded hills which, further still, ended abruptly in the cliffs of the western Blue Mountains, tinged orange in the afternoon sun.

The sight gave her a shiver of excitement. She might live in the middle of the city, but she had no doubt about where she belonged. *I love a sunburnt country,* so the poem by Dorothea Mackellar described the bush. Well, she wasn't much of a poet, but that was her world, all right. No stress, no nosy idiots, and space to get away from it all when life became too complicated. For her, it meant space to let the sparking mist flow from her and let it whip at the trees and tear bushes bare without anyone noticing. Things had become better since she figured out that she needed to do this every few days, because the tension built up inside her, especially in hot weather or if she'd spent a lot of time in the sun.

The memory of the incident with Angus still chilled her. There had never been other people in the mist, or voices.

She wiped the sweat from her upper lip.

No need to worry. Nothing had happened, right?

Jessica took a book from her bag and opened it on her knees. Sunlight slanted in through the window, spilling across pages of Japanese text. Of course she didn't need Japanese for Vet Science, but she liked languages and she was good at them. She squinted through her eyelashes, letting the patterns of the text draw themselves before her, as if floating in the air above the page. Then she hesitated. If she used the mist for seeing the patterns in the text, would the web form again and would there be someone else at the other end?

She gazed out the window, feeling uneasy.

A puff of smoke from a bushfire rose in the distance. From up here, the landscape looked grey, washed out, parched. A road sliced through paddocks directly below her, and on it a tiny white car moved. A mother collecting kids from school, a farmer going into town, a sales rep travelling to his next assignment.

Without warning the familiar landscape melted before her eyes.

She saw rolling hills covered in rainforest. Mist hung in the valleys, with wispy clouds reaching over the ridge tops. Ahead, the hills fell to a floodplain with reeds and small pockets of trees. Sparkles of light reflected off a huge stretch of water. At the horizon was the grey silhouette of an island, its outline jagged, square and stair-like, as if covered by buildings. The evening sky was deep green above, fading to yellow and orange at the horizon.

～

Bloody hell, what was that?

Jessica clawed at the armrest of her seat, heart thudding.

The hippie flipped a page in his book. The businessman's head drooped.

She looked out the window. Brown paddocks, white specks: grazing sheep. Nothing strange, just the dull greyness of the Australian bush.

It was so stuffy in this cramped cabin. Jessica turned her face into the flow of cool air from the air-conditioning vent.

God, now she was getting worried. She'd dealt with all that shit when she was younger. Her parents had traipsed off with her to countless doctors and other professionals, yet the only thing they'd found out was that no one knew what it was, and the only thing she could do was to learn to live with it. Up until now, she'd thought she was doing well, but obviously she had thought wrong. Damn it, damn it.

Something tickled the skin at her elbow. She lifted her arm to look for the culprit—a tiny spider or some such—but found nothing.

Feeling sick, she leaned back in her seat, but as soon as her elbow touched the armrest, a shock went through her. She sat up with a jolt and placed her hand on the window—a current went through it and the panel underneath it, and . . . Now tendrils of mist spread from the floor and the walls of the plane.

The two male passengers sat reading and sleeping, and the

pilot stared ahead, moving his head in a rhythm as if singing to himself.

The tickling spread from her hands to her back and her legs, everywhere her body touched the plane.

This was ridiculous. Fool or not, something was going on here.

She called out, "Excuse me." Her voice was hoarse and didn't rise over the noise of the engine.

Now the very air tickled, as if it was alive with static electricity. Jessica reached for her seatbelt, ready to push herself up and tap the pilot on the shoulder.

There was a flash, turning the world into a seething mass of white. Jessica couldn't see, couldn't breathe.

The plane lurched and shuddered.

She must have been knocked out, because the next thing she knew her eyes had gone funny and everything looked blurred in rainbow colours.

Her ears popped. Fog trailed past the window, and the only sound was the ominous rushing of air. The propeller turned idly at the nose of the plane. Her ears popped again.

The pilot's voice was loud in the eerie silence. "Repeat— reporting engine failure . . ."

Jessica sat stiff in her seat, every muscle cramped with fear. No, she didn't want to die, she didn't want to die . . . she didn't . . . Heat flowed from the seat into her hands.

The trickle of warmth grew into a flood. It made its way up into her arms and through the soles of her shoes into her legs. Pain stabbed her forehead, as if a vial of acid had exploded there, spreading down her neck, her shoulders, her arms; burning, eating everything in its path.

She was flying, flapping her arms, which had become great white wings. She was a swan, and as long as she kept moving her wings they would never reach the ground. Pain increased until it felt like her skin was on fire, and still it grew. Over the thuds of her pounding heart, the world slowed to an unreal, hypnotising pace, in which the pilot's attempts to restart the engine felt like they were part of another universe.

The businessman shouted, "Come on, fucking re-start the engine!" He grasped the back of the seat before him as if ready to do so himself.

The pilot called into his headset, "Mayday, mayday, mayday."

The burning heat inside her grew so strong that Jessica could no longer bear it. She opened her mouth to scream, but no sound came out.

The pilot turned around. "You guys wearing your seatbelts? Lean on the seat—Fuck!"

Glass exploded everywhere. Jessica was thrown into the wall. The noise was horrible: screeching, something tearing at the outside of the plane. Then a gentle cracking of wood, and the hammering of her heart in her chest. And pain, like molten lava, flowed over her skin.

Silence.

S EMI-DARKNESS, mist, the dark shapes of tree trunks.
Jagged shards of glass jutted out from above the plane's
instrument panel. Pieces of glass also glistened in the
pilot's hair. He hung sideways in his seatbelt, almost a silhouette in
the dim light.

Humidity mingled with the overpowering smell of fuel, which
clung to Jessica's skin like a film of grease.

"Are you all right?" asked an unfamiliar voice, deep and male,
muffled in the stuffiness of the cabin.

Jessica tore her gaze from the pilot's limp form and almost
screamed. Her eyes, her face, her skin burned like fire. Waves of
sparks travelled under the skin of her forearms, swirling over her
hands, disappearing under the sleeves of her shirt, where she
could feel them running up her shoulders, down her back . . .

Shit, I can't move.

"Are you all right, girl?" the hippie repeated. He had an accent
she couldn't quite place, Eastern European maybe. Diffused light
cast a silky sheen over his sweaty face.

Yes, Jessica wanted to say but she only managed a tiny nod.
Tears stung behind her eyes. She should have cheered and
laughed. Still alive. How often did people survive small plane

crashes? But she had felt this burning over her skin only once before and that was a time she didn't want to be reminded of. She worried that he could see the sparks. *Had* people seen the sparks back then, with Stephen Fitzgerald? Her parents had said nothing, and her mother was the first to see her, after . . . Shit, shit, shit.

"We're leaking fuel." The hippie turned the door handle. Branches cracked under the weight of the door as it swung down.

"If you're not injured, this is not the time to play damsel in distress. Let's get you out."

He reached for Jessica's arm. A spark crackled from her elbow, over her lower arm, down her hand to his fingers.

"Shit!" He jerked back, hitting his head on the ceiling. "Damn it, you could have blown us up."

Jessica glared at him. *Do you think I can bloody help it?*

His eyes were an eerie light blue, lighter than she would have thought possible. His face was very narrow and his skin looked as soft as that of the year-seven boys at St Patrick's College whose beards hadn't started growing.

She muttered, "Sorry."

But the spark had released some of the tension and she could now move her arms, even though it still hurt. She would need to rage at something and release the mist to fix this. Quite a bit of mist, too.

She scrambled over the seat he had vacated and slithered backwards out the door. Every time she put down her knees, a burning pain flowed through her. Sparks flew from her shivering hands, warming metal, fabric or plastic under her touch.

A knee-deep carpet of broken branches littered the forest floor. Her shoes caught on twigs, causing her to stumble on unsteady legs. Out here, the smell of fuel was even stronger.

"Help me, girl. We need to get them out." The hippie flung aside a black bag and a newspaper. The businessman leant against the window, his eyes half-open, blood seeping into the collar of his shirt.

Something clicked in her mind. What was she doing? Forgetting everything she'd learned about first aid? "You're . . . you're not supposed to move injured people. You might make their injuries worse." Her voice sounded high, awfully childish.

He shot her an irritated look. "Yes, if the victim is in a safe place—which we are not. You know how flammable Avgas is? Even a mobile phone signal can set it off. Here—get a move on. Take that somewhere safe." He shoved the first aid kit into her hands.

She had no energy to argue with him, tell him that mobile phone story was an urban myth. Besides, the sparks she gave off might do the trick and she didn't want to argue about them either.

Jessica clutched the first aid box to her chest and pushed up the slope through the tangle of branches. Pain spiked through her feet with every step, as if she were walking on knives. On her arms the sparks swirled, forming patterns, as if schools of tiny fish swam under her skin.

"Hurry up, girl," came his voice from behind her; the staccato accent heightening the unfriendliness.

Damn it. Who did he think she was? She would hurry if she could, if only she had some time to get rid of these sparks. Jessica plonked down the first aid kit and retraced her steps.

He had pulled the pilot out of the wreck and placed him against a rock. The man's chest moved in shallow breaths, and he clutched a bloodied hand in his lap.

"Girl. Help him to wherever you've put the first aid kit. Do something about his hand."

Irritation boiled. "I have a name. It's Jessica."

Again, she met those weird eyes in a moment of silence.

Like this, he didn't look like an ageing hippie at all. Much too uptight, no *Peace, Man* attitude. Maybe he belonged to a bikie gang, and was used to bullying his minions around. Not the best character to get into a fight with when you were stuck in an isolated valley.

She glanced at the silhouette of the businessman in the plane. A trail of blood ran down the window.

"Don't you want help getting him out?"

"I'll get him. You worry about the pilot."

Jessica bent down, looped her arms under the pilot's shoulders and heaved, clamping her jaws against the pain. When she lifted him to about knee-height, he became too heavy and she had to put him back down.

"You feel hot," the pilot whispered.

Jessica pressed her lips together. *Tell me something I don't know.* At least she no longer sparkled like a Christmas tree.

"Can you get up?"

Of course, she should have asked that first. *Girls,* her father had mocked often enough, *always do things before they think.*

With a groan, the pilot turned over and managed to push himself to his hands and knees. Jessica draped his arm over her shoulder, and pulled him up until he stood on his feet. Apart from his hand, he had no obvious injuries.

By the time she eased him down against the trunk of the tree where she had left the first aid box, the sparks under her skin had gone completely, although she still felt as tense as hell.

He groped behind his back. "Ouch, what's this? It's all prickly."

He was right and she only started noticing the strange trees now. The trunks of all the trees were strange, all prickly with fronds and leaves as if a piece of lawn had wrapped itself around it. Weird. Very weird.

She flipped open the first aid kit, a comprehensive affair that folded out, with bottles and syringes on the top shelf inside the lid. The pilot gave her a suspicious look.

"I'm just going to bandage your hand," she said. "Don't worry. I've done this before."

Lots of times, save that she had been working as assistant vet nurse, and her patients had been horses, breeding cattle and working dogs.

He relaxed a bit. Looked away. "Sorry. My name is Martin."

"Jessica."

"You don't look . . ."

Didn't look what? Old enough to have this kind of experience? "I'm studying to be a vet." Slight exaggeration—she needed to make the entrance score first.

"Oh. I'm sorry."

She found bandages and disinfectant—the pilot cursed when she put it on his hand—and affixed thin strips over the cuts. Then she bandaged up his hand.

A cracking of branches announced the hippie's arrival, stumbling backwards as he dragged the limp form of the businessman on a picnic blanket. He came to a halt next to the pilot, let go of the blanket and straightened, panting. His sweat-slicked face looked white. For all his bravado and bluster, she didn't think he had much experience in emergencies.

As he stood there, digging in the pocket of his jacket, it occurred to her that he was as tall as her. Few people were.

The skin on the businessman's face had faded to pasty grey, the cheekbone pushed in, the ear filled up with blood, which ran down his face, his neck and shoulder. His chest moved in slow, shallow breaths. Jessica couldn't keep her eyes from his injury. Last year, when working for the vet, she had attended a horse that was hit by a car. It had a broken leg, and internal injuries, but there was much less blood than had seeped into the man's jacket. The vet had seen no option but to put the animal to sleep.

She knew: this man was going to die.

Jessica took a wad of bandage from the first aid kit, intending to wipe blood out of his nose to make breathing easier.

"What the bloody hell . . ." The hippie's voice sounded loud in the silence. He held his mobile phone in front of him. "The battery has died."

"Try mine," said the pilot, holding out his phone.

The hippie took it, but it had the same problem. Jessica could see it in his face before he spoke. "Nothing. Not a bloody thing."

Both men faced her. She took her phone out of her pocket, but the screen was dead, too. Strange.

Jessica turned back to the businessman, but her face tingled. Nausea washed over her, black spots floated before her eyes, she swayed . . . Long-fingered hands stopped her falling into the leaf litter and propped her up against a tree. A bottle was pressed to her mouth. She gulped, stale water soothing her throat, running down her chin, onto her shirt.

"You're sure you're not injured?"

The hippie's face floated in and out of focus, his weird eyes fixed on hers; Jessica shook her head. Shit. Now he was going to think she fainted because of the blood.

He sank down to his knees, wiping her face. "Your skin feels hot . . . what's that?" Frowning, his finger traced the erratic pattern of small reddish spots on her upper arm. "Old injury?"

She pulled her arm back. It was as if he picked on all her peculiarities. The spots were not that clearly visible, and there were many odd things about her that most people would comment on before mentioning them. The words "creepy" or Dracula featured commonly in those descriptions.

"It's nothing. A birth mark. I've always had that."

Always. Not even her mother knew how those spots came to be on her skin, or the burn on her leg, now hidden under her jeans, and she had been only three weeks old when she stopped being anonymous, abandoned "baby J" and started being Jessica Moore.

She tried to soothe her nerves and convince herself that he knew nothing of the web of light she used to control animals. He knew nothing of her feelings just before the crash. He knew nothing of the sparks.

But she wasn't entirely successful.

He smiled, uneasily. "Just take it easy, girl. None of us are made of steel."

"My name is Jessica!"

He flicked up eyebrows of white hair. "Jessica." In a tone as if he didn't believe her. His gaze turned to the businessman. "You're OK to clean him up a bit? You need help?"

"No!" Spoken more angrily than she intended, but who the *hell* did he think he was, bossing her about? She was *not* a softie. She unwrapped a clean wad of bandage and drenched it with disinfectant.

The hippie turned away and spoke to the pilot. "Did air traffic control reply to your distress signal?"

The pilot gave a helpless shrug. "It was all so fast I never got a chance to talk to anyone. As soon as the lightning struck us, the radio went dead. I'm not even sure anyone heard my call."

"You're sure it was lightning, mate? Couldn't have been flying too close to power lines or anything?"

"Not at that height. Yeah, I think it was lightning. No idea where it came from, but the weather does weird things at times."

"You're not wrong there, but that would have been the strangest lightning I've ever seen."

Jessica shivered. It wasn't lightning, she was sure of that. Anyone else would know that, too, having noticed the distinct lack of clouds in the sky. What sort of brain did this man have in his head? A brain that was avoiding the obvious conclusion: that the crash had something to do with *her*.

Things had started to go wrong the moment that . . . whoever it was . . . started tugging at the web she had cast at Angus. Something had happened. She had felt the prickling sensation of a current through the plane, so there was no reason the hippie couldn't have felt it. She saw the sparks under her skin, so he might have seen them, too.

He had definitely seen the sparks leap off her skin.

He sank down on a knotted root next to the pilot, not looking at her, or avoiding her gaze.

"Any idea where we are?" he asked.

The pilot shrugged. "Not the faintest fucking clue, mate. I mean, according to the map we'd be somewhere on the western slopes, about fifteen minutes out of Lithgow, but I don't know of any country like this on the western slopes. It's like we've landed in some kind of fucking hidden valley. Like the one where they discovered this . . . this . . . flaming tree . . . oh, what's it called?"

"The Wollemi Pine?" Jessica said.

"Yeah, that's the one. A prehistoric kind of valley. I mean, aren't there supposed to be gum trees in this country? You got any idea where we are?"

Soft thuds of drops of water falling from trees were the only reply to his question.

"How long before the airline discovers we're missing?"

"Not too long. What's the time?" Eyes wide, the pilot stared at his wrist. "Would you believe it? My fucking watch has given up the ghost, too. It says it's just past four, but it must be later than that. It's getting dark."

Jessica's watch too, said five minutes past four, but the seconds were still ticking over.

The pilot looked up where tree trunks disappeared into the mist. "They'd be searching for us right now. I don't know how long it'd take." He groaned. "Shit, my head hurts."

The hippie got to his feet. "Well, it looks like we're stuck here for the night unless the mist lifts. Do we have any food?"

Silence.

He shrugged. "Suppose that would be asking a bit much. Let's see what we do have. A tent of some sort? It looks like it might rain."

"There's a tarp in the plane," the pilot said.

"Come on, girl, you look big and strong; I could use some help."

Jessica very much wanted to tell him where he could stick his patronising comments and orders, but there was nothing else to do, so she pushed herself up and followed him back to the wrecked plane, thinking that even though she and the pilot had introduced themselves, he had not. When he stopped to hold a branch aside for her, she looked into his sweat-slicked face.

"Forgive me asking, but do we know each other?"

A closed look came over his face. "Should we?"

"I didn't think we did, so I don't know your name."

"Uh, sorry. My name is Brian."

A slight hesitation. Not his real name, no way, not with that accent. Someone on the run? She forced a smile. "Nice to meet you, Brian."

He didn't reply.

They reached the plane wreck, where he crawled into the luggage compartment and extracted the tarpaulin, which he handed to her without meeting her eyes. The uncomfortable silence lingered.

By the time Jessica had helped Brian string the tarpaulin between the branches of two trees, it was almost dark. Since he had told her his name, Brian had spoken only the most necessary words. Silence hung between them like heavy syrup. He glanced at her, and she glanced at him, trying to do so when he wasn't watching, and being unsuccessful at least half the time. Those light blue eyes chilled her. He was sizing her up or something. Not quite a pervert, since he'd made no move to touch her when they were alone. But something was odd and creepy about the way he looked at her.

To get away from his stare, Jessica collected pieces of dead wood and put them in a pile, but however much Brian tried, the pilot's cigarette lighter would not cooperate. He went back down the hill to the plane wreckage and came back with a container. The look on his face spelled thunder, so Jessica was happy to get out of his way and watched from a distance as he sprinkled Avgas over the wood. The smell of fuel drifted on the air. He flicked the cigarette lighter.

Nothing.

He flicked the lighter harder and harder, his mouth set in a grim line. His lips were very thin.

After a while, Jessica started feeling sorry for him. He so clearly wanted to play scout leader. "Maybe the lighter is out of fluid."

"Don't you think I'd have checked that?"

He flicked the lighter again and again, sweat sheening his arms. It was probably not such a good idea to needle him so much. She could almost feel his anger.

"It doesn't really matter. I mean—do we really need a fire? It's not cold."

He turned around, glaring at her. He took a deep breath, held it for a second or two before letting it out again. "Look, girl, why don't you attend to the others?"

"My name is Jessica, not *girl*."

He gave her a withering look.

Jessica sat down next to the pilot under the tarpaulin, glaring at Brian's back. All right, so he didn't want to be helped. Well, fuck him.

She pulled her knees up under her chin.

"Are you all right?" came the pilot's whisper.

"Yes, it's just . . ." She shrugged.

"He's a bit odd, isn't he?"

"Yeah." She was glad the pilot volunteered.

"Do you know him?"

"No."

He raised his eyebrows. "Oh. I thought you did. You know he's the only reason we waited for you at the airport?"

"He is?" Her heart jumped.

"He told me he'd be happy to wait when I said there was another passenger coming."

A chill crept over her back. This guy kept staring at her. He made no effort to introduce himself, but picked up on peculiarities of hers that no one noticed—and yet seemed to gloss over the most obvious ones. Between that and the accident and the mysterious message on her phone . . . It couldn't all be a coincidence, or could it? Or was she being overly suspicious? Heaven knew she'd had plenty of reason for that.

No, her imagination was running away with her. She had never met anyone who knew about the mist. Why would she be sharing a plane with one?

In all likelihood, she would have asked the pilot to wait, too, knowing how hard it was to find alternative transport in the country. But somehow he didn't feel like the kind of person who would have that much concern for other people.

"I'm beginning to wish I missed the flight," she said.

"You're not the only one. I was rostered on a different flight and took this one only so that I could go to my brother's birthday tomorrow."

"I'm—ouch!" Something pricked the skin just above her sock. Something black, soft and slimy, like a slug. She swiped at it, flicking it into the bushes. "Yuk, these things bite."

"What is it?"

"Some kind of black slug. Look there, on your shoe."

He pulled his foot closer to see. His face twisted into a disgusted mask and he flicked the creature off. "Great, leeches."

It wasn't a leech, she had seen plenty of those on last year's school kayaking camp, but Jessica wasn't going to argue about it. Blood-sucking slugs were the last thing she felt like dealing with. She pulled her socks up as far as they would go and stuffed the hems of her trouser legs in them. From the sound of shifting leaves, she gathered Martin was doing the same.

A bit later, Brian joined them. He sank down in the leaf litter and heaved a great angry sigh. The pile of sticks lay like a large dark mole hill. No one spoke.

They sat in the advancing night, sharing drinks from Martin's water bottle, while drops of water *plocked* on the tarpaulin. Every now and then, Brian would get up to check on the businessman, but he never said anything when he came back and Jessica never asked. She knew the news couldn't be good.

Martin fell into some kind of fevered sleep. He mumbled and tossed and turned, every now and then letting out snorting snores that made Jessica sit up straight and strain her ears. When would the rescue team come?

The night drowned in shrills and cries and buzzes. Wings fluttered close to her face and tickling creatures ran up her legs under her trousers. Some time later, a breeze picked up and blew away the veils of mist. Gnarled black shapes materialised: the trunks of enormous trees covered in growths so they looked like yetis with arms stretched towards the sky. Mossy boulders dotted the hillside like marbles thrown by a giant hand. A patch of moonlight travelled across the treetops, showing the canopy above.

"The mist is lifting," Brian grumbled and after the long silence his voice sounded loud. It was very deep, and rumbled in his chest. "That means tomorrow the search party will have no trouble finding us."

Oh, she hoped so. He creeped her out. Seriously.

More drops of water fell on the tarpaulin; strange noises drifted from somewhere far off. Jessica scratched exposed skin at every itch. Carnivorous slugs. Furry trees. In all the time since the crash, she had not heard a single familiar bird call. The trees, with their covering of ferny plants and large branches so close to the ground, did not look familiar either. On kayaking trips with school, she had traversed rainforest gullies full of tree ferns and giant gum trees with white trunks like graceful nymphs, where the sound of whip-birds and the laughter of kookaburras rang in the forest. Here, there were none of those familiar things. Just where had they landed?

"You have a sleep," Brian said after a while. "I'll keep watch and wake you when I hear something."

Jessica was not tired in the least, but she lay down anyway. Her thoughts went around in circles. Maybe she was silly, but she didn't trust him. He was weird and made her nervous.

She couldn't stop scratching herself, checking her skin for the horrid black creatures. Every now and then, she held her breath for as long as she could, listening for the sounds of the forest, as if the slugs made a hungry sucking noise. Then she would remember the crash, the frightening sensation of falling, and she would try to piece together how it could be that the day had passed so quickly. Nothing made sense. Then she would drift off, only to be jolted by a grunt or a snort from Martin. And remember that she wanted to stay awake. And find herself covered in sweat. She would look up to see Brian's silhouette sitting there, staring into the dark. But somehow, sleep managed to claim her.

4

"GIRL, WAKE UP!" Someone shook Jessica's leg.

"Huh—what?"

She pushed herself up, seeing nothing but pitch darkness. The scent of musty air. Her hands clawed in leaf litter.

What the hell . . .

Then it came back to her. The crash, the forest.

"Someone's coming," Brian said. Leaves rustled as he jumped to his feet. He whistled so loudly her ears hurt. "We're here!"

Footsteps came closer. Male voices rang out. Jessica peered into the darkness, expecting to see the glare of torches and hear the barking of dogs, but all remained dark.

Strange.

The footsteps stopped quite close. From somewhere ahead came the sound of panting breaths. A musty scent wafted through the air, reminiscent of something that had been in stale water for days, mixed with a smell of fish.

"Who are you?" Brian asked, his voice laced with the same apprehension Jessica felt.

A man spoke in a foreign language, full of harsh and guttural sounds.

Brian mumbled, "What the hell's going on here?" He took a

step back, stumbling into Jessica. "We need help. Our plane crashed. There are four of us and one's been injured real bad—"

The rest of the sentence drowned in a blue flash. By its brief burst of light, Jessica could make out five figures on the slope below. Small and lithe, with wild mops of hair in dreadlocks. The closest one held out a fist, pointing at Brian.

"What the fuck, they're shooting—"

That was Martin's voice.

Holy shit! They must have stumbled on a group of poachers, or a drug syndicate's hide-out, or some set-up like that. Her father often talked about those and how dangerous those men were. As a police officer, he would know.

Jessica shouted, "Brian, get out of here, hide yourself!"

She scrambled up the slope, slipping on boulders, stumbling over branches and fallen tree trunks. Shadows followed her, quick and silent. Something gripped her arm. She screamed and kicked. There were shouts, rough voices, more footsteps; hands on her arms, holding her, pulling a rag around her wrists. She wriggled. One of her arms shot free and hit what felt like somebody's face.

"Let me, go, let me go! I know nothing. I won't say anything."

A wave of heat welled up from within her, rising to the skin in swirls of sparks. It flowed into her arms, up her shoulders, burning like boiling water.

Oh damn it, that was the tension still inside her coming out.

Blue-white light flowed out through her skin, engulfed her hands and crackled up her arms in a net of sparkling threads. Shapes formed in the air while the sounds of the forest dulled.

She was on the front steps to the main entrance of her inner city boarding school. There was a police car in the drive. The school principal stood under the arched entrance of the porch, surrounded by about half the girls from her year. Some were crying.

A voice said, "They found nothing?"

It was a male voice, unfamiliar, coming from her throat.

The principal shook her head and glanced up over her reading glasses. "Are you a relative?"

"I am . . ." She found herself hesitating, in her male vision-persona, and a wave of anguish washed over her. *His* anguish.

Where are you?

Jessica tried to reply *I don't know* but she was back in the forest again, in the noise, the shouting, the smell of singed vegetation.

Panting, Jessica swayed on her feet. What the hell did she just see?

Then she realised something else: her captors had let go of her hands.

She sensed them standing at close distance, hesitant. Their fear rippled over her in the same way Angus' feelings did, like a wave of cold.

Jessica ran. She stumbled because she couldn't see through the purple blotches that danced in her vision. Branches cracked and leaves rustled, slapping in her face. Jessica blundered through the forest, into trees and rocks, tripping, falling.

After a while, when no one followed her, she stopped and listened.

Wings buzzed. Animals croaked, shrilled and wailed in the night. The smells had returned to normal: mushrooms, dead leaves and the faint whiff of fuel.

And silence. For a long time, she stood there, waiting to hear footsteps and voices, but nothing came. The poachers were happy to have chased her off? They were scared and were going back to get reinforcements?

She had to get back to Brian and Martin. They needed to get out of here.

"Brian?" she whispered and when there was no answer, a bit louder, "Brian?"

Silence. A patch of moonlight touched the tree canopy. Ghostly shadows turned the forest into an impenetrable mass of black and grey.

"Brian!"

Half-blind, she pushed through the undergrowth. Branches and boulders tripped her, twigs scratched at her face. She had no idea where she was going, except down a hill—because she had run up a hill to flee the men. She lifted her foot to step over a boulder. The ground crumbled under her, and she slid, legs-first, down a gravelly slope . . . into knee-deep water.

A creek gurgled past her, murmuring and whispering in a bed of soft sand. She sat there, dazed, wet all over. In the daylight, she hadn't seen a creek. If she had, she could have refreshed the stale water from Martin's drink bottle.

Bloody hell. She could have injured herself badly. That was really stupid, to go thrashing about in the night like a chook without a head. There could have been snakes, or a ravine. Brian was a big boy, old enough to keep his head down until he could see enough to move around. She'd worry about him in the morning.

The truth was, though, the stupid oaf did have her worried. Those idiot poachers had been *shooting*. She couldn't recall hearing shots after they had tried to grab her, but Martin and the businessman were injured. No way they could run if they needed to.

The thoughts kept going around and around.

Jessica stumbled out of the creek and sat on the moss, her back against a tree, staring into the darkness. Her ears strained for sounds, she twitched with every tickle and ran her hands over her legs to check for biting insects, or carnivorous slugs. The thought of those things gave her the heebie-jeebies.

After what seemed like an eternity, the dark faded into grey and then an even lighter grey.

Only wisps of mist still hung between a gnarled, knotted tangle of trees stretching out of view in all directions. Large mossy boulders covered every bit of ground, crowded humps silvered in soft light.

Halfway up the hill, bits of white, twisted metal peeked through a mass of tangled greenery.

Just as well she hadn't tried to find the plane in the dark last night. It would have been impossible to get through the tangle of branches without seeing where she was putting her feet.

By the time she arrived at the wreckage, sweat ran from every pore of her body. The mist might have lifted, but it was as humid as Darwin in the wet season. The air smelled of compost, mingled with the ever-present stink of fuel.

In all of this, Jessica picked up the scent of burning wood. Had Brian been able to get the fire going after all? She was annoyed that she wanted to see him. Yes, he was weird, but right now it would be good to see his face, to know that he was all right; to discuss what to do and where to go. Maybe he had even found something to eat—she was starving. Breakfast. She should have been at school now, getting her breakfast from the kitchen and sitting down in the dining hall. Eggs, toast and marmalade, tea.

She pushed aside the broken branches.

In the leaf litter lay a body clad in a blue uniform, the Westways logo embroidered on the chest. Empty eyes gazed heavenward from a face with translucent white skin, spotted with adhering bits of bark.

No! Martin!

The bark pieces on his face—they *moved*. Fluid oozed from red trails on his arms and a deep hole in his cheek, where bits of white shone through—his teeth. The skin on his legs crawled with black slithery bodies. Not pieces of bark, but carnivorous slugs eating the skin.

She stumbled several steps backwards, crashed into a tree trunk.

The others—Brian and the businessman—where were they?

A bit further up the slope, another body sprawled on the forest floor, on his stomach, legs splayed. The jacket of the grey suit had ripped and his back was a mess of raw, exposed flesh and crawling slugs. Threads of his shirt, black and singed, clung to his shoulders. She didn't need to come closer to see there was no hope. His ribs and the bumps of his spine already protruded through the skin.

She barely dared look, but found a third bloodied lump a bit further up the slope, half-hidden by tree roots.

"No." Her lips formed the word but no sound came out.

A glance at her feet showed slugs crawling out of the leaf litter, swarming up her legs, on her shoes, on her jeans. She stamped her feet, hit her jeans, and kicked, again and again.

No, no, get off me, get off!

She stumbled through the shrubs, jumping, kicking and swiping at her legs.

GET OFF, GET OFF, GET OFF!

She hurled herself down the hillside, sliding, tripping over boulders. Down, down, into the creek, down on her knees. The slugs came off more easily in the water and the current carried them away.

Safe.

Safe from what? A few slugs?

She sat in the creek, taking deep, calming breaths. Water again seeped up the legs of her jeans—they had only just dried from falling in the same creek last night.

Come on, Jess, you can handle this. You're not some ninny from the city.

What was the best plan? Wait here to be rescued, until the poachers or whatever they were came back? Face them—by herself?

No, stupid idea, Jess. She'd better find a road or something leading to civilisation. It couldn't be that far away.

Which direction should she go? Instinct told her to follow the creek—at least she'd have water, but the poachers would probably think the same.

Then where?

Her gaze went up the creek bank, up the hill on the other side. Maybe she could see something from up there.

Move your bony arse, Jess. Let's get out of this shit.

That's what she did if something troubled her: work hard, go riding, clean out her mother's chook pen, fix the fence, or shoot some rabbits.

She ran to the plane, and threw all the luggage out the door. The businessman's laptop computer landed in the leaf litter, followed by Brian's weekend bag, which contained only a pair of riding boots, a shirt and a bag with a horse's reins. The pilot's bag contained running shoes and damp and dirty clothes. Did no one bring anything useful? Ah, a tool box. That was at least something. And a rope. Now to pack it.

She turned her backpack upside-down. An avalanche of school things fell out. Homework, reading assignments, diary and library books.

Now, what was in this odd assortment of personal belongings that she could use? The rope, her spare shirt and pairs of under-wear. A small saw, a hammer and a box of nails, a roll of string.

She added the water bottle, a plastic bag and the pilot's empty thermos.

No food—she had no food.

On the other hand, wherever she had landed, she wouldn't be more than half a day away from some sort of civilisation. People would be looking for the plane. If she could get clear of this ridiculous forest, they would find her. Uncomfortable words were there in the back of her mind.

This isn't the Australian bush.

She heaved her backpack onto her shoulders. In her mind, she could hear her father's voice. *If you have a breakdown in the middle of nowhere, don't leave the vehicle.* A memory: an abandoned and bogged four-wheel-drive. There had been something on the news about German tourists who got lost in the desert in Western Australia. Blanket-covered bodies in the red dust.

Stupid people, her father had said. *Never do that, Jess. Stay with the vehicle.*

"Sorry, Dad," she whispered and her voice sounded unnatu-rally loud.

She turned away from the wreck and trudged down the slope.

At the stream, she stopped to fill the water bottle. The water was crystal clear and probably fine to drink. The city girls at school always wanted to muck around with water purification tablets, but if they were camping in the mountains, she never used any.

As she straightened to screw the cap back on, someone touched her shoulder from behind.

5

J ESSICA WHIRLED around and faced . . . Brian.

"What the fuck are you doing here, sneaking up on me like that!"

He took a step back, wide-eyed. His jacket was dirty and torn, his face smudged with mud. His hair was a tangle of sticks and branches, and one of his hands was bleeding.

Shit. "I'm sorry. Did you see the others?" Why the fuck hadn't he responded when she called?

He nodded, wordless. There was a hardness to his face that chilled her. What had he seen last night? How they were killed? Had he been in hiding until now?

"Are you OK?" Her heart was still beating like crazy.

He nodded, again wordless. He didn't *look* OK to her. Had he thought she was abandoning him?

"I . . . I thought everyone was dead." Stupid. She had seen a third body on the forest floor, but she should have checked to see if it was him.

"It's OK." His voice sounded a lot more subdued than it was yesterday.

She shook her head. It wasn't OK. "I'm sorry."

A wordless silence hung between them. She studied his face: haggard, dirty, younger than she had initially thought.

She continued, uneasily, "I was about to leave. I think we need to get out of here in case those idiots come back."

He nodded again. "Do you have any water?"

She gave the bottle to him, and he took it, screwed the cap off and drank. All of a sudden, her world had changed. She wasn't alone, and someone *had* survived. Not the person she would have chosen, but someone else nevertheless, and she was glad of that.

He handed her back the bottle. While she bent down to re-fill it, her stomach rumbled uncomfortably, acid burning in the back of her throat. She was hungry, but thinking of the food they didn't have would only make it worse. She had to hang on. A day or two at the most and they would surely find their way back to civilisation. She stuffed the bottle in her backpack's side pocket and swung the pack onto her shoulder.

"Let's go."

"Where to?"

"Up there. See if we can find a way out of this bloody jungle."

She expected him to argue. Maybe she hoped he would argue, say he had picked up some sound and a rescue crew was coming. But he said nothing.

And that was weird, too. Certainly people would be out there looking for a missing plane?

This is not the Australian bush.

"Do you have a preference for which way to go?" she asked, just to make sure.

He shrugged, not meeting her eyes.

"I was going to go up the hill, because we might see something from up there. I also think that those men will think we'll follow the creek."

"Fine."

Well, he wasn't going to be much use to her if he was going to act like this. What happened to his I-know-everything attitude he'd had yesterday?

Jessica took the lead up the hill. There was no path, and the hillside was a tangle of low branches and large mossy boulders. Slippery and hard to climb. Brian would push her up, and then she would reach down, hanging onto whatever branches were close, to pull him up as well. He would grunt with each climb, his hands slippery with sweat. An odd smell it had, too, reminiscent of wood fire.

Her jeans stuck to her legs, making it even harder to climb. Riding boots were not the right shoes for this job either. The soles were much too thin and smooth.

At least half an hour had passed by the time she clambered onto the crest of the ridge. About halfway up, she had already seen that the rainforest was just as dense up here as at the bottom and they would not be able to see anything, so it was not as if she had expected a grand vista, but she felt drained anyway, looking at all those tangled trees.

She dropped her pack into the leaf litter. Shit—how much of this blasted jungle was there?

Brian clambered up behind her and sank down, his back against the trunk of a tree. His face glistened with sweat. When she pulled him onto the last few boulders, she had noticed how his hand had trembled. No stamina, no bush experience.

She handed him the bottle.

He gulped, water running down his cheeks, which she noticed were smooth-skinned, with still no trace of beard growth.

She itched to ask how old he was, but she knew even the farm boys who worked for John Braithwaite already had hairs on their chins at fourteen or fifteen, and there was no way this man was that young. Laser treatment? She had wondered why men didn't use it. How fashionable could it be to walk around with a hairy caterpillar on your face? The idiotic fact was that men somehow *liked* having to drag a knife over their skin every day. They liked their beards, and here was a man who didn't have one. At all.

A transsexual? She saw them sometimes, in the city or out in Oxford Street, and—well—you weren't supposed to say so, but usually you could pick something odd about them. Not that she cared—whatever they did with their lives was their business.

But with Brian's deep voice and his angular face—no way. His light blue eyes met hers. Jessica averted her gaze. If she knew what was good for her, she shouldn't stare at him.

The silence lingered. She put the bottle back in the side pocket, taking as long as she could. When she looked up, he was staring at *her*. Next thing he was going to ask a question about sparks, or flashes of light.

"Do you think those men will come back?" An uncomfortable question, but she could think of nothing else to distract him.

He shrugged—that seemed to be all he could do.

"Who do you think they were?" Or *what*, rather, but that was an uncomfortable thought as well.

"I don't know. I didn't see."

More evasion? Hard to tell. His eyes looked vacant.

"How did you escape?"

"I ran . . . fell down the creek . . ." He shrugged again—the habit was getting on her nerves, as was his accent. "Don't know. It was dark . . . I fell asleep somewhere."

Asleep? After all that? She thought she'd called pretty loudly. But she didn't press the point. They only needed to walk for a few days at the most to get out of this jungle. Soon, there would be a dirt road or a power line they could follow, or maybe a farm house. She didn't need to know things he didn't want to tell her. They'd be rescued and go their separate ways and she'd never see him again.

Brian met her eyes in that intense look. Piercing light blue. Eyes of an albino almost, but his hair was pepper-and-salt grey, the end of the ponytail still under his jacket. Wasn't he hot in that thing?

She pushed herself up. Her muscles screamed protest, but she gritted her teeth.

"Let's go."

He scrambled to his feet, unsteady, all thin legs with prominent knees. A grasshopper, her mother called her for that same reason. Could never buy clothes that fitted properly.

Freak, farmhands would call her behind her back.

She gestured for him to go first, and then stared at his back. He really was very tall and long-limbed. His fingers were very long, too.

They were going down the hill again. That was easier, but also more dangerous. Sometimes there were no branches to hold onto and the only way down the boulders was to carefully slide on their backsides and hope neither of them would lose grip and fall into the bottom-less crevices in between the boulders.

Another rainforest creek ran in the next gully. Across that, another slope of boulders. Bloody hell, the landscape was like a giant version of road corrugations. There just seemed no end to the dense cover of trees, hiding the sky from sight. No sign of civilisation. Not the faintest trace of anything familiar. No sound.

By the time they reached the next valley, also with a creek, the light was turning grey. Jessica's watch said 11pm. It was still doing something, but not displaying the correct time. Moisture damage?

This particular gully spread out into a mossy glade, where the creek pooled into a waterhole from which it trickled lazily over algae-covered rocks.

Brian sank down on the moss and promptly fell asleep, leaning back against a tree trunk, his mouth open. In the fading light, his face stood out like that of a ghost. Exhausted, not used to bush-bashing. His hands rested in his lap, with fine, long fingers, now green and scratched, but with clear impressions of rings he normally wore. What working man wore jewellery on all his fingers? She hadn't asked him what he did for a living, but he looked like an artist to her. Jessica wandered down to the water-hole, shivering because the back of her shirt was still wet from her backpack. Her stomach cramped from lack of food. Soon, they would have to make a decision—slow down to find something to eat, or press on towards the safety of civilisation. Except where would they find food? Bush food was not unfamiliar to her, but she had seen nothing edible, nothing even remotely familiar. No lilly-pillies, no quandongs, or anything that grew in rainforests.

She had no idea what these tangled trees were. She had never seen them before. That gnawed at her. She knew bush plants well enough to recognise a few edible ones. She knew gum trees, or ash, but they were big trees that had straight mottled or pitted trunks and leaves all the way above the rainforest shrubbery, not like a covering of fur on their trunks.

Then there were the animals. Apart from the carnivorous slugs, she had seen no animals. There should have been bush turkeys; there should have been lyrebirds scratching around the leaf litter and whip birds calling out in the shrubbery, although you hardly ever saw them.

She glanced over her shoulder. Brian was still sound asleep.

As quickly and as silently as she could, she peeled off her clothes and slipped into the water. Its freshness enfolded her. The sandy creek bed was soft under her feet. Beautiful.

There had to be a volcanic spring somewhere nearby, for the water was warm and had a faint sulphuric smell. Like New Zealand. Another chill. *There were no volcanic springs in Australia.*

Or were there? Hadn't she heard of some place near . . . she had forgotten, but it was somewhere up the coast. How the heck would the plane have ended up there?

Stop fretting, Jess. Wherever we are, worrying is not going to change it.

She rinsed her hair and sat on the sandy bottom until her body shone pale in the low light.

When she turned to clamber out, Brian was awake and watching her.

She gasped and jumped up into a crouch, covering herself with her arms. He couldn't have seen anything. She had no boobs to speak of anyway. She didn't even have the hairy bits you-know-where. There *was* nothing to see. She was ugly and boyish and bony.

Yet he was staring.

She stared back, her heart hammering. Here she was, naked, alone in the forest with a strange man. He might be exhausted, but she was a seventeen-year-old girl and a grown man would have no trouble getting from her what he wanted.

Brian didn't move. He sat there, leaning back on his hands, his legs stretched in front of him and crossed at the ankles. Damn, she couldn't see his crotch—that would be a dead giveaway. Why was he doing this? She *needed* him if they had to climb more boulders tomorrow. She didn't want to go alone, but she bloody well didn't trust him as far as she could throw him.

He said nothing, and Jessica stayed in the water, just the top of her shoulders exposed. The air was getting nippy. A drop of water plinked into the pool, and a moment later, another one.

Great. It was raining.

Eventually she asked. "Would you mind?"

"What?"

"I'd like to get out."

"Oh. Sorry." His voice was warm, bemused, but maybe she only imagined that.

He turned sideways, but not quite enough for her to be sure he wasn't watching. She crab-walked to the bank, grabbed her shirt and pulled it over her head wet and cold. Then she crawled out of the water and angled for her other clothes. God, those undies stank, but her clean ones were in her backpack which sat exposed on the bank. Bugger. She pulled the dirty ones on as quickly as possible. Getting into her jeans with wet legs was harder, but she managed it. What now? Go back to him and . . . what?

"Brian?"

"Yes."

An uneasy silence.

Then he said, "Come and sit here. I'm not going to harm you."

Suspicion rose. They all said that. Sex wasn't supposed to hurt, was it? And if they enjoyed it, the girl should enjoy it, too. Never mind that she had never enjoyed the feel of a sweating male body against hers. Men stank and they hurt her. All of them. God, that Luke at John Braithwaithe's farm had been a beast. *Women like it rough,* he had said, and, knowing little better, she had put up with it for far too long. Problem was, he was nice during the day, and he paid for trips to resorts up the coast and even Thailand. He made her feel accepted.

God, she didn't even like resorts.

And where he got the money was still a mystery to her.

Vulnerable women attracted abusive, manipulative men.

She called back through the forest, "There is a soft patch of moss here. I'll sleep here tonight."

Silence.

"I'm sorry if I upset you," he said. "I was just curious."

Curious about what?

"I didn't mean to disturb you . . . Jessica." That was the first time he'd used her name.

Well, you were disturbing me.

Jessica sat down, a comfortable distance from him, her legs folded before her as if ready to spring. She didn't know whether to keep watching him or to turn away. She wanted to do both, to make sure he couldn't sneak up on her, to make sure he didn't interpret her watching him as interest. She was *finished* with men.

He continued, "I want to thank you. You seem to be well-trained for this situation, this . . . forest."

"I've done a lot of bushwalking."

Another silence. He shifted; leaves rustled. "Where were you travelling?"

Why was he so talkative all of a sudden?

"Just to Sydney."

"Family there or . . ."

"No family. I go to school there." Maybe she shouldn't have said that. Next thing he'd want to know what school. But he didn't.

More drops were now trickling from the tree canopy. The uneasy silence lingered. A twinge of shame crept through her. All day, they had helped each other. He had pushed her up rocks, and she hadn't felt embarrassed by his touch. Why now? What was the harm in a chat? She was just being paranoid. As long as he was talking, he wasn't doing anything else.

"What about you? Were you travelling to Sydney?"

"Yes."

"Family?" He'd have a wife waiting for him somewhere.

"Business. I have no family in Australia."

"They're all overseas?"

He stiffened. Averted his eyes. "Yes."

"What country?"

"New Zealand."

No way. Not with that accent. "Where did they come from before that?"

He gave her a sharp look. She could almost hear him think *you ask too many questions.* The suspicion meter went up again.

She stammered, "Well, I thought . . . because of your accent . . ." But she let it go. Wrong subject. One obviously didn't go there with him. This man was one hell of a strange puppy.

He rose, brushing leaves from his trouser legs, a useless gesture, since his trousers were as filthy and dirt-caked as hers. "If you don't mind, and if it's appropriate, I'd like to wash myself as well."

"Go ahead." Appropriate? He'd just been staring at her while she was naked and now he asked about appropriate?

He stumbled his way to the waterhole, wincing and stiff. At the bank, he finally took off that leather jacket. He folded it carefully and put it on a rock, as if it was precious. He reminded her of one of John Braithwaite's young farm hands, who had a jacket that had been given to him by some singer or other.

Underneath the jacket Brian wore a checked flannelette shirt, as was popular with workmen. This one looked new, the red and blue stripes still vibrant. He unbuttoned it and peeled it off, discarding it in a heap on top of the jacket. His skin was ghost-white, with a tattoo on his left shoulder blade. Some sort of emblem, but he was too far away, and it was too dark for her to see exactly what it was.

Next he unbuttoned his trousers. She turned away, because there was no way she wanted to give him the slightest impression that she was interested in him.

Water rippled and splashed.

Drops trickled from the trees in increasing frequency. They

pattered on leaves, dripped down trunks. The little fern-gardens on tree trunks glistened with moisture. The pool in the creek had already merged with the night.

By the time Brian splashed out of the water, it was almost completely dark.

It was now raining in all earnest. There was nowhere to shelter—the tarpaulin had been burnt in the nightly attack. Jessica found a marginally dry spot under an overhanging tree branch, but tree roots stuck in her backside, water trickled down the trunk and she kept thinking about carnivorous slugs and then thinking about food and that made the hunger pains worse. At times, too, tingling air crept over her skin. Just like she had felt before the plane crashed. She shivered. The accident had all been her fault. The more she thought about it, the more certain she became. She stared into the dark, her thoughts tangled in mires of worry. In her thoughts, she faced a court investigation into the crash. A mechanic would say, *There was nothing wrong with the engine, Your Honour.* And then everyone in the room would look at her.

Ridiculous of course, but it kept her awake, and it stirred unwelcome memories of a time when she'd been thirteen and innocent, when the blue web was still something she thought she controlled and she was facing a judge at least four times her age in a wood-pannelled courtroom packed with folk from Barrow Creek who had travelled to the city to see her *put in her place.* She could still hear the judge's voice, speaking clearly as if he thought she was stupid. *You do understand, Jessica, that you're being accused of the murder of Stephen Lewis Fitzgerald . . .*

She shivered involuntarily.

Every now and then, she thought she heard Brian's voice, mumbling something, talking in his sleep. She couldn't make out his words, and at times she thought he was speaking in his native language. His voice scared her. It sounded like he was ready for the loony bin.

She must have dozed off a bit anyway because all of a sudden, the light was blue, and she lay on her back in the leaf litter staring up at the tree canopy. A damp smell rose from the forest floor, but it had stopped raining.

Brian was still asleep, on his side, his back facing her, his jacket covering his shoulder and body. His hair was loose and spilled into the leaf litter.

Overnight, it had turned brilliant white.

6

WHITE HAIR? That was ridiculous. No one had white hair except elves in fairytales. No one under forty at any rate.

Well, she had to hand it to him—without that dye he looked younger, his face kind of high-class with a long, straight nose, high cheekbones and thin but well-defined lips. His eyes were closed, his eyelashes half-moon crescents of silver hair. His eyebrows, too, had turned white. Albino.

He was handsome. Not drop-dead gorgeous like some sultry-eyed teenage football hero who'd be arrested for drunk behaviour and groping women by the time he was twenty-five, and fat and ugly by the time he was thirty, but the type of handsomeness that didn't age.

But why the disguise?

Who the bloody hell was he with his dyed hair and his accent and his evasive replies? Why was he on the flight, why had he suggested the pilot wait for her? Why did he seem to notice things about her other people didn't and ignore things that other people mentioned? Did he perhaps have anything to do with . . . the plane crashing, with the web, with the male voice on the other end?

As quietly as she could, she crossed the space between them and crouched on the moss next to him.

She breathed out slowly, and let the strands of mist flow from her, tentative. The blue mist snaked around his sleeping form, caressing him like ghostly fingers. It wasn't right, using it on a person, and it was something she hadn't done for a long time. He might notice; she might find out something she'd rather not know. Worse, she might go too far and that thought sent shivers along her spine. Back in the time of innocence, she had done so many things that still gave her nightmares. She had never known what harm these threads could cause until it was too late. The mist was weak—she needed energy, sunlight, food to work this trick. The strands snaked over his jacket, and sought out the warmth of his skin. Buried in his arm.

She braced for the onslaught of memories she was about to face. Animals were easy—their emotions were simple, but people . . . Painful and ugly memories, heartbreak, lies and treason, that was the kind of shit people's minds unleashed. Once she had probed a classmate and had hurt for days with what she had found in the girl's memories. Adults actually *did* that to their children?

But with Brian . . . nothing came.

He had no thoughts, no dreams. What the hell? Everyone had dreams, even if they didn't remember them. How could he have no thoughts? He'd have to be dead. No, for some reason his thoughts were inaccessible to her. She stared, heart thudding, trying to think of reasons, other than that he had some sort of training in avoiding having his thoughts probed.

His chest moved with a deep breath. In-out. The exhaled air ticked over her hands like a horse's swishing tail. He stirred and mumbled. As Jessica retreated, he opened his eyes and stared at her as if he knew she'd been doing something.

"Good morning. Slept well?" Her voice sounded too high.

He sat up, groaning. "I'm sore everywhere." He frowned at her. "Is anything wrong? Did I say something?"

"No."

Jessica couldn't meet his eyes, and turned to her pack instead. She trembled. Who was this man?

"I think we'd better be going."

Shit. He was going to notice that his hair had turned white, and wonder why she hadn't said anything. It was the sort of thing she *would* comment on, in a normal situation.

She heaved the pack up. Her shoulders protested with a stab of pain. God, not more hills to climb. More moss boulders, more tangled tree roots, there was no end to it. She peered at the tree canopy, trying to determine the direction of the sun. West—the direction they had been heading since leaving the wreck. She plodded off, but after a few paces noticed the absence of footsteps behind her. Brian still stood at the creek bank, his face turned up, looking at the tree canopy.

"Aren't you coming?"

"Is there . . . much point in going that way?"

"Should we be going any other way?" What did he know about navigation? He'd said nothing all day yesterday, had been absolutely no help whatsoever in making decisions. Why the change of mind?

He shrugged. "We don't seem to be getting anywhere."

"Tell me, where is this *anywhere* we're supposed to be getting? Out of this fucking jungle would do me." She couldn't help irritation seeping into her voice. Hunger stabbed at her belly, made her head pound. She wasn't in the mood for arguing. Having a fight would solve nothing either. They *needed* each other. She breathed out heavily, stifling jangled nerves. "Do you recognise anything? Did you hear anything?" Of course he didn't. He was just trying to play boss again.

When he spoke, his voice was hesitant. "I thought, maybe yesterday . . ."

What the fuck? "Yesterday? What did you hear yesterday? Why didn't you say anything *yesterday?*"

Does he even speak the truth? But her heart jumped in spite of her suspicions. Anything to get out of this bloody mess.

"I wasn't sure."

"What was it? What did you hear?"

"I thought I heard branches cracking. That way." He pointed downstream from the creek.

"That's a reason not to go that way. If those trigger-happy lunatics are following . . . What else could it be? If they were true rescuers, they'd call."

Shit, shit, shit.

He stared at her, as if that thought hadn't occurred to him.

"Come on, let's go before they catch up."

She started off, up the hill. This time, Brian followed.

Some time much later, when the light was turning golden, Jessica scrambled onto an area of land free of trees at the top of a hill. Cloud brushed the ground, but within a few steps of the tree line, the mist thinned and then disappeared altogether. A warm, dry breeze touched her face.

"Hey, Brian, look!"

They had arrived at the top of an escarpment, and below lay a marshy landscape. Cloud-brushed cliffs stretched to her left and right as far as she could see. Ahead, a large cloud blocked the sun, its edges ringed with light. The marsh disappeared from view in a glare reflected off the water. This looked just like . . . Yes, she remembered the vision just before the crash. That meant there would be . . . She scanned the horizon. The island, with its jagged profile, protruded from the bath of silver like the back of a barnacle-encrusted whale. Even from this distance, the square outlines of buildings were clearly visible.

"Where the hell are we?"

Brian just stared, his mouth open, green smudges on his face.

"Come on, where are we?"

Not the Australian bush.

"I . . . don't know."

"I don't believe that. You've been hiding something. What is it?"

"I don't—"

"Yes, you do. What's your name? Who are you? You have something to do with this, don't you?"

"I tell you—I don't know where we are."

"Does this look like the Australian bush to you?"

"No, but we could be somewhere north."

"Where the sun sets in the ocean? Rubbish! The sun *rises* from the water on the east coast. Who are you? Not 'Brian'. Not Australian, not even from New Zealand. You've been gawking at me all along. Just what are you after?"

"I swear, I have nothing to do—"

A branch cracked in the forest.

Jessica froze, eyeing the wall of rainforest. "Did that sound like footsteps to you?"

He turned his head and listened. "Maybe."

Shit. "Come! We have to get out of here!" How could he be so calm?

"No. Stay. We'll be fine."

"How do you know that?"

"We'll be fine, really."

"Oh yeah, you know these guys. That's why they've killed two of us, huh?"

"I tell you, we'll be fine."

"In the same way Martin and the other guy were fine? I don't think so. I don't believe you. You've been having me on these past few days. What was this about going the other way this morning? Why didn't you tell me what it was you saw, or heard? You've been telling me shit—"

"It was not my fault, I—"

"I don't care. I don't believe you anymore. I don't care if you're happy to let those gun-happy idiots get us, but I'm going to—"

Bushes rustled behind him.

There was no time to think, no time to find a place to hide. Jessica ran to the jagged edge where the escarpment fell away. Bloody hell, what a gaping drop. At least a few hundred metres, all the way down to the marshland. Small shrubs clung to the cliff face, the rock soft yellow. A bit to the right, the cliff had eroded to form a little valley. Jessica ran in that direction and hesitated again, teetering at the cliff edge.

Branches cracked, and a bush moved violently. The pursuers were at the edge of the forest. There would be twenty, maybe thirty seconds before they saw her. She glanced down the gully.

"Brian, if you want to save your arse, come over here!"

God, it was steep.

Brian turned to the forest but didn't move.

There was nothing for it. No time to wait for him. She launched herself down the slope. Her feet landed in loose gravel and slid out from under her. For a terrifying split second she realised she was falling, and powerless to stop it. Bushes and rocks whizzed past like blurs. She clawed at the rock, grabbed at passing branches, and tried to find purchase in the gravel with her feet. Her hands slid over stone; branches broke; whole bushes ripped out by the roots, spraying dust and gravel in her eyes.

With a jolt, she came to a halt in a pile of stones and was, a few seconds later, blasted in the back by an avalanche of gravel. Stones bounced around her, over the rocks into the reed bed.

When her heart had calmed and the roaring of blood in her ears had stopped, Jessica became aware of an unmusical clattering, like thousands of sticks rapped against one another in quick, staccato beats, so loud it hurt her ears.

She pushed herself to her feet.

Behind her, the cliff rose in a towering wall of yellow rock. A white trail marked the rockslide she had just come down.

A bit further along the base of the cliff the reed beds gave way to a beach, which ended perhaps a few hundred metres ahead in a spit of sand. That beach looked inviting. She could take off her clothes there, and wash them. Maybe, too, she could find some-thing to eat there.

Jessica scrambled down the gravel, shook stones out of her shoes, and pushed through the shoulder-high vegetation. The clat-tering noise was even stronger here, as if an entire army of cicadas lived amongst the reeds. Mud sopped under her feet and sucked at her shoes with every step, but eventually she made it to the beach.

At that moment, the cloud at the horizon moved away and sunlight flooded the sand, eerie and wan.

Jessica squinted into the light. Weird. The sun looked so small and blue, and such an unusual glare gilded the bottom of the cloud that had just moved away. Almost as if behind that cloud hid . . .

No, that couldn't be possible.

Jessica stared, her heart pounding.

The cloud continued to move away; the gilded edge intensified, until . . .

A second glow of light flooded the marshlands, more yellow, brighter than the first.

Jessica turned around. In the low sunlight, her body cast a long shadow over the sand. Two shadows rather, which mostly over-lapped except for a thin yellowish edge on one side and a bluish edge on the other.

Two suns.

Until now, she had the distant hope that the plane had crashed in a hidden valley. That there was a big lake whose existence had slipped her mind. That the men had been poachers. That somehow she would come across a road or a farm and find that nothing strange had happened at all.

Not any more.

Grey clouds, sunlight and white water mixed in a haze of tears. She let her backpack slide from her shoulders.

What was the point of going on? She might as well lie down and never wake up. The killers were not poachers, but some kind of alien with unintelligible motives. She remembered the small size of the figures and their dreadlocks, and their scent.

They might as well catch up with her; it made no bloody differ-ence. She was alone and she would never get back home, where she could lie on her bed reading while a fly buzzed at the window. Where the breeze brought a scent of gum trees and magpies yodelled on the roof.

In her mind, her mother said, "As long as they haven't found the wreckage, there is hope."

No, there wasn't. By now, her parents would be mourning her, her mother's eyes rimmed with red while stroking her picture on the mantelpiece. The school would have a memorial service. Mei Ling, Jacqui, her other friends, dressed in formal school blazers, clutching bunches of flowers and crying on each other's shoulders.

Kreeeek, kreeeeek.

What the hell was that?

On the sand between two bushes sat an animal about the size of her forearm. It looked like a large lizard, with popping black eyes and orange slitted pupils. Its head was pointy like a snake's, but the skin shone with sparkling gold and looked wet like a frog's.

She stared at it and the animal stared back at her. Then, as it came to her that if she could catch it, she could probably eat it, it turned around and ran off in a gallop-like gait, most unlizard-like, with an arched back, tail held high. Jessica jumped forward and crashed through the bushes after the creature, grabbing its tail with both hands.

A frightened squeal, *Kreeeeek!*

She swung the animal above her head, intending to smash it down on the sand, but somehow, it had managed to pull itself up and clamped a pair of jaws over her thumb. "Ow!" She let go of the tail. The lizard fell to the sand and scuttled away, across the beach, into the water.

Jessica stared after it, panting, her head throbbing with pain.

She rubbed her thumb where the lizard had bitten. A v-shaped red mark had appeared, but the teeth hadn't even broken the skin. Coward that she was. Anyone else would have clubbed it over the head. Anyone else who didn't spend a lot of time fixing up animals. Shooting rabbits was easy. You did it from a distance. *Bang, bang, bang.* Rabbits were introduced pests anyway. But to kill an animal by wringing its neck with her bare hands . . .

She kicked up a spray of sand in her anger. Having thought of food had made her stomach pains worse. If she was to survive, she had to slow down, find things to eat. But she couldn't even kill a lizard to save herself.

The ghost of a breeze touched her sweaty face, bringing the smell of wet mud and the clattering noise from the reeds. There was also another sound. Rustling, swishing and a whistle . . .

Jessica peered over the bushes. Something moved in the reed bed to her left.

The killers.

7

J ESSICA RETREATED into the shrubbery at the bottom of the cliff.

First one and then another figure came out of the reeds. Against the glare of sunlight, they were nothing more than black shapes. Small, dressed in rags, with mops of untidy hair like reggae singers. Five of them.

How could they have come down that cliff so quickly?

They stopped on the beach, talking and gesticulating. Any minute now and they would see her footprints and then they only needed to follow the trail.

Jessica broke a branch off a shrub and pushed backwards through the vegetation, sweeping the fine sand over her footprints as she went. It was a botch job and if these trackers were worth their salt, they'd find her in a jiffy, but what else could she do? Branches snagged on her clothes and scratched her arms. She stopped to peek. The knot of men broke up and one pointed at the water's edge, the spot where she had stopped and noticed her double shadow. Two of the men followed her tracks up the beach. They disappeared into the bushes.

Faster she walked backwards, and faster still. Step, sweep, step, sweep, step.

A whistle echoed. They would have found her backpack. *Shit.*

Jessica turned and ran as fast as she could. The men shouted; branches cracked.

She jumped over and between bushes. Something funny was going on with her right shoe. Parts of it flapped loose and her sock was filling up with sand.

If she could reach the river beyond the sand spit, swim across, she might escape if the men couldn't swim, or at least not as well as she could.

The shrubs ended abruptly.

Jessica launched herself into the open, weaving between tussocks of plants. Here she could gain speed and take advantage of her longer legs, get away from them as fast as possible. She ran up a low sand dune, around the corner of the cliff into an invisible curtain of . . . something.

Her hands tingled; the skin on her face pricked. The feeling exploded over her chest, down her stomach, her legs, like pins and needles in her entire body.

She had to stop running because her legs threatened to buckle under her.

From where she stood, a meadow sloped down to a lazily churning river. In the middle of the grassy space stood a circular wall, and on this wall about a dozen tall metal poles. Each of these poles bore a glass "eye" at the top that collected beams of light reflecting from hundreds of silver dishes attached to the cliff face behind. The eyes then directed the light to the top of a pillar in the centre of the circle. There, the light simply disappeared. Some sort of collection plant for solar power.

The collected energy from the beams made that pillar throb with power. The air vibrated with it. It crept through her veins. Warmth spread inside her, familiar, soothing, and calling for more. Every fibre of her being wanted to go to that pillar and submerge herself in the energy it radiated. If it was what had brought her here, it could get her back home.

Rough voices sounded behind her. The five men clambered up the sand dune, silhouetted by the light. One of them pointed.

Jessica ran.

Her thoughts soared to the stars, to a place where the sky was blue and a single sun beat down on the tarmac of the airstrip at Barrow Creek and her father's police car stood parked on the other side of the gate. He leaned against a fence post, a crooked smile on his face and a twinkle in his eye and hugged her, grumbling, "Welcome home, poss."

She reached the circular wall and heaved herself on top into the full blast of power from the central pillar. Every particle of her body screamed with life and with the hunger for more power.

Yes, she could do it; she had to, for the sake of her parents. She would find a way back home. She would run or hide or fight the natives, go back to the beach and catch another lizard, kill it before it had a chance to bite, eat it raw if she couldn't make a fire, build a raft and paddle to the city on the island, swim if it sank, and learn to communicate with those she found there so they could help her. If it took the rest of her life, she would find a way back home.

A long, clear note pinged across the meadow. The beams of light that passed overhead went from white to red and faded. The "eyes" at the top of the circle of posts ceased to shine. Vibrations in the air stopped and there was . . . silence.

Behind her, the first of the two suns dipped below the horizon.

Someone whistled at the ridge.

Jessica jumped off the wall. An all-too-familiar stab of pain shot up her legs as soon as her feet hit the ground. Now she had done it. In some way, this strange machine had charged her to breaking point, like when the plane went down. How stupid was that? Why hadn't she run for the river as she had intended?

Jessica crouched and pressed herself against the wall.

When those men reached the circle of poles, she would have to do something, or they would be tanning her hide. She didn't think she could trigger another flash, or at least not on purpose. She could make a web—but would that risk that person at the other end grabbing hold of her again?

What then? Make a dash for the river?

The brown water looked inviting, but there was no way she could run that far, not like this.

More whistles followed, closer this time, and the thuds of running feet. Female voices shouted in a language full of consonants, punctuated with loud snaps like the cracking of a whip.

Jessica peeked over the wall. Even moving her eyes hurt.

A line of figures ran across the field. Agile like hunting cats, they sliced through the vegetation. Glass-bladed knives glittered at their belts. They stopped, facing the approaching men.

Jessica's pursuers had come to a stop on the hillside. One of them spoke, his voice rough.

Several female voices replied with shouts.

That was a piece of luck. If these guys were going to have a conference, maybe she could still get away. She turned . . . and stared into a circle of faces. Small, lithe creatures human-like enough to call them people reached only to her chest. Their eyes were at least three times the size of a human's, pools of liquid brown. Their hair, black or greying, was rolled into dreadlocks or woven into ornate braids with beads and bits of coloured fabric. A faint muddy scent drifted on the breeze. She recognised that smell from the people she had thought were poachers.

There were about twenty of them, naked except for white aprons. Patterns of white and grey zebra stripes or leopard spots graced their upper arms, elbows and shoulders, but faded on their faces, and on their chests, which had pale, rounded breasts.

Jessica backed into the wall, holding up her hands. "Look, I'm unarmed."

Stupid. Aliens only spoke English in the movies.

The females continued their staring game. One of them muttered a word, *avya,* another repeated it, until it went around the group like Chinese whispers. *Avya, avya.*

It made her nervous.

"Well, guess you've never seen a human being before. Suppose we're kinda ugly to you." God, she was saying stupid stuff, babbling. Her head throbbed with a monumental headache. A cloud of sparks swirled under her skin.

The spectators shuffled aside for an older female. Wispy white hair hung to her waist, threaded into plaits adorned with beads. The low light from the setting suns made the grooves and wrinkles in her face stand out like canyons on a topographic map. One of the aproned females spoke in staccato tones, but the old female silenced her with a wave of her hand and faced Jessica.

Her eyes were huge. Gold spots floated in the irises, the pupils black and fathomless. Long, delicate eyelashes, white with age, blinked. She reached a wrinkled, paper-skinned hand for Jessica's upper left arm and whispered, *"Anmi."*

Jessica looked down . . . and nearly fainted. The birthmark spots that had always marked her skin had joined up to form a pattern. Two signs glowed with bright phosphorescence: one like a small 'n' with a long loop down, the other like a mirrored numeral three.

Jessica rubbed the skin, but she knew it was pointless. The phosphorescent lines matched the familiar spots on her upper arm perfectly. They could only be part of the same thing, some kind of tattoo, and something in the air—that weird installation that collected sunlight—had brought out its radiance.

It was like . . . biology class a few months ago. Their teacher had used a blacklight on a group of cowrie shells, which had looked pretty, but ordinary, in daylight, but glowed brilliantly pink under the blacklight's rays.

That's how the tattoo on her arm shone.

Holy shit didn't half describe it. And those stripy-skinned humanoids still stood staring at it, bright pink dots reflected in their huge eyes. What the bloody hell did they think she was?

The old female pointed at Jessica's chest and repeated, "Anmi." Then she pointed to herself and said something like, "Ikay."

Did it matter what her name was? These looked like the same type of people who had killed Martin and the businessman. They had captured Brian. They were going to kill her anyway. Kill her and eat her like cannibals and feed the bones to the lizards.

"Well, you got that wrong. My name is Jessica. You hear that? Jessica. Jess-i-ca."

The old female pressed her finger to lips. "Poh-poh-poh-poh —Anmi."

"Suit yourself. Can I go now? Those guys over there are after me. I need to get to the city to catch the next spaceship to Earth. You see, I've got an appointment with the basketball team, but now I'm a bit late, I sort of got lost along the way and ended up on the wrong planet."

She didn't even know what she was saying. This was ridiculous. Completely and utterly ridiculous. She stumbled a few painful steps, grasped the top of the wall to haul herself over, get out of here, but something glittered at her chest. A knife; no, more like a machete, the blade clear as glass. The female holding it was a fierce creature. Black zebra stripes on her shoulders gleamed with a coating of oil. Lean, muscled and ready to spring, a fighting Amazon.

The white-haired female Ikay gave a harsh command that sounded something like, *Alll.*

The Amazon relaxed her hold but something wound around Jessica's arm and held it in an iron grip; some kind of snake-like thing, banded black and white. Jessica attempted to prise her fingers between the coils and her skin, and found its end: a small, white-haired tip. She realised where it came from. These people had tails.

"Let me go, I tell you—let me go. I'm not going to harm you."

She struggled against the tail's grip. Swirls of sparks raged under her skin, but if the Amazon saw them, or if she felt the heat, she didn't show it. Pricks of pain went across Jessica's shoulders, her stomach and her legs. Strands of light snaked when she breathed, forming into the familiar web.

Jessica tried to withdraw it. She could make Angus do what she wanted, but he was a bull, and there was only one of him. Now the web wove over the entire group of natives and there was no way she could control all of them.

Ikay grabbed her arms, and shouted harsh words.

Jessica's skin burned. She struggled. Every movement hurt. There was pressure inside her looking for a way to escape. She wanted to scream, but her mouth wouldn't move. Before her eyes, the blue-veined web formed out of strands that came not from her body, but materialised from Ikay's skin. As they curved and reached out for Jessica, she retreated.

Ikay gave a sharp command. The Amazons took hold of Jessica's shoulders, and brought her to her knees, until she faced Ikay, who bent forward until her huge black eyes filled Jessica's vision.

Jessica closed her eyes. She could not let that web connect with her. She could not let that woman do whatever she did with those blue strands. Read her mind. Erase her memories. Kill her. Those things she had done herself.

But closing her eyes made no difference. The web not only shone through her eyelids, but it strengthened. The force at the other end pulled at the heat inside her.

Jessica wanted to scream, but her voice didn't cooperate.

Images flowed into her mind. She saw some huge, hive-like structure in the forest. A boat floating to a jetty. There were houses in the background, and people hauling nets. Children, their skin completely striped. A group of white-haired elders in heated debate. Snapping tails, furious hand gestures. *Invaders have come. We must kill them. They fell from the sky.*

And then she was in another place entirely . . .

Grey light filtered through a window, over empty tables and chairs in some sort of eating house. Not normal tables—the surface was a crystalline screen with strange characters . . . which she could read. The menu.

It was raining heavily outside, a curtain of water that obscured the view beyond a grey building on the other side of a street. A man sat by himself in the corner near the window, his spidery hands—the index and middle fingers much longer than the others —clutching a cup.

He looked up; a smile crinkled the skin around deep-set eyes, the irises yellow with a black rim. "Daya."

Jessica drew back a chair. Once again she was in the body of the strange man—that's why she could read the menu.

"How are you, Wonan?" the man asked, and it was strange to have the sound come from her mouth.

"You seemed in a hurry to talk to me."

"I am—thank you." The last words to the woman who deposited a glass on the table. It contained a vivid blue drink, a trail of vapour rising from its surface.

Daya picked up the glass. Jessica felt it as he held his breath and took a large gulp. His mouth burned, and when he swallowed the feeling tracked all the way into his stomach. Warmth spread through his body. He sighed; he needed that.

Wonan blew steam off his tea. "So, what is the problem?"

"I'd like to have your thoughts on something. I've tried a lot of other things, but I keep coming back to the same conclusion." He twirled his glass. "Say you wanted to fool the Exchange, how would you do it?"

"Fool the Exchange?" Wonan leant back in his chair, frowning. "To what end?"

"To make an aircraft disappear. A craft that is unaware that it's being transferred."

Yellow eyes fixed his. "You're talking about unilateral translocation."

"Yes." Daya cringed. Like the fifth dimension and the eighth sense, unilateral translocation was one of the subjects philosophers liked discussing but no researcher in the sciences seriously believed existed.

"That's impossible."

"I know. Yet it happened. Something fooled the Network into accepting reciprocity for a craft that had no ability to do so. A craft that had no Exchange capacity, no anpar control, and no communication."

Wonan's frown had deepened. "You're sure?"

"As sure as I can be."

"If you're right, why has no one made a big fuss about this?"

"They have, on the craft's home world. But it's not a Union

world and they have no idea even of the existence of the Exchange."

Wonan's eyes widened. "Where is the craft now?"

"If I knew that, I'd be halfway to answering my questions. I need access to the translocation records."

The web crackled and shivered.

Damn, damn, damn. She couldn't control it. Just when it was getting interesting—he was talking about what had happened to her, wasn't he?

The restaurant exploded amidst a blur of images that were not Daya's, but belonged to the tailed people. A boat bringing in a huge fish. Tailed and stripy-skinned people carving it up on the beach. A young male climbing a tree to pick fruit. The images came faster and faster until they blurred together in a stream of colour.

Strands of light flailed and whipped about, until they, too, merged and became a seething stream of white that flowed through her and eroded the knot of energy inside her, like a river eats at a sandy bank. When the light dimmed, all she saw was two large brown eyes that seemed to swallow her. The blue strands and sparks under her skin were gone. So was the pain.

8

A SNAP BROUGHT Jessica back from the trance.

She blinked. Stared. Blinked again.

Orange light gilded Ikay's face, bringing out gold spots in her huge irises. Behind her some curious females still lingered, but most onlookers had gone back to work.

Doors were open at the bottom of the installation's central pillar. Jessica could see wire cages inside, with lots of balls that glowed like radioactive caviar. A group of females were wearing gloves and loading those balls into bags, which others carried towards the river.

The air was humid, heavy with the minty scent from the females' bodies and the wet smell of mud. A breeze caressed Jessica's skin like soft fingers. The most beautiful thing in the universe. Gone was the burning, the pain, the madness and the recklessness. Gone was the web and the man's voice and the stranger in the restaurant. With the heat that had fled her body through the web, the anger had melted away.

How had this alien female done that? Because when their minds connected, there had been no doubt: Ikay had done something to drain off the pressure, something none of the doctors she had visited on Earth had ever been able to do.

Jessica stared at Ikay and the remaining onlookers as if, for the first time, really seeing them.

Yes, they were the same type of creatures as the ones who had been following her, the ones who had taken Brian and killed the others. Those men still stood motionless at the ridge, mere silhouettes against the darkening sky. A group of hunting females waited halfway between them and the wall. Why the men should let themselves be stopped when they had fire-spewing weapons was a question Jessica couldn't answer, but the fact was they didn't come closer and so it seemed for now she was safe, at least from them. And if these females had plans to kill her, they could have done so a hundred times already.

A wave of fatigue rolled over her.

"I'm sorry to be so rude, but would you have something to eat?" Jessica mimicked eating.

Ikay repeated Jessica's mimicking, speaking a single word that sounded something like *okkik*, with short vowels and deep guttural "k" sounds.

Jessica nodded, but at Ikay's blank stare repeated the gesture again. "Please?"

Ikay beckoned, and led Jessica away from the wall, waving the last aproned workers back to their jobs. The two Amazons followed, still looking wary.

At the gap in the wall another Amazon waited. This one was much younger, her body graceful with female curves and supple, striped skin. Large, long-lashed doe-eyes met Jessica's in a questioning look. A gorgeous, feminine creature, even in the way she held her knife.

Her voice, young and childish, rang like a bell.

Ikay pointed at the chest of the black-haired Amazon and said a single word that sounded like *"Alllll."*

The Amazon's name?

Jessica tried to repeat the word, but couldn't produce the thick "l" and said, *"Alla."*

The Amazon's glare met hers. Her tail swayed at knee level. It probably meant *mildly annoyed.*

Ikay moved to introduce the older woman with the leopard spots. This one took Jessica's bastardisation of her name into *Maire* without any emotion, gazing into the sunset.

On the other hand, after hearing Jessica call her "Dora", the young Amazon let forth a barrage of snorts and gurgles that sounded like she was choking. It seemed this was their version of laughter. Jessica chuckled, launching Dora into another set of snorts.

Alla gave her a cold look, and spoke a few harsh words.

Ikay waved around the small group and said something that sounded like, *"Pengali."*

So that's what they called themselves, Pengali.

Jessica repeated, "Pengali." And then pointed at her own chest. "I'm Jessica. I'm human." Well, that sounded stupid.

Ikay raised her hand and wagged her finger. "Poh-poh-poh-poh—Anmi."

Whatever. As long as they gave her something to eat.

A well-worn path led from the power installation to the river bank. Yellowish brown water flowed sluggishly past a line of about ten dugout canoes, tied to each other, into which the working females were loading their bags of glowing pearls. A delivery of charged batteries to the island city she had seen?

Another boat lay on the muddy beach a bit away from the others. The grey-haired Amazon, Maire, took the rope attached to the bow and heaved, dragging the canoe into the water. Dora sprang into the bow, picked up a stick and poked it hard into the sand to keep the boat in place. Jessica stepped in; Ikay settled behind her.

Alla and Maire pushed off and the canoe glided into deeper water. They turned upstream, where the rainforest edged the river like silent walls of green. Dora splashed the stick with well-trained rhythm. Even from the back, her figure looked more feminine than that of the other Amazons. Earlier, Jessica had noticed her full breasts and a curved belly. She could be pregnant.

Jessica looked over her shoulder. She wondered where Brian was and how far upriver these creatures were taking her. She could still hear Brian's voice. *We'll be fine.* She was angry for having lost him. Yes, it was his own stupid fault that he had been left behind. He had probably been caught by the other mob, the poachers, or whatever they were. He should have come with her, but still . . . it didn't feel right, what had happened, and she should try to go back and find him. By now, the boat had gone so far upstream that the top of the cliff where she had left Brian was almost out of sight.

The canoe entered a lagoon, where the river emerged from a deep gorge in a large pool of mirror-like water. Images of trees and vines reflected in the surface. The beach at the lagoon's edge looked unnaturally white. A row of boats lay in the shadow of the trees. There were also racks made from sticks with something that looked like seaweed hanging on horizontal beams to dry. The dizzying smell of cooking hung over the water. Jessica's stomach growled.

As soon as the bow of the canoe hit the sand, a lone figure strode out of the forest, clad in a cloak of material that shimmered blue and purple in the dying rays of daylight. Coloured beads glittered in his greying hair. His protruding pot-belly hung over a jewelled belt around his waist, adorned with ornaments made from hair and seeds. His flaccid penis, the skin dark brown, left no doubt about his gender.

His eyes met Jessica's while he exchanged a few words with Ikay and the Amazons, during which Alla gestured towards the ridge, where the silhouettes of Jessica's pursuers were no longer visible. The male's voice sounded angry; his tail waved behind him, causing his dangling penis to swing from side to side. His pubic hair was white and straight, hanging down between his sinewy legs like a goatee. His balls protruded from it like black marbles, the skin shiny and stretched.

Again, his eyes met hers and held them for a few seconds during which he turned aside, giving her a full view of his genitals, the penis no longer entirely limp.

Jessica shivered. Oh, no, he had no doubt about her gender.

The Amazons dragged the canoe up the beach, while Ikay beckoned Jessica into the forest.

It was dark under the cover of the huge trees. The smell of decaying leaves brought back the first escape through the forest after the crash.

And Brian. She shouldn't have left him, she really shouldn't have, mysterious and creepy as he was. She should have grabbed him by the arm and dragged him down that rock slide.

The sound of many voices talking, children calling, whistling, came from somewhere between the trees.

Ahead was a huge structure, as tall as the trees and blending in with them. Greenish light spilled from an archway entrance. Two sentries stood on either side, no more than shadows in the gloom. Ikay replied to the men and they let the group pass into a huge hall made up of living trees. These trees, in a rough circle, formed the pillars for a roof at least a couple of floors above.

A second circle of tree trunks, ghostly green in the eerie light, supported wooden structures, like balconies surrounding a town square. Jessica counted at least four levels above ground. Specks of light dotted the delicately-carved balcony railings, the tree trunks and ceiling. It took her a while to realise that they were sparkly reflections from the opal-like floor, smooth as a floor in a suburban shopping centre.

The greenish light originated from glowing bulbs suspended from ropes strung from one tree trunk to another.

People spilled from every nook and cranny. Small, large-eyed, their shoulders and backs striped like zebras, or spotted like leopards, all of them waving and signalling with tails. Young males, old males, young females, mothers carrying babies, old females, children. In contrast to the adults, who only had pigment stripes on their shoulders and backs, the children were striped or spotted all over, like wild piglets. All stark naked, whispering, pointing at her. The smell of their musty bodies was so strong that Jessica felt sick.

Ikay guided her across the floor, ushering curious onlookers aside. They went through another archway made from carved wood, where the smell of sulphur and the press of humidity hung thick in the air. This room held a large indoor pool.

A few stone steps led to the edge of the water, dark and murky. Eerie light shone from balls similar to those in the main hall. The surface rippled from splashes on the other side of the room, where children yelled and laughed. Adults stood in the water, talking.

Ikay tugged Jessica's shirt up. Jessica grabbed the hem and pulled it back down.

"I don't want to bathe, I'm hungry."

Ikay shrank back, her tail curling before her. Children stopped splashing. Adults stopped talking. Everyone crowded around to watch her. Shoulders glistened with moisture. Breasts cast small, half-moon shadows on female chests.

Jessica stared into Ikay's huge eyes. "Sorry, I didn't mean to scare you."

The tail lowered; Ikay mimicked eating.

Jessica nodded, flooded with hope. "Yes, I'm starving."

Once more, Ikay tugged her shirt. Clearly, Ikay wanted her to bathe before eating. Jessica pulled the shirt over her shoulders and let it sink on the steps. Dora hastened to pick it up.

Onlookers pointed, murmured and snorted. Yes, she had no breasts to speak of. Did they have a problem with that?

She kicked off her shoes. Her right shoe bounced down the steps, the loose sole flapping, and fell in the water. Oh bugger.

A boy dived under the surface and came up a moment later with the shoe in his hand. A few of his little friends mobbed him, and he swam off across the pool, holding the shoe above his head.

"Hey, that's mine. Give it back."

The boys paid her no heed.

Jessica turned to Ikay. "I need my shoe. Make him give it back."

Ikay just stared.

Jessica bent to pick up her other shoe, but dropped it just as quickly. God, it stank. But without shoes she could do nothing; her feet were much too soft to go barefoot. And where was her shirt?

Dora was gone. No shirt.

Ikay gestured at her jeans.

Jessica bristled. What? Take them off, too? And then what? Would she get them back?

A breeze carried the smell of roasting meat. Jessica's stomach churned. What was more important? Her pride or her survival?

Slowly, she undid the button on her jeans, and pulled down the zip. The fabric felt greasy and stiff under her hands, and when she pushed the waist band down, the stench made her gag. God, if these people had noses half as sensitive as hers, no wonder they wanted her to bathe first.

Her jeans fell on the floor, followed by her underpants. She used her foot to scrunch them into a little heap, not daring to look at the crotch of her undies. Maybe she could give her things a wash before she put them back on. Surely no one was likely to run off with this lot of clothes.

Ikay led Jessica into the water. It was quite warm and enfolded her tired body like a comforting blanket. The chatter of the Pengali faded into the background. Someone tipped water over her head, and hands rubbed her hair, lathering in a soap-like substance with a strong smell of mint.

In between buckets of water upturned over her head, Jessica glanced at the steps. Her clothes had gone.

9

ATHED AND smelling of mint, Jessica followed Ikay and her Amazons back into the main hall. A mass of people gathered, talking and waiting around steaming pots. The white in their skin patterns showed up brightly, as if the light had a strong ultraviolet component. Large eyes glinted. Jessica felt vulnerable. After coming out of the water, Ikay had given her a thin belt to wear around her waist, so there was nowhere to hide. She was so tall, and her skin was so white it almost glowed. People stared—they always did. A seventeen year old girl in the body of an adolescent boy. No curves, no femininity.

Hands, tails and other body parts slithered past her as she struggled to keep up with Ikay. Air stroked her skin in places normally well-covered. Drops of water ran from her still-wet hair down her spine into her bum-crack, leaving her with the uncomfortable feeling she had pissed herself.

She scanned the ever-moving crowd for a sign of her clothes, but there were so many bodies and with their stripes and spots it was hard even to tell them apart.

Under the first floor gallery, a group of older males sat amongst bowls of white and black paint, using fine brushes to accentuate skin patterns on the backs of those seated before them. Others threaded beads into each other's hair.

Ikay pushed Jessica down on pillows amongst the group. With a chatter of vowel-deprived words, two males crawled over to apply black paint to her shoulders, one using his tail, while the other passed her a bowl from which rose a rich spicy smell. Finally, food. Jessica was so hungry she gulped the fishy balls and gooey sauce without wondering if they might contain poisons her body couldn't digest.

She gave the empty bowl to a young boy who walked past collecting them. Ikay and her Amazons had disappeared.

Jessica tried to get up, but a wave of dizziness came over her. She stumbled; the belch welling up from her stomach tasted of rancid fish and acid.

Sweat broke out all over her body. God—she wasn't going to spew, was she? What would she do? Over the heads of Pengali she identified two emergency exits: the main entrance, guarded by two sentries, and an archway into a dark room on the other side, where a steady stream of people came and went.

In the middle of the hall, a couple of youths dragged out drums and an impromptu dance started. Males and females lined up to meet on the floor. Under loud cheering, each couple so formed danced together before moving aside for the next couple. Jessica was jostled to join in. Onlookers brayed laughter, pointing at her fake skin patterns.

She shuffled in the heaving mass of bodies smelling of the gunk that came from the bottom of her mother's outdoor fish pond. Thinking of what to do when her stomach would no longer obey her orders, of what to do when she got to the end of the line and was supposed to dance. And the line before her kept getting shorter.

On the floor, a leopard-spotted male met a young giggling girl, took her by the hands in a whirling dance. The girl, eyes wide, laughed clear like crystal. Then the man stopped, put his hands on her hips and kissed her. The onlookers cheered.

The grey-haired Amazon, Maire, who took the floor next,

wasted no time in getting herself into the arms of the handsome young male fate dealt her. Sharing passionate kisses, they moved as one across the floor, rocking in time to the drumbeats, their tails intertwined, curling around their hips. When the onlookers cheered, the young male grabbed Maire's hand and pulled her after him through the crowd.

The next couple took the floor. Jessica panicked, felt bile rise in her throat. Hands pushed her forward. No, she would not throw up. At least not here.

Between the mass of bodies, she glimpsed Maire on a pillow near a tree trunk, her unmistakable leopard spotted back undulating in slow rhythmic movements, her tail curling around hands that gripped her sides.

Blood rushed to Jessica's cheeks.

Drumbeats roared in her ears, reverberated in her chest. She swallowed hard. Once, twice. Tried, driven by a mixture of revulsion and fascination, to catch another glimpse of Maire's spotted back, the young male's tail stroking it, in that same rocking movement.

The crowd surged and Jessica found herself a few steps onto the dance floor. Looked up. There, facing her, stood the pot-bellied male from this afternoon. A wide grin splitting his face, he held his arms wide to welcome her onto the dance floor. But she saw only his swaying, no longer flaccid penis.

No. She took a deep gulp of air. *No way.* Took a step back.

He grinned, held out his hands, came closer.

The crowd cheered.

Drumbeats and cheering mingled in deafening, throbbing noise.

Her mouth flooded with saliva.

No!

Clutching her stomach, she turned away, and pushed herself between the onlookers. She brushed past sweaty bodies; grasping tails and hands slid past her. They were all cheering and laughing and their voices rose in crescendo above the thumping of the drums.

Away, away!

A tail gripped her arm and a fierce-looking figure blocked her path. Alla. The pot-bellied male waited behind her, a grin on his face. Jessica hit at Alla's tail. "Leave me alone! Let me go!"

Somewhere behind her, a loud female voice shouted over the music, followed by a sharp whistle. The drums fell silent.

Ikay walked slowly to the centre of the floor, where people shuffled back to form a circle around her. In the eerie light, her hair looked almost green. She gestured to Alla, who pushed Jessica forward. The pot-bellied male had retreated to the edge of the circle and glowered at Ikay. His tail swayed, brushing the males behind him in the face.

Ikay spoke. In that tense silence, her voice sounded loud. Heads appeared in the voids behind the gallery railings: wide-eyed faces of young children. Four layers of tribespeople, all looking at Jessica, and listening to Ikay.

The sound of Ikay's old voice carried well in that space. She gestured with her hands like a politician giving a prepared speech. Jessica strained her ears for the meagre words she had picked up in their guttural language: *okkik*—food, *enggit*—the creatures that produced the incessant noise in the reeds or *mohok*—settlement or tribe. Ikay's speech pattern flowed in a repetitive cadence, with short breaks after every three words. Vowels, if any, were only short. Nothing of what Ikay said made sense.

And all those eyes glanced at her, especially those of the females. The pot-bellied male leaned against a tree trunk, his arms crossed over his chest. Every now and then, he would lash out his tail with a crack like a whip.

Then Ikay mentioned the name she had given Jessica: Anmi. Others repeated it, until it travelled in a whisper around the hall. *Anmi, Anmi, Anmi.*

Pengali around Jessica backed away from her, as if she had some sort of disease, or as if she was the subject of immense respect.

Oh yeah, I'll be like the Spaniards who were worshipped like gods by the South American tribes.

But hadn't some of those explorers been killed to prove they were not gods?

Whatever these people thought about her, she didn't want to deal with it. She'd almost rather have been captured with Brian by gun-toting aliens. Well—maybe not. *Oh, Brian, why did you have to be such a stupid stubborn oaf?*

Ikay gestured for Jessica to come forward.

There was no choice—what else could she do? Her legs felt like rubber, wobbly in the knees. The whisper in the crowd surged around her.

Anmi, Anmi, Anmi.

Ikay sat down, nimble and agile like a cat. Jessica remained standing on the edge of the circle. There was a pattern inlaid in the stone—a five-pointed star in black and cream mosaic, with symbols at each point, curled loops.

"What is this?" Her voice sounded unnaturally loud.

Ikay pointed to the stone and said something that sounded like, *Akkar.* Then she raised her finger to Jessica and said, *"Avya."*

She motioned for Jessica to sit down.

Jessica hovered in indecision. Stared at the floor patterns. The symbolism of the star gave her the creeps.

Her father's voice sounded in her mind. *Never sign a deal without reading the contract first.* Well, it was not as if this setup came with a how-to manual.

She didn't want to do this because she didn't understand, and she did want to do this because it looked like Ikay understood the web. But really, she wanted to make her own decision. What could Ikay do to her? Hypnotise her? Impose the tribe's will on her with the web? There was only one of her, and so many of them.

Jessica sat down. The stone felt smooth and cool under her naked skin.

Ikay folded her legs under her, and pressed her hands together in front of her face in a kind of Buddhist monk position. She spoke a few words, and when Jessica didn't react, her tail wriggled out and pushed Jessica's hands up.

Ikay's mouth twitched into an expression that might or might not be a smile, if these people smiled at all. Large gaps showed between her yellow teeth, the two incisors much larger than the surrounding teeth, not unlike a rabbit's.

Ikay closed her eyes; her face relaxed.

The air tingled.

A rush of warmth floated past, tugging at Jessica's senses.

Ikay opened her eyes and moved her hands apart . . .

Strands of light snaked into the space between her hands and were sucked up into a single bright spot of light.

Jessica tried to fight the strand that curled around her, but she couldn't. Her senses warped, the web tugged at her. Strands of sparks flowed from her unbidden, and flowed into that bright light. She sensed not just one person on the other end of those strands, but many. One of the focus points was much stronger than the others. It pulled her, stronger than she could resist. Her awareness slid and then she was in the mind of that man again.

He sat in a room gloomy with artificial lighting. His elbows leaned on a metal surface. Another man sat at the table, and a solidly built woman stood behind him near something that looked like a stove. In a corner, a pot hovered over a patch of glowing mist. Lights blinked on a wall panel. The walls were shimmering purple.

A kitchen, but not one like she had ever seen.

The man, Daya, put his cup on the table with a clunk. He met the other man's eyes. His uncle, Jessica knew.

"By the way, I'm going to be away for the next few days." Nerves tightened his voice, even though he tried to sound relaxed.

His uncle raised heavy eyebrows. "You've just come back. There's the year reports to be done. There's a board meeting on tomorrow, and—"

"The board can meet without me. I'll send Ilrith; she knows as much as I do. The year reports are on my desk. I did them last night." He rubbed his cheeks. Smooth and hairless, Jessica registered. The line of lights on the communication hub on the wall danced in front of his eyes. Damn, he was tired.

Jessica sent a thought, *Who are you?*

Daya hesitated.

Could he hear her?

The frown on his uncle's face had deepened. "But Daya . . ."

The woman, his aunt, reached over the table, setting a bowl of steaming broth before her husband. He smiled at her. "Thanks."

She then came to Daya, set the bowl down, stepped back, an expression of disbelief on her face. "You're not going to work like this, Daya?"

His eyes met hers, challenging. *Like what?*

"You've been drinking."

Daya pushed away a wave of irritation. So what? Yes, *zixas* had a potent smell; he'd wash and get changed before he left. Big deal. He needed it to keep him awake. All night he had spent going over the Network records Wonan had given him. He had found one irregularity, well-hidden amongst hundreds and thousands of data lines.

His uncle fixed him with a stern look. "Is anything wrong?"

"No."

"Where are you going?"

"Picking up someone." He enjoyed the puzzlement in his aunt and uncle's faces and added, "When I come back, I'll be moving into the apartment I bought."

"By yourself? But what message will that give the workers? There is too much of a housing shortage for people to live by themselves, even us."

"I won't be alone."

He imagined leading the girl into the living room, which had a large window that looked out over the central hall where lights glittered in the fountain and people sat around the pond. He imagined whispering her name, her *real* name, not the name those people who had looked after her for the last seventeen years had given to her. She would look up to him with those dark eyes, so like his. Then he'd tell her all he knew about their kind. He pictured her happy smile.

He had almost lost hope when she had gone missing.

Jessica's heart hammered. He was talking about *her*.

A deep silence fell in the kitchen. Children's laughter drifted in from the hall, where the oldest of Daya's nieces and nephews were getting ready to go to school. The nanny scolded them; footsteps thudded up the stairs. A door slammed.

His aunt was the first to speak. "What do you mean—you won't be alone? Daya? Is there a woman?"

Daya shrugged, trying to push away uncomfortable feelings. He wasn't absolutely *sure* where the girl was, and his interest in her was not of the nature his aunt imagined.

His aunt harrumphed and thrust the spoon in the pan with a too-loud clang. "You could have told me about this earlier. I've been talking to Ennai's family again. It seems she's sorry—"

Daya snorted, perhaps with more anger than he intended. He knew his uncle and aunt meant well and he appreciated how they had taken him in, but they didn't understand what it was like to be zhadya-born, a freak. They didn't have to put up with the resentment against his high position at the company, the implication that he somehow didn't deserve it; they didn't hear the rumours that he was supposedly bending the minds of all the board members to his will—something he couldn't do, even if he tried. They didn't hear all the slanderous rumours about him; they didn't have to pretend not to have heard. They still thought, or hoped, that by entering a contract with a *normal* girl, he could have a normal life, but it was too late for that.

"I told you I wanted nothing more to do with Ennai. She may say she's sorry, but that wouldn't happen to have something to do with my inheritance, would it? She was pretty clear: she wanted children, so she was going to negotiate a contract with another man to—look, why am I even discussing this? I'm no longer interested in her."

Jessica's cheeks glowed. *Are you interested in me?*

His uncle chuckled. "So that's what all this is about, huh?

Daya's in love. No need to be so mysterious. Who's the lucky lady and what's her name?"

"I'll introduce you when we get here." And whether it would be *that* type of relationship remained to be seen. She didn't know him; he didn't know her. Not really, after all these years. He shifted nervously. After all the taunting, he wasn't the type of person who easily opened up to others. Not at all.

A shiver went through Jessica's mind. *Who are you?*

But her connection slipped away, like a bright dot of light gliding along the strands of the web. She fought to hold on to it.

No. Stay here. Tell me who you are.

Control slipped further.

"No." She reached and grabbed Ikay's hands. "Tell me who you are!"

He didn't listen. Reality rushed back. The tribe. Thousands of eyes on her, many of them staring. Had they seen the man, too? Did the web connect to him through Ikay?

Images rushed through her mind. A dark cave, long shadows trailing over carved walls. A ceremony. Ikay standing on the beach, surrounded by females from the tribe. In the golden sunlight, she held aloft a bowl with steaming noodles and meat balls inside. She set the bowl down in the sand, and retreated up the beach. Making an offer. Waiting, but no one came.

The strands of the web faded.

People were getting up, yelling and shouting. They whipped their tails, and made frantic gestures with their hands. *Avya.* That word surged around and around.

Jessica pulled her knees up to her chest, not wanting to be part of the uproar, not wanting to be noticed. She didn't understand; she wasn't sure if she wanted to understand.

Something warm and hairy snaked over her shoulders: Ikay's tail, pulling her closer. She spoke, her old voice soothing, stroked Jessica's shoulders and caressed her skin.

10

"ANMI."

Jessica stirred. Something firm and hairy touched her arm. She rolled onto her back. Ouch. The floor under the thin mat was like concrete.

Afternoon light, warm and golden, filtered through a slatted wall, over rough timber floors and rows of humps—thighs, backs, buttocks—on sleeping mats. Arms draped over waists, tails curled around legs, heads of braids with glittering beads, shoulders and backs marked with zebra stripes or leopard spots.

Ikay sat on her knees by the side of her mat, folding a thin sheet and placing it under the pillow.

Jessica struggled to sit up and rubbed her leg muscles. Her head throbbed. Her mouth tasted like raw sewerage.

Ikay got to her feet in a cat-like movement and beckoned. Jessica pushed the thin cover aside. A soft breeze tickled her naked skin, still sticky and greasy from the white and black paint applied to it last night. She rubbed her upper arm, but the stuff was very resilient.

She clambered to her feet, her first steps wooden. Oh, her legs ached.

Now where the hell were her clothes?

Not next to her mat. Not anywhere else between the other mats, or on someone's body.

Damn it.

And yesterday, she had lost her backpack, too. With her spare clothes, and her first-aid kit, and her rope and tools and everything that might provide proof, however feeble, that she had come from Earth.

She picked up the thin sheet. It was too big to use as sarong, and when she folded it over, it was too short.

Double damn it.

Well, bugger that. Everyone went in their birthday suits here, so apart from the usual stares, she wasn't going to attract attention for not having clothes on. She flung the cloth down. Never mind that if ever she got back home she'd need clothes. Lucky it was late spring in Australia, huh? Not too cold. Summer on the way. Why worry about walking in the nuddy when there was that little problem about how she was going to get back in the first place? Her eyes pricked.

She joined Ikay on a ramp which led from the sleeping gallery into the large hall. There was a silent throng of striped bodies on the other side of the floor. A smell reminiscent of porridge drifted from a steaming pot from which a young boy scooped long white things into bowls. His eyes were red-rimmed and puffy, and every now and then he yawned, showing his rodent-like teeth. Well, look at that. These Pengali were a lot like people—they got hangovers, too.

Ikay pressed a bowl into Jessica's hands.

The white things were noodles, bluish and slightly transparent. They were slippery like wet spaghetti and kept escaping the small tongs Jessica was given to eat them with.

Ikay's fighting Amazons were already eating. Alla wolfed her food down and then took her knife from her belt, and proceeded to clean her nails while sitting cross-legged on the floor, her back straight as a cattle prod. Her black hair in tight braids glistened with oil. A single drop ran down her forehead.

Maire ate much more slowly, droopy-eyed and slumped over

her bowl. Every time she yawned, which she did a lot, a teardrop formed in the corner of her left eye. Eventually, it grew so big it ran down her cheek. Alla scowled at her.

If Jessica closed her eyes, she could hear the deep drumbeats and see Maire in the heaving mass of bodies clutching the waist of some young male. The smell of Pengali male sweat—fishy and stale—still lingered in her nose and so did the pungent stench of Pengali urine and semen, or both. By the end of the long night, most Pengali had been drunk and all over each other, cheering and whistling at bestial grunts of males having their way with females, watched and cheered on by the entire tribe. All night, Jessica had remained as close to Ikay as she could, until the light outside grew blue and everyone retired to the sleeping galleries.

A soft breath of air tickled her skin. Dora had come up next to her. In her arms, wedged against her stomach, she carried a basket of woven reeds from which drifted the smell of spiced meat.

Alla and Maire climbed to their feet, Maire with much groaning, which earned her another scowl from Alla.

It seemed they were going somewhere. Frankly, anywhere would do, as long as she didn't have to attend another orgy. She followed Ikay and her Amazons out the entrance, past the guards into the forest.

Golden afternoon light tinted everything yellow. Animals buzzed in the trees.

Jessica followed, her steps clumsy. Her feet were too soft to walk on the leaf litter of the forest floor. Every muscle in her body screamed its protest. Leaves and branches brushed against her naked skin. Her eyes pricked with fatigue and tears of frustration. She felt so helpless. With the bushwalking and abseiling and canoeing she did with school, she thought her bush survival skills were good, but what was she without clothes, without shoes and without regular food, all those things humans of the 21st century took for granted? It would take her weeks to build up enough energy and skill to even contemplate leaving the tribe if they let her.

They arrived at the beach. The sand was soft under her feet, still warm from the day's heat. The smell of fish wafted from the drying racks, mingled with the more gentle whiff of mud and the ever-present minty smell.

The suns hung low over the horizon, cloaking the opposite bank in a glow of gold.

A number of boats lay in the water. Young females hauled baskets with brown lumpy things up the beach. Others had collected nets of white waxy flowers, which floated in a string behind one of the boats.

A whistle echoed over the water. Another boat had rounded the bend into the lagoon. The occupants, three older females, all pushed off the bottom with sticks. A couple of younger females on the beach set down their loads and helped the boat ashore. Tied at the back hung the biggest fish Jessica had ever seen. It was an eel-like creature, its skin dark green. The pointed head sported formidable jaws, dagger-like teeth poking out at odd angles. It stared into nothingness out of a lifeless eye, the pupil slitted like a cat's. It was at least twice as long as the boat.

And she had been so stupid to think that she could swim to the island city? If these things lived in the water, that sounded like an exceedingly stupid idea. Another avenue for escape cut off.

Jessica started when Dora touched her shoulder.

Ikay sat in the bottom of a canoe at the water's edge. Alla waited on the beach, the stick in her hand, and Maire held the bow, standing in knee-deep water. Maybe they were taking her to the city after all. Oh hell, she hoped so.

As the boat glided across the lagoon, again with Dora pushing, Jessica looked over her shoulder. The females on the beach had all produced glass knives and were cutting the skin from the eel, peeling it away from the white flesh.

The canoe rounded the bend, bringing the solar plant into view, its "eyes" dark and lifeless now the suns had dipped below the horizon. Like yesterday, a line of boats lay in the water, all filled up with bags. A female with a stick sat in each boat. More still stood on the muddy beach, shouting and whistling at the Amazons. Tails waved and cracked like whips, communicating their wordless signs.

Hello, where are you guys going?

We're taking this weird creature back to where she belongs.

Something like that.

But as soon as the current carried the boat out of the river mouth, Dora steered the boat into the reeds, into the harsh clattering noise and the overwhelming scent of mint.

"Hey, I want to go that way." Jessica pointed at the island, which poked out of the mist on the horizon.

Ikay pushed down her outstretched arm. "Poh-poh-poh-poh."

The boat moved swiftly parallel to the escarpment, away from the island.

Jessica balled her fists in her lap, burning with frustration. *Tonight when there is another party, I'll sneak out, find some way of distracting the guards, steal a boat. I've got to get out of here.*

For a long time, she stared at the bottom of the canoe, thinking of ways to get past the sentries at the entrance to the settlement, how she would retrieve her backpack, and climb back up the cliff to look for Brian.

Light turned grey and then blue. The air cooled and softened. A blue haze, heavy with mint, settled over the water. The clattering noise in the reeds faltered and then stopped. After the monotonous racket, silence was painful.

Dora's stick splashed in a slow rhythm. Maire and Alla spoke in soft voices. The boat rocked; reeds brushed against the sides.

Jessica rested her head on her knees.

Water splashed in Jessica's face. With a jerk, she lifted her head off her knees.

And stared into a landscape cloaked in darkness. A small, red-tinged moon hung almost directly overhead, casting eerie golden light over the water. Beds of reeds showed up like patches of black.

Moonlight hit the beach barely a hundred metres ahead.

Behind it, the cliff towered into the night sky, a wall of sheer rock turned dark brown in the reddish light. Bushes clung to the cliff face like bits of black cotton wool. To the right, a white cloud hung over a copse of trees, moving and billowing like a ghost. Thumps and hisses coming from that direction suggested there was a geyser behind the trees. Behind the boat, the marshland vanished in the darkness. Pinpricks of light shone on the island, now even further than it had been when they left the tribe's settlement.

They were moving towards the shore. Ikay pointed and spoke a few words. Moonlight edged her white hair in a reddish glow. Jessica couldn't see her face, but her eyes glinted with alertness.

Dora's back bobbed up and down with each push of the stick. They were going through a thick patch of reeds, which made for hard going. The stems scraped the bottom and sides of the boat. Maire pulled handfuls of stems to help the boat along.

They were very close to the beach now. Directly ahead, a cleft in the rock face of the escarpment showed up like a black stripe, the mouth hardly wider than one metre. In that place, there was no beach and the reed field led right up to it, although Alla and Maire had to get out of the boat to push it across.

The boat slid into the gorge, dark and silent, past rock walls close enough to touch. Every breath sounded a hundred times magnified. The passage opened out into a small lagoon surrounded by sheer rock walls. Moonlight slanted onto the rock to their left and the water just at its base. The rest of the lagoon bathed in ink-black shade. A group of insect-like animals, about the size of a thumb, detached themselves from the surface of the water. With startled splashing, they flew up into the sky, their wings glittering in the moonlight, and transparent, like a dragonfly's. When their flapping had died away, only the sound of rippling water past the bow of the canoe disturbed the silence.

A shiver crept up Jessica's back.

What the hell were they doing here in the middle of the night?

The canoe bumped into a beach of large smooth boulders. Alla jumped out and pulled the stern up with a dull scraping. Jessica stepped out of the boat, straightening her stiff legs.

Maire and Dora carried the basket up the steep incline and set it down in the moonlight, at what looked like the mouth of a cave. Heaving a sigh, Dora sank down on a rock and leaned against the cliff face, the pushing stick still in her hand.

Sure, it was rude to stare, but Jessica had never seen anyone pregnant up close, let alone naked and pregnant. She had dispensed even with her belt. Grey skin stretched over the bulge in her belly, a flat bellybutton just under the widest point.

Dora met Jessica's eyes. She reached out and laid Jessica's hand, palm flat, on the top of the bulge. Her skin was warm and slick with oil. Something moved inside. A knee or a heel or an elbow. It felt quite big.

There was a memory, unbidden: a sweaty-faced woman reclined on pillows in a white bed, the camera directed ungraciously between her pulled-up legs. A gush of fluid squirted from between masses of dark curly hair. A pink rim of skin stretched to show this massive black slippery thing, then the squashed face and grey skin of the baby emerging from her body. Jessica shivered. Why had their biology teacher thought the girls would benefit from seeing that? The memory of the woman's howls still gave her the creeps.

Dora spoke a few soft words and placed her hand in the same spot on Jessica's stomach. Goosebumps spread all over her body. She also remembered the woman's tears of happiness at holding her newborn son, and the reporter's question: would you do it again? To which she answered, without hesitation: yes.

She withdrew her hand from Dora's skin and turned away. Did she have to come here to be reminded that she was infertile? Doctors had told her so many times. No boobs, no periods, not even a real woman. A freak.

Ikay dug in the basket, producing a parcel wrapped in leaves and a curious contraption that looked, for all Jessica could think, like some kind of egg-whisk, except the metal bars at the top encased a pearl the size of a billiard ball. Ikay laid it on the rocks before unwrapping the parcel. It was far too dark for Jessica to see what was inside, but a rich smell of spiced meat drifted in the breeze-less night.

OK, picnic time.

Nobody spoke while they ate. There was something about this place that made talk seem trivial.

When Ikay had finished eating, she heaved herself to her feet, picked up the egg-whisk thing and plodded towards the cave entrance. The white patterns on her back only just stood out in the dark. Jessica hesitated.

"I hate caves!" Her voice sounded unnaturally loud.

Then she hated herself for allowing her emotion to show. *Never show your fear.* Her father's words. He talked a lot about dealing with criminal men. She wasn't scared of raging bulls or bucking horses. She'd catch a koala with an attitude problem, or shoo a brown snake out of the hay shed. Leeches, she wasn't so keen on, but one thing really gave her the willies: dark enclosed spaces.

Ikay returned, put a gentle hand on Jessica's arm, but tugged her further into that maw. Jessica strained her muscles, ready to yank herself free, run back into the lagoon, outside, where the air was fresh, where she could breathe.

Ikay breathed threads of glittering mist; she was using Jessica's own tricks against her.

But she couldn't fight it, or maybe she could, but she wasn't sure it would be a good idea. *Click.*

Bright light flooded the cavern, from the pearl in the egg-whisk thing in Ikay's hand, which she now held aloft. Sheesh—it was a torch.

The cave was a few metres wide, high ceilinged and strewn with rounded boulders. Further into the rock, the passage narrowed and turned a corner.

Now that the light allowed her to see, her fear seemed silly. It was only a cave. Rocks and sand, nothing else.

Ikay led further into the cave. The ground was very wet here, and the boulders that lay scattered over the ground sank into the mud when Jessica stepped on them. Her feet were disgusting in no time.

When they had turned the corner, they came to a large cavern with a huge pool. A muddy beach sloped down into water so black it absorbed the light of the torch. To the left and right of the beach, rock formations lined the water, their surface glittering with tiny crystals. Across the pool, a sheer rock wall rose into the darkness of the cavern roof, beyond the reach of the light.

Deep grooves marked the surface of the rock and through the blackened covering of algae, Jessica recognised a five-pointed star. Like the one on the floor of the tribe's hall.

She'd been right that this place held some sort of tribal significance.

Ikay planted the torch in the ground and walked into the water, gesturing for Jessica to follow.

What? In there? You have to be kidding.

But Ikay gestured again, this time with her tail.

Jessica stuck her foot in the black water. The mud of the bottom was slimy and squishy on her feet. Her skin crawling with goosebumps, she let herself sink into the water. Cold closed around her chest like a vice.

Her movements stirred up wells of even colder water from the depths, bringing with them smells—stale, oily, unnatural, with a scent of plastic.

Ikay waited, treading water, on the other side of the pool, where the algae-covered rock wall loomed over them.

Without warning, Ikay's head disappeared.

Large ripples and rising bubbles disturbed the water. Panic rose in Jessica's chest. "Ikay." Her voice sounded small. "Ikay, please."

Ikay's head bobbed up again, muddy water running from her hair. Before Jessica could protest, Ikay's hand grabbed hers and dragged her under. She just managed to suck a lung full of air. She struggled, she kicked, but Ikay was surprisingly strong and pulled her deeper and deeper into darkness. Jessica's lungs ached to bursting. Patches of colour grew before her eyes. Up she pushed, kicking off a rocky bottom, swimming in desperate strokes. Ikay's hand slipped from hers. Her head broke the surface of the water. Gulping the air, she looked around.

Nothing.

She held a hand above the water, but couldn't see it, nor could she see the surface of the water, or the shore.

Jessica stretched out her hands, feeling nothing but water surrounding her—water everywhere.

"Ikay—help. Where are you?"

From quite close by came the sound of splashing of water and Ikay's voice, and then the slap of wet footsteps on rock.

Then a small pinprick of light winked on, floating above Ikay's forehead. It showed another cave, smaller, and filled with water. Slicks of an oily substance floated on the surface.

Jessica swam to the side and clambered onto the rocks. Had Ikay brought her here just to play tricks with lights again?

But no, as soon as Jessica had joined her, Ikay turned and led the way out of the cave. The tunnel climbed steeply and grew ever more narrow. Fortunately, the ground was even, or Jessica would have stumbled and fallen many times. Still they climbed, up, up, up. The air changed, became drier, stale, dead.

After what seemed hours, but was probably no more than fifteen minutes, Ikay stopped so abruptly that Jessica almost crashed into her.

An archway reached across the passage. Ikay's light cast long shadows over the pillars that supported it, so straight they could only have been made by a stonemason.

The pillar to the right of the path bore three carved signs. Topmost, an arrow; below it, two suns; and below that three people. Ikay stepped aside, gave a short bow and gestured for Jessica to walk under the arch, like a butler bows to his master.

Unease made Jessica's skin crawl. She shuffled forward into the pitch darkness of the room. The floor here felt smooth under her feet. Her breathing echoed unnaturally loud in the chamber, as if all sound inside it bounced endlessly from wall to wall. The air was heavy with the smell of dry stone, like an Egyptian tomb. God, how old was this?

Ikay entered the room and came to stand next to her, still

carrying the torch. Ancient reliefs covered every bit of wall space. Life-sized figures carved in yellow stone.

The panel facing the door showed a landscape of reeds and a few trees that Jessica was sure depicted the marshland outside. A stream-lined futuristic shape sat in the middle of the reedy field. Not an aeroplane, but a vehicle with a sleek triangular delta shape. Two pointed flanges at the back were tails. Bulges in the rear of the delta wing looked like engines. A large window wrapped around the front of the cabin. Three lines of rectangular portholes ran over the craft's side.

The craft didn't fit in the landscape, the treeless plains of reeds. It didn't even fit the ancient feel of the frieze. It was too modern, too futuristic. Yet, it was there, carved in perfect smoothness, in the reeds like an enormous beached whale.

To the left of it lay a makeshift camp, sheets strung over sticks.

Around the tents, people sat on the ground and stood talking. They had stern and proud faces, straight noses, high cheek-bones. . . . Human, very human, no tails, no striped bodies.

At the foreground of the picture stood a woman with a gauze shawl draped over long hair. Both hands reached out to a much smaller figure with large eyes and a tail: a Pengali male carrying a knife and wearing a cloak. He held a bowl out to the woman. Other Pengali people stood behind him, life-sized figures coming up to Jessica's chest.

In contrast, the human woman was her own height. Jessica let her fingers glide over the carved folds of her dress and stopped at the woman's chest. It was flat, like her own. Her heart skipped a beat.

There was another woman, but she stood behind a child. A third woman also had that masculine, triangular body shape, and so did a fourth. She moved along the frieze, studying every woman. Broad shoulders, tall figures. Narrow faces with high cheekbones, strong lips and pronounced chins.

To her left, another frieze depicted a city of low, graceful build-ings surrounded by airy verandas and topped with steeply thatched roofs.

People in the streets gathered in knots, pointing at the sky. Faces showed mouths open in expressions of horror. In the sky hung a bright star whose rays outshone those of the two more muted suns.

In an open space lined by large buildings stood the same craft amongst more people. A man hung a pendant on a chain around the neck of a woman. A young man clutched an older man, his face contorted with grief. A few people stood inside the craft, looking out the door. Others around the edge of the carving were being held back by armed guards.

Tears pricked in Jessica's eyes as she understood the horrific history told in these two pictures. That bright star was a celestial object, a meteorite or rogue planet, that was going to hit the home of these people. They had fled the disaster and come here, a long, long time ago. They had carved this room to preserve their story for the future and because she resembled these tall people more than the Pengali, Ikay thought—

She shivered.

These images were so life-like. To her left, a line of workers laboured to carry supplies on board the space craft. Broad-shouldered men wearing no shirts. Shadows pooled in v-shapes across the centre of their backs, formed by the pull of muscles which ran from both shoulder blades diagonally to his spine. Jessica's mouth went dry.

So often had she stood in front of the mirror and flexed those muscles, watching them alternately push up the skin and relax. She had hated them as much as she hated her white skin which never tanned or burned, and her flat, boyish chest. None of her friends had funny muscles across their backs like that.

And these people . . .

In the middle of the frieze was a flat panel with carved text, curved loops and characters that looked like a small letter n or u. She knew those shapes. They still burned in her mind like pink fire: the characters on her arm.

God.

Could it be?

She staggered back. Thousands of questions shot through her mind. What? Who? Where? Why? But most importantly: *who am I?* Threads of glowing mist leaked from her skin unbidden, and spread around the chamber.

Someone clutched her in a blanket and carried her. The person's panting breaths sounded loud in the stifled silence of a stone staircase. Sandals slapped on stone steps. Down, down, down.

A door creaked, footsteps shuffled. The door shut with a soft thud. The person who held her heaved something aside with the grating of stone on stone. A deep reverberating thud. Jessica wrestled in the constriction of the blanket. She was very young and didn't understand what was going on around her, only that something bad had happened. A small light flickered into life above her. Wan and eerie, it lit the face of a woman she felt she should know. The woman's straight nose and long eyelashes threw ghostly shadows over her face. Her skin was pale; she had high cheekbones and hollow cheeks. Deep black eyes stared down at Jessica, unblinking. A single tear tracked across dust-stained skin. Jessica reached for the woman's hair. The woman bent over and planted a soft kiss on Jessica's forehead, enveloping her in a scent so familiar, so much like home.

A deep rumble shook the ground. The woman stumbled; the light flickered. Her eyes widened. She tightened the blanket around Jessica with one hand, while lifting her chain and pendant over her head with the other. The earth rumbled again.

Cold metal touched Jessica's skin when the woman put the chain around her neck. Her lips moved. *"Am taali isverian."*

Jessica whispered those words, "Am taali isverian. I am equal." Her fingers traced the characters carved in stone.

The woman bent further down and lowered Jessica into a basin. Water ran over her belly, her chest, rose up to her chin and then covered her face. The blanket floated around her like some slimy sea creature.

I can't breathe.

Jessica struggled. The world had gone hazy green.

I can't breathe.

Fluid filled her mouth with an acrid taste. Green and black mingled before her eyes. She kicked and kicked, but the firm grip of the hands that held her did not fail. Blackness closed in.

In the cave, Jessica fell to her knees.

11

"ANMI, ANMI." Ikay's whisper sounded like a roar in the silence in the chamber.

Jessica stared at the frieze, the carvings lit in sharp relief by Ikay's light. She didn't know when she had started crying, but her cheeks were wet with tears.

With trembling hands, she ran her fingertips over the shapes of the woman taking the bowl from the Pengali man. Her ancestors? Her mother?

"Am taali isverian; I am equal."

Her hand caressed the skin on her own upper left arm where the characters of the tattoo had faded—the same script as on these walls. A clue to her past she had carried with her all her life.

She had questions—thousands of them. How old was this frieze? Who were these people? Where had they come from? Were any of them still here? If they were not, could she find them? How had she ended up an abandoned baby in a derelict building in a small town in Australia? Did that—could it possibly—mean her real parents were still alive? That woman who had carried her down the stairs was her mother? What was with the water, and why would a mother drown a child?

"Anmi." The light hovered just above Ikay's head, highlighting her hollow eyes, the pupils wide. Grooves on her face showed black like deep canyons. Her light looked faded, strangely weak. She pulled Jessica's arm with her tail.

But Jessica couldn't leave. Not now, not while there was still so much to see. A whole room full of carvings to study. If only she had a camera, or a paper and a pencil even.

She gestured to Ikay. "No, I'm not coming. I've got to know. Who are these people? Where can I find them? What does all this say?"

The echo in the chamber repeated the "s" sounds in her speech.

"Look, this is you—Pengali." She pointed at the man with the bowl. "This is me." She pointed at the tall woman. "What is she? Where did she come from? Where are her people?"

Ikay's mouth fell open, but it was not a look of surprise or misunderstanding. Her huge eyes went empty like holes. The light, now hovering a mere handwidth over her forehead, faded to eerie green.

Jessica grabbed Ikay's rough-skinned arm. "Ikay. What's wrong?"

Ikay's skin felt cold. For a second or so, a pulling sensation tugged at the warmth in Jessica's hand, as if Ikay's body was trying to draw reserves.

"Ikay, say something."

Ikay's eyes glazed over. She swayed on her feet and staggered. Her skinny arm slipped from Jessica's grip and her body crumpled to the floor. The light faltered and failed. Pitch darkness.

Oh, shit.

Jessica fell to her knees and groped around in the dark.

"Ikay! Ikay!" The echoes of her voice laughed at her. The stony smell of the room became suffocating. Visions spun through her mind. Her breathing sounded ragged just like the woman's breathing in that vision of her young self. Any moment now, she would hear a thudding door and the earth would shake, and this cave would fill up with water.

Don't be bloody ridiculous. We're way above the water.

She crawled over the stone floor, feeling her way. Her hand found Ikay's arm, relaxed and limp.

Jessica forced herself to calm down. "Panicked people are dead people," was her father's mantra. He had explained it so well, sitting in front of her class in primary school, talking about emergency evacuation procedures, in case of a flood or fire or some such. Her father knew everything so well, but reality was so different. How would he like to be in a cave on an alien world in the pitch dark?

Come on, Jess, you're bigger than this. If those people escaped the blowing up of their planet, then you can get out of this bloody cave.

She heaved herself to her feet, pulling up Ikay with her. Just as well Pengali were so small.

She shuffled sideways, waving her hand in front of her until it touched stone. Then she followed the wall to where it opened into the archway. One hand on the rock, one arm supporting Ikay, she inched down the slope.

Ikay moaned and stirred. "Anmi." She grabbed Jessica's hands, clasped them and held them to her chest.

"Yes, I'm here, I've got you." Here in the passage, her whisper sounded quite normal, even a bit muffled. "Come on, let's go."

Ikay held both her hands in a tight grip.

Jessica tugged gently. "Let go, don't be afraid, I'm trying to get us out of here."

Ikay moved her hands up Jessica's arms until their forearms touched in a firm grip, like trapeze artists. What on earth was she—

The skin on her arms warmed. Then she knew what Ikay wanted: to borrow some of her internal energy to make a light.

Jessica hesitated. *I have no control over it. When I let go, people get hurt.*

A prick of heat stung her skin, an impatient prodding.

Ikay pulled herself closer, her breath warm against Jessica's chest. A minty smell rose from her hair, homely, trusting. The soft tip of Ikay's tail stroked her cheek, and pushed her eyes shut.

Oh, all right, if you insist. Don't say I didn't warn you.

Jessica breathed out, trembling from head to foot. In her mind, she imagined herself, her being, her essence, flowing out through her breath. At first, the mist fought her will, dispersing in all directions like it usually did. Then it wove into a web, and it came to her that maybe this was necessary to get it to work properly. This ability was not some sort of weird trick—it was a form of communication. She concentrated on her arms. The skin flushed with a burst of heat. Ikay gasped and tensed. Jessica opened her eyes. "Sorry, I didn't mean to hurt—"

Soft light lit Ikay's face from below.

Both their arms glowed with a blue aura.

"Holy shit." She lost concentration.

Again, total darkness enveloped them.

"Wait," Jessica whispered, flushed with excitement and purpose. "I'll do it again."

That, however, was not necessary. A moment later, the passage once more lit up with the steady glow of Ikay's light.

Ikay said a single word, *"Ikim."*

Jessica was sure it meant "thanks."

Ikay's eyes met hers and her wrinkled face creased into a smile. Just like a teacher would smile at a bright pupil.

Arms clasped around each other, they continued down to the water.

When Jessica and Ikay stumbled out of the cave, the waiting Amazons greeted them with anxious shouts. The boat already lay in the water. High above them, the patch of sky visible between the rock walls had turned orange; bushes up there glowed with early sunlight.

Jessica helped Ikay into the boat. Dora in the bow pushed off, back through the narrow entrance and into the marshlands.

A bluish haze hung over the marsh, merging water and sky at the horizon. Sunlight was no more than a pink tinge on the tops of the trees poking through the mist, their branches drooping and perfectly still.

No one said much. With relentless monotony, Dora moved the stick—up, down, up, down. *Splash, splash, splash.* Alla leaned over the side, knife poised over the water, tail held high and twitching for balance. Every now and then, she plunged her hand in and tossed a wriggling animal into the basket behind her. Jessica couldn't see what she caught, and couldn't get up to look, because Ikay had fallen asleep, using her knee as a cushion.

Jessica stroked the old female's shoulder in mechanical movements, without really seeing anything.

Instead, she was six years old again and saw her father's face as he had sat her down on the couch, and began his confession with the words, "I would have liked to have told you when you were a bit older . . ."

He showed the folder with newspaper clippings, of an abandoned baby girl and pleas for her parents to come forward. Pictures of a baby with piercing black eyes. There was a bandage on her right shin. A burn, doctors said, from which she still bore the scar. He showed her advertisements in magazines, and posters hung at supermarkets, police stations and hospitals.

He told her no one ever came, so he and her mother had applied to adopt her.

Then, she had told her father she didn't care and at the time that was true. She remembered his bear-hug and how he had said he would always love her. But the unknown gnawed at her. She wanted to know where she came from—wasn't that natural?

Her friends from world-wide chat groups for overseas adopted children confirmed her feelings. Those girls had one thing she didn't: they knew they had come from China or Vietnam or Korea; that their parents had been too poor to look after them. Some even had little mementos: a grotty, hand-written birth certificate, a singlet they had worn, a grainy photograph taken by an adoption agency. The lucky ones knew their mother's name. Jessica had nothing.

She had posted pictures of herself to the chat groups.

You look Eastern European, a boy had said, and she had spent days reading up on the Romany people.

How about South America? someone else had suggested.

Reading about both parts of the world had left her empty. Did you *feel* something when you found your ancestry?

Yes, because she felt it now. Everything she had seen in the cave was true. This was what she had been looking for all her life.

I'm not even human.

A tear ran down her nose.

Goddamnit, I'm an alien. A fucking alien.

She bit her lip in a desperate attempt to keep herself from crying, but resistance was futile.

Another tear trickled down her nose. Jessica freed her hand from under Ikay's head to wipe it away, but it splatted on Ikay's face before she could do so. Ikay stirred and opened her eyes, meeting Jessica's with a look of concern. Her tail moved up to stroke Jessica's knee. Jessica laid her hands on top of Ikay's and Ikay curled her tail around them. Warmth flowed through the skin.

Ikay blew out a long breath and closed her eyes again. The first rays of sunlight touched her face.

A whoosh of air went over Jessica's head; Dora's tail cracked like a whip. Ikay shook her head and heaved herself up from Jessica's lap.

Dora in the bow stood still, watching the river bank with the eyes of a bird of prey, every muscle tense, her tail quivering at waist-height.

Clearly, something was wrong.

The beach of the lagoon stretched before them, edging the rain-forest with a silver margin. Boats lined up abandoned in neat rows, fishing nets folded over their bows. But another, larger boat lay at the water's edge, reed baskets on its floor.

Dora and Alla jumped out of the canoe as soon as it bumped into the shore. In swift strides, they crossed the beach to the strange boat. Footsteps led from it into the forest. Large, deep and booted.

Alla shouted something; Maire replied.

Wondering what the heck was going on, Jessica followed Ikay and the others up the beach, along the rainforest path to the settlement. The structure of rough wood and branches—like a bee hive several storeys high—blended in perfectly with the forest. Some lights still burned in the large central hall, visible through the arched entryway. The sound of many voices drifted from this entrance. Cracks of whipping tails split the air. Above all that din called a male voice. "Jessica Moore, I'm looking for Jessica Moore."

What?

Jessica ran inside, past the guards at the archway and into the crowd of onlookers that had gathered in the hall.

A group of Pengali carrying huge knives had assembled around a much taller figure: Brian. He struggled against the Pengali who tried to tie up his wrists. "Oh, fuck off. Can't you see a man's harmless?"

"Brian!"

"Oh, you are here after all, good—" His eyes widened. His white eyebrows rose.

Jessica's cheeks grew hot. Damn, she was still completely naked.

She shrank back, crossed her arms over her body, stammering, "They . . . they took my clothes." Speaking English, or even hearing the sound of her own voice was so strange, but so familiar and homely.

Now the Pengali let go of him, and he came out into the light. Yes, it was Brian, but he looked so different that she hardly recognised him.

He no longer wore the stained shirt, or the jeans. His hair was combed and neat. In the shaft of light falling through the roof, it looked like quicksilver. He wore a tight-fitting khaki shirt, fastened with hooks down the front; sturdy khaki trousers, held up by a broad belt with metal studs; and boots halfway up his calf, lined with dark mottled fur. Golden loops glittered in his earlobes. He looked like . . . she didn't know, but whatever someone with the name "Brian" was supposed to look like, it wasn't anything like this.

Without a word, he shook out the cloth the Pengali had been using to try and tie him up, muttering, "Honestly, what were these people thinking? Letting you run around naked. No dignity at all."

He tossed the cloth to Jessica. "Get that around yourself. As interesting as those, um, body paintings are, you won't be allowed in town like that."

Face burning, Jessica whispered a barely audible "thank you."

She proceeded to wrap the cloth around her body while the uneasy silence lingered.

"What happened to you when we—"

"When you ran off?"

"Excuse me? When *I* ran off? Those guys were after us—"

"Those guys were rescuers."

"Rescuers? And how did you know that?"

He just looked at her.

"Come on, tell me. You seem to know an awful lot all of a sudden. I bet your name isn't Brian. You've been lying to me."

Tribespeople watched from all around the hall; tails swishing, ready to spring. He looked uncomfortable, sad almost.

"I'm sorry, but I was lying for a reason."

"And what is that reason?"

"I thought you'd appreciate some help getting home."

"So you admit you know where we are."

"Yes. I do. I honestly didn't know when we were in the forest, but I know now."

"Tell me."

"Later."

"No. Now."

"Listen. I don't want to sound like I'm pushing you, but we should be going. I'm lucky I got here. If you think this adventure is over, think again. We've landed in a tribal war. We really, really have to go. It's . . ." He glanced up at the ceiling windows, "already mid-morning and we *have* to get into town by dark.

You've seen the killers following you after you got to the beach. They're hiding on the other side of the river."

"We came past the river mouth twice today. No one was waiting for us there."

"So it seems to you. They're hiding. Waiting for their mates to arrive so they have enough force to come into the tribal lands. They don't belong to this tribe. They're outcasts who work for people in the city. And these people are *nocturnal*. They can't see much in daylight, but once it gets dark, we've got no chance at all. We have a dangerous journey ahead of us. Let's get out of here."

"To the island city?"

"Yes. Come."

He gestured and made to leave, but Ikay ran across the floor and threw herself into Jessica's arms with a fierce blow that made her stagger back, while paper-skinned arms enveloped her in a hug and her characteristic minty smell.

"Anmi."

"Oh, Ikay, don't be silly, he's not trying to attack me."

But the voice of her subconscious said, *Who is he? He still hasn't said.*

Another part of her rejoiced. No more sex orgies, no more stares from leering males. He might not have been truthful about his identity, but in three days with Brian alone, he hadn't done any more than stare at her. And he did look different now. He knew what was going on. He knew how she could get back. With all the will in the world, and off it, she couldn't see Pengali in command of a space craft.

She pushed herself out of Ikay's hug. "I . . ." She pointed at her chest. "Go with him. He will help me now."

Ikay waved her finger. "Poh-poh-poh-poh."

Jessica pushed the finger down. "No, you don't understand. He can help me. He understands what I want."

Ikay waved her other finger and spoke a few unintelligible words.

Jessica turned. "Brian, do you speak their language?"

The way in which he gaped at her was probably answer enough. "How come you're so friendly with them?"

She hesitated on the verge of telling him about the cave and the carvings, but didn't. If he knew *she* had caused the accident, would he still be willing to help?

"They saved me. Without them, I would not be alive."

She stroked Ikay's arm, whispering, "Thank you."

"Come on, let's go," Brian said. "We've got a long way to travel."

Jessica hesitated. Well, that was a shitty choice. Stay with natives who knew something about you but whose language you couldn't speak, and half of whom wanted to fuck you, or go with a stranger who knew stuff and who could get you home, but who had been holding back the truth?

Home won.

"Sorry Ikay."

Ikay slowly lifted her hand. Her eyes, dark as the night, bore an expression of immense sadness. Her whisper carried through the silence. "Anmi."

After one last look, Jessica followed Brian into the forest.

12

T HE UNKNOWN BOAT on the beach, of course, was
Brian's.
A bundle of rags amongst the baskets moved, and
revealed itself to be a Pengali youth. He climbed out of the boat
and stood, holding the rope attached to the bow, wide eyes roving
the opposite river bank. Eddies of water gurgled around his knees,
tugging at the hems of his turquoise trouser legs. With his skin
patterns covered under a thigh-length tunic, also turquoise, and
his hair cut short, he looked almost human. And where was his
tail?

Brian stepped in the boat and shoved some crates aside.

"You take this."

He passed Jessica a small object, which felt cool in the palm of
her hand. It looked, for all she could think, like one of those
gadgets her father used to clean his telescope: a brush on a tube
attached to a rubber balloon that hissed air when you squeezed it.
Except this thing was made from silvery metal and had no brush.

"What's this?"

"It's a zapper. What do you do with it? Blast the living
daylights out of anyone who follows us before they blast the living
daylights out of us." And at her horrified look, he added, "Sorry

about this, I know, it's no job for a lady, but we can't take any chances."

Holy shit—was this trip going to be that dangerous?

"How does it work?"

He beckoned and she held up the device.

"It's easy. You point. Wait until they're about thirty yards away. You press this button with your thumb. It shoots a narrow beam of energy. You won't see the discharge until it hits something. Don't get frightened by the flash and drop the weapon in the water. Give it to me after you've discharged. It only fires once and I'll reload. The important bit is the distance. Don't discharge too soon. They're not powerful at a distance. But they're the only weapon you can legally own."

Jessica pulled her thumb away from the button, oval and also made of metal.

"Is this how the others were killed?"

"Most likely. They're very effective at short range. Pengali messengers are stealth killers. They'd use knives and catapults before anything else. Proper charge guns are illegal anyway. They do a lot more damage. They flash blue."

"But . . ." The flashes in the forest had been blue. Hadn't he seen them? "Is this . . . the only weapon you have? What about if they come from the air?"

His eyebrows flicked up.

"We'll be fine. Get in."

Well, he'd said that before, and maybe she would have been fine if she hadn't jumped off that cliff. But without any explanation, she had no way of knowing. It was all about trust and, right now, she wasn't entirely sure if he deserved it.

Jessica clambered into the boat and wriggled sideways against a stack of baskets, pulling her knees against her chest. He might have given her a cloth to serve as dress, but she still had no underwear and couldn't sit cross-legged.

As soon as Brian had settled himself, the turquoise-clad youth jumped into the bow and pushed off with his stick.

The expanse of slowly churning water between the boat and

the shore grew. Behind the beach rose the rainforest like a wall of green. Ghosts of shadows moved between the trees, small figures blending with the forest.

A chill crept over Jessica's back. The look on Ikay's face still lingered in her mind. Her lips moved in a soundless whisper, *Avya*.

The secret of the link between them might forever remain a mystery.

Who were these tall alien refugees?

Her thoughts whirled in circles. Maybe she should have stayed. Maybe she could have found out who she was. Whoever these tall people were, they had never cared about her. Why should this discovery change it? She might want *them,* but they sure as hell didn't want *her* or they wouldn't have abandoned her.

The man Daya is looking for me.

Well, he'd had seventeen years to catch up with her.

What if he never knew where I was?

Just bloody shut up, right! A decision was a decision.

"How long is this trip going to take?"

Brian didn't reply and motioned for her to be silent. He scanned both riverbanks, the forest and the tops of the escarpment, his face tense.

The boat drifted past the solar station. Beams of light intersected the air like needles. Here on the river, they were too far away to feel its power.

Only when the boat had drifted well out of the river mouth did he speak.

"First, let me apologise for not being straight with you before. I've been rude to you."

"So—where did you go when I went down the rock slide and where are we now? Who came for you? Who are you?"

"A lot of questions."

"Yes. I think I have a right to know, because your name sure as hell isn't Brian, and you're not from New Zealand, either."

He slowly shook his head. "I'm sorry about that, too, but you have to understand. According to the law we have to hide ourselves, so on the plane I was Brian, because I was on business and that's how people know me."

"You are saying that . . ." Heck—these alien people lived in Earth cities?

"We are required to have a local identity. I have a passport in the name of Brian O'Malley."

"But your real name is. . . ?"

He dug in the pocket of his trousers and pulled something out that glittered in the sunlight.

"My name is Iztho Andrahar. Trader."

He held out the glittering object—a medallion of some sort. There was a symbol on it, and writing she didn't recognise. Some kind of proof for his statement probably, never mind that she had no idea what it meant.

It shook her. There was no denying that. To accept that she had somehow ended up on another world was one thing, but to suggest that there were people who regularly did this . . .

Her heart hammered.

"Can you say that name again?"

"Iztho."

She repeated it a few times. *Iztho, Iztho.*

"You are from here?"

"No. If I was a local, I would have recognised immediately where we were. I would have spoken the local language. I would have known who those gun-happy rogues were."

"Can you tell me where we are?"

"The city-enclave of Barresh, jurisdiction of Miran, colony of Ceren."

"What . . . what does all that mean?"

"Barresh is the name of the island city. I presume you have seen it."

She nodded. "And where is that? Not Earth obviously?"

Sunlight glinted in his hair with the barely perceptible shake of his head. "Ceren."

Blue eyes examined her face, his expression guarded, as if he expected some kind of horrified reply. He wasn't going to get it. Not from her.

"You . . . you're taking this well."

"I've lived with the Pengali. I've seen the two suns in the sky. Am I still supposed to be surprised?" She pushed down the rest of her irritation. Of course he didn't know about the cave and about all the things that had made the truth easier to accept.

"Well, no, I guess not . . . not exactly. It's just that—"

What did he expect then? That she was a helpless damsel in distress pleading on her knees for him to help her?

He spread his hands in a helpless gesture.

Awkward, she thought.

"I apologise for all this, for getting you involved. It's been such a grave mistake."

"Mistake?"

"A mistake indeed. A stupid, silly mistake made by the local node of the Exchange—that's how we travel from one inhabited world to another. I don't suppose you've heard of it."

She shook her head. "How does it work?" She knew it was impossible to travel faster than light. Even so, what had happened to the plane could hardly be called travel. "Is it like a wormhole?"

"In a way, yes, 'wormhole' is probably a good description of the process. Wormholes large and small occur naturally where anti-energy that is plentiful in the universe coalesces into strands and meets normal energy. Remember that all objects are made up of potential energy, which is the energy that went into creating those objects. The Exchange shapes that anti-energy. The Exchange network nodes are in constant contact with each other, and create holes where they are needed. All wormholes, natural or artificial, form a flux strong enough to carry messages, images or objects over huge distances with little loss of time."

"You're saying that our plane accidentally got caught in this . . . network?"

He hesitated, glanced at her, probably thinking his explanation made no sense to her. But it did. It made far too much sense. It described more accurately than any previous explanation she had heard what her web did: strands of energy that connected with other strands, and occasionally with other places and other people. The man Daya was clearly in another place. Maybe on this world, maybe another. That's what Ikay had tried to teach her, the weaving, and forming the strands into a ball that became a light. Concentrating energy, which they called *avya*.

Hadn't he felt the pricking of this cross-dimensional-whatever energy that made the web? She thought back to the few seconds before the accident. The businessman—asleep; the pilot—humming to himself; and Brian—Iztho, whatever his name was—reading, without the slightest care in the world. Because he *hadn't* felt it, or because he pretended he hadn't?

He gave a grim nod. "There's going to be trouble. It should never have happened. There should have been three checks carried out before the translocation was completed. By the look of things, none of them were done. They picked up a craft on a domestic flight in a non-Union world. It's a disgrace. There's going to be an investigation. The city of Barresh could lose its Exchange Node and that will stop everything: trade, export, travel. The whole economy of the city depends on it. Worse—its independence. That's why they want to get rid of us. That's why those guys came after us in the forest: to get rid of the proof of their mistake, to shut us up—forever."

"Kill us, just to save their economy?" Because of something *she* did?

"I'm afraid so."

"But—hang on, let me get this straight. You're saying that the people in this city want us dead. So what is the logic in travelling there? We'll be going right where they want us. Shouldn't we be going somewhere else?" Maybe that was what Ikay had been trying to tell her.

"Where to? Barresh is surrounded by water. On the other side of the city is nothing but a sandbar and beyond that, the sea. Behind us is the rainforest all the way to the border. There are no other towns in the enclave and you can't cross into Miran on foot anyway; the border is sealed. As dangerous as it is, to travel into Barresh and leave by air is the only way out."

"And you can arrange that for me?" She wasn't sure if she meant it to sound as sarcastic as it did. He didn't pick up on it, or ignored it, whatever was the case.

"I have to. Don't think I'm doing this for pleasure. My name is on the line, too. We're lucky those rogues who came to the plane didn't find either of us. They were sent by the people in the council. Mercenaries, to kill us. The council now thinks that all the passengers are dead and the situation has been dealt with. You didn't make it easier when you decided to run off when I was telling you not to. Not to go down those rocks. The people who caught up with us were a search party, but now the whole tribe knows as well."

"You could have told me all this a bit earlier."

He snorted. "I knew as little as you. This backwater of a town is not that familiar to me."

If she hadn't gone down, she wouldn't have found out about the Pengali, or the frieze. The meeting with the Pengali *was* accidental, wasn't it?

Jessica muttered, "I'm sorry," and a bit later, "Thanks for coming."

He sniffed, but she guessed the apology was accepted.

"How would it work, getting home?"

"The actual process is not the problem."

"But I'll have to get onto some sort of spaceship."

"Aircraft."

"OK, aircraft. And then?"

"You'd be transferred by the Exchange."

"You mean . . ." That was absurd. To go into some kind of alien craft, which would then land somewhere on Earth. "Why doesn't anyone on Earth know about this?"

"There's a lot of sophisticated technology involved. There are craft with engines that make no noise at all and that run a current through the outer shell of the craft, making it near impossible to see, even by radar. The Exchange is well-hidden. Plus they only fly out at night. And a few people know—only they've sworn not to reveal anything. No one would believe them if they did, anyway."

Something, *something* about his words didn't quite add up. The process sounded too easy. His words seemed rehearsed. Who was deceiving whom?

13

THE TRIP TOOK a few hours, according to Jessica's best guess. She wished she still had her watch, but it had disappeared with her clothes. She stared at the passing water, reeds and floating weeds in uneasy silence.

How long was the day on this world, she asked, and Iztho produced a little gadget that told her twenty-eight hours. That explained how her watch had seemed to lose huge chunks of time each day.

At long last, the boat glided into the long shadow cast by the island. On both sides of their watery thoroughfare, small figures waded through fields of grey grass or floating lettuce, cutting or picking crops and loading them onto barges.

The clattering sound that had been so incessant since she had stumbled down from the escarpment died away. Other noises took its place. People talking in the Pengali language, voices of children, footsteps on timber, thuds, hammering.

A sea of flat-roofed buildings rose from the waterline to form an anthill of civilisation, dotted with pinpricks of light.

Hundreds of boats lay tied up along the timber platforms of a jetty. An overwhelming smell of fish drifted from the shore, occasionally mixed with whiffs of rotten eggs.

The Pengali youth in the bow stopped splashing his stick in the water. In a purposeful glide, the boat drifted sideways and clunked into wood.

"Here we are," Iztho said. Jessica stretched her stiff legs. With an inelegant step, waving her arms, she half-fell onto the jetty.

The sound of heavy booted footsteps and a deep voice made her look up, straight at a fearsome metal arrow perched on a crossbow held in the crook of a man's arm.

He inclined his head, blond curls tumbling over his forehead, framing an angel-like, heart-shaped face with eyes of the clearest cobalt blue. Human and yet strange.

He was dressed in a long-sleeved grey tunic and leggings with a white sleeveless tunic over the top. It reached halfway down his upper legs and was held by a belt around his waist. A red and silver emblem adorned the centre of his chest. If it hadn't been for his strange face, he might have been an actor in a medieval play. A horse, a helmet and chain mail would have made the picture complete.

Jessica climbed to her feet, while the man spoke in a language with rolling r-sounds to Iztho, who climbed out of the boat. He replied, in a confident tone, friendly almost.

Jessica held out the zapper. "Do you want me to walk ahead with this?"

"No, we'll be right." He glanced at the soldier. "He's here to keep an eye on us."

"A guard?"

Jessica's gaze returned to the arrow on the crossbow. Nothing like any arrow she had ever seen, this was a shaftless construction of two very long double-edged blades crossed length-wise. From the needle-sharp tip, serrated edges ran down each of the four flanges. Take a hit from that and you would be cut into ribbons. The arrow sat at the end of a metal slide. Two thick metal springs, stretched taut, strained to hold it in place.

"What good is a crossbow against some sort of laser gun?"

He gave her a sharp look. "Take it from me: never underestimate the power of a Mirani crossbow."

OK, wrong remark, Jess. Geez, the guy had toes from here to Timbuktu.

The planks of the jetty creaked under their feet as they walked towards the shore, the soldier first, Iztho and Jessica directly behind him. Their approach put an end to many waterside conversations. Fishermen dragged their nets aside and put down their baskets. They were all Pengali, but their hair was cut short and their skin patterns covered with shabby clothing. Jessica looked at their backsides, but could see only one, a young male, whose trousers clearly hid a tail.

A young boy pointed at Jessica, but the adult male who sat next to him pushed his hand down, and went back to mending the net on his lap. His eyes, though, glanced at Jessica from under hair swept over his forehead.

Jessica asked, "Is the whole city like this?"

"No. This part of the city is a separate island called Far Atok. Any Pengali without a high-class family to look after them live here. Barresh proper is very different."

"Are all of the people in the city Pengali?"

"Can you see Pengali flying an aircraft?"

True.

"The guys in power in this place are the keihu people. They're shorter, dark-skinned. You'll see plenty when we go to the other island. That's where they all live, in their huge mansions. They are the ones who are in the council and who run the Exchange. We want to avoid them for the time being. That's why we're here. Any arrivals on the main island attract more attention. We'll walk from here to the other island, but first, I'll have to borrow some clothes for you. A customer of mine owns an apartment here. It's a bit rough, as you see, but pretty good for our purposes. He normally uses it for storage, so I hope you don't mind a bit of mess. You can stay there tonight, well away from the council."

What? By myself?

Two more soldiers were waiting when they reached the shore. After a small nod of acknowledgement, they fell into step behind them.

There was a kind of market here, people selling things out of baskets. A small crowd of Pengali congregated around woven mats spread out on the compacted earth under a tree. Between legs and baskets, Jessica caught a glimpse of water creatures, barely deserving the name "fish", lined up for sale. They were black bristly things with protuberant frog-like eyes at the top of a wide-mouthed head and four lizard-like limbs spread-eagled on the mat.

The soldier at the front shouted at the crowd of shoppers. Towering over the Pengali crowd and standing out in his white uniform, he had little trouble clearing the path. Pengali males stepped aside, their eyes on the soldiers' crossbows; females squeaked and pulled their children out of the way.

After they had passed, however, many stopped to look at Jessica. Some even muttered her Pengali name, Anmi.

She pushed away unease. For people who seemed primitive, they sure communicated fast.

"Why are these people so scared of these guards? Where do they come from? They're not from the . . . whatever people rule the city?"

"Keihu. No, they're conscripted soldiers from Miran. Here to keep order. Sad and sorry as it is, Barresh isn't truly independent. It relies on Miran for almost everything; the surrounding nation is a powerful ally. The soldiers are our friends."

The Pengali clearly thought differently.

On the other side of the square, an alley stretched into the approaching darkness up the crest of a steep hill. Here, the crowd petered out.

The air became unbearably hot and stuffy now they were away from the water. High walls on either side radiated heat that had collected during the day. Soon, sweat trickled down Jessica's stomach, and down her temples into her neck.

When they had almost reached the crest, Iztho stopped at a door to the left. He produced a dark-coloured cylinder from his pocket, inserted it into a hole at chest level in the centre of the door, and twisted it. Something grated on the other side and then the entire door started curling and rolling in like a garage door mounted sideways.

Walking through, Jessica stared at the mechanism of closely positioned slats joined by a mesh of twine or metal wire.

The soldiers stationed themselves in the alley.

As the door rolled itself back into position with a clatter, Iztho led Jessica across a dark courtyard into a doorway.

A short hallway led into a larger room, packed with all manner of goods. There were crates of glass bowls, baskets of coloured sheets, bundles of coloured thread, woven rugs, cooking and eating utensils, jewellery, and a thousand other things, the functions of which she could only guess.

There was a low table in the middle of the room, surrounded by dirty cushions. On the table stood a basket covered by a rough blue cloth.

"My customer's servants left some food for you. There is a bed in the other room. I'm really sorry about the state of this place, but . . ." He glanced at her, his face almost in pity. "You simply can't go through the city like this without attracting too much attention. I have to be careful enough to find someone I can trust to explain the situation and borrow some clothes."

"And then?"

"I'll make some investigations to find the best way of getting out unnoticed. I think we'll want to use some kind of disguise, but I need to see who I can bribe to get the documentation."

Jessica pulled the cloth off the basket, and found a bowl of noodles underneath. She lifted it and put it on the table, pretending to be busy. Her fate was in his hands, and she still wasn't sure if she could trust him. The silence in the room lingered.

"Thank you for doing this." Hopefully it didn't sound too strangled.

He nodded and walked to the door. "I'll be back as soon as I can."

Before Jessica could say anything else, he left. The gravel in the courtyard crunched with his footsteps. The door squeaked then slammed shut. Locks rattled.

Jessica took a deep, shuddering breath. She ate quickly, barely tasting anything. Then she heaved herself to her feet and crossed to the single window in the room: a square hole in the wall, with no frame or glass or curtain.

Outside, the city stretched down to the water in a mass of black, dotted with islands of light. The smell of dry stone mingled with the scent of cooking and a faint, ever-present whiff of sulphur. Sounds of talk, music and other noises cut through the heat of the night. Not a single merciful breeze.

In a courtyard about three storeys below the window, light flooded from a door onto wispy steam rising from a basin. Hot water springs. She should have known. Only last year her parents had taken her to New Zealand, to places where mud bubbled, vents hissed steam and hot water pooled in silent, deadly springs. That sulphuric smell clung to everything there, too.

A myriad of stars, some clear, others barely visible, stretched overhead in a broad band, as if a painter had shaken out a brush of white paint on the dark canvas of the sky.

When she was little, her father used to take her into the bush to watch the night sky. Then, she hadn't believed it when her father told her stars were all great flaming balls of gas. Suns in other systems, he had gone to pains to explain. Had two of those pinpricks of light represented the suns of this planet? Was one of those lights in the sky above her, now, her own familiar sun?

Then another thought came to her: by showing her the stars, had her father been trying to tell her something? Her parents said they knew nothing of her origin and that she was found wearing only a nappy and a cheap romper suit bought the previous day from the department store in Pymberton. But was that true?

How much of a coincidence could it be that of all those flights in the air on that day, the "accident" had to involve her; someone who wasn't really a stranger to this world?

The skin of her arms puckered into goosebumps despite the heat.

Feeling uneasy, Jessica turned away from the window and went into the darkness of the hall, where it was quiet except for the sound of water dripping into a pool. A stone bath was set into the back wall. Steaming water dribbled from a spout fed by a stone duct that came in through a small window near the ceiling. The bath overflowed on the other side into a similar duct that left the house through another little window near the floor. The water was warm and smelled of sulphur. Jessica took off the sarong, climbed into the bath and scrubbed her shoulders until her skin glowed and most of the Pengali-applied paint was gone.

She wound the sarong around her and went in search of the bed. The air in the second, windowless room smelled of must and other staleness. It was hot in the room, and breathless amongst more boxes and baskets and all kinds of merchandise stacked in piles. She stopped to admire sarong-like pieces of cloth, painted with exquisite geometric patterns in vivid colours.

In one corner lay a mattress with some folded cloths she presumed to be bedding.

She sat down on the mattress, legs crossed, back straight. She pressed her hands together in front of her face, closed her eyes and concentrated on her palms. Everyone else was telling her what to do. Iztho was so keen to have her in this city that frankly sounded dangerous. Ikay seemed to want her to stay at the tribe, or at least not go with Iztho. She had no idea who was right; she was going to find out herself.

She was going to weave her web into a light—because that had to be the wormhole—and was going to try to talk to this Daya guy, and ask him what he knew, since he was clearly looking for her, and perhaps didn't even realise that she was listening in. Whatever he wanted with her, she'd get it over with so she could decide what to do and who to trust.

She pulled together all her strands of concentration and poured them into her hands. Drops of sweat trickled down behind her ears. The burning feeling stirred inside her. A ghost of a breeze touched her skin, making her shiver. A warm glow travelled to her hands, but stopped there. There was the usual amorphous mist, but no blue aura, no sparks, no light, nothing. The mist even refused to weave into strands.

Well, so much for that idea.

She really should have learned while she was at the tribe. And she shouldn't have left, and . . .

Shit. *You really fucked up, Jess, admit it.*

She blew out a deep breath.

Yeah, Mum, sorry about the language.

For now, she had better catch some sleep.

The light on the wall next to the door was a glowing pearl sitting atop a metal coil. One of those pearls that were charged at the plant that the Pengali operated.

The light stand had a long handle, which she presumed was for turning it on and off. It wouldn't go further down, but when she lifted the handle up, a small spoon-like contraption flung up and lifted the pearl off the metal frame, and the room went dark. Dark as the inside of a whale in fact.

Jessica fumbled her way back to the mattress, spots dancing before her eyes, when she became aware of a bluish glow from behind.

Somewhere down the bottom of a stack of boxes near the door, blue light spilled through a crack, so bright that when Jessica tried to peep in, she couldn't make out anything for the glow.

Holy shit. Was this something she should worry about? Something she should turn off before going to sleep?

She heaved the boxes that stood on top onto another pile, until she uncovered the source of the blue light: hundreds of transparent balls like the eyes of dead fish. She picked up one of them. It was heavy, about the size of a marble, and perfectly smooth. She clamped her hand around it. The surface remained icy cold.

Strange.

She opened her hand. The marble stared back at her, glowing blue light, its smooth surface revealing none of its purpose. There were no holes to thread a string, or indentations of any kind. The touch of her hand did not warm the surface. This was one heck of a weird thing. She wanted to drop it back into the box, but it clung to her palm.

What the. . . ?

Jessica held her hand upside down, but the bloody thing wouldn't let go. Sparks and waves of heat whirled under her skin, and disappeared into the glass-like material, which glowed ever brighter blue with each bit of energy it absorbed from her. She tried to wipe the marble on her knee and take it off with her other hand. Sparks flew from her fingers. The glass glowed red, then white and then sang with a deafening tone until it shattered. Jessica screamed. Pieces of glass flew everywhere. Clattered on the floor, against the walls and ceiling. The light near the door had turned itself on again.

Silence.

Jessica gasped. The palm of her left hand was red. Blood dripped from small cuts the flying glass had made on the skin of her arms. There were also cuts in her shins and feet. Very carefully and still shaking, she sank to her knees and, using a corner of her sarong, wiped fragments from the floor. She hoped to hell these things weren't valuable. Things that collected energy were bound to be.

14

J ESSICA WOKE with a shock. She sat up, peeling sweaty
sheets from her legs, wondering why she was awake, since
it was still pitch dark. But then she heard faint shuffles from
the darkness of the hall—and a giggle.

She heaved herself up and groped around the crates on either
side of the door. The bottom crate still glowed faint blue, allowing
her to see enough to find a makeshift weapon: a metal bar of some
sort. She closed sweaty hands around it, and she waited, pressed
against the wall next to the door.

Voices came closer, Pengali voices, female voices. Familiar.

Jessica lowered her makeshift weapon. That sounded like . . .
"Ikay?"

A moment of silence, and then a couple of dark figures came in
through the doorway. "Anmi, Anmi." Ikay enclosed her in a hug,
with her characteristic minty smell, and her paper-skinned arms,
and the rough touch of a tail.

Jessica dropped the metal bar.

It *had* been wrong to leave the Pengali settlement.

She stroked the old female's hair, recognising the rounded
shape of Dora over her shoulder.

Ikay led her into the living room. More dark silhouettes stood next to the window, or sat on boxes or on the table. There were at least six of them, and others were coming in from the courtyard.

How had they come in? What had they done with the soldiers who guarded the door? And what were they doing here?

But there was a more important thing she wanted to ask now she had the chance. "Show me how to do this." She pressed her hands together before her face. "I need to talk to this man."

Ikay spoke enthusiastic words, and pushed Jessica down on the table, settling opposite her, also on the table. Backlit by light coming in through the window, Ikay looked like a ghost.

Jessica willed the heat into her hands. It fought her, sparks breaking out all over her skin, eerily visible in the dark. Pengali voices chatted in urgent tones. Jessica kept her hands together, clenching her jaws.

Sparks floated from her hands in an incoherent pattern. The heat went everywhere except into her palms. She gave a frustrated cry. "Why can't I do it? Why?"

Ikay took Jessica's hands in hers, speaking soothing words. A long index finger traced a path over Jessica's inner arm, leaving a faint glow in its wake. She did the same thing with Jessica's other arm, then put her palms together and traced paths along the outside of her arms. When she had reached Jessica's hands, she started again at the elbows.

Jessica closed her eyes and tried to push heat up her arms each time Ikay traced her fingers along her arms.

There was something calming about the touch of Ikay's fingers.

Jessica tried to dip into that feeling of purpose, pouring all her being into just a small spot between her hands. Her nose itched. It irritated her and she broke her concentration to rub it with her arm. Ikay spoke a few admonishing words.

Jessica steeled herself.

Try again. This time, calm came over her as soon as she closed her eyes. The spot where the light was meant to go stood out clearly in her mind. Her skin warmed. Images swirled before her eyes. Darkness, spots of light, a sensation of movement. There was that man again. She tried to draw her consciousness to him, but a current dragged her along a different strand, as if she had fallen into a fast-flowing river. Her hands warmed, glowed and seared with pain. Damn it!

She jumped up, flapping her hands to cool them.

Ikay spoke a few stern words; the others just watched.

Was this painful for Ikay, too?

Well—painful or not, she was going to learn how to do this. She pressed her hands together once more, closed her eyes and again focused on a spot between them.

The room faded.

Cold. Snow. A howling wind.

Jessica shivered.

Daya pulled the hood of his fur cloak down over his forehead. His field of vision became restricted to the broad back of the woman in front of him. He stood in some sort of line. The biting wind carried shards of talk over the high scream of propulsor jets and the howl of hot air cannons. Daya stamped his feet, wishing those cannons warmed him instead of the shuttle's engines.

Just his luck that a passenger service had come in on his tail. By the time he had shut off and cooled the engines of his craft, packed and locked up, the line of waiting passengers stretched out of the building.

Jessica probed into his thoughts. *Who are you? Where are you?*

He drifted off into thought, and his mind was filled with sloshing water, and boats, and warm air.

She tried, *Are you looking for me? You're in the wrong place.*

He looked at the soldier standing guard at the building, and she could sense he felt like someone had called his name.

That's right—can you hear me?

"Hey, friend." The man behind him tapped Daya's shoulder.

A large gap had opened in the queue in front of him. The broad-backed woman and her companion were at the door to the hall. Daya covered the distance in a few strides, meeting a stiff-faced soldier. "Identity, please."

Daya produced his Union citizenship card from his pocket. The man raised his eyebrows, took it, and went inside the building.

Another soldier, a group commander judging by the dots on his tunic, waited at the door, and now spoke to the couple. "How long do you plan to stay?"

"Not freakin' long at all," the woman said, while her companion muttered, in a heavy accent, "We stay two days . . . sister-daughter's wedding."

A junior soldier sat at a table copying the man's reply onto a card by hand. By hand. No wonder this took so long. At the entrance to the Hedron settlement, a simple show of Daya's amber-stone earrings would let him through the first line of controls, a communicator strip on the back of his citizenship pass automatically registered his presence. No need to show anybody anything.

The soldier who had taken Daya's pass came back. He nudged the senior soldier at the door, whose blue eyes glanced at Daya, and moved the couple on with an impatient wave, then pressed Daya's citizenship card in his hands. He extended both hands palm up in a formal greeting. "We are highly honoured that a businessman such as yourself graces us with a visit. Would you like to accompany my men to your accommodation?"

Daya returned his official greeting but wondered what had earned him this attention. He had not come on an official mission and had not let anyone know he was coming; his uncle didn't know he was here, he had not even applied for a permit before he left.

Jessica tried again. *Were you looking for me? You're in the wrong place.*

Daya's thoughts didn't waver. Official accommodation was a lot better than spending the night in a crowded guesthouse and eating bean soup and mass-baked fish bread. Sticky, doughy, pale rolls, heavy with the rancid tang of fish meal.

The two soldiers led the way into the hall, parting crowds of waiting people, luggage hastily dragged aside. Three more guards idled at the building's exit into the city streets, metal crossbows slung across their backs.

The thick-walled buildings of the old city lined the street beyond, whitewashed walls with slits for windows. Grey clouds scudded low over the roofs.

By the time they had come to the city's central square, flakes of snow bit into Daya's face. The dark shapes of the council buildings and library rose on the other side of the Foundation monument, a pentagonal platform with pillars on the corners. Merchants and buyers shuffled in and out of the market hall.

The soldiers led Daya up the steps to the council buildings under an archway. Glad to be out of the wind, Daya lowered his hood. In the courtyard, fire light flickered behind the upper floor windows of a turret; all the other windows were dark. One of the soldiers bowed and gestured at the door to the turret, beyond which a spiral staircase led up out of sight.

Daya climbed, his footsteps echoing off the portrait-studded, and tapestry-hung walls. The special guest quarters.

At the top of the stairs, he came out into a large high-ceilinged room. Directly opposite the landing, a roaring fire burned in the fireplace, its orange glow gilding the dark slate, fur rugs and soft couches arranged around it. A low table was laden with books and a bowl of fruit. The smells mingled with the scent of smoke. Juni, hanga, feruzan, pricey foreign goods which, like the heavy wooden table, would have been imported by Miran's formidable Traders.

On another table stood a covered tray and a basket of fish bread. The scent of well-made bean soup mingled with that of burning straw bricks.

One of the soldiers had followed him up. He bowed. Snowflakes in his hair had melted into diamond-drops of water. "I hope these quarters are to your satisfaction. You will find the private rooms off the hall."

Daya forced a smile. Why had they decided that he was an official visitor? "Thank you. I'm actually here to visit someone who has recently relocated to Miran—"

Not relocated. I'm not where you're looking for me.

"You will have to speak to my superior about that."

"That's very kind, but not necessary. I know my way around."

"My supervisor insists you shouldn't go out by yourself. We've had some problems here concerning . . . foreigners. Only a few days ago, a visiting merchant was killed just outside the markets. Please wait until we can provide an escort." He gestured at the table. "Your meal is ready. It's warm in here."

Daya glanced at the window, where the glow of the fire in the hearth reflected against the backdrop of the leaden sky outside. He nodded. "All right."

The soldier bowed again. "Then have a good night."

Daya sat down on the floor by the hearth. He held out his hands to soak up the warmth, held his hands closer, and closer, until the flames licked his skin. Heat flowed through him, through her.

Jessica whispered, "What—" The Pengali in the room stared at her. Her cheeks throbbed with heat. She brought a hand to her ears; they felt hot, too.

Once more, she pressed her hands together in front of her face. She closed her eyes and concentrated on the spot between them. Her skin grew warm. She braced herself for pain but if there was any, she didn't feel it.

A steady stream of energy flowed into his hands. His skin glowed soft green. The light peeped through the cracks between his fingers. When he moved his hands apart, it flooded the room with brightness.

And flooded the dank apartment's living room. Jessica took in its eerie beauty. She cupped the light in both hands, her lips moving in a whisper, "Yes. Yes, yes, yes."

All the strands of energy curled into one. They no longer flailed where she couldn't control them.

Soft spots of glow lit up here and there amongst the Pengali in the room, weak like candles in the floodlight hovering above her outstretched hands. "I did it. Ikay, I contacted him." No matter that she hadn't yet managed to get a reply. That would come with practice. She rose, holding the light aloft. "I did it, I did it."

The Pengali spoke in excited voices. A young female kneeled on the floor, her head bowed. Another Pengali, a male, unwrapped a parcel, spreading a hearty scent of soup. He came to stand next to the female who still crouched on the floor, and held a bowl out to Jessica.

Her legs trembling, Jessica clambered off the table, holding the light aloft. The other Pengali had lined up on either side of the male, who still held out the bowl. She recognised the scene from the frieze. Goodness knew how many years ago, her ancestors had fled and when they arrived in this area, hungry and dishevelled, the Pengali had offered them hospitality.

She had seen a memory of Ikay on the beach, offering the bowl to an imaginary person. The Pengali might repeat that ceremony every year, until someone from those people came back.

I am here now.

Jessica took the bowl from the male's hands. The soup tasted salty, with the tang of fish. While she drank, no one spoke, but more and more Pengali slipped into the room from the courtyard and even through the window, some adding their lights to the increasing glow floating near the ceiling. They stood, silent, watching her sip the steaming soup. History replayed. Her name was Anmi and she represented her ancestors. After so many years, Jessica had never expected to find out anything about where she came from. Tears pricked in her eyes.

A man's voice disturbed the silence. Footsteps. A slamming door. Someone shouted in the courtyard.

Lights flickered and went out, returning the room to darkness. A tall figure entered the room, a mere silhouette. Someone clanged down the lever on the light, bathing the room in a harsh glow.

The figure was a soldier, his crossbow raised.

Pengali scrambled to their feet, and tripped over boxes in their efforts to get out of the way. A male flung himself under the table, a female ducked behind boxes, a few made for the door. One jumped onto the windowsill, and then up onto the roof, until his tail disappeared from sight. The soldier shouted. A male voice in the courtyard replied.

Jessica thunked down the bowl and jumped forward, pushing the Pengali back from the door, her arms spread wide. "No, no, stay here. There're more soldiers out there. Someone will get hurt."

A young boy ducked under her arms. He reached the door only to crash into a second soldier, who clamped a muscled arm around his neck until the boy made choking sounds. Then an older Pengali female burst in, shouting a war cry. She grabbed a stool from next to the door and hit the soldier over the back. He released the boy, swung around and backhanded her across the face. She shrieked. With a great cry, another female jumped out from behind the boxes: Alla. There was a glitter of a knife, and the guard fell back against the wall, clutching his shoulder. Blood spread over his tunic.

The other soldier shouted and raised the crossbow, which didn't appear to be loaded.

Alla and the soldier regarded each other in complete silence. Alla's tail waved threateningly at shoulder level. The soft moans of the soldier's injured colleague as he attempted to get up were the only sounds in the room.

The soldier's hands tightened around the release mechanism of the crossbow. With a metallic *zhing*, a metal bolt shot into position from a magazine underneath the slide. A tingle drifted on the breeze, and chilled Jessica's skin. Somewhere close by something drew energy.

"Alla, get out of the way," she said in a low voice.

The Pengalis' eyes widened, as if they felt the tingle of energy, too. In that moment, the young boy ran into the courtyard.

All remaining Pengali scrambled after him. The injured soldier tripped up a female, causing another Pengali to stumble, but they jumped up, or were dragged up by their kin, and kept going. The soldier with the crossbow shouted, moving the weapon to get an aim on the flow of targets, but the Pengali were already gone. Some into the courtyard, others into the hallway. Splashes of water made Jessica realise how they had come in: through the ducts in the back wall. The soldiers ran into the courtyard, shouting, and the next moment someone ran into the room, panting.

"What happened here? How did they get in?" Iztho. His eyes wide, nostrils flaring.

"I don't know. I woke up and they were inside."

"There were two guards outside your door. I told you to warn them, didn't I?"

"Calm down. They were only Pengali. Harmless. They were helping me."

He flung his arms wide. "Helping you with what? Helping you be noticed by the council? Helping to make sure you never get out of here?"

"No. I don't know. They don't seem dangerous."

"*They don't seem dangerous.* I'll tell you something: those guys who killed the other passengers—they were Pengali, too. They were harmless primitives? And here I am, risking my reputation to get you back safe, and you—"

Jessica folded her arms over her chest. "These Pengali are not dangerous."

For a moment, he glared at her, then he harrumphed and stomped across the room. "All right. Go ahead. Be stubborn about it. We can't reverse the damage. By now all the town will know that you're here. Go back to sleep. In case you have any more stupid ideas, I'll stand guard myself."

He strode out of the room. Gravel in the courtyard crunched under his feet. "That's the last time I'll do anything for an obnoxious woman." The door slammed and rattled shut behind him.

15

N OW SHE FELT guilty. He was right about one thing: it was true that she didn't know much about this world. She sat back down on the mattress and glared angrily into the dark, her arms folded over her chest.

Well then, maybe he should tell her. Whose fault was it that she didn't know much anyway?

She let out a forceful breath.

Acting like a spoilt teenager was not the answer either. She hadn't exactly been friendly to him, and maybe he hadn't been sure how much he could tell her. Perhaps he suspected she might not be what she seemed to be either. And maybe he had a whole lot more to teach her than the Pengali could. She could at least speak to him and find out what he was willing to share.

When he returned in the morning, she would apologise to him, and from then on, she would not let his arrogance rile her so much.

But when he swept into the room in the morning, apologies were long forgotten.

"Time to get up." The heels of his boots sounded like gunshots on the stone floor.

Jessica groaned, rolling on her back and staring into the semidarkness. All her muscles ached and felt stiff from the hard mattress. "Is it light outside?"

He flipped on the light, which shone mercilessly in her face.

"It is light now."

He now looked even less like a faded hippie. His hair rippled over his shoulders like mercury. He wore, of all things, a fur cloak —in this heat! The medallion he had shown her yesterday was now prominently displayed on his chest. He also wore earrings, golden loops through his earlobes. He looked in his element, groomed, comfortable.

"Did you sleep well?"

"Well enough." But even as she said this, a wave of fatigue engulfed her.

He raised his eyebrows. "You look tired."

Look tired? She was tired. Damn Pengali, damn different days, damn everything. Her whole body was out of whack, but she was not going to crumple and let him play the knight in shining bloody armour. "I'm all right."

"I've brought some breakfast and you better eat it quickly. We have a lot to do today."

"Doing what?"

She stumbled to her feet and followed him into the living room, where a bowl stood on the table. Some sort of translucent noodles.

He explained while she ate.

"I had some excellent results yesterday. I used some of my contacts in town, and I'm fairly confident I'll be able to get you out."

"You mean—take me home?"

"It will be the first step, but we're not there yet."

Jessica took a bite. Noodles dangled down her chin. "So what comes first?"

"I have to apply for a permit for you to leave town, and that isn't as easy as it sounds, because you have no documents and the entire town is looking for you. So obviously you will have to travel in some sort of disguise, and I think I've found a solution. But first you need to be made presentable, and you need to learn to behave in a way fitting to the personality your documentation will say you are."

Geez, he was speaking in legalese. "And that is?"

"As my wife."

Fucking what?

"Traders' wives travel with their husbands, often under the same licence, and unless they plan to travel separately, they don't need their own documentation. However, Traders' wives are refined women. Polite, educated, softly spoken, cultured."

Everything you are convinced I'm not. Fuck you. You're doing this on purpose.

He turned to her, pointing his finger at her chest.

"Don't get any ideas. I don't like it either. It's my reputation on the line. Everyone in the Trader Guild knows the Andrahar heir does not have a woman. I don't intend that to change, so you keep quiet, and we might get out of here without too much trouble—"

"You know what? I don't like your threats, and I don't like being intimidated."

"Do you want to go home or not?"

"I do, but I don't want to sell my fucking soul to do it."

His nostrils flared. "Lady, don't you *dare* suggest that I will *ever* lay a finger on a woman who is not willing."

She stared at him. Believed every word he said.

"If you are a lady, don't use that sort of language either."

"So it's OK for you, but not for me?"

He stared at her, blew out forcefully through his nostrils. "You are truly like no woman I've ever met."

"Then you've only ever met dishrags, not real women."

"I *didn't* mean that as compliment."

"I didn't expect it to be. Do whatever you like. Just don't expect me to follow mindlessly."

Again, a wordless stare. Longer this time. Something she couldn't quite put her finger on softened in his stance.

He sighed. "Meanwhile . . ." He dug in a basket on the floor. The cloak fell aside and strapped to his arm was, clearly visible, a metal contraption that looked too much like a gun to be anything else.

The only weapon that's legal to own. Yeah—right. What was that, then? A water pistol?

He put a bundle of fabric on the table. Red, thin woven cotton. "I borrowed this dress."

Jessica picked it up. Folds of fabric tumbled onto her lap, releasing a musty smell. It was a simple dress made of thin material, straight, long-sleeved, the material crumpled beyond redemption.

"Put it on."

She gestured at the sarong. "Can't I just wear this?"

"No. That's what I'm trying to get through to you. You have to dress appropriately. Covered shoulders, no bare knees. Dress code is very important."

Jessica glared. But there was nothing for it; she didn't have the energy to fight over it. She picked up the dress and went to the bedroom. In the darkness she slipped off the sarong, folded it, and pulled the dress over her head. It reached only to just below her knees and the hem hung much lower at the back than at the front. Pulling the front made the sleeves twist around which caused the seams to cut into the soft skin under her arms.

She ran a hand through her hair, fingers catching in knots. The action freed a whiff of the gooey soap Ikay had used.

Her mind filled with doubt. The way Iztho was talking, she would soon be out of here and would never find out who these people were, where they had come from and where they had gone.

When she entered the living room, Iztho pulled a face. "I'm sorry. That really *is* dreadful."

"I'm glad you agree with me for once."

He met her eyes in a wordless stare. Was it pity she saw there? Well, she didn't want his pity.

"Yes, we will have to do something about that as soon as we can. Here, put these on as well." He passed her a pair of sandals.

Jessica dropped the sandals on the floor and wriggled her feet into them. The straps cut across the tops of her toes, but they fitted better than the dress; they were probably a man's.

Then they were ready to go. She followed him into the courtyard and out the door into the alley. They started off down the hill. The suffocating heat of the previous night had dissipated and the alley was bathed in cool, blue-tinged shade. Sunlight only touched the very top of the wall to their left, the light still yellow and feeble, the shadows ringed with a distinct double edge.

Three soldiers joined them, one in front, two behind.

It seemed that Iztho really had organised their safe passage, if even she'd had doubts about him. Jessica remembered that she had intended to apologise for last night, although she didn't really want to broach the subject of the Pengali. It would only lead to more arguments.

Jessica asked, "How far are we going?"

"To a guesthouse on the other side of town. It's a fair walk."

"Doesn't this town have gliders or shuttles or trains, or boats?" She looked down the alley, where she could see nothing except walls interrupted at regular intervals by timber doors. When she arrived last night, she had seen no form of transport other than boats. No engines, no motorised equipment, no technology other than the rechargeable pearls used as light source.

"No. No trains or boats."

"What sort of place is this?"

"It's Barresh. It's poor, it's a backwater and it's total anarchy. You don't think this stuff-up with the Exchange could have happened anywhere else?"

"Anywhere else? How many other places are there? Other . . . planets?"

"Colonies. There are many."

"How many?"

Giant space ports with large ships going in and out. Modern equipment, blinking lights. Like in that kitchen she had seen in Daya's mind. He was now in another place where it was cold. She eyed Iztho's cloak. Obviously intended for a cold climate.

He met her eyes, a wary expression on his face. "The less you know, the easier your return will be."

"You mean you can't tell me, or you're not allowed?"

"You don't give up, do you?"

"No." Now she was getting angry again. Never mind the bloody apology. The man was an arrogant prick. "You told me I'm here because someone did something wrong. Don't you think that means I'm entitled to know a bit more about what happened?"

Another sharp glance. He said nothing. It seemed the conversation was over.

His eyes scanned rooftops and alleys, his hand under his cloak, where his weapon was hidden. The sunlight glinted off the crossbow carried by the soldier in front. The two soldiers behind them had caught up.

At the bottom of the hill, the small market lay deserted at this early hour. Only a giant lizard sat under the tree, scratching the dirt where the fishmonger had displayed his wares yesterday. It scuttled up the tree trunk at their approaching footsteps.

The soldier in front led them around a corner to the left, away from the water. Here, they entered a wide, tree-lined street bordered by hills where every bit of ground had been built on. In addition to that, the hills seemed to be hollow. Tunnels led off the street at regular intervals and inside Jessica could see the lights of markets, eating houses and shops.

Pengali ambled in and out of these entrances. No one was in a hurry. Older males gathered in groups, their jaws working as they chewed some green substance; mothers carried children and youngsters laughed. They wore rags and walked bare-footed, showing none of their skin patterns.

Many of them watched the small procession of non-Pengali from the corners of their eyes. At Jessica's passing, hands moved in unspoken signals, first close, then on a balcony, then further down the street. As if through an inaudible radio system, the news spread through the city faster than they could walk.

There was no getting away from their stares.

On and on they walked. The soldier in front, Jessica next to

Iztho in wordless brooding, and the other two soldiers behind. Most of the people on the street were Pengali, but some were taller, and looked more like short and stocky Earth people, except for their strangely round faces with closely-spaced eyes and large nose. Every now and then they would pass a Pengali male or female who was well-groomed and dressed in turquoise. Most of these lugged bags filled with various items of produce, bulbs, bundles of leaves and fruit. They didn't stop to speak to anyone except vendors and then only briefly. But they signalled just as much as the others.

Jessica chanced a question. "Why do they wear that unusual colour?"

"They're servant colours. It means they're employed."

"Who employs them?"

"The ruling class—the keihu people."

He had talked about the ruling class before. She suspected they were the short and chubby people.

But what about the tall people from the frieze? "Are there any other type of people in the city?"

"There are no other people from Earth—"

"What about other kinds?"

He raised his eyebrows. "The largest group are the Mirani army. Most of them look like these soldiers here—"

"What about others?"

Again, that sharp glance. "Why are you asking? Did you see anyone in that forest except Pengali?"

She shook her head, then decided to plunge in. If she didn't ask, she would never find out anything. "No, I didn't see anyone. It's just that the Pengali showed me this rock carving of these people . . . tall . . . and . . ." She gave a helpless gesture, not willing to say *like me*, ". . . arriving at the Pengali settlement in some kind of spaceship, and . . ." She shrugged, and tried to sound careless. "I just thought they might still be here. Just wondering . . ." Hell, what a lame argument.

His frown deepened. "A rock carving?"

"Yeah—in the cliffs over there."

"In one of their sacred caves?"

Jessica cringed. Maybe it would have been better not to mention it. She didn't like his tone when he spoke of the Pengali activities.

He asked, "Did it look old?"

She nodded.

"How old?"

"I don't know."

Then his face closed again. "I have no idea what you're talking about. I've never heard of people on rock carvings. Not here in Barresh anyway. But you should know that the Pengali are masters at craft. I mean—you saw all the stuff in the merchant's apartment unit. Individual masterpieces. Their cloth, their glass-stone work. Sells very well. I wouldn't put it beyond them to produce some rock art."

He laughed, but it didn't sound genuine.

"It's not like that." Jessica shook her head, pushing down her irritation. "This was old, really, really old. Thousands of years."

He shrugged. "Well—then I don't know."

And with that, the conversation was over.

Jessica stared at the uneven pavement passing under her feet. With every step, she walked further away from the truth about these tall strangers. And somewhere out there in the universe was a mother, or maybe a whole family, who had lost a baby.

Somewhere out there was a man called Daya who was looking for her, who wanted to pick her up, but was in the wrong place, and whom she could almost contact through the web, but not quite. She must try again as soon as she could.

They came to a bridge over a canal. Lazy water flowed between its straight sides, reflecting the yellow morning sky. Pengali boys were jumping off the railing into the water below, cascades of laughter following them through the air.

Four soldiers stood sentry on the other side of the bridge. Their blond heads bobbed as they exchanged greetings with the guards who accompanied Jessica and Iztho. Like cherubs in uniforms, they looked. Similar to each other, deadly but silent like stone. Cobalt blue eyes glanced in Jessica's direction.

Away from the canal, the scenery changed abruptly.

Large leafy trees lined the street, interspersed with flower beds and benches. Gone were the rubbish mounds, street stalls and compacted dirt pavement. Two-metre walls lined both sides of the street. Elaborate, albeit sometimes rusty, gates offered glimpses of the houses beyond.

No more large apartment blocks, but single blocky houses, two or three storeys high, surrounded by gardens and high walls. Mosaic paths inlaid with glittering stones, flowering bushes clipped to perfection, fountains dribbling steaming water into ponds, porches supported by carved columns, leading up to double front doors with metal ornaments.

The people changed, too. The short and squat ones were in the majority here. They were olive-skinned with dark curly hair and deep-set eyes. Many of the men had big double chins and wide spreading bellies; women sported several layers of hips. Taller than the Pengali, they still reached only to Jessica's shoulders. Most of these people were dressed in clothes from drab khaki material. They wore a lot of adornments. Their short, sausage-like fingers were hidden under jewellery. Multiple chains of beads glittered around men and women's necks. Their hair was braided into plaits interwoven with beads.

The only Pengali here were the turquoise-clad type, who moved like silent ghosts, bustling, carrying things, wheeling trolleys.

Then houses made way for larger buildings, two or three storeys high, external stairs going up to higher levels, with galleries, and colourful displays in open façades. Shirts and dresses hanging on racks. Shawls or sarongs folded up on shelves. Cushions of all shapes and sizes, rolls of fabric stacked up to the ceiling.

The smell of food drifted from a shop where people sat at tables and chairs. It could have been a café in an exotic place on Earth, until a Pengali wove between the tables carrying a basket-like tray crammed with bristly-skinned fruit that had been cut open, scooped out, and filled with red and green spotted leaves.

Soldiers in twos or threes guarded every corner. They stood rigid at their posts; their eyes didn't miss a single movement in the street. Most citizens ignored them, walking past stone-faced. A Pengali, carrying a sack on his shoulder, spat on the ground. Equally stone-faced, one of the soldiers unslung his crossbow and slipped it into the crook of his arm. His hand tensed and with a metallic click that caused sóme women to gasp, an arrow unfolded from the magazine. The soldier held the weapon aimed at the old man while he shuffled down the street, ignoring the weapon. When he had gone, the soldier made the arrow disappear into the magazine again.

The street opened out into a large open square, a desolate and empty place with cracked and uneven pavement. Directly opposite, behind a line of bushes, the land fell away. Jessica spotted glimpses of marshland. To the right were huge trees with market stalls underneath their overhanging branches.

Behind them, a two-storey building stood half-sheltered by giant pink-flowered trees. A wall surrounded the complex, crumbling where the roots of the trees had worked their way into the brickwork, bulging from cracks like varicose veins.

An opening in the wall led to the entrance, where a glass dome, many of the panes missing, protruded above the building's roof. On the first floor, to the left of the entrance, a large window looked out over the square.

Iztho grumbled, "That's the Barresh Exchange. See what a disgrace it is?"

Yes, Jessica saw that. The centre section with its large window was the only part of the building that looked in any kind of habitable condition. In the wings to the left and right, windows glared like empty holes, the glass absent or broken. Walls were weather-eaten, pock-marked with what looked suspiciously like bullet-holes. Crowning the walls, exposed roof beams pointed up at the sky like dead fingers.

"That place made the mistake that brought us here?"

He nodded, his face grim. "We don't want to go in there, or anywhere near the council until we're convinced they are going to believe what we're telling them you are. They're going to deny everything about their mistake."

"But how does it work, if the building's here and we crashed all the way in the forest?"

"The craft are transferred to a point above the city, supposedly outside the atmosphere, but that clearly didn't happen with us. The network requires a three-point check: one each from the on-ground nodes, like in this building; and one from the aircraft. If the Network doesn't get a legitimate response from both the receiving node and the craft, it shouldn't translocate. That's the simple version of the story. The fact that this has happened is an outrage. I'll make sure that the Barresh council won't be allowed to cover it up, but only once we're out of here, when you're safe. I wonder how many other wrecks are in that forest."

They crossed the square to the line of bushes. There was a gate, where four soldiers stood guard. One soldier opened it to let Jessica and Iztho through.

They came to a wide expanse of weed-dotted land on which stood a single aircraft, velvet black, like a crouching panther. Two red lights blinked on the wing tips, which nearly touched the ground. A line of oval portholes ran from the front wraparound window to the tail section, where broad flanges looked like exhaust outlets. The door was open.

16

_____

J **ESSICA GULPED** and stopped. "Where are we going? Where are you taking me?"

If he thought she was coming in that thing, he would have to think again. She would agree to nothing unless she fully understood it.

His blue eyes met hers. "Do you have a single trusting bone in your body? I told you we need to make you act the part of a lady."

"Where are you taking me?"

"Nowhere. Do you think I'd risk my licence by going off without a permit?"

"I don't know about permits. You don't tell me anything."

"And you would do well to accept what you're given once in a while." There was that accusing finger again.

She was going to say _You don't give me anything,_ but that wasn't true at all. He wasn't giving her some information she dearly wanted to know, but he had explained how he wasn't free to share everything. He could just as easily have left her to fend for herself with the Pengali. He didn't really need to take any risks for her. He was right. She _wasn't_ a lady; she was a mangy dog expecting a kick. Crawling under the table, but positioning her teeth so she could inflict the most painful bite possible when the foot came again.

She'd built a shell for herself that looked like a tough cowgirl on the outside, but the armour was close to breaking and inside she was a mess. If she wasn't human, then why did she feel so much pain?

He stopped at the door of the aircraft. Sunlight made his hair glow like gold.

"It is a truly poor place where you've grown up. I hope to show you that there are places where someone's word is just that: his word. I promised I would help you, and no matter how stubbornly and stupidly you behave, I will do just that."

He opened a panel next to the open door. At the press of a button, plates of black metal unfolded from the recess and fashioned themselves into steps.

A gust of wind blew Iztho's hair across his face. His rings glittered in the sunlight as he raked it back and gestured for her to go inside. Like a gentleman holding open the door to a lady. His expression, though, said otherwise; he hated her, with good reason. She'd behaved like a brat.

Jessica felt dreadful.

She climbed the steps and plunged into semidarkness of the aircraft's cabin, a single space the size of a small room. When her eyes had adjusted, she saw control panels, blank screens, dials and other instruments on a panel that looked like the craft's controls. A red light blinked every two seconds or so.

A table surrounded by a semicircular bench and padded seats, bolted to the floor, was directly opposite the entrance. Cupboards, made of what looked like dark-coloured wood, lined the walls, their glass doors showing stacks of documents, small boxes and instruments, all individually strapped to the shelves with neat ties threaded through golden eyelets and secured with gold clasps.

Iztho opened a door, slid the cloak from his shoulders and hung it on a hook inside.

"Is this all yours?"

"Yes." He crossed to the table and set something down: a flat, tile-like object. "And before you accuse me of having known that we would end up here in advance: I had a member of my staff bring it here."

He slid in the seat opposite her.

"Now, firstly, you'll need to at least pretend you can speak to me in my own language. That is Mirani. I don't suppose you have ever heard of it."

"No."

He slid the tile-like object towards him, pressed the corner and pushed it back to her.

It was a screen of some sort, like a tablet, but much thinner and more flexible.

Two black characters, if the assembly of circles, lines and triangles could be called that, occupied the centre of the light blue background. He shook his finger, the Pengali signal for *no*, and he said *"Doi."* Then he touched the screen, where a single character appeared. He made the Pengali hand signal for *yes*, the downward movement of the hand, and said, *"Eni."* A different character appeared on the screen.

"Repeat this until you remember."

Geez, this guy didn't muck around.

Jessica had no idea how much time had passed when she stretched and looked up from the screen. The brightness of sunlight that fell in through the window and hit the craft's instrument panel made her squint. On the other side of the window, the wind stirred clumps of weeds dotted over the expanse of barren land that was the airport. God, she had a headache.

"Keep working." He spoke Mirani. The screen translated, but she didn't need the translation anymore. He had said it so often that the patterns in the text almost jumped at her.

He sat on the opposite side of the table, keeping her company as she worked at his screen. A carpet of yellow cards spread out before him. He held a thin pen, with which he wrote out characters in immaculate precision. A jar with three more such pens stood on the table.

"I'm hungry," she said.

He grumbled, "In Mirani."

Jessica clenched her teeth and repeated in Mirani. "I'm hungry."

"Have you finished?"

Jessica glared at the rows of sentences, verbs, nouns and conjugations that filled the screen. Whenever she completed one exercise, the next one appeared. It was never-ending. "I think I've finished."

"I think you can do a few more pages. My younger brother did better than that in most of his language courses."

Jessica clamped her jaws. What did she care about his younger brother? The man was a slave-driver. In one morning, she had learned more Mirani than she had learned Japanese in four years of study. But all right, if he wanted to be stubborn, she could be stubborn, too. She returned to her work.

Give ten examples: <verb> <action> <place>.

Her fingers danced over the lower half of the screen, where she had long since become accustomed with the circles, angles, dots and lines that made up the Mirani alphabet, and the combinations of those that formed syllable-characters. There was an advantage to being naturally good at learning other languages. She squinted against the screen's soft glow, letting lines flow through the text. The patterns weren't quite as strong as they had been this morning —she was tired indeed—but still clear enough to be visible to her. In angry keystrokes, she typed out the sentences, murmuring them to herself. *Gammari . . . jimara . . . talin.* <I want> <to go> <home> *. . . Gammari . . . dolo . . . palin* <I want> <to eat> <dinner> *. . . Gammari . . . jimara—*

A clunk on the wooden tabletop made Jessica gasp. Iztho rose from his seat, his face set in a scowl. "Is there a less childish way to make your point?"

"I tried. I think I learn enough today."

"Learned."

"Learned!"

He dragged the screen across the table. With an experienced touch of this thumb, he flicked back through the pages Jessica had completed. His light blue eyes moved as he read each page, and although he said nothing, he gave a tiny nod each time he progressed to the next page, and the next one, and the next one. Finally he rose, flicked the curtain of hair back over his shoulder and retrieved his cloak.

"In all honesty, I should tell you that my younger brother scored very rare perfect results in his Trader exams. And he already had a basic knowledge of the languages he learned."

Jessica balled her fist under the table. Ha—he was impressed; he was just too stubborn to admit it. And somehow the look on his face was worth more than all the praise she had ever received at school. Because no one at school had ever told her that her work wasn't good enough. At primary school, she'd pretended to be working, while secretly sending out coils of mist trying to find out who had a crush on whom. Now, in the last years of high school, she was doing subjects not due until next year, but the teachers let her set her own pace. The teachers couldn't keep up with her. They kept telling her they had no more study material for her, and she was bored.

So—right. Bring it on. She *would* learn his language as quickly as she could. She *would* learn to be a lady, and whatever other challenges he dreamed up. Because she would not let herself be shown up by this arrogant arsehole.

But the afternoon was long. She supposed it would be, if the day was twenty-eight hours, but it felt like time had crawled to a stop. Even though there was some sort of cooling system going, the door was open, and hot humid air wafted into the cabin.

Jessica was tired, and when she rested her head in hands she must have dozed off.

The sound of a door creaking. Soft footfalls on the floor.

She hadn't seen any threads, or mist, but somehow, she was in Daya's mind again.

He lay on a bed in a dark room. A thin strip of light fell in through a crack of a door which stood ajar. Something shuffled nearby.

What the. . . ?

He pushed himself up.

Firelight edged the rug and the blankets on his bed in gold.

No one.

Daya jumped up, throwing off his blankets, and went into the hall.

His footsteps echoed hollow in the staircase, the walls only lit by the glow of the fire above. The downstairs hall lay deserted; the large metalwork door was closed. Daya moved up the latch and pushed.

He couldn't move it.

What was this nonsense? Wait—he'd get someone to unlock the door.

Taking the steps two at a time, Daya ran back up the stairs, grabbed his bag off the table, took out his reader, turned it on . . .

A soup of grey and blue dots sizzled over the screen. The only other place he had ever seen this happen was inside the refugee camps, where scramblers prevented unauthorised Exchange access by camp inmates.

His heart thudding in his throat, he walked to the window. Drifting snow lashed against panes set in their metalwork frame. None could be opened; the window had no ledge on the outside, and below was a three-storey drop to the ground.

He ran to the bedroom, but the situation was the same there. Trapped. He sank down on the bed. How could he have been so stupid?

Just as he sensed a person moving in the room, the figure lunged at him from behind. A hand closed over his mouth.

Jessica jerked up. The rich interior of the aircraft came slowly into focus. Iztho was still working with his cards.

She stared at the screen, but turned her concentration inwards.

Who are you? Where are you? What can I do to help?

There was no reply.

17

IZTHO STOPPED in the street and gestured. "The dressmaker."

In a shop on the right side of the street, lengths of fabric hung from beams suspended from the ceiling, waving like flags in a gentle breeze. Orange, bright pink, yellow, blue, red, the colours of an African market blended into a tropical tapestry of colour.

A man in a flapping orange robe squeezed himself from the narrow aisle. He squinted against the light, chest a-glitter with chains and bangles. "Trader Andrahar!"

Iztho spoke to the man in the local keihu, waving a hand at Jessica. The dressmaker's eyes widened, then beckoned for Jessica to come forward, staring up at her as if she were some weird creature.

"You . . . like . . . colours . . ."

Guess he wanted to know which material she liked. In the shop, the smell of food from the street stalls mingled with a musty, organic scent. It was cramped in here, and she had to bend her head to avoid colliding with beams displaying lengths of fabric. What did she like? She ran her hand over one gaudy-coloured bundle after the other. Certainly not orange, or hot pink, bright yellow or translucent white. Against her white skin, most colours simply looked dreadful. She was hot, wanted a bath more than anything else, and she had always hated shopping. Especially clothes shopping.

Then her attention fell on a shimmer of blue against the side wall: a silky fabric in the clearest of cobalt blues. She squeezed herself between two piles of bundles, and touched it. The fabric ran through her hands like satin. Rich, smooth, soft. She looked over her shoulder, where the dressmaker waited in the aisle.

"I like this one."

Iztho pushed himself forward. "Allow me." He pulled the fabric down from the beam and draped it over Jessica's shoulder. He nodded, stepped back and nodded again. "That will do just fine." He handed the bundle to the dressmaker, whose face contorted with the effort of suppressing a smile. At this, Jessica was convinced she had chosen the most expensive fabric in the shop.

Iztho dumped an armful of fabric bundles next to the blue one. A soft yellow, a light blue woolly fabric, a satin black, a peach orange with tiny glittering drops, and a shimmering deep magenta, each one more exquisite than the other. "Do you like those, too?"

"Yes." Jessica wondered how from her choice of just one fabric, he had determined her taste. Maybe that was part of his profession. This man had many strange qualities. Being a faded hippie wasn't one of them.

He pointed out the fabrics one by one. "I'll ask him to make a second dress, a tunic, a nightshirt, a warm overdress, underclothes . . ."

Jessica didn't like it. All this was going to be expensive, and she had no money or whatever these people used to pay. He had to expect something in return.

The dressmaker pressed a few sheets of cardboard-like material in Jessica's hands. Photographs, or some such thing. "You stay . . . we make dress—"

Vivid lively colours showed three women walking in a treeless meadow bursting with flowers. Sunlight played in the women's silken hair. In the background, a landscape of rolling hills stretched away under a stark turquoise sky. "Where is this?" she asked Iztho, although the women's light-coloured hair made her think she already knew the answer.

"This is the meadow just outside our great capital city of Miran, which bears the same name as the nation. See the clear mountain air? The view over the highlands? Smell the flowers and the freshness of molten snow. That, Lady, is life."

In the oppressive heat, humidity and the overpowering smell of tropical flowers, it sounded wonderful.

The dressmaker tapped the picture. "Which one? We have a lot of work to do."

Jessica tore her gaze from the scenery. Wide flowing skirts, narrow waists, tight bodices, not unlike Victorian ladies' fashion. What was Mirani for *I hate dresses?*

She flicked through the pictures and eventually picked a simple design with a straight body piece and straight sleeves. Once again, Iztho seemed appreciative of her choice, but the dressmaker's face bore traces of disappointment. He took the pictures from Jessica's hand, put his fingers in his mouth and whistled hard.

A Pengali female shuffled from the darkness at the back of the shop, clad in a turquoise servant dress. She carried a basket, and several lengths of white tape around her neck. Her huge eyes met Jessica's. Dark lips moved in a soundless whisper. "Anmi."

Jessica cringed. Not that again. She didn't want to disturb this man's staff and attract more attention to herself than necessary.

The servant took Jessica's arm and guided her towards a curtained door. On the other side was a covered patio, a well-lit, large, half-open room where bundles and rolls of colourful material stood stacked against walls. Half a dozen Pengali, also dressed in turquoise, sat on pillows, each of them surrounded by a circle of fabric pieces in one particular colour. Gazes went to the door, but hands continued to work. Pushing glittering needles, cutting patterns with tiny glass shears.

The female servant sat Jessica down on a stool—the only piece of furniture in the room. She took the tape from around her neck and measured Jessica's shoulders, arms and waist, then motioned for her to stand up and measured shoulder height, for which she had to climb on the stool. In between all this, performed without uttering a single word, she scribbled markings on her measuring tape, while her boss looked on. Under his glare, the servant then took the blue fabric, spread it out over the floor, and, using the markings on the tape, drew shapes on it with a piece of chalk-like material. Finally, she ran the shears along the lines, lifting loose pieces out of the fabric, forming a pile of shimmering silk.

With a final glance and a loud sniff, the dressmaker turned and went back into the shop.

As if someone had pushed a button, shears clattered on the floor and needlework crumpled in heaps as all assistants abandoned their work, and crowded around Jessica. Rough-skinned hands touched her left arm and pushed up the material of the borrowed long-sleeved dress, ran up the skin to the tattoo on her arm, which had faded back to its usual red spots. Speaking in whispers, they repeated over and over "Anmi."

Jessica tried to push them aside, sick with the thought of the previous night. She said in Mirani, "Stop. I don't want trouble."

The servants retreated. Six pairs of huge brown eyes stared up at her. One female, possibly the youngest of them all, stepped forward, speaking in faltering, heavily accented Mirani. "You . . . Ikay."

"Yes, I know Ikay."

The female waved her finger in the way Jessica had come to understand meant "no". The young female thought, bit her lip, thought some more, her eyes at the ceiling, where racks held yet more rolls of fabric. "Ikay . . . tell . . . us . . ." She made a vague gesture. "You . . . here . . ."

Jessica frowned. Ikay had told them she had come here? "Why?"

The young female continued, "Ikay . . . says . . . meet."

"Ikay wants to meet me?" The last time hadn't ended so happily.

The servant moved her hand down in a sharp gesture that

meant "yes" and that Pengali at the settlement had made with their tails.

A relieved smile spread over the young female's face.

"Ikay knows where are . . . old people?" Damn, her Mirani wasn't much better than the girl's.

Huge eyes widened. "You . . . old people. You *Akkar*."

"I am? What is Akkar? Where from? Tell me."

"Akkar fell from sky." Her voice was little more than a whisper.

"Where from? Where did they come from? Where are they now?"

The young female shrank against the wall, fear in her eyes. She whispered, "Ikay."

"Does Ikay know?" This was so frustrating.

But at that moment, voices sounded in the shop, and all servants scurried back to their pillows, picking up their work just in time before the curtain moved.

Another Pengali servant came in, accompanied by a young keihu woman, who looked like she'd spent the night in the rain. Rat-tails of dark hair hung loose over her back. Dark eyes burned in a face paler than those of other keihu people, as if she rarely saw sunlight. Her broad lips muttered inaudible words. A khaki tunic hung off her bony shoulders like a poorly erected tent. She wore no jewellery; her lower arms bore angry red marks of recently healed wounds.

No matter how much Jessica wanted to look away, she couldn't.

The dressmaker's assistant held up an exquisite pink dress before the woman. Other assistants smiled and talked, presumably about how good the dress looked, but the girl just stared, hollow eyes directed at the back wall.

"Anmi." The dressmaker's youngest assistant held out the keihu girl's hand, motioning for Jessica to touch it.

As soon as Jessica's fingers made contact with the scar-crossed palm, a wave of heat shot into her hand. She gasped. Yellow sparks swirled under her skin. Holy shit.

The young female whispered, "Avya."

Yes, Jessica had gathered as much, but . . . a keihu girl? "Are many like her?"

"Many. Many, many. Pengali in city, keihu children locked up by parents. Say is mad. We do not know what to do."

Children locked up in rooms for being abnormal, children who might one day, when forced, or abused . . . She saw the limp form of Stephen Fitzgerald's body in the sand of the riverbank. That was a dark place in her past where she didn't want to go. She'd been thirteen. He had been fifteen, drunk and challenged by a friend to make advances. He'd grabbed her, and tried to drag her into the dry river bed. Parts of her memory had never come back, but she knew there'd been a flash, and that Stephen had fallen into the dirt. A bright spot of light hovered over his limp form before winking out. He had failed to get up. Drug overdose, the police had said. Stephen's parents refused to believe it. Jessica didn't believe it either.

It was self-defence—he'd been drunk. He'd tried to rape her.

That was before she could make the web, before . . .

It was no excuse. No bloody excuse. Her only luck was that she had supportive parents.

These girls didn't.

"But Ikay . . ." Surely Ikay knew what to do.

"Ikay can help only strongest. Ones who have avya spilling out."

Like her. "What happens to the other ones?"

"Usually die. See?" She held up the girl's arm, showing the large red marks on the inside of the wrist. "She cut. Kill themselves. No one can stopping them. Not Ikay even . . . She is losing many children of herself."

Jessica pushed away a shiver of discomfort. The pain and burning inside her seemed like years back, but her crazy run towards the central pillar of the solar station had not been long ago. That action might easily have killed her. She, too, had been on the path to self-destruction. She took the girl's hands, fine-boned and cold in hers. "Can you hear me?"

Nothing.

Jessica turned to the servant. "Does she speak Mirani?"

"Yes. Very well. She helps father and father's brother in business. Speaks Mirani, and Coldi and Damarcian, and . . ." The servant counted off on her fingers.

An intelligent girl with a natural talent for languages, just like herself. But she had never gone into unresponsive moods like this. If anything, her fits had been just the opposite.

Damn it—what could she do?

The answer was as simple as it was scary: use her body to draw off the built-up energy. Ikay had done it, when they had first met at the tribe.

She closed her eyes and focused her own strength. Then she opened her eyes again and met the girl's brown gaze. It was empty, as if all life had withdrawn. Yet somewhere deep within Jessica sensed a knot of heat, so tightly bound it resisted Jessica's probe. She needed more energy, and that had always come to her on hot and sunny weather, because she absorbed energy from the environment.

She broke eye contact and turned to the servants. "Bring me something very hot."

One of the females left the workshop and the others continued to work without speaking. The girl rocked gently to and fro, still muttering her inaudible words.

Within a minute, the servant returned carrying a bowl of steaming water. Sheesh—those volcanic springs were handy—hot water on demand. The servant placed the bowl on the floor in front of Jessica. Sulphuric air rose from it in wisps of steam.

She stuck out her hands, rubbing them nervously as steam enveloped them. She placed one hand flat on the surface of the water. For a split-second, she wanted to scream. Heat seared her skin and pain flared up her arm, but pain turned into warmth and warmth produced tiny flecks of light which moved up her arm like twinkling stars in the night sky. Her body drank in the energy. Greedy for more, she plunged her other hand in the water. Then she went back to the girl's unfocused gaze. She found the knot of power and tugged at it with a flush of energy.

The girl's mind-voice spoke. *Go away.*

Jessica replied. *I'm here to help you.*

I don't want to live like this any more. Images of a dark room with a high window passed through Jessica's mind. A broken chair lay in one corner. Bed sheets had been torn to shreds. Stains of red marked the walls.

Your family will miss you. Jessica forced herself to think of her mother years ago, giving her cups of warm milk when Jessica emerged, raged out and tired from her temper tantrums, from the old shed. Tears threatened in the corners of her eyes.

A flicker of surprise went through the girl's mind. *My family says I'm mad.*

I can help you control this. Jessica thought of how she had learned to make the light with the help of Ikay.

The knot loosened. *Who are you?*

They call me Anmi. Let me help you.

I've had enough.

No, come. Jessica gritted her teeth and wrenched the knot of heat apart. A wave of sparks swirled before her eyes, bringing a blast of power that flowed from the girl's body. She gasped, concentrated on a spot in the air and directed as much of the spare heat into it as she could. The spot glowed, and grew, and grew, out of control. Jessica tried to clamp down on the energy flowing from her, but it was as if another mind, *a third power,* had taken possession of it. The girl's face vanished to be replaced by the face of a man.

Daya. And for once, she wasn't inside his head, but experienced him as if she was next to him, and for the first time, she could see him, but still feel his thoughts and emotions.

Black eyes stared at her out of a pale-skinned face framed by dark curly hair. Yellowish light gilded long eyelashes, which blinked. Moisture glistened on dark lips, slightly parted. God, he was so much like her.

His feet slapped on a smooth floor. Freezing air stung through his tunic.

A dim light on the other side of the room reflected in the smooth surface of a table top or a bench. In one corner stood a shallow metal dish, some instruments protruding over the edge. A man busied himself in the corner under the light, pulling on smooth gloves that reached to his elbows.

A slight figure dressed in white approached from near the frost-covered window. The silver embroidery of the Mirani emblem glittered on his chest. His uniform was adorned with so many other coloured and glittering markings that he had to be someone high-ranking. His grey hair was cropped short and framed a sharp face with a pointy nose, a jutting chin and skin stretched taut over high cheekbones. His eyes had the colour of a glacier in early morning light.

Daya said, through shivering lips, "What are you doing with me?"

The small man passed him with slow footsteps that clacked on the tiles, his hands behind his back. His breath steamed. "No need to worry. This won't take long. We won't harm you."

Someone grabbed Daya from behind. "Come, over here." The man pushed him against a wall of metal, cold biting into his back. "Hold still."

He tied a strap around Daya's arm.

Daya yanked. "Hey!"

The man restrained his other arm in a similar strap and went to pick up the metal bowl from the table. From this he took several medical instruments. The man had to be a medico; he squirted a spot of cold spray on Daya's arm. Then there was a sharp prick and the medico was taping a needle to Daya's arm, with a thin lead attached to a machine. "What's all this?" Daya asked.

"It doesn't harm you. Relax."

The medico sprayed cold stuff on his other arm. "Hold him."

Someone else pushed his arm into the metal wall, one hand on his upper arm, the other on his wrist. Another sharp prick and biting pain spread from his lower arm.

"What are you doing to me?" In the dimness, his shoulder pushed against the metal, Daya only saw the medico's hands, attaching a long strip of tape to his forearm, and untangling a length of wire.

The pain, the pain, the pain.

Jessica wanted to jump out of the vision and grab him, take him to safety. He was hers, and hers alone, one of her kind.

The keihu girl's face appeared again, no longer empty, but her cheeks wet with tears. She threw thin arms around Jessica's shoulders, resting her head against Jessica's chest. Her whole body shook with anguished cries.

"You must go and rescue him." The girl had *seen* Daya?

Jessica patted her back awkwardly, her whole body still glowing and throbbing. Damn him. She was in no position to rescue anyone. She didn't even know where he was.

A deep voice behind her said, "You've quite finished breaking each other's hearts?"

Iztho stood there, leaning against the doorframe, his thumbs tucked in his belt. Blood rushed to her cheeks. How long had he been watching?

He jerked his head at the door opening. His face betrayed no emotion. "If you're ready, I have something you might find interesting."

18

I ZTHO WENT TO a couch against the side wall in the shop, where he had left his screen, and turned it towards Jessica. "The markings on the walls in that cave you were talking about—did they look anything like this?"

He spoke Mirani and made no attempt to simplify his speech for her sake.

So he *had* been interested in her story about the cave. She made a note not to underestimate him again.

The screen displayed an image of a stone, like a brick in a wall. Carved grooves in the surface depicted, under each other, an arrow, two suns and three people. Her cheeks flushed, Jessica nodded.

He touched the screen. Another picture displayed an overview of a chamber with a flat dais in the middle, just like in the chamber she had visited with Ikay. The walls were covered in carvings. She whispered, "Yes, like that. Where is this?"

He cursed, or at least she thought he did because she didn't recognise the word he uttered. "This is one of the chambers they found on Asto."

"Where is that?"

"It's the inner world in this system. I'll show you tonight. Asto is very bright in the evening sky at the moment."

"Have you seen this cave?"

"I can't. It's too hot to go there."

"Too hot? But . . ." She searched for words. "Can I do this in English?"

He gave her a withering stare that said *I thought you were made of tougher stuff.*

All right. Not in English then.

His attention returned to the screen. "Asto wasn't always the desert it is today. Many years ago, a great civilisation, the Aghyrians, inhabited the planet. They invented many things we use now; they invented things we don't even half understand. They started space travel at the time Ceren was only a jungle inhabited by savages."

The people from the frieze. "Were they tall and. . . ?" She didn't know how to say *broad-shouldered.*

"Yes."

"What happened?"

"The legends say a star fell from the sky, but in reality, it was a wayward asteroid. For all they peered into space, luck was not on their side. It came from behind the larger sun and by the time they saw it, there was little time left to prepare. Our own Mirani legends say the cloud of dust around the planet took thirty years to clear."

Jessica's skin broke out in goosebumps. That's how scientists said dinosaurs had become extinct. A massive impact, clouds obscuring the sun for years. What a horrible way to die. At the same time, she remembered hearing running footsteps on stone, panting breaths, a slamming door and the rumbling of the earth. She'd thought it had been a vision when she was in the cave with Ikay, but could it be a memory? She clamped her arms around herself.

"Did anyone survive?"

"At first, it seemed not, but then, many, many years later, another kind of people appeared on Asto. They called themselves Coldi. No one is quite sure where they came from. Their own history tells of them arising from the dust, and when you couple legend and known history, it seems they are right. Certainly there is no evidence of Coldi presence anywhere else in the inhabited worlds dating from before the disaster. There are rumours that the Coldi are not a real race but were created by the Aghyrians specifically for survival. Others say they're descendants of those Aghyrians who survived in the caves under the destroyed city of Aghyr, but there's no proof of that. Wherever they came from, the Coldi have adaptations that help them survive the heat. They came to Asto, or were already there, they found Aghyrian knowledge still buried under the ruins of cities. That's why we have the Exchange network: the Aghyrian people invented it. They never built it in its current form, but they discovered the principles."

"But none of them survived, even though they could travel into space?"

"They had only just started a large-scale space program. They had nowhere near the capacity to get everyone off-planet in time, but yes, some fled. In the old works, there is mention of three ships leaving Asto before the disaster. No one took those records seriously, because no one has ever found out where they went."

Jessica raised a hand to her mouth. "Barresh."

He nodded, his face grim. "So it seems. Or at least one of them did."

"And they're no longer here."

While he shook his head, she wondered if this was true or how else would both Pengali and keihu share avya, a characteristic that had to have come from this old race, if she and Daya both had it, as well as some Pengali and keihu girls.

"Maybe we should ask the Pengali about the caves."

"Yes." He finally turned his gaze from the screen. "Yes, that sounds like a good idea." He stared at her in a way that made her uncomfortable, and she realised that he hadn't addressed her relationship with these people, nor was he surprised that she was interested in history that, for all he knew, was far removed from hers.

And indeed, all signs said to her that he *did* know what she was and he chose not to address it. Why? Good question. Because he knew avya had triggered the transfer of the plane?

"Um—lady?"

Only then did Jessica see the dressmaker's assistant behind her, holding the dress. Blue folds of material shimmered in her hands. The bodice fastened with bows at the back. A decorative vest, its edge scalloped, hung over the front. Elbow-length sleeves were adorned with small plaits, secured at the hem with tiny embroidered flowers. From the waist flowed several layers of material, frilled like a petticoat.

Another Pengali servant held up a singlet and shorts made from the black silky material, tied with a ribbon.

Iztho nodded at her. "Go with them. Put it on."

Jessica followed the assistants to the back of the shop, where she slipped the too-tight, and by now very smelly, dress over her head.

Jessica put on the satin-like shorts and singlet, the material cool on her skin. One of the assistants tied up the ribbon at the back, while another lifted the dress over her head. A rustle of blue material cascaded to her feet.

Another servant climbed on the stool. She combed back Jessica's hair and tied it in a bun with a broad blue ribbon of the same fabric as her dress. Yet another servant approached with a wooden box, which contained all manner of small pots. Jessica protested that she could manage very well without make-up and had done so all her life, but the Pengali were not to be distracted. The servant on the stool took a thin brush from the box, dabbing it in a pot of black to outline Jessica's eyebrows. A round brush with dark brown accentuated her lips. Then he took a larger brush and brushed powder on Jessica's face, followed by sprinkles of glitter around her eyes.

Finally, the servants led her into the shop and pushed her in front of the glimmering black stone wall that functioned as a mirror.

Jessica stopped.

And stared.

Fought to restrain tears that threatened in the corners of her eyes, lest they run over the so carefully applied powder.

The dressmaker walked back and forth behind her, making approving noises, but she barely heard him; she could only stare at her mirror image.

Had that dreadful Stephen Fitzgerald, his friends, her own friends at school, even her parents ever suggested she was ugly? Had she herself ever thought she was ugly? This awkward, skinny, pale, lank-haired tomboy?

The young woman who stared back at her, who moved her hand when she did, looked like a princess, a tall and straight figure, a proud and aristocratic face, a black piercing gaze.

The dressmaker came to stand next to her. More than a head taller, she towered over him and compared to her, he looked like big fat toad.

The dressmaker nudged her. "You . . . like it?"

Like it? Her reflection blurred in a haze of tears as her gaze once more roamed the magnificent dress. It accentuated all the good parts of her, her narrow waist, her strong shoulders, but unlike dresses she had worn before, it didn't make her look like an adolescent boy in women's clothing. She wondered what—

Where was Iztho?

Just as she had noticed the screen left on the couch, still turned on, he strode in from the street, carrying a large blue flower.

He stopped. His mouth fell open. He looked from her hair to her bare feet and back again. Jessica's skin pricked.

The dressmaker smiled and spoke to him in keihu. Iztho ignored him, stepped forward, took Jessica's hand and bowed. "Lady. May I offer you a small gift to compliment your beauty?"

Jessica wished she could laugh at his silliness—how dreadfully formal he sounded when he spoke his own language—but a deep blush had risen to her cheeks.

She took the flower from him and noticed it was the same colour as his eyes.

Lost for words, she tucked the flower in her bun; he still

watched her in the mirror. Once again, she ran her hands over the dress, looking at her mirror image, her mind aglow with a sense of pride that was new to her. Why the hell had she spent the past seventeen years thinking that because she didn't look like the other kids at school, she was worth nothing? Why had she thought that because specialist doctors knew no solution to her mental problem, none existed?

No, there would be no more presumptions, no more barriers. She smiled at Iztho, who still watched her.

"Thank you."

He accepted a parcel from the dressmaker that presumably contained the other items he'd ordered. Then he held out an outstretched arm, and Jessica put her hand on it like a noble girl accepting a dance. His skin felt cool under her palm.

Like this, her back held straight, she accompanied him out of the shop to the astonished and curious gazes of others.

From now on, things would be different.

19

J ESSICA STOPPED in the shadows and peered through the bars of a gate. The broad, furry silhouette of Iztho came to a halt behind her. His voice rumbled somewhere near her shoulder. "In here."

An abandoned garden. Reddish moonlight gilded creepers trailing the rim of a dry fountain, a statue at its centre. Not a single pinprick of light lit the dark form of the house. Exposed roof beams clawed at the night sky like the ribs of some dead creature.

Iztho pushed her gently aside, sliding his hand under his cloak. "Let me go first. I don't like the look of this."

They had gone back to speaking English; for this night only, he said.

Jessica pushed him back, a bit rougher. "No. She said no weapons."

His eyes met hers in a stern look, the glacial blue irises faded to lifeless grey. "This situation could be dangerous. You don't know what they want. It could be a trap."

A shiver crept over Jessica's arms, but she refused to be put aside by him. When he opened the gate—it creaked—she was the first to enter the garden. Long shadows slid over the pavement as they walked up the path and the steps, Iztho behind her, his hand again under his cloak.

Jessica glared.

He said, "I swear I have never met a woman as stubborn as you."

"Then what are the women like where you come from?"

He muttered a curse and pushed himself in front again.

She followed him, up the path, between broken statues, up the steps to the porch, into the darkness of the shadows. His fur-clad back moved in front of her. Really—now whose idea was it to come here? Who was trusted by the Pengali?

Something shuffled in the dark.

"Watch out!" Jessica sensed the presence of others, their warmth radiating amongst the stone pillars of the porch. "Is this the Pengali hide-out?"

Shit—Iztho's charge gun glinted in the shadow under his cloak. Jessica made frantic gestures for him to put it away. If she could see the gun, the Pengali with their much better night vision would see it too.

"I am Trader Iztho Andrahar of Miran. I have come in peace. However, if you will not show yourself and talk to me in an honest way, I'll have to assume you're hostile."

Oh, the pompous arse.

A small figure emerged from between two pillars, the head ringed in white hair like a ghost. She wore a too-wide gown of uneven length that looked like a worn nightgown. A familiar voice whispered, "Anmi."

In two steps, Jessica had crossed the distance between them. She threw herself into Ikay's arms, and would have lifted the old female off the ground had she not been wearing that silly too-wide gown, which slipped off her shoulders in Jessica's hug.

When Iztho took a step towards the house, two Pengali jumped out from behind the pillars, one cried, "Only Anmi." Knives glittered.

In a flash of metal, Iztho raised his gun in a two-handed grip.

Jessica jumped between them, facing the Pengali. "Oh, stop this nonsense. He's helping me. He can come."

Pengali eyes glinted in Ikay's direction. She made a hand signal; knives lowered.

Iztho glanced at her.

Jessica mumbled, "Put that bloody thing away, or they're not even going to talk to us."

"You really do want to be difficult, do you?"

Jessica stepped past him.

Ikay preceded them into the house. Two once-great doors, the wood now rotten, sagged on elaborate hinges. A short hallway led to a carved arch, and opened into a hall. Silent figures crowded on haphazardly-placed couches and mattresses.

Pengali shuffled aside. Hands or tails reached up to touch Jessica's legs as she walked past. Occasional whispers drifted on the air, "Anmi."

In the middle of the hall, red moonlight fell through a broken ceiling window on a couple of cushions. Ikay gestured for Jessica to sit down. She was glad that she had changed out of the dress in the room of the guesthouse Iztho had rented for her earlier that afternoon.

Iztho remained standing while his gaze roamed the crowd, like a vigilant body guard. He still held the bloody gun.

Jessica raised her voice so everyone could hear, and said in rehearsed Mirani, "We have come because I want to hear the story of the people who made the chamber."

Iztho translated into keihu.

Ikay spoke to him; he replied.

A younger Pengali female joined Ikay, with Ikay having to translate what she said for Iztho, him asking questions and Ikay translating it back again. After a few such exchanges, the young female went to stand amongst the seated crowd. Jessica noticed that all of the Pengali wore old and ill-fitting clothing, and she remembered Iztho's comments about the importance of the state of one's clothing.

Iztho faced Jessica, moonlight falling on his silken hair. "She's going to tell the histories. It's a formal sort of thing; they don't write. The elder will translate into keihu for me, and then I'll translate for you."

The young female began her story, speaking in rehearsed tones and hand signals; Iztho translated in his deep rumble that tickled the hair against Jessica's ear. "The Akkar who fell from the sky told this story to repeat to our children so no one will forget what happened to them.

"One day when the Akkar people still lived in their beautiful home, a star came too close. Their elders said it would fall and their whole world would burn. There was much panic amongst the people. Many took their lives. Many took all their possessions and buried themselves under the ground. Many of them fought. But the wise elders who ruled the world appointed two groups to look after the survival of the Akkar people. They told the first group to leave. Three silver ships left the ancient city that was the hub of their people, each for a different destination. Then they told all people who had newly born children to bring them to chambers under the city. Here they set up a pool that halted their growth to sustain life—"

"Wait." Iztho held up a hand.

The storyteller shot him an annoyed glance.

"I want to make notes of this." He finally sat down, clicked the gun in the bracket on his arm, took his reader from under his cloak and turned it on.

Jessica leaned forward to see the screen. "Is this what you thought?"

He typed while he spoke. "I've heard the story of the buried children and the three ships before. That's almost standard knowledge on the history of Asto, as far as oral history is accurate. The children were mostly discovered when the Coldi civilisation grew and they started building. Most of them died as soon as they were taken out of the chambers. The last one was found about three hundred years ago. But I've never heard there was any kind of planning involved. The known history says that all of Aghyr was in such panic that government—they didn't have elders of course

—disintegrated and within days an entire society was reduced to the level of beasts: everyone for themselves, and that the rich people with connections to research appropriated the chambers which had been used to store artificial humans they had created. The Aghyrians might have been smart, but they were damn selfish." He turned to the storyteller again, speaking Mirani for Jessica's benefit. "How have these stories been passed on? Are they told at gatherings and then repeated by others?"

Ikay replied, while the storyteller folded her arms over her chest.

He said, "If that's the case, how do you know this is the truth?" Then he translated his own question.

Ikay gave a sharp response. Iztho frowned at her. "You mean—all of it is written down in rock? And you can read it?"

The storyteller jumped forward and argued with Ikay. Her tail had escaped her clothing and waved at waist level, brushing the hair of several of her kinsmen. Large eyes shot vicious glances at Iztho.

Ikay soothed her and spoke with Iztho. He translated for Jessica. "They are upset because they do not like our questions. This is how it was, they say, so one cannot argue with it."

"But we're not arguing. We just want to know what they mean."

"I know, Lady, I know. You and I view history as something that has to be rediscovered, over and over, reinterpreted by generations to come. They think there is only one version of history, which is how they tell it. We'd best keep quiet if we want to hear the rest of the story." He sat back and nodded to Ikay.

The storyteller continued. "The ship that carried Anara and her followers came here when the elder of our tribe was the great Orrid. All the tribe watched when the silver machine flew over a few times and landed on the water. The creatures emerging from it —for strange they were, no tails, so pale, so tall—had drifted the skies for days. They had found no landing places and had run out of food. Their silver machine was damaged when it slid through the marshes. Orrid offered them their first meal in days from our plentiful supplies. They were grateful and said their people would always respect the Pengali. In turn for our food they taught us to read their signs. The Akkar settled on the island and a time of great prosperity followed."

After waiting for Ikay's signal that she could speak, Jessica whispered, "How come none of those people are left here?"

"There are. Akkar live in us through avya."

Iztho asked, "Why do you think this young woman is one of them?"

From somewhere in the dark room a fierce voice in heavily accented Mirani said, "We do not *think* so. She *is* one of them."

"Can you prove this?"

Ikay whistled. A small boy ran forward to drop a glowing pearl in her hand, which she rubbed over the skin of Jessica's upper arm. Warmth spread out from it, and tendrils of energy. When Ikay took the pearl away, the characters glowed pink once more.

Elegant loops, the distinctive character like the inverted number three. His mouth open, Iztho reached out and traced the characters in the air without touching her skin. "What . . . what does it say?"

"Anmi." The fierce voice belonged to a servant female, a young woman perhaps Jessica's age.

"And that means?"

"Anmi. Her name. Like the Akkar who fell from the sky. They all had their names written on their skin."

Anmi, my name.

Jessica closed her eyes and let the threads flow through her arms. She reached out for the web, for Daya.

Did you know that, about my name?

There was no reply, no images, no one on the other side. Last time she'd seen Daya, he'd been captured. Where was he, and what did these people want from him?

Iztho had taken his reader on his lap. A deep frown on his face, he flicked through images and turned the screen towards the onlookers. Jessica recognised one of the pictures from the cave he had shown her that afternoon. "Read for me what this says."

The young female didn't hesitate. "May life guide you in the future, Cara Ivedra Arellan."

"Ivedra!" Iztho's voice boomed through the hall.

At the sound of the name, a wave of goosebumps went over Jessica's back. "What is it? Is anything wrong?"

Iztho's eyes met hers in an intense gaze. "No, she's right, that's the problem." He gestured to the screen, displaying the picture of the circular chamber. "This was the chamber in which three hundred years ago on Asto one of the last surviving buried children was found: a baby girl, Cara Ivedra Arellan. The Coldi woke her up and raised her on Asto until she died at nineteen when the heat became too much for her. For most of that time, she was locked up because of her strange mental abilities. It was said she could kill a person just by looking at them."

Jessica pulled up her knees against her chest and rocked to and fro. She wasn't sure if she wanted to hear the rest, but everything he said made too much sense.

"I am a survivor from those chambers, aren't I?"

Daya, did you know that?

Iztho closed his eyes and gave a single nod. "The characters on your arm are clear enough."

"And the images I see."

He raised his eyebrows. "Images?"

Jessica spoke in a barely audible whisper. "When I was in that cave . . . Someone runs down the stairs with me and puts me in that water. My mother, I think . . . and then the earth rumbles . . . and I drown and . . ." She fought back tears in her eyes, hearing, again and again, those footsteps, that thudding of the door, the panting breaths. Her mother saving her while she herself had perished?

Iztho stared at her, his eyes wide. "You . . . you remember that?"

Jessica shrugged. "How long ago did this happen?"

How long had she floated, hovering between life and death in some dark, watery place? Could any of her family still be alive?

Without speaking, Iztho groped in the pocket on the inside of his cloak and produced a disk-like piece of equipment. He fiddled with it until red lights danced across the screen; he held it out to her.

At first, the simple characters made no sense, but then she recognised a clumsy attempt at roman script. Blazing across the screen was a date: 17 April 47,513 BC.

What?

He had to be kidding.

No way she could have survived for—

Iztho inclined his head. "My Lady."

Jessica jumped up, blood rushing to her cheeks. "Oh stop that, stop that! I'm not a lady, I'm just Jessica. Just ordinary Jessica!" But she knew her protests were futile; it all made far too much sense, and she had left ordinary Jessica behind long ago.

She took a deep shuddering breath.

All Pengali around the hall stared at her with huge eyes which glinted in the dark. Ikay knelt at her feet and someone murmured, "Anmi." Before long the murmur travelled through the hall. Anmi, the name which, years beyond understanding, someone—her parents?—had tattooed on her arm.

Jessica just stood there, ignoring voices around her, shaking uncontrollably. Tears flooded her eyes, trickled down her cheeks. She wiped at her cheeks, but new tears fell. Her mouth trembled. She sank down on the floor, biting her lip. All alone. There would never be any relatives of any kind.

20

WHEN JESSICA stumbled up the steps of the guesthouse, clutching Iztho's arm, a wave of fatigue washed over her. It must be well past midnight. Most of the windows facing the street were dark, and only a faint glow of light radiated from the archway into the entrance hall. That afternoon, when Iztho had taken her into the guesthouse after their visit to the dressmaker, the hall had bustled with activity and patrons of all races and sizes lined up to talk to a keihu woman with an enormous bird's nest of hair. Now, the lectern-like table that held the matron's booking system—a concertina-folded stack of paper tumbling to the floor—stood empty and deserted, lit only by a small light in a sea of darkness.

Iztho's high boots clacked on the mosaic floor. He hadn't said much on the way back, as if he sensed she wasn't up to speaking. She was thankful for that.

Now he led her up the stairs to the first floor balcony, where he had booked two adjacent rooms overlooking the courtyard. Jessica longed for the softness of the bed. Yet she didn't want to be alone with the truth.

He stopped in front of the door to her room. "Are you sure you're all right?"

The ghostly light from a single pearl on the wall a few rooms down cast deep shadows over his face.

"I can understand if you are upset."

Jessica turned away. "No, really, I'm fine." *Just shut up or I'll start crying and I'll never stop.*

"All right, sleep well."

The door to her room rolled open. A rectangle of moonlight slanted through the window, edging the oval, dog-basket-like bed in a golden glow.

Jessica froze in the doorway. Alone. Her mother and her father had died millennia ago, saved her life. For . . . for what? So that she could lead her life in loneliness?

Except for Daya who lives only in my mind. But he wasn't replying, and maybe he, too, was only a vivid memory.

She stifled a choking sob.

A few footsteps and Iztho's hands were on her shoulders. "You are not fine."

His moonlight-edged face blurred in a haze of tears. He led her into the room and sat her down on the couch in the corner. "Let me get you a drink."

Jessica bit her lip, fighting tears, staring blindly at the opposite wall, but seeing only black eyes and a gentle male face surrounded by dark curls. A memory. He was nothing but a memory. What was the point of knowing her history if none of her people were left? What was the point of anything in her life?

The door rattled and Iztho came back, carrying a carafe, two cups and a large case, the strap slung over his shoulder. Jessica frowned through her tears. "What's that?"

He set the cups on the stable, unstoppered the carafe and poured. A scent of sweet flowers drifted on the air. One cup he passed to her.

"Just sit and drink for a while."

He clicked the case open. Folds of blue satin-like fabric glimmered in the moonlight, cradling an instrument like a lute, the body trapezoid with rounded corners. Its metal surface shimmered with delicate engraved patterns. He picked it up by its short neck, caressing the strings with a soft musical tingle. Eyes closed, he took his cup from the table, drank deeply and put it back down. Then he set his fingers on the strings and music filled the room. A soft, lilting melody; baroque-like, but with a hint of something wild and untamed.

Jessica sipped from the sweet drink, not daring to make the slightest noise. His eyes were still closed; a strand of hair had slid off his shoulders, part-obscuring his face. He hummed, then whispered words which formed into song, his tone deep and warm.

The Mirani words were too archaic and formal for her to understand, but every now and then he repeated the lines:

My heart goes where I know
I will always be at home
Where my love smiles at me

Tears pricked in Jessica's eyes. When the song ended, he reached out for his glass.

The sudden silence unsettled her. She wasn't sure if he expected a reaction, so she said, "You play beautifully." It sounded clumsy.

His eyes didn't meet hers. "A Mirani folk song."

He set his fingers on the strings again. "Do you want to hear more?"

"Yes."

He played a few notes, then looked up at her. "I'm a Trader. I talk about buying and selling. I'm afraid I'm not much good at talking about . . . personal things."

"Neither am I." She fiddled with the hem of her tunic. "But your music speaks beautiful words."

He played another chord. "That's an accident. Life would have been a lot easier for me if I hadn't . . ." He sighed and put the instrument aside. "But that's me. Let's talk about you, your incredible history—"

"There is nothing incredible about it!"

"Yet there is." His voice was soft.

"But I'm . . . all alone." She fought to keep her voice from breaking.

"I don't think so."

"What do you mean?"

"There *are* others. Men, mostly."

"There are?" *Daya.*

"Yes. You see, it is clear that the Coldi race somehow arose from the Aghyrians, and it happens that every now and then a Coldi couple will have a child, a boy usually, who is unlike his parents. He will be thin and tall, and cope poorly with the heat. Most of these children die young, but the few who survive are men with feared abilities. The Coldi call them zhadya-born and treat them like they're abnormalities. You see, most of them . . ." He made a helpless gesture. "Most of them suffer terribly in the mind, and they're not quite normal, but . . ."

He looked away. "I could take you to meet them. I think you could help them." He drank from his glass, not meeting her eyes.

She didn't know what to say. What did he expect? That she would jump at the chance of meeting a group of mentally unstable men?

What if Daya is with them?

She shook her head. "I'd like you take me home."

He frowned. "Home?"

"Yes. Where I came from. The family where I grew up. They may not be my real family, but no one else has ever looked after me." Tears again threatened in the corners of her eyes. Home, where she could go on being a freak. How could she explain her absence, how could she forget this world?

"I could take you home, but you would need to be . . . treated, so you won't remember where you've been. The Union is strict with its secrecy laws." His voice sounded hesitant.

"You mean—if I go back home, someone will give me some kind of drug?" Anger flared in her. No, she didn't want to forget any of this.

"Yes, that's true, but there is another option. I would never have thought to offer this to you, but your history simply can't be forgotten. I'm offering to sponsor you for Union citizenship."

Now it was Jessica's turn to frown. "What does that mean?"

"Union citizenship is awarded to the most trustworthy people of the Union entities. You must be of good character, you can't have a criminal history, and you must have enough intelligence to learn Union Law; there is an exam. When you've passed, there is no limit on what you can do. You can be called to judge on minor disagreements, you can teach, and you can even sit on the Union Assembly in the Union capital Damarq. They deal with inter-entity matters, most importantly the Exchange, and coordinate responses to major crises or conflicts. On the practical side, once you're a Union citizen, you can travel." He inserted his hand under his cloak and withdrew a black card a bit smaller than a credit card. "This gives you the right to travel wherever you want."

Jessica took the card. The surface was warm with the touch of his skin and completely smooth. "You mean, if I have one of these, I could see my parents . . ." He raised his eyebrows at that word. ". . . and still come back here to see what else the Pengali know?"

"Whenever it is safe. Barresh is not very stable, I'm afraid. But I'm sure a visit to the men of your race would be appreciated."

She could look for Daya.

"If I agreed, how long would it take before I get this pass?"

"Not long, about a year. You could do most of the work in Miran. My family owns a large house in the noble quarters. You could stay there. You'd have your own servant, of course."

"A year?" How long was a year? "And I can't contact my family all that time?"

"Strictly, no, but I know how important family is. Who is your family's heir?"

"I don't have any brothers or sisters. My parents—adoptive parents—never—"

"Just as I thought—it is important that they know you are alive. If you give me the details, I will make sure that they are told."

Jessica opened her mouth, didn't know what to say and closed it again. It was as if the revelation about her past had changed his opinion of her. She was no longer a nobody, but someone to be held in awe. A different awe from the way the Pengali treated her.

The Pengali wanted to reconnect. He just wanted to . . . sit and watch her, with a far-off look on his face.

It was all so strange, and she didn't know what to think. His offer sounded good, although she still didn't know what he wanted from her in return. Sex didn't seem to be it. Maybe she was being paranoid in thinking that he *should* want something in return. Maybe he just wanted to do the right thing by her. Maybe it was what these people did.

Sheesh, what did she know?

"You can think about my offer, if you need. With the need to get you a permit, we won't be going anywhere for a while, at least until tomorrow."

Tomorrow! That was only a few hours away. "I . . . I like it, I . . ."

"That's good, then."

He finished his drink in one gulp and slid the lute back on his lap. When his fingers hit the strings, it was with a sense of determination, and the song flowing from his lips jumped with life.

Yes. Let's do this.

21

J ESSICA JOLTED AWAKE when Daya woke with a gasp. Hazy flames danced before his eyes. The back of his arms puckered in gooseflesh, but shone with sweat.

He stood tied to a wall that was cold like a block of ice. Broad bands looped around his chest. Tight bands held his arms and legs in a spreadeagled position. A thin tube led from his left arm to a machine where a red light blinked; a thick bandage covered his right arm, the wires protruding from it and leading to a box attached to a glass-stone vessel filled with what looked like beads. Whatever they had stuck up that arm still hurt like burning acid.

Jessica called, *Daya.*

How long had he been out?

Men spoke in soft voices somewhere in the room.

". . . and you got how much from the others?" Daya was sure he had seen this man before: an army commander of some kind, somewhere in a field shouting orders at soldiers. The sharp-faced man looked so familiar, even in the way he was much shorter and thinner than his subordinates, but the man's name wouldn't come to him.

"With all the attempts combined so far, we've only charged up half this jar."

"Only half?" The commander's voice came like a bark.

"I know, there are all the other jars still to go. Priming these beads takes a lot of energy. Some of them just can't do it." This was a medico, pulling on gloves.

Another soldier slipped a blindfold over Daya's eyes. "Ready? This will be easiest if you don't fight it. Relax, and do as we say."

Jessica felt Daya brace himself.

The next moment, a large quantity of water splashed over his head. Pieces of ice slithered down his neck, between his tunic and his skin. Water dripped from the fabric onto his legs.

Cold, cold, cold, damn it.

Jessica shivered and caught a brief glimpse of her dark guest-house room where she sat on the couch. She needed to get into the bed. But Daya needed her.

Don't give them what they want. Whatever it was.

He straightened his back, as if he heard her, determined not to show his shivering.

Small flares of heat leapt from within the core of his body, but barely reached the skin. His mind cast out for the warmth of the body behind him, but the water thrower had retreated behind the metal wall.

Footsteps came closer again.

An impossibly warm hand touched his cheek and thin fingers caressed his wet skin. "Relax. We won't hurt you." The commander's voice, so familiar.

When Daya breathed in to argue, he got a mouth full of iced water instead, as another bucket was upended over his head. He spat the water in as big a spray as he could. "I want you to let me go. This will be reported to the Hedron Mines board, and they'll refuse to do business with you ever again. You hear me?" Patches of purple rose before his blindfolded eyes. Chest heaving, he yanked at the bonds, straining muscles Jessica was unused to having.

I am you. Tell me what you want and I'll do it.

Still, her thoughts didn't connect.

Another load of ice water crashed over Daya's head, so cold it hurt.

A raw, uncontrolled howl escaped his throat. The ice burned like boiling water. Worse, he was now so cold that his bladder had contracted to the point where all he could think was the need to pee.

"I . . . don't . . . care . . . about . . . your . . . foul experiments. I'm . . . freezing . . . to death."

"Not quite. We'll stop before you get to that point."

The commander asked, "Anything yet?"

Somewhere in the room a new voice replied, "No. It usually takes a while, at least it did with the others, but I'll say this: I think we'll need a lot more of these guys to produce enough energy."

"How many more?"

"As many as you can get, really, unless we find a less crude process."

"I'm sure we can find more of these poor men. It's not as if they have anything to live for. Everyone thinks they're crazy." The commander gave a chuckle. "Would it help if I brought you a girl?"

A girl? His girl? It had to be. There *were* no other girls.

Jessica chilled to the core.

"Hold still." The medico pulled the strap holding Daya's right arm. "A girl? Hmmm—we could get two, no maybe four babies a year from her, if she could be made to carry twins—"

The commander interrupted. "No, that'd be a waste of her strength. I'd want you to try harvesting her eggs. Prepare yourself for when we bring her."

Bring her? His girl? Where was she?

Tell me where you are! I'll help you.

Another load of iced water hit Daya's head. Ice heaped on his hair, his shoulders. He strained his arms, the bonds cutting into his skin. He arched his back. Fabric ripped. He tore one arm free, then the other. He sensed the commander's hasty retreat.

"Restrain him!" someone shouted.

Daya stumbled and splashed through the puddles of iced water. Tripped when the leads attached to his arm held him back. Smelled the distinctive tang of urine in the humidity rising from the floor. Fresh and stale, mixed with the lingering scent of cleaning agents. How many of the zhadya-born men had been reduced to animals before him? Where were they now?

Were those men imprisoned in the same place? Jessica asked. Iztho had talked about them, too.

The medico's voice sounded from far off. "This is a tough one. Stay right there, boss, I'll tie him back up. We're almost done."

Another load of iced water hit his skin. Cut into his mind, sent searing pain into his limbs. Anger flared. Heat rose inside him, spilled out of his skin, drew energy from the air.

And sucked at the strands from Jessica's web.

He ripped the bandage and needle from his left arm. The blindfold fell from his eyes. A window flew open by itself; wind whooshed into the room, tearing at the soldiers' uniforms. The light blew out. The fire flickered and it, too, went out. Energy crackled, charged through his body—Jessica's body, Daya's body. The air lit up in a net of blue lightning, which funnelled into the wires still attached to his right arm into the huge jar of glass-stone balls. The entire vessel lit up blue. Someone screamed. "Get out of here!"

Still more energy crackled into the vessel. Daya writhed on the ground, his back arched and muscles stiff. Light blazed from his eyes, pulsing with his heartbeat.

The air flashed and crackled. A beam of white-hot energy streamed into the vessel of balls. It shattered into thousands of diamond-flecked pieces.

～

Silence.

Soft sleep.

A faint heartbeat.

Daya?

Daya groaned and pushed himself up. There was snow under his hands. He was in some sort of alley, with blind walls on either side. How had he ended up here?

His head hurt. His hand hurt; his muscles hurt, his eyes hurt. Pain spiked up his leg. He now remembered: that was from when he had twisted his ankle jumping down from the room where the soldiers were all unconscious. Damn—he was a mining executive, not a bandit; clumsy and awkward even as a boy.

Sparks swirled under the skin of his hand. Traces of ash still adhered to his clothing. His trousers had ripped when he had climbed out the shattered window. Blood trickled down his leg where glass had cut the skin. He dared rest only now, this far from the council building, but it was far too cold for the clothes he was wearing, and his eyes kept seeing what had happened to him.

The explosion. The cold water, the flash, the jar of balls. Wide eyes, cramped muscles, a pulsing heartbeat.

Daya knew: they were harvesting life energy from the bodies of those with the ability to collect it and storing it in those beads. It was crude, but they would find better solutions to collect the most dangerous and most powerful energy of all. Life energy was everywhere. It could be harvested from the air, even from depth of space by people with his ability. They knew where the girl was. He saw her strapped against the metal wall, screaming as the medico stuck a thick needle into the soft skin of her lower belly.

Daya hurt, hurt so much inside that it made him breathe in shallow gasps. He had to save her, except he didn't know where she was.

Jessica reached out for him. *I'm here. Listen to me!*

But either he couldn't hear her or her voice was not strong enough in the way it needed to be focused to reach him.

Fresh snow blew across the entrance of the alley, heaping on the lee side of a blind wall. He sensed danger moving everywhere around him. The whole damn army was after him.

"Don' move!"

Daya froze. A soldier held a crossbow pointed barely a hand's length from his face. A typical Mirani with cherubic blond curls.

"Looks like I'm going t' get th' prize." His breath stank, and his teeth were brown.

Daya shrank away, running his hands over the wall at his back, searching for anything to use as a weapon.

"Now—get going." The soldier gestured with his weapon. As the point of the crossbow traced a line in the air, a chill followed it. Heat flared inside him and sent waves of sparks to his skin. What was causing that?

A rough hand grabbed Daya's arm. "Y' move when I tell y—ouch!" A spark flew up the soldier's arm. It singed a path over his tunic, across his chest, from where it jumped onto the crossbow. The soldier stared, letting the point dip away from Daya's face.

Daya jerked up his knee, hitting the soldier hard between the legs. The man screamed. The crossbow flew from his hands. Daya kicked against the wall and pushed the man's shoulders. They fell. The soldier's back hit the ground with a dull thud.

Daya crashed on top, forcing air from the soldier's lungs in a loud *oomph.* "Where is the girl?"

"What girl?"

"You know what girl."

Fear stirred in the man's eyes. He took a gasping breath, coughed. "There's no girl."

Nonsense! Daya pushed, thudding the man's head against the frosty ground. His whole body trembled with rage. "Liar, liar. You know about her. Where is she?"

The man coughed. Splatters of slime flew onto Daya's hands. The soldier's breath wheezed. "You're . . . killing . . . me."

"Damn, I will kill you if you don't tell me the truth. Where is she?"

More coughing. "I don't know. I swear!"

"You know, you know, you know." With every "know", Daya smacked the man harder into the ground. Blood marked the snow. Blue eyes met his, unfocused. Knowledge whirled in those eyes.

Knowledge of standing guard and watching as men were tortured.

Zhadya-born men, like him.

Tell me tell me tell me tell me.

A flash of images whirled before Daya's eyes. A senior soldier. A bucket of water. A jar full of glass balls. Black-haired men sitting around the hearth. Men only.

"Where is the girl? Where is the girl?" His scream echoed in the alley.

Silence.

The soldier's eyes, wide open, stared at the sky. Above his face floated a bright spot of light.

Daya let go of the soldier's hair. Trembling, he stumbled to his feet, wiping golden locks from his hands. Splatters of blood marked the snow. *A life for a life marks the start of a war.* A Coldi proverb. Well, as far as he was concerned, this was war. War on everyone who wanted to mistreat him and his race. Just as they had killed Ivedra. It was time to fight back.

But he felt sick. In that moment, faced with the pointy end of the crossbow, he had lost control and he knew it. He who prided himself on keeping a tight rein on his ability. Worse, it had achieved little. He still had no idea how to get out of here, and soon someone would discover the body.

Voices shouted in a street nearby.

Daya scooped the light out of the air. A blast of heat hit him. He bit his lip to stop himself screaming out and sagged against the wall, clutching his chest, gasping. His skin lit up with swirls of sparks.

Damn, oh damn, oh damn; how could he ever have forgotten how much this hurt?

I know, Jessica told him, *I know, I know.* And she saw her pale thirteen-year old hands reach for the light that was the remainder of Stephen Fitzgerald's life force.

It was an accident! She could still hear her voice screaming those words, pummelling her fists into her father's chest.

No one listened. No one had even considered that she *might* have been responsible.

Now Daya *was* responsible, and she was a witness.

Self defence, a voice murmured in her mind. The soldier would have killed Daya.

That wasn't what disturbed her. It was the ease with which he killed; the ease with which *she* could kill if she chose.

Daya closed his eyes, letting images of the soldier's memories wash over him. Lines of soldiers in the snow. The crunching footsteps of a senior officer. The hard slap of a hand against bare skin.

Stand up. Slap. *Wash yourself.* Slap. *Pull your uniform straight.*

A soldier clutching his face, blood running between his fingers.

Daya edged down the alley. The storm of images inside him had calmed. Now he only saw a dirt-streaked building—the soldier's house, he presumed. From it spread a network of imaginary lines along the streets. A bar, a market, another house, the soldiers' barracks. The man probably knew the city backwards. Daya's mind followed the map to the central square. A wall topped with metal spikes surrounded the airport. The only way in was through a low building. The only way to the building was through the city gate, which would be guarded by soldiers.

Trapped. No way to get out. Unless . . . he eyed the hole in the snow where the soldier's crossbow had fallen. Remembered the crackle up the soldier's arm. Remembered the jar of glass-stone balls. He picked up the weapon. If they wanted fireworks, he'd give them fireworks.

He slung the strap over his shoulder and left the alley. Soft morning light edged snow-covered roofs in shades of blue and green. Every time snow crunched under his feet, Daya cringed. Already, his fingers were numb from cold.

In the main square, the first buyers streamed into the markets. A couple of soldiers stood sentry near the entrance to the government buildings, but they were quite far away and they looked bored. Daya waited until a group of merchants crossed the square and walked behind them to the other side.

In the street leading to the city gate, shop owners were sweeping snow into heaps. A few gave Daya strange glances as he walked between them, clutching the crossbow under his cloak. Too soon, he stood before the wide arch of the gate. On the other side, the airport building beckoned; and behind that the wide expanse of the airport, where his craft stood—the gateway to freedom.

Everything looked so normal. Daya fingered his Union citizenship pass in his pocket, and wondered if the guards knew to look out for him.

Then one of them shouted and pointed. In fluid movements, the others raised their crossbows.

Daya fumbled to untangle the weapon from under his cloak and raised it to shoulder height.

Rough voices shouted, "Drop the weapon. Surrender yourself." More soldiers had come out of the building. Too many—there were too many of them. With trembling hands, Daya pulled the release catch halfway in. With a metallic click an arrow unfolded from the magazine underneath the slide. He focused . . .

The air tingled with a feeling he knew all too well. A feeling Jessica knew.

Avya—the power of life, burning through his veins, swirling over his skin.

Blue light flashed at a small bead at the top of the crossbow's slide.

His hand contracted. The release snapped, setting free the arrow with a metallic *zhing*. A sizzle of blue drew from his hands, following the flying arrow like a shaft of lightning, over the heads of the soldiers—he'd always been a bad shot—into the doorpost of the building.

Blue lightning exploded from the door, engulfing the building in a net of crackling energy. People screamed. Glass shattered, walls blew outwards. The guards dropped into the snow. People were screaming and running from the shattered door to the cover of the city wall.

Daya tucked the crossbow under his arm and ran. Past both checkpoints, into the gaping hole in the building, past passengers crawling out from under benches, out the other side onto the open space of the airport. The soles of his shoes slipped in the powdery snow. Still, he ran, expecting to hear the shouts of soldiers and the *zhing* of fired arrows, but the eerie silence accompanied him all the way to his aircraft.

Panting, Daya swiped as much snow from the window as he could reach. No time to clean it. No time to defrost the engine.

He jumped up the stairs, switched on the controls. Red text flashed across the communication screen: *Warning: Miran Exchange closed.*

He hit the instrument panel with his hand.

Damn—damn, damn, damn. He should have known. What now? He couldn't stay here. He pressed the ignition. The engines fired, but ran irregular. A light flashed *insufficient power.* Yes—he knew, he was meant to defrost the engine.

No time. No time.

Dark figures ran onto the snow from the building.

Daya laid his hands flat on the instrument panel, sending as much heat as he could muster into the metal, but the flash had drained him.

Please, don't desert me now. Please help me out of here. Please, anyone who's listening, help me get out of here.

Jessica jerked up. Morning light silvered the empty cups on the table before her. A soft breeze brought the sounds of servants talking in the courtyard. She'd fallen asleep on the couch.

Iztho looked up from the reader on his lap. The glow of the screen lit his face from below. "What did you say?"

Jessica frowned, wiped her cheeks, the folds of her tunic impressed in them. "Did I say anything?" Had he sat there working all night while she slept?

"I heard you speak."

"I didn't." She closed her eyes and let her head sink back on her arms. Someone—something—had called her. Someone was in trouble.

"Come on, come on!"

Daya pushed down the propulsor test lever. The propulsor engine uttered a sickly hiss; the floor shook. A row of three lights flashed orange. *Insufficient power.*

Damn, damn, damn!

The running figures had crossed half the distance from the building to his craft. Daya closed his eyes and fed more heat into the metal. One of the lights turned blue.

Voices shouted outside.

Please, someone help me.

There it was again. Jessica sat up, looking around the room.

Iztho had left his reader on the table and was at the door, talking to a servant. ". . . yes, bring it in here. The Lady doesn't feel well."

Large Pengali eyes met hers past Iztho's fur-clad back, pleading.

"I . . . I feel fine, just tired," Jessica stammered. To demonstrate how well she felt, she pushed herself up from the couch.

Daya pressed the lever again. Another hiss. The whole craft shook. Steam drifted past the window. Lights flashed on the instrument panel. Two orange, one blue.

A warning beep filled the cabin, followed by a female voice. *The Miran Exchange is closed—you cannot leave. I repeat: the Miran Exchange is closed.*

Two blue, one orange. The floor stopped vibrating.

Daya leaned on the metal of the instrument panel. Heat, more heat.

Please help me.

Jessica stumbled, clutching her head. "Stop, stop it!" She tore at her hair, loosing it from the bun.

Please help me.

Footsteps crossed the room; hands grabbed her arms. "Lady, what's wrong?" The scent of wood fires filled her nose; the fur on Iztho's cloak tickled her arms.

I need to get out of here.

"Let me go!" Someone was in danger, someone wanted her help. Jessica struggled, but Iztho's grip tightened. "Lady, you will hurt yourself."

Jessica yanked her hands free, stumbled back.

"Lady, Lady, what is wrong?"

Daya's black eyes met hers. *I need heat.*

Heat. She could do that. She turned her face to the ceiling and closed her eyes. Iztho's agitated voice faded in the background. Her chest moved with calm breaths while she focused heat in a point inside her head. A questing probe tugged at her, tickling her senses. She latched onto it. It found the spot of heat and flowed away into nothingness.

Daya gave a cry and punched the air.

Three lights blue.

Daya slammed his hands down on the steering panels. The engines roared, causing a sheet of ice to slide from the roof over the front window. It fell at the feet of approaching soldiers, who threw themselves down in the snow. The propulsors screamed; a cloud of steam exploded around the craft. A jolt forward and the airport vanished from sight. Snow streaked past the window. Up, up, up, out of here.

Pressed back in his chair, Daya turned off the still-flashing communication channel. Even if the Exchange was open, he couldn't use it. The craft's power level was still only a bit more than half what he needed. But Barresh, on the other side of the continent, had an Exchange, too. Moreover, he had recognised the source of the power that had helped him.

He had also seen the slim form of a Pengali female. Barresh. The girl was in Barresh.

But he had to hurry. He had also seen the white hair and fur cloak of a Mirani Trader.

Miran already had its hands on the girl.

22

J ESSICA LET IZTHO lead her down into the courtyard of
the guesthouse, where the patrons sat at tables for breakfast. Still in the tunic and trousers she had worn to the
Pengali hideout last night, she felt hot and sweaty. While he
pushed her into a chair, she tried to mumble something about a
bath, but her tongue wouldn't work.

Her brain felt like someone had been at it with an axe, trying to
split it in two.

Iztho poured light green juice in a cup and passed it to her.

"I think you and I should leave as soon as possible. You are in
shock. You are in need of a Healer and I wouldn't trust the ones in
this pitiful town. As soon as we have finished our meal, I'll go to
the Exchange. I think you are ready to pass as a local."

He didn't say *my wife.*

Jessica attempted to wipe haziness from her eyes. In the
mirrored stone next to the door in her room, she had seen that she
looked even paler than normal. If the glances were anything to go
by, fellow guests who shared this corner of the courtyard with
them had noticed as well. Two petite red-haired women turned
frequent glances on her, hazel eyes ringed by bright orange
eyelashes. A man on a table next to them cast severe yellow-eyed

looks over the top of his reader. Goodness knew what they all thought.

She took a bite from the bread. Its nutty, minty taste exploded in her mouth—and images of trees lining a riverbank bursting with green. Drooping branches tickled the water. Children playing. The soft murmur of a woman's voice. Her mother; she recognised the tone. Memories, as if these past few days had unlocked them from somewhere deep in her mind.

Jessica took her cup, brought it to her mouth with a trembling hand. Was there anything she could do without getting visions and hearing voices?

"Lady, do you want me to bring you to bed?" Iztho's face looked pale.

His blue eyes turned into black ones. Loose curls tumbled about his face. The soft glow of early morning light glistened in amber stones that dangled from his earrings. Below him flickered lights on an instrument panel similar to what she had seen in Iztho's craft; sleek and smooth. Much more modern.

I'm coming. Hold on tight. I'm coming for you. The power of the engine sang through her veins.

Blood rushed to her cheeks.

Iztho just caught the cup before she dropped it, but a gush of juice went over the front of her tunic. "Come, I'll get a Healer to come out right now." Iztho's eyes were wide with concern.

"No, really, I'm fine." She rose from the table. *I'm here. I'm waiting. Tell me where you want to see me.*

"You're not. You're disturbed. Please, let me help you."

"I'm not disturbed!"

At the tables around them, conversations halted. People turned around.

She said in a lower voice, "He's coming for me."

Daya's dark lips twitched into a tiny smile that accompanied his twinkling eyes. A wave of happiness washed over her. *His* emotions. The link between them was complete. He was coming.

"Who is coming? Let me take you—"

Come to me. You're in danger.

"No." Jessica pushed Iztho's hands aside. She was not going to any doctor to be prodded at. If there was anything *wrong* with her, there was only one person who could fix it.

She ran from the table across the courtyard, although she barely saw where she was going for the image of Daya's face in her mind. *He's coming, he's coming.*

Iztho called after her, "Come back! Who is coming?"

Jessica ran out, into the foyer, past a line of guards into the street. She turned left, at random, had no idea where she was going or why. A group of Pengali stopped and watched. Jessica ran. She didn't want to become entangled with them again, she didn't want to . . .

She didn't know.

She ran, without aim, without taking notice of where she was going. She ran, and ran and ran. No one stopped her until the visions faded and she found herself soaked with rain and exhausted, in an alley.

Empty, dulled, staring at the rain-soaked pavement. The surface of puddles stirred with raindrops. Sometimes, larger drops falling from the trees made bigger rings. She clamped her hands around herself; her tunic was soaking wet. The memory of Daya's voice repeated in her mind. *Come to me. You're in danger.*

He didn't just speak in her mind, she could *hear* him, *feel* him, *smell* him. His voice left her no option, no energy to question, no opinion of her own. He called, she obeyed. He *was* her, and she *was* him, except right now, she was alone, rain pelted down on her, and she had no idea where she was.

Daya, what now?

Wait. I'm coming.

Well, that wasn't much help right now. Her hair dripped into her eyes; she shivered and she was hungry.

She pushed open a small door to what looked to be a shed.

The scent of rot wafted out of the dark space beyond. Great. A rubbish tip. But it was the only dry place and she simply had to get out of the rain. She sucked in a deep breath, ducked and crawled into the darkness, then pulled the door as tightly shut as it would go. A thin sliver of light lit mounds of rotting vegetables. Bloody hell, what a stink.

Her eyes closed, she sought the energy within her. Cold had released much of her reserve, but she found enough to make a light. The cramped shed had two doors, one leading to the alley, the other presumably to the house on the other side of the wall. She might find a cleaner shelter there, or better, some Pengali servants. Where there were Pengali, there was food. She pushed the second door, but it didn't move. Locked.

So much for that idea.

Heavy boots marched past, splashing in puddles. A voice shouted orders in Mirani.

Jessica held her breath and pressed herself against the damp wall, ignoring its putrid stench.

If you want to talk to me, please let me know where you are.

~

Daya shivered, righting himself against the hard wall of the house. In the stuffy warmth of the room, he had dozed off. His backside hurt from sitting on the floor. He longingly thought of the bottle of zixas in his bag, saw himself pulling out the stopper and taking a big swig, but no. He wanted to have a clear mind when he met her.

On the other side of the room, the Pengali fell quiet and turned to him. "What did you say?"

Daya shook his head, banishing sleep and weariness. "I didn't say anything." Or did he? A voice asking a question lingered in his mind.

The Pengali male held up an unidentified piece of lizard. Thin bones protruded from half-eaten flesh. "You want some?"

"No." Daya shuddered. As Coldi, his family only ate worms and other creatures that lived in soil or compost. Even though he had discovered that his body was quite different, he still found it hard to accept meat of larger animals.

He went back to staring out the window, wishing the voice would come back. She was here somewhere.

The smell of cooking lingered in Jessica's nose, although around her was only damp and rubbish.

Another group of soldiers marched through the alley, or were they the same ones coming back for a second look? Where were the Pengali?

Where are you?

Damn!

Daya jumped up.

On the other side of the room, the Pengali stopped talking. Large eyes observed him.

"Be patient," said the male.

Daya spoke through gritted teeth. "I can't be patient. She needs me now." *And there is a whole army after me.*

Outside the rain came down incessantly and water clattered from overflowing gutters.

He clenched his fists in his pockets.

The footsteps came back again, much slower this time. Men spoke in Mirani, but their speech was uneducated, too unlike that of Iztho for Jessica to understand.

She crouched behind the door. Soon they would discover that it was open and look inside, and she would have to run.

Daya opened the door into the courtyard, letting in a cloud of droplets. Water dripped from the leaves of the tree into deep puddles between its roots. No one, not even a creature, stirred in the yard or the alley on the other side of the gate.

He balled and unballed his hands, kicked at the rotten planks at his feet.

A Pengali behind him said, "Leave the door closed; someone will see us."

Leave the door closed—with him on the inside or the outside? In one jump, Daya grabbed one of the broad-rimmed rain hats that lay in the corner. Too small to fit him, he sat it atop his hair, its oiled cloth curtain dangling over his back. Another jump and he was in the courtyard. He slammed the door behind him.

Closer the footsteps came, and closer. Jessica crouched, preparing to spring. She shut her eyes, gathering strands of energy in her mind. When that door opened, she would have to do something, dazzle them with light or burn them with sparks, but making a light was not that simple. It required time and concentration. Not something you could do while running.

Whoever's out there, please help me.

The door into the house opened again. A Pengali looked into the courtyard, squinting against the grey light. "Wait until dark."

Daya was opening the gate into the alley. "I can't wait any more. If you're going to sit here and do nothing, that's your problem, but I won't."

"Anmi is in guesthouse. We go there after dark."

"It is almost dark. And she's not in the guesthouse."

Daya pulled the veil down from the hat and launched himself into the alley. True, he had no idea where to go, but when he closed his eyes, a picture formed in his mind.

It was dark and smelly and soldiers walked outside a door. Somewhere, not far away, she waited for his help.

Jessica drew deep breaths, feeling warmth flow into her. Warmth that came from somewhere else, outside her body.

The soldiers had come closer still. Branches rustled, footsteps splashed in water. "No, not here."

The door rattled.

It opened. A rectangle of grey light fell over rubbish-strewn ground.

A cherubic face peeked in.

At the moment the soldier shouted, "Ya, found her!" Jessica jumped and pushed his chest. The soldier toppled, crashing bottom-first in the mud. He swore. Three others shouted.

Jessica shoved them aside and bolted for the end of the alley, gambling they wouldn't shoot because she'd be no use to them when dead.

Daya clutched his head, pressing the wet cloth from the hat's veil into his face. The mental scream of panic pounded inside his skull like the beat of many hammers.

Running footsteps sounded in the alley to his right. He rounded the corner.

Three soldiers ran away from him; one scrambled to his feet, the back of his uniform stained with mud. The girl ran to the other side of the alley.

Another patrol stepped out from around the corner.

His mind screamed, *Anmi!* Threads of energy escaped . . . formed a strand of lightning . . . arcing, sizzling and crackling, through the air . . . over the soldiers' heads.

Jessica stopped and turned around. Stared at the tall figure at the other side of the alley. His call pierced through her mind. She held up her hands and caught the arcing light.

For a moment, it seemed like the world stood still.

Then the air exploded around her. A flash bleached her vision brilliant white. A gust of wind tore through the alley, carrying leaves and sand.

The soldiers shouted. Fell against the walls. Sagged onto the ground.

Silence.

Nothing but the soft hiss of rain.

The girl stood there, dazed and shocked, staring at the soldiers who lay in the mud. Her tunic clung to her, wet and streaked with dirt. Her hair fell in wet strings over her shoulders, but her eyes burned. A rush of heat rose to Daya's cheeks. Her scent drifted on the breeze, the scent of an Aghyrian woman. No longer a girl, a woman. The scent of laughter, of eyes looking only at him, of picking her up and—no, he couldn't do that. He had to protect her.

Daya reached out a trembling hand. "Come."

Jessica ran.

Jumped over the bodies. Splashed through puddles. Threw herself at him. Buried her face in his sodden chest. Cried out in deep gasps, "Are they dead? Are they dead?"

He flinched and pushed her off him. "Whoa, not so fast. You're all wet. Calm down. I'll get you somewhere dry."

Jessica asked again, "Are they dead?"

"I don't think so."

His voice was as warm as she remembered. Yes, it was him. Eyes as dark as hers, his face equally high-cheekboned and pale-skinned. He was even taller than her.

"Here, take this." He draped his hat over her head, arranging the rain shield that hung off the rim over her shoulders. His touch burned through her tunic. Then something registered in her foggy mind. "You . . . you speak English."

A melancholy smile crossed his lips, full and dark like hers. Her heart jumped. "Come. Let's get out before the entire Mirani army turns up."

"Where to?"

"I know a safe place where we can hide until dark."

For a while, they walked with large strides. The rain hissed, water clattered from gutters, whirlpools rushed down street drains. Many times, Jessica glanced up at him. There seemed no need for words. In her mind, images whirled of a riverbank, trees with drooping branches which trailed in the water, the sound of children's laughter and her own face, bright with a smile.

There was a boy with black curly hair in a circle of other kids. He was taller than the others, but thin and gaunt in a way the others weren't. The skin on the back of his hands shone and stretched from sunburn, and on his nose and cheeks blisters wept yellow ooze.

The same boy sat at a table and a man shouted at him. A woman wept.

The boy ran through dusty streets.

Whoa not so fast. What is all this?

Questions made up of common words lagged eons behind what she saw. They were memories, of his life, and hers.

Through the haze in her brain, a fundamental question came to her. "Who are you, precisely?" How young, innocent and childish her voice sounded; how strange the sound of English in her ears. How utterly absurd the words.

She recognised his scent; she had known him all her life.

"That is a question not easily answered." Just the faintest trace of an accent marked his upper-class British speech.

She smiled at him, meeting those dark eyes. "Your full name would help a great deal."

"What is a name but a place marker in society? Does your name reflect who you are?"

She opened her mouth to say that was a silly question but then realised how his remark had hit at the core of her problem. Out of all the personalities in the universe, she couldn't possibly be Jessica Moore.

She laughed and hated how she sounded like a giggly girl. Blood rose to her face; her cheeks must be glowing. "You're weird."

Another one of those mischievous smiles that made her heart jump. "You're not the first one to say that. Anyway my name, as such things are considered important, is Daya Ezmi."

How much he was like her: his broad shoulders, his pale skin, high cheekbones, long arms and long-fingered hands. Loose curls framed his face and tickled the collar of his tunic. His hair looked softer than hers. She wanted to bury her fingers in it, smell it. Images flooded her mind. Herself as a little girl learning to ride a bike, herself on horseback galloping through the sandy river bed. She whispered, "You were there?"

His eyes grew sad. "All the time and not often enough."

"But . . . but why?" She didn't know what to feel about that. He'd *stalked* her, or kept her safe?

"I was going to tell you, and I was waiting to meet you."

She stared at him, as her mind went through events of the past. Leaving the showground to go back to school. Climbing into the plane. Her phone beeped with a message. "You mean that message was you?"

"Exactly. It was time that you were told the truth."

She gasped. "Are you my family?"

"I told your carers that I'm an uncle of yours—"

"But you're not."

"No."

"But we're both survivors from an ancient race which once lived on Asto."

If possible, his eyes widened even further.

"Is it true?"

"Yes, it is true. We are Aghyrians, more human than anyone in the universe. We are the root of all humans and human intelligence."

Jessica trembled on her legs. "Is it true that I was found in some sort of chamber where I survived for . . . for almost fifty thousand years and . . ." Her voice grew more unsteady.

"Yes, that is also true."

"And that I was submerged in some kind of fluid in a basin and that my name was written on the wall?"

He nodded. Red patches had risen to his cheeks. His voice sounded hoarse. "May life guide you in the future, Anmi Kirilen Dinzo."

Jessica froze. *What?*

"Anmi Kirilen Dinzo. Your name. I promised I wouldn't speak it until I could do so to your face."

Her lips moved in a soundless whisper. *Anmi Kirilen Dinzo, my name.* Her name: the word she always wanted, but never seriously hoped to hear. Tears pricked in her eyes.

She saw an entryway carved in stone, the gaping hole of a dark tunnel beyond, a small light casting long shadows over carved walls. The silhouette of a skinny boy holding a bundle of cloth in his arms. She realised the truth. "You found me."

His grip on her shoulder tightened. A white-knuckled hand on her upper arm. He averted his gaze.

The boy held a baby swaddled in blankets clutched against his chest. He ran down a tunnel, with the power of millennia peeling away from him. The mad dash into the burning hot desert heat. His hands on the instrument panel of a battered aircraft. The sound of a baby crying. His slender hand, the skin burnt and peeling, pulled back the blanket to reveal a line of blisters on the baby's right shin. She bent down and ran her fingertips over the scar. Burns, the doctor had told her parents. How right he was.

"You saved me."

His voice came as a whisper. "I'm sorry."

Sorry about what? She didn't say anything, sensing his inner turmoil.

For a while they splashed through puddles in the tree-covered alleys. Big splats of water dripped on the rain hat. High walls towered up on both sides of the wet gloom.

Finally, he spoke. "I'm sorry. I should have come earlier. I should have told you all this myself. I shouldn't have left you alone for that long, but you were happy with the people who looked after you and it wasn't until these strange things started happening." Meaning: Stephen Fitzgerald. "But when I found you . . . I was too young to look after a baby, and I didn't know what to do. You see—you are an original survivor, but I was born as a freak child to my parents. They never wanted me. No one ever wanted me. People were scared of me. Others like me had all been admitted to institutions. I was scared they were going to do the same thing to me. I didn't want that to happen to you."

Jessica turned to him, held up her hand to touch his cheek, but didn't. "Stop, stop. Slow down. You're making no sense at all."

Despair and anguish radiated from his eyes. "You don't want it to make sense. I could have prevented this whole mess."

He stopped in the shadow of the wall and pushed open a timber door on the side. They emerged into another, narrower alley hemmed in by high walls with more doors. Behind the walls loomed large houses, some part-shaded by trees.

Here, the water ran ankle-deep and the ground underneath was soft and slippery. Daya stopped in front of the door at the end. He faced her, his black eyes intense. "But I did it for one thing: you would not become another Ivedra. I would not have you locked up and investigated until you died in a prison."

He pushed this door open. On the other side was a small court-yard dominated by an enormous tree. Gnarled roots had burst through the pavers, which lay haphazardly around its base as if they had been lifted by an explosion. Daya shut and barred the door.

She whispered, "Ivedra was the woman who was found three hundred years ago, wasn't she? One of our kind."

"She was. The Coldi at Asto locked her up when her strange-ness became too obvious. You'll have noticed that your inner energy builds up more quickly when it's hot. Imagine what she went through, living on Asto."

Jessica shivered.

"Ivedra had a daughter in prison. Stories go that she survived and that I and people like me are her descendants."

She stopped him under the tree and faced him. The hat hung askew on her head. She flung it off, over a low branch where it dripped water into a puddle. She reached for his hair, but he pushed back her hands. "Hey, what are you doing?"

"I want to smell it."

He raised his hands like a shield before him, backing into the trunk of the tree. "I'm not sure if that is such a good idea—"

She searched for his thoughts, but a wall had gone up around him—to protect himself from her, she realised. "Don't worry. I'm controlling it now. No more sparks or anything." She laughed, meeting intense dark eyes, the irises so black that the edges of the pupils showed up only as a ghost of a ring.

"I still don't think . . ."

"Please, I need to do this."

He closed his eyes, blew out a forceful breath through his nose and leant back against the tree, his chest heaving.

"I won't harm you."

Slowly, he undid the fastening of his collar and pulled aside the fabric. His hands trembled; a vein throbbed in his neck.

Jessica leant closer. She breathed humidity. Then the smell hit her . . . fresh rain in a forest, running hand in hand with a lover, rolling in the grass. Blood throbbed in her cheeks. The glow spread down her chest.

She leant closer still, breathing on his pale skin. His curls tickled over her cheek.

His voice rumbled close to her. "Are you convinced we're of the same people?"

She nodded, unwilling to withdraw. The glow now crept over her shoulders, down her arms. "Can I feel your back?" Her voice sounded hoarse.

"Oh no." He slid a step sideways, holding up his hands again.

"Please. I need to know if you have . . . those muscles over your back."

His dark eyes met hers, and seemed almost desperate, bewildered. She still received no images from his mind.

Finally, he nodded. "Make it quick, then." He looped his arms over his head.

She reached behind him and ran her hands flat over his back, feeling the depression created by the V-shaped muscles. Saw herself standing before the mirror as twelve-year old girl, saw herself swimming through the eyes of someone else.

He whispered, "Wait," and took off his tunic. His skin, pale but firm, almost glowed in the dim light. Soft under her hands, the muscle tensed and relaxed, and tensed again. Just like hers. He stood perfectly still, his eyes closed, his chest heaving with deep breaths. Breathing her scent, like she breathed his. He let out his breath in a long hiss, lowered his arms and ran his hands over her back. His touch sent shivers through her.

Her tunic was wet and dirty and clung to her shoulders when she tried to take it off. She wrestled it up as far as her chest before she realised what she was doing . . . outside . . . in the pouring rain.

Daya gave a sheepish grin. "You better keep that on. They're not keen on public nudity in this town." But his hands slid over the naked skin on her back.

She whispered, "It's dirty." Before turning away. The blood pounded in her ears. Rain ran down her forehead into her eyes. She rested her head on his shoulder.

He mumbled, "We better go inside."

She nodded. "Yeah."

He didn't move except his hand, which drew small circles over her side in a mesmerising rhythm. His cheeks had gone red.

Jessica turned her head towards his neck so his curls tickled in her face and her breaths were laced with his scent. The most beautiful thing she had smelled in her life. The only thing she ever wanted to smell for the rest of her life, most precious, most special, most—

He traced his nose from the top of her head. Moist and warm, his tongue licked raindrops from her forehead, her brow, her nose. She turned her face up. He didn't waste the opportunity. His wet and cool lips tasted like rain. His tongue pushed inside her mouth. A soft groan rumbled in his chest.

Her body acted as of its own accord. She replied to his kiss with all the vigour she could muster. Arched her back so she pressed against him, raking her fingers through his hair, feeling his readiness through the thin fabric of his trousers.

His mind-voice spoke inside her, *Do you want to go inside?*

Jessica didn't protest.

23

J ESSICA OPENED one eye.

A soft noise had startled her, as if someone was in her room.

The first thing she saw was a very tall ceiling that was definitely not the one in her guesthouse room. There was a window in the room—very dirty. She lay on a bare mattress on a dusty and cracked mosaic floor. There were other mattresses around the perimeter of the room, where Pengali slept, rendered in shades of grey in the semidarkness.

What the. . . ?

Jessica pushed an elbow under her. Her stomach gave a protesting growl, bringing with it a surge of bile. Sweaty skin puckered into gooseflesh as a heavy and warm weight slid off her thigh: a male arm, which twitched with her movement.

Daya. His eyelids relaxed and closed, his long eyelashes arranged in perfect sliver-moon crescents. Bluish light silvered the curve of his shoulder, moving slowly up-down-up-down with his deep breaths.

A black tattoo of thorned branches encircled his upper arm. She hadn't seen that last night. Then again, she hadn't seen much at all.

Hell, she didn't remember half of what had happened last

night. Only shards of images and fragments of conversation. They had gone inside the house, where a group of Pengali silently retreated. Daya had offered her a drink. The blue stuff was called zixas and its acrid smell hit her face like a cloud of chloroform. He had downed it in one gulp. Laughing with the effects of his maddening scent, she had tried to copy him, but the stuff was so strong she couldn't help coughing. He had licked the coughed-up splatters from her face and chest. Hell, when had her shirt disappeared? It lay in the dust on the floor.

The images. There was something about images they shared. Images in his mind, and hers. Something about soaring through clouds and thundering rivers, and her face, her hair backlit by golden sun.

How had she ended up on her back on the mattress, his skin sweaty against hers?

She breathed with him; her heart beat against his; his lips explored her naked skin.

How could this have happened? *I don't even know who he is.*

And what were all the Pengali doing here, sleeping curled up on mats along the walls?

A shiver went through her.

She reached for her tunic, but as the fabric unfolded, an empty bottle tumbled out and rolled *clang, clang, clang* over the stone floor.

Shit.

Daya's eyelids fluttered and opened. He looked around, confused, and smiled as his eyes met hers. Warmth flooded through her. Not her warmth.

That's how it happened. His mind addled hers. His smell clouded her senses. His blue drink had completed the task. She'd been his for the taking, and he had taken her.

He pulled her closer. His mouth still tasted of that vile liquid. She wanted to push him away, but stroked his hair instead. Soft, gorgeous.

If he noticed the confusion in her, he didn't show it. His lips glistened when he broke the kiss. "Let's get dressed and go."

Jessica stiffened and wanted to ask *go where?* But she was afraid of waking up the Pengali. She scrambled to her feet and yanked on her tunic.

Even the corridor was full of Pengali, sleeping two or three to a mat. Seeing them brought uncomfortable memories. The Pengali featured in the happenings of last night. They'd come in, *worshipped* her; they had *watched*. In the dark, Jessica stepped across legs and bundles of clothes. Somewhere outside, a gutter overflowed.

Daya opened the door to the courtyard.

Raindrops made concentric circles in puddles. Clouds scudded over the city like grey-purple fluffs of cotton wool.

The door rolled shut behind them.

Only then did Jessica dare speak. "Where are we going?"

"Out of here." He sloshed through the puddles. "I have a unit at Hedron. You can stay with me."

A feeling of discomfort crept over her. "But I need a permit. That's why I haven't been able to leave so far. I was going to—"

"Don't worry about permits. I've got an override code."

"You . . ." Jessica gulped. This was all going way too fast for her. She still didn't understand the rules that kept her here. *If there were any such rules at all.* Her brain felt as thick as porridge. That damn drink.

Now at the door into the alley, he beckoned. "Come on, let's go. There won't be much time before we're discovered. We really should have left last night, but . . ." A sheepish grin crossed his face. God, he looked gorgeous like that. His scent, the love in his eyes, the warmth in her mind that possessed her, soothed her . . .

She shook it away and clamped her arms around herself. Get real. A man who said he'd known her all her life, but had never talked to her, who said he knew her parents, but lied to them, and then fed her some sort of drug so he could sleep with her.

He spoke in a whisper. "Come. I love you so much it hurts. I've waited so long for this moment."

"Then why didn't you tell me before?"

"You don't accept the apology I gave yesterday?"

Jessica couldn't remember an apology, just a lot of talk about things he had done wrong; a lifetime covered in five minutes before that smell had overwhelmed her senses.

He tugged her arm. "Please come. If we're to get out of here before anyone finds you—"

Anyone. The soldiers—Iztho, who was going to help her get Union citizenship and then go home. The Pengali and the keihu women who still had a story and knowledge to share. "Leave? Just like this?"

"Yes."

"And can you take me home, too?"

"Your home is with me. Now come."

"And then what?" Where did he get the idea that because of one night spent together—

"We'll discuss it later, when we're out of here."

"No—now. I want to know what's going on. You . . . took advantage of me. You gave me this blue stuff that made me all dizzy and—"

He held out his hands. "Don't you feel the bond of kinship, the smell of sharing, of being the same? Didn't I share my memories in your thoughts? Didn't you ask me to take you? I didn't fight you; you wanted it, too."

Memories of his smell clouded her. Throwing back her head, casting sweaty hair over her shoulders, while she sat astride him . . . She shuddered. "I was drunk, for God's sake."

He crossed the sodden courtyard and took her in his arms, stroking hair out of her face. "I am still drunk. Drunk for you, drunk with happiness."

While he spoke, a string of memories assailed her: a metal door set in stone, sliding the lid off the basin and finding the baby inside, floating in a bath of green, his hands shaking as he dipped them in the green fluid, her limp body enmeshed in arcs of life energy and her piercing wail as she drew her first breath. That's where he had found her, and saved her, and hidden her away for his own use.

Clenching her jaw, Jessica gathered strands of energy and

pushed them down the mind link. *Stop that!* "And that is a reason to assume that I belong to you? Just because you . . ." The words *raped me* were on her tongue, but he hadn't really raped her. This was something else, something much deeper than that, for both of them. It scared her.

She stared up into his eyes, their black depths swirling with longing. Just like last night. She remembered his beastly cry of pleasure when he spilled himself inside her. A cry of conquering, victory. Breath tickled over her face. His earthy scent enveloped her before warm lips met hers in a hungry kiss. For a moment, Jessica forgot her objections. She pulled him closer, shivers of desire running down her back.

He released her, chest heaving. "We've got no time for this. You've got to come. We're in danger here."

Jessica pushed him away with all the strength she could muster. "See, you're doing it again!"

"Doing what?"

God—he was so addled he didn't even notice. "Bewitching me with that smell. It makes me want to . . ." Rip off her clothes, and his, too. Throw him on the bed. Feel his tongue between her legs. Hear his laughter. Be thrown on the floor. Scratch and hit and bite him while he slammed deep into her. Revel in his conquering howl. Again and again. Until she bled and he cried and begged for forgiveness and they fell asleep in his other's arms. And whatever else had happened last night. No, it wasn't rape; if anything, he had more scratches and bruises than she did.

A look of understanding came over his face. "It's the scent. It's hormonal and it drives you mad. You'll get used to it."

And he expected her to come with him? Like this? He'd kill her within days, if she didn't kill him first. "Please get away from me."

He grabbed her arm. "Come on! I swear you'll get used to the scent. There is no time for this. Miran is after us. I almost ended up a prisoner there. Come with me before that Trader finds us here, or the soldiers he's sent. If they do they'll lock us up, or kill us."

Iztho, kill her? "He told me they would take me home."

"And you believe his promises?"

"Why the hell shouldn't I?"

"Because I've seen what the Mirani are doing. I've just come from there. They use weapons powered by life energy. I saw it. I fired one. And they're using us to get the energy. Please, for the last time: come with me."

"And what do *you* want with me?"

If he caught her sarcasm, he didn't show it. "We are Aghyrian. We can study our ancestors' knowledge, rebuild our civilisation, our cities, rebuild our race. All of the other known Aghyrians are men. With you—"

Blood rose to Jessica's face. "So that's what it's all about? You've been following me all these years because you want me to be your breeding cow?" *Wait until I tell you I'm infertile.*

He stared at her, his mouth open. When he spoke, his voice was soft.

"Oh. I should have left you to be examined by researchers on Asto? Left you to die a painful death like Ivedra? Or I should have left you to face a prison sentence for Stephen Fitzgerald's death? Is that what you wanted?"

Jessica reeled back, choking. "You did—what?"

"When that boy died because you lost control—"

"He tried to rape me."

"You lost control. He died. You don't want to know what I did to fix it up. That boy's insides were cooked. The parents demanded a postmortem. I falsified *all of it.*"

"You—what?" A wave of dizziness took hold of her. Deep inside, she'd always known that she'd been responsible. *But I had no idea what I was doing.* She felt the blood draining from her face.

"Now come. There won't be another chance to escape."

Jessica ducked to escape his grasping hand. Was he going to hold the threat to reveal her guilt over her head whenever she disagreed with him?

"Regardless of what you think, you don't own me. Leave me alone and stop bothering me."

She turned on her heel and ran out the gate.

24

JESSICA SPLASHED through ankle-deep puddles, kicking up sprays of water. The high walls and doors on either side of the alley blurred before her eyes. It was so dark today; with the thick cloud cover, everything ran into shades of grey and black.

She charged around a corner, almost crashing into a group of Pengali. Although they sported the short haircuts of domestic servants, males and females wore only skirts and wreaths of white flowers.

One of them held out a hand and whispered, "Anmi."

For a moment, Jessica felt like joining them in whatever they were celebrating, shoving a wreath of flowers on her head, stripping off her sodden clothes and dancing in the rain, showing her bruised and scratched body for all to see.

See what he has done to me? He only wants me to be his breeding cow.

But it wasn't that simple. What he had done to her was deeper than that, and he was still there, in the core of her mind, a seed that would once more grow into passion, or violence. He was still listening.

And I invited him in. It was the truth, and if she had a chance to go back in time, she would do it again. She'd had no other choice. His maddening scent still lingered in her clothes, begging her to go back. She *wanted* to go back.

Tears flooded her eyes.

The Pengali male extended his hand further.

"Oh, just leave me alone." Jessica ran on, down the street where more Pengali were setting up food stalls. Others had put out baskets with garlands made from white flowers. Others still had climbed up trees and were hanging out decorations.

In the shops, young keihu women tried on white dresses. Pengali females sat on benches re-braiding each other's hair.

Some major festivity was in the works.

In her mind, Jessica heard the thumping drums and the shouts and yells of the Pengali tribe. A small circle cleared in the heaving mass of striped and spotted bodies where a young male danced with Maire, bodies intertwined, moving to the beat.

A hot rush came over her.

. . . wet lips pushing hers apart, her hands sliding over soft skin, feeling the V-shaped depression in his back . . . his memories flowing through her while the earthy scent of his body enveloped her . . .

She wanted him so badly.

He only wants to use me.

Jessica sank down on the pavement in an alley, knees drawn up against her chest. Water seeped into her underwear, the only place of her that was still dry. She didn't care. She buried her face in her hands but tears wouldn't come.

Stupid. *Stupid, stupid, stupid.*

There were footsteps in the alley. A familiar deep voice rumbled, "Looks like I've found the little bat who flew away." Iztho.

His voice sounded like home, like cups of lukewarm tea taken in the civilisation of a colourful courtyard, like sumptuous dresses and talk of lessons and learning, promises of education, Union citizenship and returning to her parents. Civilisation, real help, reliability.

He was alone like a big, wet, forlorn grizzly bear. No soldiers, no gun. Just a long-fingered hand with many glittering rings reaching out for her. Dark patches under his eyes stood out against sallow and pale skin.

Jessica scrambled to her feet. "I'm sorry. I shouldn't have . . ." Her voice would no longer cooperate.

"I've found you, Lady. That's all that matters. Let me take you back to the guesthouse. I'd say you could do with a good meal and a bath. I've spoken to the authorities. I think I have a good chance to get us out of here soon."

Jessica didn't say how glad she was to hear this news. She walked in step with him, letting silent tears run down her face. When her nose started to run, Iztho passed her a cloth that smelled of fresh flowers and mountain air. "Come now, Lady. I don't like crying women." His voice had lost its edge, like it had done when he sang.

The entrance hall to the guesthouse was dark. The matron had moved her table out into the courtyard under the balcony, with the stacks of concertina-folded records against the wall, as far as possible from the rain. She was writing something and squinted up from her work as the footfalls of Iztho's boots echoed in the corridor. He spoke in keihu, remarking on the lack of light, and the matron said the servants hadn't been able to get fresh recharges.

Jessica thought of the line of boats carrying sacks of crackling pearls all the way from the Pengali settlement.

With the rain, the dining tables had been moved from the courtyard to the overhang of the balcony. Patrons sat at empty tables, their silhouettes black against the rain-swept pavement. The air hummed with discontented voices.

Iztho led her up the stairs. "The next few days are what the locals call the Bachelor days, the eclipse."

"Eclipse?"

"When one sun goes behind the other. It's a strong one this time. The Day sun completely behind the Evening sun."

Something clicked. "That's why it's so gloomy."

"Not really. The eclipse only lasts for the morning. The gloominess is because of the monsoon, but yes, it will be extra gloomy if it's overcast like this during the eclipse. Most cultures on Ceren or indeed on Asto have old superstitions that relate to occultation. Most involve rebirth or cleansing or a wake. A start of new life."

Jessica could just about imagine what Pengali would make of that.

"Anyway, the lady owner of this guesthouse apologises. She says it's not usual for so many of her servants to run off. She says that usually, the promise of money keeps them here for the festival, but many of them have taken unscheduled leave."

The Pengali. They're up to something. Jessica clamped her hands around herself. As if she didn't have enough trouble already.

"It also seems the supply of recharged pearls has dried up."

"I know—I heard."

"You . . . heard?" He frowned. "You understand keihu?"

She shrugged. "Just a bit. That woman uses her hands and eyes a lot. It's not all that hard to follow what she talks about."

"No, Lady, don't be so indifferent about it. You have a special talent for languages. I have been pushing you as hard as I can, but I'm stunned. I have never met anyone with an aptitude for languages similar to yours. It is a very rare and useful talent indeed."

A hot blush crept over Jessica's cheeks. She averted her eyes. "Words make pictures in my mind. They're all the same in every language. When I find the pattern, I see the picture; I don't hear the word."

The corners of his eyes crinkled with his smile, although his face never lost that intense look. He inclined his head and gestured to the door to her room. "Will I see you at mealtime, Lady?"

She responded with a nod, rehearsed and polite as she had seen him do, but she restrained an urge to rub her cheeks. What was wrong with her? Just about every comment by a man made her blush these days. A few steps brought her to the door of her room. There she stopped and turned around.

"I told you before: call me Jessica." The words had left her mouth before she could stop them, more out of habit maybe than anything. Jessica—was that her identity? Even though she had found out that Anmi was her real name?

Anmi, Anmi.

Daya's voice echoed in her mind. Anmi Kirilen Dinzo. Survivor of a disaster way before written history on Earth.

There were others, Daya said. Would they look like her, or him, tall and lank and pale?

She scratched her arms, which came out in red stripes from nail marks. Damn, she was so itchy. There must have been something in the last meal that caused hives. Come to think of it, her last meal had been ages ago and she had consumed nothing except that vile blue drink with Daya. Good. She was allergic to it.

Iztho stared at her. Drops of rain ran down his face and glistened in his hair like diamonds. "Go and get changed. You'll get sick if you stand out here wet. Put on your pink dress. I would like to see it on you."

Jessica spent a long time in the bathroom, trying out all the jars on the shelf for something that would wash away Daya's smell. The bottles contained powder, or tonic, or little nodules and with every container she opened, her hands trembled more. She didn't know what she was doing. There was no way that she would just go back home and everything would be fine. Her former life no longer had a purpose. She'd live in constant fear that Daya would reveal the truth.

And then Daya's assumptions . . . if he truly knew so much about her, he should also know about that visit to a specialist with her mother, a thin man with glasses who had, while looking only at his papers, assured her that her blood lacked female hormones.

I couldn't give him any children, even if I wanted to.

Did she want to? Of course she didn't.

No, that was bullshit, talked into her head by feminist teachers at school who insisted that all girls *should* want a career, and that family was less important. OK, so she could have all the careers in the world; she was smart enough to get into any course she wanted. But without purpose, school bored her. Daya had said that the two of them were more human than anyone else alive. The human mind was conditioned to want most what it couldn't have, and what she wanted most was family.

The bathroom blurred before her eyes. Some goop from a bottle ran from her hand, dripping down her leg. Jessica sank down into the water and cried.

Anmi. Daya's voice was clear as if he sat next to her.

Jessica didn't reply.

Where are you?

Again, she made no reply.

I need you. I'm . . . sorry.

Well, he needed to come up with a better apology than that. *I need you.* What about her?

I love you. I'm sorry. I don't know what happened either. I lost control.

Lost control of your drinking, more like.

Can I come to see you?

No!

Look, you need to get out of here. There's something afoot in the city. It looks like the Mirani army are using the Bachelor festival as cover for some activity. I'm afraid they want to bust you out.

Don't give me any of that bullshit. I'm in safe hands.

With that Mirani rescuer of yours?

Iztho? A chill went through her. *Stop seeing threats where there are none. I've been safe here.*

But you've seen what the Mirani did to me?

Again, that chill of doubt. Was the snowy city that was Iztho's home the same place where Daya had been tortured?

But no, he was diverting attention away from the problem. She was with another man and he was jealous. Simple as that.

Just stop bothering me.

With that, she cut off her end of the communication. And stared.

There was no water in the bath. The water, steaming and

bubbling, arced in web-like strands from one side of the bathroom to the other. Just a second, and then the whole construction collapsed. Jessica gave a squeal and curled up in the bath. She only just managed to brace herself for the scalding of near-boiling water.

What the fuck?

Trembling, she clambered out of the bath and mopped up the mess with a cloth. Her body had gone berserk. Dangerous, deadly. No wonder Ivedra had been locked up all of her short life. No wonder an army was after Daya.

What does that mean to me? That I should be locked up like the criminal I am?

Stephen's death was an accident.

What if I, like Daya, can't always control accidents?

She'd watched him kill the soldier. The man had been trying to kill him just as Stephen had been trying to rape her, but that didn't make it all right.

In her room, the pink dress hung over a chair. She slipped it over her head and examined herself in the mirrored stone next to the door. She didn't like the deep magenta as much as the blue, but the colour accentuated her eyes. Still, she didn't quite look as good as she had in the dressmaker's shop. For one she didn't know how to roll her hair into a bun and had no make-up.

Secondly, her guilt marred her looks. No matter how much she prettied up the outside, she was still a murderer.

No longer an innocent girl. Face the truth, Jess: you're a monster. You've always known that.

There was a knock on the door.

She went to open it. Iztho stood there, carrying a jug, the strap of his lute case slung over his shoulder. "I thought you might want some company, Lady."

"Yes, thank you." Anything to get away from those horrible thoughts.

He came into the room and put the carafe on the table. Familiar, like he belonged here. He felt like such a steady presence, not taken with nonsense and speculation.

While she brought over the glasses, he unpacked the instrument. Soft tones drifted through the room. He sat down on a chair, his back to the window so his silver hair glistened in the light. He poured the drinks, his blue eyes meeting hers as he passed her the cup.

Jessica settled on the couch, cradling her cup against her chest. Damn that blush! "If we leave from here, where are we going for this . . . training I need?"

That was Daya asking the question. *Get out of my head, you creep.*

"My home city of Miran."

See, there you have it. His voice sounded sarcastic.

Shut up.

Iztho went on, oblivious. "You will like it there. Miran is a breath of fresh air. Clean, cool and strong. We value knowledge and learning." Iztho strummed a chord and played sweet lilting notes while he spoke.

"Where will I stay?"

That intense look again. "I live with my family in the noble quarter of the city. I want you to stay at my house. I hope that would not be viewed as inappropriate."

"Inappropriate?" Jessica wiped furiously at her cheeks. She had to be almost glowing in the dark.

He played a few more chords before answering. "In the Mirani nobility, there are many rules. In Trading families, there are even more. For an heir of a Trading family—the oldest son of the oldest son." A soft melody flowed from the strings, slow and haunting. Jessica sipped from her cup, closing her eyes to listen. Suddenly, Iztho played a few angry, discordant notes. She opened her eyes, shocked, but he sat bent over the instrument and continued with the gentle song.

The water in the river flows down
But my heart wants to go up until
The weight of the water crushes
My desire to be free

He stopped playing to empty his drink; he slammed the cup on the table.

Jessica whispered, "Iztho?"

His shoulders went up and down with a deep breath. He slouched over the lute, not looking at her.

Finally, he spoke. "Trading is a hard business. There is no time to relax. The reputation of the family has to be held up. My father was a Trader, and his father before that, and so on, all the way back to the foundation of the Trader Guild." He played a few more notes, staring at the table.

Jessica whispered, "But you'd love to play music instead?" She picked up the carafe to refill his cup.

"I've always been different. From my brothers, from my nephews . . ."

How Jessica could relate to that. She passed him the newly-filled cup, seeing only his crystal-blue eyes. "I love your music."

God, her arms itched, her chest burned and the feeling now crept from her palms to the soft skin on the underside of her fore-arms. She scratched and scratched.

A long-fingered hand came into her field of vision and grabbed her wrist. His deep voice rumbled, "Don't. You'll make it worse."

Damn. She yanked her hand free and continued to scratch. "I think I've got something—some sort of disease." Even her voice sounded funny, all hoarse and husky.

"No. You're flushing."

"I'm—what?"

"Flushing. Coldi women flush, too. It seems your race is related to them. It's the first time this has happened to you?"

She nodded. "What does it mean?"

"It means, my Lady, that you are now a woman, ready to be married and have your first child. Your body knows it's ready. This . . . flushing is how it responds to . . . your desires." He cleared his throat.

"But . . . I can't have children." The doctors had always said so. The hormone levels in her blood were too low and didn't vary enough to produce a menstrual cycle . . . for a normal human . . . "Or does this mean I can?"

"Maybe, but who will know? You will need to find a male survivor of your race to find out."

Double holy shit. Daya. "How often does this happen? How does it work?"

"Coldi women can flush every ten days or so. They're fertile for a day afterwards."

Ten days. If her skin flushed now, it couldn't have done so yesterday. Phew. "Does that mean that every ten days I'll go like this?" Jessica scratched red patches on the inside of her arms. That would be *so* embarrassing.

He grabbed her wrist. "Don't scratch. I told you—you'll make it worse." He met her eyes briefly, then looked away.

His mouth worked. "No, you don't flush every ten days. You'll only flush when you're near a man you . . . feel attracted to." He pushed himself up, putting the lute back in its case. Patches of red had appeared on his cheeks. "I'll leave now. This isn't right."

Looking at her with every step, he walked to the door.

Jessica continued to meet his eyes. He was so gentle, so proper. She was still unsure of his motives, but he'd done a lot for her that he hadn't needed to do, including this explanation of what was clearly an embarrassing subject for him.

She rose. "Please stay." Her head was throbbing. Damn, she wasn't going to faint, was she?

"But you're in a scandalous state."

"It scares me."

He stared at her, his hand on the doorknob.

"Just to play music. I'll sit over there." She gestured at the bed, at a safe distance from the couch.

He hesitated. "You're certain?"

Jessica nodded.

Of course "playing music" was only the beginning. He told her that women of the Coldi race could control the flush of heat and she tried very hard. But then their discussion got to family and the harder she tried to push Daya away, the more he invaded her mind and repeated over and over again,

Come with me. You're in danger.

How could she be in danger with someone who cared for her while nothing required him to do this?

Come back to me. You're in danger.

She shouted, "Shut the fuck up!"

Iztho jumped up and held her to calm her down. Their eyes met. He was so close that she could see the peachy hairs on his chin. Her cheeks felt like they were lighting up like a glow-worm's butt. She was long past the itchiness and gone to a state where every touch on her skin felt much more sensitive than normal. Her heart was pounding and to be honest, she had enough of fighting the flush. It was not going away unless she gave in to it.

Through the watering of her eyes and huskiness of her voice, she said, "Please. Sit next to me." To Daya, she said, *That will teach you to eavesdrop on me. You don't own me.*

Her intention was to spite Daya, but the evening turned into something luxuriously relaxing and lazy. They had a meal brought up to the room, they bathed. He washed and touched her in all her private places and the next step seemed only natural. He assured her many times that she could back out if she wanted.

But, no. It was relaxed, gentle and pleasant.

Very pleasant.

25

D AYA PACED across cracked and dusty pavement, lifting up broken tiles with strands of energy and smashing them against walls and floors.

Shadows of Pengali hid in the corners of the room, or in the corridor. Sometimes they whispered. When Daya tried to talk to them, they scurried away, but always returned. Watching, observing him. Whispers of her name echoed in the empty rooms. *Anmi, Anmi.*

Why did they want her?

Ask them, and you might find out.

There was a shout outside, and Daya ran to the door, hoping against hope to see Anmi's tall figure. He stared into the darkness of the yard. A group of Pengali ran out the gate. Where were they going? Did they know something he didn't? She was at the guest-house, in bed *with the Mirani Trader.*

The thought burned, ate at him. Yesterday, she had coerced him into doing what he hadn't intended to do. It had been good, but he suffered for it; she suffered for it. And now . . .

∽

Jessica lay awake, staring at the ceiling. The patter of rain was only disturbed by the sound of Iztho's breathing. He lay on his side facing the door, his hair fanned out over the mattress. Strands of it stuck to the sweaty skin on her stomach.

Jessica peeled it off and swung her legs over the side of the bed. Heat washed over her in waves. In her chest, in her cheeks and face. Her skin had stopped itching, but now glowed and throbbed as if it was some sort of aftereffect of the flushing.

She staggered to the bathroom, where she scooped handfuls of sulphur-scented water over her naked skin. Goosebumps spread from her arms to her stomach, but underneath, she still felt hot.

Damn that flushing. Coldi women controlled it, Iztho had said, but she wasn't Coldi. More and more, she worried about it. Was yesterday afternoon really the first time it had happened to her? She had felt hot right from the moment she had met Daya. She sat down on the edge of the bath, rough stone on her naked buttocks.

Stay calm.

She pressed her hands together in front of her face. The flow of energy came easily and no longer hurt. Bright light flooded the bathroom.

In the darkness of the alley, Daya stumbled amongst a throng of Pengali. Lithe bodies squeezed past him into a square ahead. Floodlights cast their ghostly glow over a sea of people, dancing, moving, writhing; many with wreaths of white flowers on their heads. Heavy drum beats reverberated in his chest. Whistles, shouts, patterned skin gleaming with oil. Rain hissed down, but no one took any notice.

Daya leaned back against the rough trunk of a tree, contemplating how he was going to cross the square without being dragged into some dance. If one more of those leering female creatures touched him with any part of her body . . . He shuddered.

Anmi was in the guesthouse; he could feel her. Except he

couldn't go that far; there were Mirani guards at the entrance, far too many for him to overpower by himself.

Everywhere he went the natives spoke her name *Anmi, Anmi*. Questions hovered in their eyes. Where was she? Why wasn't she with him?

Because I stuffed up.

He had failed, and he didn't understand why. *You have no idea how to relate to people.* Ennai had said that, in the fight that led to their break-up. His relationship with Ennai had been a mistake from the beginning, but living amongst the Coldi at Hedron, he had once entertained the illusion that he could be like them, that he could be *normal*, accepted.

Wrong. He had never been like them. He would never be like them. His life belonged not to his parents who had cast him out, not to his uncle's business, but to the girl, to Anmi. It was his task to protect her, to keep her safe, so she didn't end up like Ivedra. And he had failed.

Daya pushed forward, shivering from sweaty bodies pressed against him. The females brushed up to him, stroking him, giving him suggestive smiles. Their body odour hurt his nose.

It's called peppermint, Jessica told him.

And it was the male Pengali who stank, not the females.

She shivered with that statement: Daya's *life* belonged to her? She didn't belong to anyone, didn't want to own anyone either.

But you already do.

The ghost of Daya's scent wafted through her memories, making her shiver, making her want to run out and look for him, to complete that part of her that was missing. Something had happened that night. *Pheromones,* her analytical self said. An involuntary, uncontrolled response; something that made no rational sense. Like falling in love, but worse.

She had started that sexual fight. Daya had been trying to hold back. It wasn't that he had hurt her; she had hurt him, too.

"Are you all right, Lady?"

Iztho had raised himself onto one elbow; his other hand shielded his eyes against the brightness of the light. He swung his feet over the side and came into the bathroom.

"I feel so hot."

He remained at the door, looking up at the light. "I never believed this when I first heard of it."

Jessica inclined her head, unsure how to respond to the tone of awe in his voice, unsure if she liked it, or if she liked him being here. It might be dangerous. *She* was dangerous to him.

He smiled and entered the room. "Once everything has settled, your future will be bright. Once we are in Miran . . . Lady, I can see you doing very well in business. Very well indeed." He closed her in his arms. "I'll help you through your citizenship exams and then I'll sponsor you to get your Trading certificate. You can work under the Andrahar licence."

There was a dreamy look in his eyes that brought a twinge of discomfort. Whatever happened to *going home?*

He cradled her face in his hands and bent forward for a kiss, but Jessica found the prospect of that and maintaining the light at the same time too much. She called the light back before meeting his lips and when she did, she saw a pair of dark eyes.

Do you have to look into every part of my private life?

Daya just blinked. Light flashed over his face. A Pengali female sidled up to him. One of the servants, tailless, wearing only the shortest of short skirts. She rocked her hips, rubbing the curve of her thigh against his. He shuddered.

Iztho's hand slid over Jessica's stomach. "Yes, you are right, you do feel hot. Come under the window."

He led her back into the bedroom. The thin cover whispered over her as she settled back on the pillow, her head on his shoulder.

Soon Iztho was fast asleep, his heavy breathing deep and regular, but Jessica lay staring at the ceiling. Damn, she was still hot and the lingering scent of Daya's skin would not go away.

Pheromones. A physiological response, like a stallion smelling mares. Not a bloody thing she could do about it. At least she didn't do the weird lip thing.

No, they only scratched each other to bits when they had sex.

It scared her. *The man is a monster. I am a monster.*

Jessica was back with Daya in the crowded street.

There was a bark of a voice on the other side of the square. The square emptied with amazing speed. Pengali-shaped shadows jumped onto walls, in trees, abandoning the drums.

Four figures came into the middle of the square. A Mirani patrol, hands on their crossbows.

Daya pressed himself against the trunk of one of the trees that lined the alley. All the natives around him sank into a silence that . . . tickled.

Jessica prodded him. *Go ahead, connect with them.* He could see for himself why she couldn't leave the Pengali.

But Daya just stood there.

Ahead, the barking voice spoke. "You are sheltering a dangerous criminal. Give him up, and none of you will be harmed."

In the shadows, a voice yelled, *"Kusi."*

Two of the soldiers raised their crossbows. Jessica didn't know what *kusi* meant, but she guessed it was nothing good.

"You are showing disrespect to officers in uniform."

More Pengali took up the call. *Kusi, kusi, kusi.* It came out of the trees, the yards, the alleys surrounding the square.

The crossbows went up, the soldiers trying to take aim, but shadows flitted through trees; leaves rustled.

Kusi, kusi, kusi.

The patrol leader was now speaking into his receiver, asking for backup no doubt. Daya grabbed the arm of the closest Pengali, a young male.

"Come. You can't win this; they'll kill you. Get out of here."

Kusi, kusi, kusi.

There was a *zhing* of a crossbow, a chill in the air, and the next moment, the flash of a knife. One of the soldiers dropped his crossbow, a dark stain spreading out from his chest. A lithe figure came out of the shadows.

No, Alla!

Another knife flew, but missed the soldiers.

There were running footsteps and shouts. A second group of soldiers came out of an alley, having restrained a group of Pengali youths.

The leader shouted, "Right, let's bundle these guys up and take them to headquarters—Hey!"

A loud crack reverberated down the street. One of the soldiers clutched his throat, making choking sounds. Another lunged for the black and white banded tail wound around the soldier's neck, yanking it free. Two others restrained the youth.

"Hah, don't you know what the laws of this city say about tails? Tails for thieving and murdering?"

The youth stared up at him, wide-eyed.

The soldier nodded at a colleague. "Go ahead. Teach him a lesson."

Daya pressed himself against the tree trembling with the force of anger and fear, not knowing where it came from.

He saw a flash of metal.

Pain.

Someone screamed, and the scream seemed to come from his mouth. There was a sickening thud. The square exploded in shouts.

Daya peeked around the tree trunk.

The youths ducked under the soldier's arms and ran. The female retrieved her knife from the chest of the fallen soldier. As many people ran into the square as were trying to get away. People shouting, shadows flitting over walls and through trees. Stones flew into the square.

~

Jessica jumped out of bed and ran to the window. Wind whipped the tree in the courtyard. Over the roof of the guesthouse wing opposite, strands of light reached for the sky, flailing, calling for help. Pain radiated out from them. She drew a strand to her.

The soldiers vanished into the street, running after the mob of Pengali, leaving behind a small figure on the ground. A Pengali youth, shivering and whimpering. Blood covered his back and ran onto the pavement. Daya took gasping breaths. Pain radiated from the youth and he had no idea why he could feel it, but he could, and the pain made him feel sick.

Daya couldn't *not* do anything, even though he had not the faintest clue what to do. In his mind, he heard the screams of a baby. *She's going to die.* He was a clumsy youth again; helpless, useless. That time, he had done nothing, except run faster, but the searing air had still burned her. She still had the scar.

He knelt next to the young Pengali male, shaking his shoulder. "Come, get up."

The youth rocked to and fro, panting and clutching his lifeless tail in his hands, blood running down his arms.

"Please, get up." Daya's eyes blurred, seeing the skin peel away from the chubby leg of a baby only three days, but fifty thousand years old. *It's my fault. They were looking for me.*

He turned around, but the natives who had been in the alley with him had gone. Again he tugged at the youth's arm. "Please get up and tell me where to go. I can't carry you by myself."

A silent shadow jumped down from the wall behind him. He felt the presence before he could see it. The shadow crossed the distance to him in two steps and enfolded him in an offensive smell that hurt his nose. White hair hovered like ghost in the darkness. The female face at the height of his elbow was old and paperskinned. Familiar somehow.

Her voice sounded familiar, too, even the harsh, vowel-less words that meant nothing to him.

Ikay.

He pulled the youth up, smearing blood all over the front of his tunic. The boy swayed.

Without a word, the female grabbed the youth by the feet. In this manner, they struggled down the length of the main street, keeping to shadows where moonlight wouldn't show them so clearly, but where tree roots bulged through the pavement, pushing up the street tiles. Several times, one of them stumbled. Groups of Mirani soldiers marched past, holding their crossbows.

Finally, the female pushed open the gate and they entered the haven that was the overgrown yard of an abandoned house. A dry fountain, cracked pavers, hedges that had grown into small trees. Daya felt like he had been here before, too.

It was the house where Jessica had heard the truth about herself.

The young male moaned some incoherent words.

Daya tightened his grip on him. "Shh, we're almost there."

They ran up the steps to the porch and the female pushed the door.

At least a hundred Pengali sat on the motley collection of couches, chairs and mattresses which sprawled haphazardly across the hall.

No one spoke. Pengali were masters in stealth and hunting. Waiting was their game.

Daya lowered the youth's shivering body, belly down onto a couch. Even with the female's gentle coaxing, he would not let go of his tail. Daya undid the ties to his shorts and wriggled the blood-soaked material off his buttocks, feeling the prick of hundreds of eyes in his back. Someone brought a light.

The black and white striped skin of his buttocks was smeared with blood. A white fragment of bone protruded from the stump that used to be his tail.

Daya reeled.

"Nothing I can do," he whispered. "I can't help, I can't. I'm not even a healer. I don't know what you think I am. I can't put their tails back on. It's impossible—" His voice spilled over; he wasn't even sure what language he spoke.

The female held the bowl of water. In total silence, she helped him clean and bandage the stump. Back in his youth, he had never done this for the girl. He had chosen to leave her care to others. Wash his hands of the responsibility. No wonder she cared more for these tailed people than for him.

I was too young to understand, too disturbed.

He saw his father, saying those words that haunted him, *I have no son.* The culmination of years of pain and desperation.

Awkwardly, he took the youth's hand.

I did as best as I could. But it wasn't good enough.

Another youth rose and spoke to the assembly. His words were like darts of venom, amongst which the girl's name stood out. Shouts echoed in the hall, fists were raised. Several people shouted, *Anmi, Anmi!*

What was it about her that these people wanted?

Ask the one they call Ikay, and you will see.

The old female sat next to him, looking up as if she expected he would ask. Had she heard the girl's mind-voice? He put his hands in her old, paper-skinned ones. She stroked his cheek with her tail. Then she closed her eyes.

The web spread out from her forehead. Weaker than the girl's, but strong enough to carry memories. There was a cave in the rocks close to the tribe's settlement. There was a chamber with friezes carved in the stone walls.

Daya saw; he understood why the Pengali felt for him and Anmi, why he saw these images in Ikay's mind . . . why the soldiers were keeping Barresh under siege. Oh, the implications.

The contact between him and Jessica fell away.

There was silence.

Jessica slept.

26

JESSICA RESTED her head on Iztho's shoulder. Languid steam rose off the surface of the bath. Its sulphuric scent mingled with the perfume in his wet hair.

Her heart still thudded with the afterglow of lovemaking. Lazy, relaxed, luxurious. Getting better all the time. That's how it was meant to be: a relaxation, not a fight.

He trailed a finger over her back; her skin broke out in delicious goosebumps.

"What do you say? Shall we do this for the rest of our lives?"

Jessica met his light blue gaze. She couldn't help a twinge of unease stirring inside her. Since coming to share her room yesterday morning, he had spoken of little else—gaining Union citizenship, joining his business, travelling the universe— "I do want to learn."

Not really an answer at all, but *yes* was not an answer either. The assumptions he made based on the fact that they slept together frightened her.

"You will learn. Whatever you want."

"And I want to be something, not just . . ." She understood Miran was a very patriarchal society. Iztho had said, *You can be Miran's second ever female Trader.*

Although that left too many questions yet unanswered. Like what those soldiers had wanted from Daya. *Us Traders belong to a very different society,* Iztho had said. He said, he said, but what should she believe?

"You can be anything you like, my Lady. I can even see you on the council."

"I want to see my parents."

"As often as you like. I'll make sure of that."

He had made this promise many times over, too. She tried to imagine him walking up to her parents' house. No way. With his fur cloak and uniform, he didn't fit. Even in his hippie outfit, her parents would be horrified. He was much too old for her. Now that would be very different with Daya—

Damn Daya. Why did she think about him?

Because I worry.

Because, after she had lost contact with him, she had heard nothing more. Because he knew why they had a bond with the Pengali, and now he chose not to talk to her.

Because something had happened to him?

She turned her face to Iztho's; their lips met in a kiss tasting of sulphuric water. For now, she was spared from having to answer his inevitable question.

There was a loud knock on the bedroom door.

Iztho broke the kiss. In one movement, he rose and clambered over the side of the bath.

Jessica stiffened. "What is it?"

He grabbed a towel, wiped himself and wrestled his arms into a tunic. "There might be news from the Exchange." False papers or such, whatever he was arranging. Papers to get out of here, *as his wife.*

He wrapped a cloth, sarong-like, around his waist. The material was tight and left little to the imagination as to what he had been doing. Had she not felt so uneasy, it would have been funny.

Instead she felt worried. She still didn't understand what was happening with the local authorities, if there was even such a thing. Daya hadn't made any fuss about satisfying regulations. He'd acted as if leaving was easy.

There was another knock.

"Yes, I'm coming." Hair dripping over the back of his tunic and on the floor, he hurried out of the bathroom. There was the sound of the door rolling open, and a male voice—a question asked, not in a friendly way.

Iztho replied. They spoke Mirani, but their voices were too low for her to make out more than shards of meaning.

". . . haven't seen anything . . . ran out and couldn't find her . . ." That was Iztho's voice.

Damn, he was telling his own countrymen that he didn't know where she was.

"We received this . . . don't know who else to give it to."

Jessica heaved herself out of the bath and grabbed the cloth Iztho had left on the floor. The skin on her stomach and chest glowed soft pink and as soon as she was dry, heat again flowed through her. Damn it. Would it ever stop? She wrapped a cloth around her.

The door to the room rolled shut.

When she entered the bedroom, Iztho stood a few paces inside the door, staring as if he'd just seen a ghost. She went up to him, but his muscles were tight and didn't relax under her touch.

"What is it?"

He didn't reply.

"It's those soldiers—they're after me aren't they?"

"They're meant to keep you safe."

Well, that was an obvious lie. He was trying to hide her from them.

"Is there a reason we haven't left this room for more than a day? Is anything going on outside?"

"There's a lot of natives in the street. There's some sort of festival going on." Not really an answer either.

"Any fighting?"

He gave her a sharp glance. "Not that I know."

She thought he was lying, but no point in pressing the fact.

Somehow, she would have to get out of this room. Who knew what had happened outside in the past two days? There were probably guards outside the door.

She sent out a careful tendril of mist. *Daya? I could do with some advice.*

Fancy that. For all she knew he'd tell her to take a hike—that's what she would do.

Shit, Daya. I'm sorry. Just talk to me all right?

There was no reply.

Then she noticed that Iztho held a folded piece of paper. "What's that?"

"You best get dressed, Lady. The Barresh council has asked for your appearance. They declined my application to take you to Miran and want to question you in person."

A cold feeling went over her. "Why?"

"I'm guessing that they found out that you might have been a passenger on the plane."

"You said they didn't know. How did they find out?"

"Your tailed friends probably had something to do with it."

Or could it have been Daya?

"It seems the Barresh council can't accept their incompetence and must have someone else to blame for this disaster."

"But . . ."

He gave her an intense look.

Jessica hesitated. "Tell me the truth. Do you think. . . ? It *was* my fault, wasn't it? Because of my . . ." She held up her hands. "Because I stuffed things up. With the lights and . . . *Avya.*"

He put a hand on her shoulder. "That is only one possible explanation and not one that will impress officials responsible for the Exchange network. The incompetence of this town is well-known."

"But it *was* my fault, though. Don't you think?"

"Possibly." Meaning *yes.*

Jessica sank down on the bed, feeling very small. Tears pricked behind her eyes. She'd killed three people. Four when counting Stephen. *I am a monster.*

Iztho took her hands in his. A smile crossed his face. "You are strong, Lady. Whatever happened to that craft, likely no one will ever know. Even if you are responsible, no one will ever believe you. No one believes this ability is real. No one knows how powerful it is. But if you follow my instructions, you should be fine. I will tell you exactly what to say."

Jessica nodded; she had been afraid of that. She was getting sick of people telling her what to do.

He closed her in his arms.

She wanted to push him away. She wanted to understand what was going on, really understand it, not just listen to things people told her, however well-meaning.

His lips met hers in a soft kiss. "You still feel hot, my Lady, are you all right?"

"I . . ." A breeze came into the window; she shivered. "I don't know." She was beginning to feel very unsure about this whole flushing business, too. It lasted for a short period every ten days, he had said, not for two days on end almost without stopping.

"You are not catching a sickness?"

Jessica shrugged, considering the thought of a fever. Whatever diseases occurred here, she would be totally unused to them.

"I will arrange medical help as soon as we're out of here."

In the streets and alleys of the city, the festival's parade was in full swing.

Whistles rent the air, rising over the squealing and trilling voices of Pengali girls, the chants of boys, the cheering of the crowd and the deep thumps on the huge drum carried by four males.

Jessica rubbed her arms, where the skin had broken out into goosebumps.

A group of young males walked past, hair adorned with the same white flowers that grew all over the town's gardens and neglected planter boxes. Some of the boys danced, wriggling their hips. Their white skirts did little to hide their swaying pride. Others, especially the younger ones, looked terrified.

Soldiers watched the proceedings from the street corners, brooding, silent. So many of them.

Iztho tightened his grip on her shoulder. "Come, my Lady, let's go. We don't want to give the council the wrong impression by coming late."

Iztho led her into a side street where merchants wheeling trolleys held up the flow of Pengali children taking a shortcut to the next main street, where the head of the parade was yet to arrive. Jessica clutched Iztho's arm in the effort not to be separated from him.

Lining the street, a rusty fence had almost collapsed under the weight of a climbing plant with orange seedpods. Above it rose the roof of a building: a grey and featureless dome that, with an adhering cover of flakes, looked like it had once been painted, but it was impossible to tell in what colour.

Iztho leaned over her shoulder, his breath tickling in her ear. "The glorious residence of the Barresh council."

That building? It looked like a prison.

Two lines of soldiers linking arms made a futile attempt to keep the crowd away from the gate into the complex. Bejewelled keihu citizens entered at a trot, harassed looks on their faces.

Iztho, too, guided her through the gate, passing soldiers who nodded at him.

In a dark hall where their footsteps crunched on broken and loose floor tiles, a man in the black outfit of the Barresh council pointed them in the direction of an arched walkway, much like that in the guesthouse. A series of murals adorned the left-hand wall, depicting flowers and fountains and beautiful buildings, bridges, gardens, all filled with smiling people from times past. In the central mural, on a balcony overlooking this splendour, stood a man. Sunlight played in his copper-coloured curly hair and drew lines of experience in his stern face. The picture intrigued Jessica. This town clearly had a rich history. Why had it gone backwards?

The soft murmur of many voices came from a set of double doors at the end of the walkway. The meeting hall.

As soon as Iztho led her into the hall, a glow of warmth went through her. Familiar, happy, it felt like home, like arms surrounding her, a familiar smell surrounding her. Unsettled, she held tight onto Iztho's arm, while her eyes adjusted to the semi-darkness.

Shadows moved where people found seats on benches set in an amphitheatre-like arrangement. A large pentagonal table in the centre of the hall was bathed in bright light. It was empty.

Iztho led her down the stairs. Heads turned and gazes followed her; a hush fell over the crowd. Jessica stared ahead, lifting her chin, trying to ignore the prick of gazes and the increasing feeling of warmth.

A keihu man in a dark green robe waited at the bottom. He spoke briefly to Iztho and marked him off a list displayed on a reader. Jessica fiddled with her dress.

A woman directed Jessica and Iztho to an empty spot on a bench at the perimeter of the floor, lit by the glare reflecting from the central table.

Jessica sat down, clamping her hands between her knees. A flush of heat went through her, making sweat break out on her brow.

Iztho put a calming hand on her knee. "Just tell them what we practiced."

She returned a rehearsed smile, still feeling all those gazes on her. "What are all these people doing here?"

She had imagined a much more private affair.

"The ones sitting on this bench I would expect to be the Barresh council."

Next to her sat two enormously fat men, in light blue robes resembling tents. On Iztho's side, a couple of younger men balanced readers on their knees. Scribes or journalists maybe. A group of robed and jewel-laden men stood talking to each other using lots of hand gestures. Half-hidden behind them sat a tall figure.

A shiver crept up Jessica's arms as she finally recognised the reason for her unease.

Daya. What are you doing here?

You will see soon enough. The cool and professional tone surprised her. Why wasn't he angry?

There's no time to be angry. There are many things happening that are not good.

Someone rang a bell at the back of the hall. The knot of men in front of Daya dissolved, giving Jessica a clear view of him, dressed in sober navy blue. Clear black eyes met hers. His hair had been combed and fell in loose curls about his face. Dark lips curled into the faintest of smiles. Warm, mesmerising, gorgeous.

You look beautiful.

Jessica inched closer to Iztho.

He rumbled, "Don't be nervous. I'll help you."

But her gaze was still on Daya. One of his feet was bandaged and so were both his hands. What had happened to him? She hadn't bitten him that badly, had she?

"Is anything wrong, Lady?" Iztho stiffened. "Is that him? The man who hurt you?"

Jessica averted her eyes.

"Is it, Lady? Tell me and I'll make sure he's removed from this meeting."

Jessica cleared her throat. She glowed with heat. "It doesn't matter."

Iztho jumped up from the bench. "It does matter. This meeting is important for you and I will not have you intimidated by anyone. I'll tell him to mind his own business and stop ogling you."

Jessica grabbed the bottom of his cloak. "No, stop."

"Why? If he has hurt you, he shouldn't be here. This is a place where we deal with respectable people."

"Please, don't make a scene."

Past Iztho, Daya had gripped the edge of the bench. *Why do you let that dressed-up clown overpower you?*

She glared back. *That dressed up clown is . . .* No, she had a better idea. As strongly as she could, she thought of Iztho kissing her.

A burst of heat shot through her, so strong she gasped.

He was jealous. Good.

Iztho pulled his cloak from Jessica's grip. "Leave this to me, my Lady. I see he upsets you and I'll deal with this."

In slow paces, he crossed the floor. A council attendant waved him back, but he ignored her. The chubby and bejewelled keihu councillors halted their conversations. Iztho stopped a few paces from Daya and languidly crossed his arms over his chest. His deep voice carried in the hall. "Why are you bothering my Lady?"

Daya rose equally slowly. He was taller than Iztho, though not by much, but his lack of a big and furry cloak made him look younger and more vulnerable. "She is not your Lady." He spoke Mirani almost without accent.

Languages—another characteristic of their race.

Iztho's hand shot out to grab Daya by the front of his tunic. "Say that again and I'll smash your face in."

Jessica cringed. *No, don't hurt him.*

Daya coolly yanked his tunic out of Iztho's hand and met Jessica's eyes; a flow of warmth went through her. "She belongs to no one. If you think otherwise, you're fooling yourself."

"Don't give me that rubbish. I've seen what you did to her. I picked her up off the street after you were done with her. Crying, wet and covered in bruises. That may be the way you lot look after your women but in my language, it's abuse. If I see you as much as look at her again—"

The two men faced each other, barely an arm's length apart. White facing black, rational facing emotional, there could not be a greater contrast between them.

Daya was the first to break the tense silence. "Is that a threat?"

"Fuck it is. I want you as far away from her as possible or you will face the consequences. Why don't you piss off and leave us alone before I get really angry. The Lady has chosen. She doesn't want you." He half-turned back to Jessica.

In a flash, Daya grabbed Iztho's cloak and pulled him back. A wave of sparks flowed under the skin of his arms, escaped and flew into the surrounding air. His cheeks had gone bright red. In his eyes burned such hatred that the whole hall chilled with it. Warmth sucked out of Jessica's skin as if an iced wind stroked past her.

No, Daya, no!

In two steps, Jessica had crossed the floor. She pushed Daya away from Iztho. "Stop! Stop it!"

Daya stumbled back a few paces.

Jessica placed herself between the two men, hands planted at her sides. "Don't you dare attack someone with your mind. If you must, deal with me." *And if you do, I'll never look at you again.* But she was already looking at him and in that brief moment, a burst of Daya's warmth flowed through her. *I love you I love you I love you.* His scent made her heart thud against her ribcage.

Jessica reeled back, into the fur of Iztho's cloak. His voice rumbled. "Come, my Lady, let's stay well away from him."

As he led her back to their seats, Daya did not avert his gaze. Her vision went dark, and full of cold. The metal of a wall at her back almost froze onto her skin. Someone emptied a bucket of ice water over her head. A male voice screamed.

Jessica balled her fists. *Stop it!*

I won't. If nothing else, I will make you believe what happens to people of our kind in Miran.

He has nothing to do with it!

A bell rang.

Iztho settled on the bench on her other side and shifted forward so Jessica could no longer see Daya, but she could still feel him. He was talking to the man on his other side, reminding him to speak slowly and wait for the translator to do his job. Daya sounded calm and confident, as if he had forgotten the argument already, as if he accepted her choice. He was *helping* the council?

Damn you.

He didn't reply.

The bell rang a second time and murmur ceased. With difficulty, Jessica forced her thoughts back to the statement she and

Iztho had practised in the guesthouse. She would tell of the accident, the killing of the other passengers by rogues presumed to be
sent by the council, her trek through the jungle, her meeting with
the Pengali, how Iztho had helped her come to the city and end
with a plea to be allowed to return to her family, at which time
Iztho would step in and say that he would sponsor her for Union
citizenship.

It all sounded so simple.

At some stage, when she hadn't been looking, a woman had
settled herself at the pentagonal table. Light glittered in the gold
embroidery around the rim of her tunic. A mediator, Iztho had
explained, from the Union, and another world. She spoke in slow
sentences in Coldi, the Union language; Jessica understood none of
it. Iztho provided quick translations of her formal welcome and
explanations of the rules of the hearing. And the question: was the
Barresh node of the Exchange responsible for the death of these
offworlders who had landed in the forest?

She introduced the others of the committee, and they took their
places at the table one by one.

She then called the first witness.

Jessica had never seen the brown-haired man who took his
position behind the lectern-like table. His hands trembled, and he
stumbled over words, repeatedly wiping his face as if he was so
tired he had trouble remembering what to say.

Jessica closed her eyes and sent out a tendril of energy. Images
oozed from him. Three people bent over long lists of data on a
screen. Despair etched their faces and hung thick in the room. Rain
lashed the window. It was dark outside.

"He's the head of the Damaru family, the bunch of incompe-
tents who own the Exchange," Iztho grumbled and went on to
translate the man's declaration: that the Exchange records held no
evidence of a wayward translocation and that this implied the
translocation had been doctored.

"Rubbish," Iztho added. "They're drowning in their own
mess."

But he *did* believe she had caused the accident and the man's memories confirmed it: they hadn't been able to pinpoint the cause of the plane's translocation.

The woman at the table asked a few questions, in response to which a woman came onto the floor to deposit a stack of documents on the table.

"What's that?"

"Proof of his word, according to him," Iztho said. "Proof of his incompetence more like."

The man continued to plead to the committee, his eyes wide as a zombie's. Every second sentence, he repeated the words *elish kamoraa o gamaru*, which probably meant something like *please believe me*, but Iztho peppered his translation with lots of disparaging remarks about the Barresh Exchange.

Iztho might not think much of the man, but his tone sent chills through Jessica and she was glad when he finally sat down.

This is wrong. He gets the blame for something I've done.

The mediator raised her voice, and a translator repeated her words in Mirani. "If what this man says is true, we should ask the only person who can answer this question. In this hall is a surviving passenger of the craft. Stand up, young lady, come here." Her eyes met Jessica's.

Jessica gulped and threw Iztho a panicked glance.

He stroked her side with a gentle hand. "Answer the questions as I said. You know nothing."

Too right she didn't, and then she wondered if, as fellow passenger, he would get a turn in being questioned. He had told her, *Tell no one that I was there. It would only complicate the investigation.* She didn't like it.

Jessica stumbled from the bench. A wave of heat hit her as she stepped into the light. Her voice uncertain, she asked in Mirani, "I will need a translator."

The mediator threw her a suspicious glance, but continued in Mirani. "You were travelling in this craft?"

"Yes."

"We are talking here about a local flight, where none of the passengers or pilot had knowledge of the Union?"

"Yes." Cringe.

"How did your craft end up here?"

"I was flying home. There was a flash and all of a sudden, we were in a rainforest. At night—"

"Good. Sit down."

"But . . ." What about the killings?

"I've heard enough." Her face was hard. "You have rehearsed this. Your Mirani is far too good to be believable. I discount you as a witness."

A councillor at the bench yelled out, "This is unfair, Delegate! Let her speak. The Pengali say that she—"

The mediator hit the table. "Enough, Chief Councillor Semisu. We will proceed in an orderly fashion."

The councillor puffed out his chest. In his heavyset frame, this rather looked like his belly increased in size. He stuffed be-ringed hands in his pockets, scowled, but said nothing. Didn't go back to his seat either.

Jessica sat down on the bench, trembling from head to foot. Iztho put a warm hand on her knee. "You did well, Lady."

"I did?" That was news to her.

"You did. She doesn't believe a word you said. That's good."

With all the will in the world, Jessica couldn't see how that was good, but she sat back down, glancing in Daya's direction, but Iztho leaned forward and she couldn't see him.

The councillor argued with the mediator, then someone on the other side of the hall shouted something in keihu that caused a sharp intake of breath of many in the audience.

Jessica leaned forward. "What? What did he say?"

Before Iztho could translate, a new voice spoke, in Mirani. "You accuse Miran of what?" A man in Mirani uniform strode onto the floor. Grey hair cropped close to his head, he was thin and fairly short. His uniform glittered with silver dots.

Jessica whispered to Iztho, "Who is that?"

But a chill took hold of her. She *recognised* him from somewhere.

"Commander Nemedor Satarin, of the Mirani army," Iztho's voice rumbled next to her.

The man walked across the floor in a regal glide. He stopped before the table and inclined his head. "Delegates."

The mediator returned his polite gesture and spoke a few words.

The Commander smiled. "Thank you for the opportunity to conduct this hearing in Coldi. I, however, prefer the local language."

The mediator's hand wave cut off a roar of protest from the floor; Mirani *wasn't* the local language. Commander Satarin copied his gesture, but directed it at the applause from the soldiers at the other end of the hall. "Calm down, calm down. Let us remember we are guests in this city, here on the invitation of the Barresh council. An orderly solution to this problem benefits us all. It was my intention to just observe this meeting as a show of solidarity with the city of Barresh. However, I'm surprised by the seriousness of the allegations against our nation of Miran. If such . . . murderers dwell amongst us, they must be punished. Chief Councillor Semisu, could you please bring forward the proof for your allegations."

The councillor stood there, mouth open. Whatever solidarity Commander Satarin had hinted at obviously didn't include informing the Barresh council. And what had he said? That the army was here at the invitation of the council? Why?

To control the Pengali.

"What are they talking about?" she asked Iztho.

"Someone made the suggestion that the murderers were Mirani."

"They weren't!" Jessica half-rose.

Iztho pulled her back down. "Sit down, Lady, You don't want any more attention drawn to yourself."

"But it's not true. I *saw* the murderers. They were Pengali."

"I know, Lady. No one is going to believe this allegation anyway."

Shouts and whistles died down. The councillor was still standing, fiddling with his robe. "I trust the Barresh council has evidence for this statement?" the commander asked.

"Witnesses saw Mirani soldiers come out of the forest." The councillor's dark eyes glinted defiantly.

"Can you present these witnesses?"

"No. They're Pengali and your soldiers wouldn't allow them in the building."

"If you can't produce the witnesses, please be seated."

A bout of laughter went up almost drowning out the voice of the mediator. "Excuse me, I determine if the witness can be seated."

Commander Satarin smiled at her and bowed. "Of course, Lady, my respect. Apologies for my interjection. Before I return the meeting to your capable hands, let me tell you that we must ensure that this situation is resolved and those guilty punished. We must also ensure that this young lady, caught up in this matter, is returned to her place of origin."

His eyes met Jessica's.

"Meanwhile, my theory is one of incompetence." He waved at the bench in a rhetorical gesture, ignoring the sharp look from the mediator. "Look at these men here. When you arrived, honoured delegates, you saw the state of this city. Crumbling buildings, naked people performing beastly acts in the streets. You only need look at the state of the Exchange building to know it can't function properly. The city of Barresh needs an injection of investment. Miran has offered that. Remember that in your judgment." He turned around in a theatrical gesture and made to go back to his seat. A roar went up from the audience.

Jessica shivered. There *had* been at least two groups of people in the forest: the Pengali, who had found them and might have been in the pay of the council, or, more likely, might simply have been tribespeople defending their territory. And there had been the rescue party Iztho had met up with at the top of the escarpment, people she hadn't seen. Were they Mirani soldiers?

There was a loud crash and shouts from the back of the hall. A beam of wan daylight pierced the darkness showing a great mass of people flowing in, small people, smelling of mint and fish and the flowered wreaths some wore on their heads. The tide of striped and spotted bodies washed down the stairs, pushing aside the guards who attempted to stop them.

At that moment, all the lights went out.

27

P EOPLE SHOUTED, rose from their seats and scrambled for the door.

Iztho grabbed Jessica's hand, his palm moist with sweat. "Come, Lady. Stay close to me. If I'm right, that was the last of the council's recharged pearls. The council doesn't even have enough light to keep their meetings going. That's how well they control their people."

Men in white uniforms moved in the grey beam of light that streamed in from the door. Crossbows glittered. Soldiers shouted orders, pushing fleeing members of the audience back into the stands.

Then, amidst the chaos, a small light flickered on halfway down the stairs. A mind light. Not Daya's, but Ikay's. Within a few moments, another light followed.

People stopped their mad stumble for the doors and stared at the centre of the hall, where the lights converged above the mediator's table, lighting her face with a ghostly glow. Most of the council members stood next to their seats.

A gust of warmth flooded Jessica and a pinprick bright as sunlight rose into the air. Daya.

Come, help us. We need to have this meeting. These people need to hear the truth.

In the eerie light, the ring of white uniforms surrounding the floor stood out clearly. Jessica eased herself out of Iztho's grip and pressed her hands together. The flow of energy came easily now. Several people around her gasped with the brightness of her light. She let it float up, hovering over the heads of the audience. The closer it came to Daya's light, the stronger the radiance of his energy became. Warm, steady. She let the light circle Daya's, like a pair of courting dancers, twirling and teasing. Jessica thought of soaring through the clouds.

"Don't encourage him, my Lady." Iztho's face looked wary.

Jessica bristled. Encourage what? Didn't he want the hearing to be concluded, so that he was free to take her out of the city?

At least fifty other lights had floated up, joining those already in the centre of the hall. Most of them were little more than weak glowing spots, but all of them combined cast a steady, even glow over the table. Not a single noise disturbed the silence.

Her eyes on the conglomerate of lights, the mediator sat back down, her face ghostly pale. "It seems we can continue now that the, um, problem with the lighting has been solved."

Thumbs hooked in his belt, Commander Satarin glided across the floor. The heels of his boots clacked on the wood and with each footstep he came closer to Ikay, who stood at the bottom of the stairs. "You know this state of undress is illegal in the city, as are any appendages?"

Ikay faced him, her expression defiant. She snapped her tail.

"After the hearing, I will make sure that you and all those who have come in here to disturb a civilised meeting are charged with public nudity and flouting of this city's laws."

His face was a mask of hatred. All of a sudden, Jessica remembered where she had seen him before: in a vision. This man had been in the lab, ordering Daya to be tortured, collecting the energy from him. And *he* was the man who supported her being brought to Miran. She heard his reedy voice *What if I brought you a girl?*

And the medico said, *She could be made to have two, maybe four children a year* . . .

She breathed deeply, trying to dispel the black spots that danced before her eyes. Her light came rushing back to her and jumped into her skin.

Iztho's voice rumbled. "My Lady, are you all right?"

Dark images flashed before her eyes. The snarling face of a Mirani soldier, running footsteps through the snow, the firing of a crossbow, an explosion, the voice of a Mirani soldier *He's still alive.*

Jessica pressed her fingers against her temples. *Stop! Stop it!*

A man strapped against a cold metal wall, wearing a thin tunic while the ground was covered in snow, a blast of iced water over his head, pain burning down his back. He struggled, but his hands were tied.

Stop it. "Stop it!"

A warm arm passed over her shoulders. "Lady, you're not well. Let's go back to the—"

Jessica pushed his arm aside. "I'm fine." Although she felt like she would throw up any minute, but to prove her point, she re-formed the light and sent it back up to the others. Daya's warmth brushed past her. *Hang in there.*

Iztho raised his eyebrows. "You don't look well, Lady." With his ashen-grey face he didn't look so well himself.

"I'm fine." She wiped sweat off her upper lip. Slowly, she walked onto the floor, into the pool of light. There was utter silence. Every eye in that huge hall was on her.

At the pentagonal table, the mediator raised her eyebrows.

Jessica spoke, her voice wobbly at first, but then more certain. "I want to know what is going on here. It is my life we're talking about, my co-passengers who were killed, my family who are waiting for me. And . . ." She swallowed and glanced at the lights floating above the table. "As you can see, I have an ability that may have mis-fired your Exchange equipment."

The audience broke out in shouts. Commander Satarin jumped up from the bench. Pengali whistled, and those who had them snapped their tails.

The mediator slammed her flat hand onto the table, shouting, "Ashi, ashi."

She had done that so often that by now, Jessica thought she knew the Coldi word for quiet.

When, after at least a minute, silence of some measure had returned to the hall, she turned her eyes to Jessica.

"So, you do know more than you let on. Interesting. What is your role in this story? Do you still maintain you were on this craft?"

"Yes."

"Can you tell us what happened?"

"We were flying, there was a flash and we crashed in the forest. None of us knew where we were. At night, three of us were killed. By . . . people . . . Small ones, with dirty hair and rags. They smelled like fish—"

The rotund man, Chief Councillor Semisu, broke in. "Tribal rogues."

The mediator repeated the word stiffly. "Rogues?"

"Young outcast men who patrol the borders of the tribal lands."

Jessica continued, "They came at night and shot at us without question."

"But not you." The mediator's dark eyes fixed hers.

"I escaped. I frightened them." The dark horrors of that night came back to her. The shouts in the forest, the screams of the men, the blue flashes of light.

Iztho sat there, his light blue gaze on her with deep intensity. He wanted her to come to Miran with him. He had been on the flight with her . . . and he didn't want that to be widely known.

The mediator spoke again. "We have a strange situation here. If your version of events is true, you would in effect give yourself up as illegal. Do you have Union citizenship?"

"No."

Iztho jumped up. "I'm sponsoring her for Union citizenship!"

Daya's voice cut through her mind, *The hell he is. I'm sponsoring you. I'm not letting the Mirani get their hands on you.*

"Lady, tell the delegation you intend to go to Miran with me." Iztho turned a pleading gaze on her.

The Mediator cut in, "A moment, Trader Andrahar. You can discuss your plans after we have concluded our investigation and have no more questions for this woman regarding the matter of the Barresh Exchange."

Iztho sat back, his nostrils flaring. Across the hall, a tiny smile curled Daya's lip.

"What is this ability you're talking about?" she asked.

Jessica called her light down and let it float above the palm of her hand. "The Pengali call this *avya*. It is the same energy that powers the Exchange."

"Hmmm."

Jessica couldn't read the expression on her face. Did she believe it?

"That is . . . interesting. Tell me, where is your family? What is your ancestry?"

At this question, both Iztho and Daya jumped up. Daya shouted, "Her background has nothing to do—" Before Iztho's deep voice drowned him out. Then they both fell quiet, glaring at each other.

The mediator raised her eyebrows, looking from one man to the other.

Daya spoke first. "Her present-day family is irrelevant."

Iztho added, "As much as I disagree with him on other matters, I agree here. We are investigating an illegal transfer by the Barresh Exchange. The Lady is clearly disturbed. She suffers illusions and must be taken to a hospital. I ask for your leniency."

Jessica bristled. Disturbed? Illusions?

"She is *not* disturbed!" Daya strode onto the floor. Patches of red had risen to his cheeks. "And I have no idea who told her that this pitiful amount of gathered energy . . ." He flung his light at a group of Mirani soldiers across the hall; they scrambled aside. ". . . is anywhere near enough to complete a bilateral translocation of a craft that has *no* Exchange capability. Anyone with the faintest understanding of Exchange technology knows about the mutuality and reciprocity needed to self-perpetuate the signal. The suggestion that a person could handle the amount of energy needed is ludicrous."

The mediator nodded, once.

Daya whirled around to face the Pengali and other citizenry. "This is what we have to put up with, being called lunatics, being ridiculed. It is time this came to an end. I will shout it at all those who want to hear. We are not aberrations, monsters or freaks, but we are the old Aghyrians, the people who first developed space travel. We developed the Exchange. We are the reason you even exist. And we may not be many, but we will no longer be discriminated against—"

Iztho's deep voice drowned him out. "Discriminated? You treat the Lady like dirt and talk about discrimination? Your ridiculous jealousy knows no boundaries. My Lady, do not listen to his ranting lunacy. Miran will solve your situation. I wish to help you more than anything. I am willing to risk my reputation; no, my life for that. Watch this." He crossed the floor, unfastening the clip to his cloak as he walked, slipped it off his shoulders and in a flourishing swoop, draped it across hers.

Deep silence.

Jessica's breath caught in her throat.

The weight of the cloak hung on her shoulders like a heavy pack, while Iztho's familiar smell enveloped her. With the gazes of all those in the hall on her, fear grew inside her. She took Iztho's outstretched hand and whispered, "What's all this about?"

A loving smile crossed his face. "This, Lady, the offering of the cloak, is the traditional way for a Trader to offer himself in marriage. I'm yours, my Lady."

Jessica stammered, "Marriage? Me?" She stared at the lips which over the past few days had kissed hers, had caressed her naked skin. "Please don't do this to me."

He bent closer. "Lady, forgive my rashness. It's the only way you can be free." His breath tickled in her hair; he kissed her cheek softly, running a hand over the line of her jaw.

Part of her screamed to embrace him, to give in to her desire, huddle forever in the safety of his arms, but it wasn't quite as simple as that. Not at all.

She met Commander Satarin's gaze across the hall. Intense, almost as if willing her to agree. On the other side of the hall she met Daya's eyes, wide and disbelieving, too horrified to even send her a hot jolt of jealousy.

"Lady, I beg you, please. Take my hands and press them to your forehead."

"I take it that is the way to agree with your proposal?" She hadn't quite intended it to come out so petulant, but damn.

"Lady, please."

"I have to know what you want."

"Isn't that obvious? Ever since I saw you, my heart has burned for you. I tried to be distant, I tried to be proper, but I cannot deny it any longer. Have I not shown you my total commitment, my undivided love? Please, for now just do as I say. We can talk later."

Jessica took a step back. "No."

"Lady, please, however much I love your independence and the way you think for yourself, this is not the time to be stubborn. Whatever happens, you will be coming to Miran anyway. Commander Satarin has brought undercover soldiers to force you to come with him. His promises of taking you home are untrue. They want you for what you are, for what you can do. Why go with him and live as prisoner, while you can live in luxury with me and still contribute to our great nation?" Light blue eyes met hers out of his sweat-slicked face. Lips parted, his breath came in shallow gasps that made the medallion on his chest glitter.

Jessica pushed his hand away, remembered how he had spoken of opportunities, of learning, of power and wealth in Miran. She felt sick. "How long have you known all this? Did you know about the Exchange—that it couldn't be my fault?"

Silence. His throat moved when he swallowed.

"Tell me. Were you playing the game?" And she had been so blind to believe him? To believe that *she* had been the cause of the transfer?

"Lady, I confess I was playing the game, in the beginning."

"You were on the flight so you could kidnap me?"

He looked down. "Yes, I was, but—"

"You knew who I was all along?"

He nodded, once.

No, no, it couldn't be true. "You were? Tell me! Tell me. Was it because of you? Did you take something in your luggage that caused it?"

His eyes didn't meet hers. "I'm not proud of it, my Lady and you have every right to be angry. Commander Satarin sent me to pick you up for considerable . . . payment. It is complicated to explain, but he holds considerable power over me—over my family's business. I was to travel with you, and bring you here. Things went wrong. We weren't meant to crash, a craft was waiting to pick us up, but it was too foggy and we didn't quite appear where it was planned. We didn't plan landing in the Pengali territory either. The plan was just to get you, drug the others and send them back."

"And I was a thing to be picked up?" Her shout echoed in the hall. Daya watched her, tenseness on his face.

"Please Lady, I'm asking for your forgiveness. Yes, I meant to deliver you to him at first, but . . . You, my Lady, are a treasure. No one should claim or use you. I've come to see that now . . . I love you. Please accept my love as a man, not as an agent of Miran." He added in a whisper, "We will escape the army."

However much he might have meant them, to Jessica, the words rang hollow. *Never agree to anything you don't understand.* Her father's straightforward policeman's advice. And she damn well wouldn't. She might be young, but she was not stupid.

She slid Iztho's cloak off her shoulders and dumped the furry bundle into his arms. "If you really knew me, you would know why I can't accept this."

For a few long seconds, his light blue gaze met hers. Before a sob could rise in her throat, before she would lose control, she turned and strode to the stairs. Two soldiers jumped to block her path. She swiped at them, sparks swirling over her arms. "Why the fuck don't you leave me alone?"

Eyes wide, they stumbled back.

Behind her, Commander Satarin yelled, "Don't shoot!"

There was a crack of something hard hitting the wooden floor and a wave of cold swept the hall. Jessica turned. A small object on the floor drew all the Pengali mind lights into a twirling vortex, sucking all strands of light into it. People stumbled for the doors in increasing darkness. Jessica yanked her threads free just in time, and stood panting, gaping at the last remains of the tornado of lights. What the bloody hell did that?

Daya's voice jolted her. *Run, my love, run.*

Jessica bolted up the stairs, out the entrance before the soldiers at the gate could even question her.

In the street, the groups of dancing Pengali had gone. So had the food stalls, the musicians, the flower sellers. Screens of slats covered shop doors. An abandoned turquoise shirt lay in a puddle, amidst trampled flowers. Where was everyone?

A voice shouted behind her. Jessica gathered her dress around her buttocks and ran. Her sandals splashed in the puddles. Around the corner, down an alley. Low-hanging branches of trees slapped wet in her face. She jumped over roots, puddles and piles of rubbish. Booted footsteps followed close behind.

Into the next street. Two half-clad Pengali youths ran towards her, carrying sticks and looking over their shoulders, where figures in white linked hands, blocking off the road to the crowd on their other side. Yells and shouts echoed between the houses. Shit—a riot.

Jessica hesitated and in that moment, her pursuer shot in front of her, blue eyes wild with triumph. "Don't move!" The point of his crossbow aimed at her chest.

In a fluid motion, one of the Pengali youths turned. He lifted the stick and brought it down on the soldier's head with a frightening thunk. The man's eyes glazed over; he slumped sideways.

"Anmi." The boy reached barely to her waist. Jessica needed no encouragement; two other soldiers had emerged from the alley. She ran to the door held open by the second youth.

As soon as she was through, he pushed it shut and shoved a

metal bar across. Yells echoed in the street; the door thudded. Jessica leaned against the rough wall, catching her breath and attempting to knot the flowing petticoats of her dress out of the way. She hated dresses.

They were in a neglected courtyard surrounded on three sides by a high wall. The house rose two floors above them, the walls covered in green slime. A door into what must once have been a kitchen hung limp on rusty brackets. Inside, broken shards of pottery littered the floor. How many abandoned houses were there in this town?

"Come!" The older boy waited in a dark alley between the house and the wall. A wooden crate stood on its side. He jumped on top and then on the wall, then held out a hand to Jessica.

Another thud shook the timber door; the wood cracked.

Jessica stumbled into the alley, onto pavement slippery with green slime, but she climbed up the crate with ease, being so much taller than the Pengali. The younger boy jumped on the wall, quick and supple like a cat. Balancing on top, he took off his shorts and put them on his head. Then he ran off over the top of the wall and jumped down in another yard.

Jessica heaved herself up. Wobbled on her feet. Oh God. She wasn't meant to run along this ledge, was she?

Yells rose from the street, blocked from her view by low-hanging branches of a tree. Thuds of rocks hitting the ground and rolling over the pavement. Running feet. Another thud on the door. A slab of render fell from the wall.

Jessica took a step, waving her arms, ran a few paces, almost fell. Her sandal slipped into the yard on the other side.

Shit.

The Pengali boy nudged her.

She muttered, "Yes, I'm going." In the street behind them, rocks and sticks flew through the air, followed by the *zhing* of discharging crossbows. A deep cold tore through her. The boy pushed her again. "Come on!"

Jessica ran. Over the top of the wall to a junction where three walls met. The older boy waited for them in the yard beyond,

next to a trapdoor from which a smell of rot and stale water
rose up.

God, what was that?

Jessica pressed her hands together, concentrated and let the
light float down into the hole. Globs of unidentified matter floated
lazily in a foam-flecked underground stream.

The eldest youth jumped in; water splashed.

Holding her breath against the stench, Jessica followed. She
almost slipped in whatever sludge covered the bottom of the drain
—or should she say sewer? She hitched up her dress, tightened the
knot to make sure it wouldn't come undone. The younger boy
jumped in and closed the trapdoor before the two of them took off.
Jessica had to run, bent over double, to keep up.

Gushing water spouted from drains on both sides. Sometimes
they came out briefly in the open air, at other times timber planks
covered the passage. At one stage, the voices of soldiers and
yelling Pengali drifted in from above. Running feet. Stones
bouncing over the pavement. The sounds of a fight.

Finally, some time after Jessica would have been totally lost, the
first boy pushed open another trapdoor. Jessica stuck her head out
into an alley she recognised. A few days ago, she had run its length
after her fight with Daya. The Pengali safe house. Ikay, smiling
widely, waited at the door. Jessica scrambled out of the drain into
warm and minty-smelling arms. She caressed Ikay's bare leather-
skinned shoulders, too out-of-breath to speak. Ikay led her into the
house. "Safe here."

When Jessica had come in with Daya, she had only been to a
room at the back, where a jumble of mats littered the floor. Now,
Ikay took her through a narrow hallway which opened out into
what once must have been a grandiose entrance hall. Wan light fell
through a ceiling window, casting grey light on two flights of
stairs, two galleries around the perimeter and a large circular
ground floor area. Pengali sat on the steps, on the railings, on the
floor and the edge of a circular basin directly under the window.
Many of them still wore wreaths of white flowers on their heads.

At Ikay's entry, many voices rose up. Some in Pengali, some in keihu. Jessica picked up single words. "Anmi . . . fighting-men . . . council . . ." The youngest of the boys who had come with her answered questions, gesturing wildly with hands and tail. He still wore his shorts on his head like a beanie.

Jessica stood in the middle of the hall. She wished she knew what they were all talking about; she wished her stomach could make up its mind as to whether it wanted to get better or have a good spew. She wished . . . no. No more men. No more lovers who wanted to use her. No more lame apologies.

A group of men entered the hall from the other side. Muddy trousers, dishevelled robes, pale faces, bruised cheeks or injured arms, wet hair plastered to their foreheads. Their long robes and twinkling jewellery seemed out of place. Jessica recognised the rotund form of Chief Councillor Semisu, although the rain had made his curly hair limp and stringy. An increasing murmur went up amongst the Pengali. Many wondered aloud what the councillors were doing here. A Pengali male said in a loud accusing voice, "The fighting-men stopped the parade."

"They hit two of my friends for not wearing a shirt," another added.

"My sons were in the parade," wailed a woman. "I haven't seen them since."

Councillor Semisu lifted his hands as if to start a speech, then let them sink by his sides again.

"I'm sorry."

His robe was wet and he sported a dark smudge on his cheek.

A young man yelled, "Sorry? You invited the fighting-men. You let them cut my tail! Sorry is the only thing you can say?"

A female yelled, "Liggi, hold your breath and let him speak. The councillor who signed for the fighting-men to come here died long ago. This man comes in peace."

The young man scowled at her but sat down.

Councillor Semisu heaved a deep sigh. "I don't know what else I can say. The Mirani are everywhere. I don't know how they got that many soldiers into the city. They did not just stop the parade, they stationed troops in front of every public building. They're checking everyone who goes in or out, everyone on the street, but the only ones they've picked up are women—women! Would you believe!"

Keihu women. They were ones with *avya*, as the clothes makers' Pengali assistants had said. Daya had been right. They were after people with strong abilities. To get her had been the intention of the plan all along, from the moment she left Pymberton airport . . . Dizziness came over her.

"Anmi!"

Jessica started, running her hands over rough mosaic tiles. How the heck had she ended up on the floor? Ikay's face swam before her. A wave of heat swamped her, causing bile to rise in her throat. God. She clamped a hand over her mouth.

"You . . . sick."

Under the gazes of hundreds of Pengali, Ikay pulled her up, dragging her back through the corridor, where the walls moved in and out of focus, into the room with the mattresses. Pushed her down.

Ikay held a bowl of water to her lips. Jessica lay back on a soft pillow. She protested weakly and tried to get back up.

"I want to know what's going on."

"No. You stay."

Ikay massaged her skin all over, starting from her head and working their way down to her neck, shoulders, breast, stomach . . .

She took in a sharp breath.

Jessica raised her head. "Anything wrong?" Her heart thudded in her chest. She half-knew what Ikay was going to say.

"I feel . . . another . . ."

Damn. She was not mistaken. Sweat broke out on her forehead. Involuntarily, Jessica hands slid down her stomach; she sent out a weak signal.

A flutter of life energy responded.

Shit. Shit, shit, shit!

Daya. Damn Daya and his possessiveness. His actions had

managed to do what his words couldn't. A breeding cow. No fucking way. She was no one's possession.

She grabbed Ikay's arm. "Can you help me, please? I can't . . ."

Face grave, Ikay nodded. "Is right. Can't have . . . man . . ." She rolled her eyes in frustration. "White hair."

"No, I can't." Although the child couldn't be Iztho's. "Can you help me please?"

Without a word, Ikay left the room.

Jessica lay on her back staring at the ceiling. This was the room where she had spent the night with Daya, the room where the child was conceived.

Daya. She hated him, his arrogance, his outrageous assumptions, she hated, no, she loved his smell, his touch, his untamed and violent passion, his wild mind voice and the way he'd been prepared to fight for her, how he had stood there and declared that their people would not be discriminated. Daya would toe no one's line and would be no one's fool.

All too soon, Ikay returned, carrying a cup. Jessica followed her back through the narrow hallway into another room which must once have been the kitchen. Steam rose from a basin in the corner and stone benches surrounded the walls, empty except for a bundle of folded cloth.

Ikay set the cup on the bench in the centre of the room. Dark liquid sloshed around inside, syrupy and oily. She handed the cloth to Jessica, speaking in halting words. "Drink here . . . wait . . . be sick . . . bleed."

Jessica nodded, grimly. Ikay had understood all too well what sort of help she wanted.

Apprehension must have shown on her face, because Ikay said, "Man . . . white hair . . . bad."

She squeezed Jessica's hands before leaving the room. The door rattled shut, leaving a deep, hollow silence.

But I'm not having Iztho's child! Although Jessica wished she would, just to annoy Daya, and imagined his surprise at a little girl with honey-blonde hair and golden eyes. But that was impossible. Aghyrians didn't interbreed with other races.

Hands trembling, Jessica picked up the cup and walked to the basin. A foul waft rose from the liquid, reminiscent of rotting cabbage. *You will be sick.* Even the smell was enough to make her gag.

Better be quick, then.

Jessica held her breath, set the cup to her lips . . .

Soft voices of Pengali talk drifted in through missing slats in the door. She remembered the tribe, the tumble of striped bodies of children playing in the steaming pool. Heard their cheerful voices.

Hesitated.

Could she willingly kill a tiny flutter of life which would grow to be her only living relative in the universe?

She eyed the towels Ikay had provided. Imagined clots of blood on the khaki fabric. Blood and a tiny foetus.

Her hands trembled so much that drops of liquid ran over the side, spreading more of the vile smell.

Daya's voice sounded in her mind. *You would not be another Ivedra.*

Didn't he see? She was already another Ivedra, wanted by everyone, including him.

Three hundred years ago, Ivedra had been eighteen when she had given birth in prison. In three more months, Jessica would be eighteen as well. Not quite in prison, but trapped in Barresh, where people shared her ancestor's abilities, where their history was written in rock.

Tears flooded her eyes.

Her arms relaxed. She lowered the cup to the level of her chin, her chest, her stomach, allowed it to tip so the contents poured into the basin.

She sank to the floor, her face in her hands.

28

J ESSICA HAD NO idea how long she had been sitting like
that when Ikay rushed into the kitchen, speaking in rapid
Pengali, grabbing the towels, folding them out. Her eyes
widened. No clots of blood, no strands of mucus, no vomit.

Jessica stared up, mouth trembling. "I can't do it, Ikay, I can't."
The enormity of her decision fell over her like a wave. Tears came
anew.

Ikay knelt beside her, cradling her and muttering, "I help." She
ran her hand over Jessica's stomach in calming, soothing movements. For at least five minutes, neither of them spoke, united by
their bond and the life of a tiny baby. Then Ikay rose and gestured
at the door. "Go. Visitor."

In the dingy corridor, Jessica undid the knots that still tied her
dress around her buttocks. She smoothed the material, hand
lingering on her stomach, wondering how long it would be before
the slim waistline became too tight.

Most of the house's refugees had gathered around the pond in
the hall. Large eyes glinted at the archway when Jessica came in.

A couple of men she recognised as councillors of Barresh gathered under the gallery, a small light on the ground between them.
Still-wet robes strained around their bulky forms, knees and legs

poking out at clumsy angles. Obviously not used to sitting on the floor.

A man in dark clothing sat ramrod-straight in their midst, long-fingered hands on his knees. Oh God, Daya. What was she going to say?

She didn't have to say anything. One of the men in khaki rose, grumbling and cursing. Dark eyes met Jessica's. "I don't think we've been introduced." From close up, the Chief Councillor had a coarse-skinned face, with a curious groove down the middle of his nose. His hair looked like a bird's nest of uncombed curls. A head smaller than her and carrying a fair amount of excess weight, he was neither attractive nor handsome, but the smile in his eyes was genuine. "I'm Jisson Semisu, Chief Councillor of Barresh."

"I'm Jessica—"

"No." Daya's voice sounded clipped. "Your name is Anmi Kirilen Dinzo."

She bristled. "My parents call me Jessica."

Then she felt irritated that she defended a name she had never liked, not even as a child. She did like her real name, it was just that she didn't like the way he was so definite about it, as if the previous seventeen years of her life had been worth nothing.

For a moment, their eyes met. She received no feelings or images from his mind, as if he had walled himself off.

On the floor before him lay a crudely-drawn map of the city, the stiff sheet held down by the weight of a Mirani crossbow.

Daya rose gracefully, picked up the weapon and dumped it in Jessica's hands. It was so heavy she almost dropped it.

She glared at him. "What am I supposed to do with this bloody thing?" Wasn't he going to talk to her at all?

"A little demonstration. Let's go outside."

He preceded her through the corridor, out the back door into the yard.

Puddles glistened on the pavement in the advancing night. Somewhere a few streets down people yelled.

"Stand there." Daya gestured at the corner, where someone a long time ago had dumped a pile of old wood. "Aim there."

Jessica glanced at the metal slide—empty. "This thing isn't even loaded."

He rearranged the weapon in her arms, her right hand fitting the handle. The soft skin of the underside of his forearm lingered against her knuckles. His eyes met hers and some of the warmth in them returned. His alluring scent drifted on the wind.

Please, do this for me. Only you can show this to them. It's important.

Her thumb found the release. He continued in a business-like tone, "You hold it like this and press there. Stand back." This to the Pengali who had swarmed into the yard.

They shuffled against the wall of the house, surrounding the small group of councillors, who had remained on the stairs and inside the door.

Jessica's arms trembled from the strain of lifting the metal crossbow. "I can't aim." Drops of rain ran down her forehead.

"Doesn't matter. Just shoot." *The secret is to aim with your mind.*

Jessica squinted at the wall on the other side of the courtyard and pressed the release. In a metallic click, so fast it was impossible to see how it happened, an arrow shot up from underneath the slide. Jessica gasped. Yes, she now saw that the arrows consisted of two pieces of metal at a ninety degree angle which could be folded flat and stacked inside the handle. *Fold-up automatic reload arrows?*

Daya nodded. *Shoot.*

Jessica took a deep breath, lifted the crossbow in trembling arms and pressed the release again.

A chill tore at her senses, growing into a whirlwind of energy. Sparks flew from her skin as with a long metallic *zhing,* the arrow shot loose. Jessica panicked and clamped her hand tighter, sending another arrow flying, and another one and another one in a metal stream that sucked a vortex of sparks in its wake.

The arrows hit a broken crate. Blue light sparked over its surface, down the pile of rubbish, up the wall behind it. Lightning crackled. Splinters of wood and sandy grit flew everywhere, mixed with steam and dust and droplets of water.

Pengali screamed and pushed back into the house in a tumble of bodies.

Jessica stood there, staring at the gap where the wall had been. Holy shit—an automatic fire-spewing crossbow.

It uses avya. Daya's face was white, but he sounded composed when he spoke. "I think we can go back inside now."

Jessica couldn't wait to get rid of that horrid weapon. Daya took it from her and once back inside the hall, laid it on the floor. He knelt next to it, undid the springs, removed the slide and took out a small object, which he held up between thumb and index finger. A simple glass bead the size of a marble. Dark eyes met Jessica's over the top of it. "Have you seen this before?"

Yes, Jessica had. That first night in the city, in the apartment. She remembered the blue glow of the beads in the crate, picking one up and having her heat flow into it until it exploded.

Daya held it out to her. "Here."

She shook her head. No way she would touch one of those again.

Instead, he passed the bead to Ikay, who took in a sharp breath and dropped it. It rolled over the floor and came to rest in a hollow where a tile was missing, radiating soft blue.

Jessica licked her lips. "What is it?"

Daya picked up the bead. "This stone can be enriched to collect life energy, which it releases into the arrow when the crossbow is fired. A normal crossbow is a dangerous weapon, but limited and old-fashioned. These, however . . ." He let the bead roll onto the floor again; it sparked with energy. "You saw what happens. I suppose you felt the cold chill, too?" A touch of his warmth laced his eyes.

Jessica nodded.

"Life energy is the most powerful form of energy we know. There's only a tiny bit in these beads; imagine what a larger weapon could do."

A hoarse voice said, "A larger weapon? You mean a bigger one of these?" Councillor Semisu stared at Daya with wide eyes.

"Like this, or something else, but equally or more destructive. If you load a projectile with enough of this energy, one throw of a stone brings down an entire building. If the conditions are right, it attracts more energy and starts a chain reaction."

Jessica tried to recall what Iztho had said about Miran, but remembered only statements about clean air and honest values. She had been so stupid and ignorant. "Is Miran at war?"

"Not at war as such, but Miran's relationships with several other entities are always tense. Miran has been involved in plenty of wars."

"Who were they fighting?"

"Asto mostly, or any of the other Coldi entities."

Councillor Semisu said, "Where do you stand in all of this? I thought you hated the Coldi."

Daya's face grew emotionless. "I grew up on Asto, and being zhadya-born, was a second-rate citizen amongst the Coldi. I've since lived at Hedron, which is mostly Coldi, too. My father . . ." Councillors' faces tightened; talk died down. "All right—I'll say it once and let everyone in this town know it, and keep their silence hereafter. My biological father is Thania Lingui, who holds the position of Chief Coordinator of Asto, but that doesn't mean I condone Asto's position or actions, nor does it mean that I align myself with those who call themselves Asto's enemies. I represent the displaced Aghyrians, and we have no position in this ongoing conflict between Asto and Miran."

No, Jessica saw it now. The Coldi hated the zhadya-born Aghyrians, but the Coldi also had a bad relationship with Miran. Now Miran wanted to entice the Aghyrians to fight the Coldi as revenge.

Daya continued, "The Mirani have found that only some of the zhadya-born have our abilities, and they need more. Here in Barresh is a whole population of people who have inherited from our forefathers the ability to draw energy in their bodies. Miran is behind this investigation into the crash. They're pushing for the closure of the Barresh Exchange to increase their control over Barresh. When Barresh becomes an official part of Miran, people can be forcibly relocated and there's not a thing anyone can do."

"But Iztho just admitted to me that the translocation was his fault."

Daya raised his eyebrows at her, as if she shouldn't refer to this man by his first name.

"Miran will deny it. They will destroy the evidence. They already have, since the Barresh Exchange hasn't been able to find a rogue translocation in the Exchange records. If Iztho Andrahar speaks out, Miran will shut him up."

Jessica felt sick. She remembered how Iztho had lied to the Mirani soldier who had come to the door. *Shut him up.* No, she didn't want that either. Iztho made a mistake, but she refused to believe that he was a bad man. "You mean this hearing with the council was all for nothing?"

"No, not for nothing. You have given Pengali hope." This was a softly-spoken voice, belonging to an older Pengali male who had been sitting silently amongst the councillors.

Jessica whirled to face him. "Hope? What sort of hope is this? We uncover the truth, and in the end we achieve nothing?" She spread her hands; her cheeks grew hot with anger.

Councillor Semisu still looked at the crossbow. "If Miran has weapons like those, do we have a chance at all? We, Barresh, are only this big . . ." He held his thumb and index finger a hair width apart, ". . . and they are . . ." He spread his arms, nearly hitting the councillor next to him in his face.

"All the evidence in the case of the Exchange will be covered up. No one could prove Mirani involvement. And now the Mirani soldiers are all over the streets."

Daya nodded. "Our only hope is to get help from outside—we must bring this to the attention of the Union Assembly."

Councillor Semisu snorted. "What can the Union do? Do you think they care about an entity as small as Barresh?"

"The Union cares about one thing: peace and stability. Barresh may be small, but the issue is not. Think of it: what we have here is an invasion of an independent entity. If the Union sends its peace guards and Miran is caught outside its mandate before the eyes of all Union members, or if it even obstructs a Union inquiry, the

Union Assembly could vote to suspend Miran from the Exchange network."

The councillor harrumphed. "Another one who believes in the Union as the source of all good."

"I believe the Union is fair, or at least attempting to be so, to those who obey their laws. No acts of war, no inciting unrest in other entities. Think of what happened to Indrahui—they suffered total isolation for more than ten years. No Exchange, no travel, no export, no import. I don't think Miran wants to follow them into that abyss. Yes, I think the Union is our best option. The only problem is getting to Union headquarters without the Barresh node in operation."

"You can fly to Miran and use their Exchange"

"Yes, I think that would be a good idea." Daya's tone was wry but his face showed no emotion. "Although it's my experience they have an interesting way to deal with foreign visitors—"

The Pengali male interrupted, eyes wide. "But going to Miran would be most unwise. You—" The rest of his speech was drowned in laughter.

Councillor Semisu patted the man on the shoulder. "Sheida, you Pengali must learn to recognise when someone is joking." More laughter went up at Sheida's puzzled face.

Daya motioned for silence. "How long would it take to get the Exchange going? What do we need? Which parts are shut down?"

Councillor Semisu shook his head. "Everything has shut down. I presume the core could easily be reconnected, if the Exchange had pearls to run the auxiliary equipment." He cast a fierce look at Sheida.

The Pengali straightened his back. "Us Pengali were not going to be mistreated without a fight."

"*We* keihu weren't mistreating you."

"You keihu introduced the law about Pengali working in the city having to cut their tails."

"You know why it was introduced. City Pengali agreed with it."

"It was three hundred years ago. You should have revoked the law before someone used it to cut the tail of an adult—"

"Enough about that now." Daya held up his hands. "Is there any chance we can get an energy source going soon?"

Sheida turned to him, avoiding the councillor's glare. "We have stockpiled our supply of pearls in Far Atok."

Daya frowned. "Far...?"

"The other island," Councillor Semisu explained. "But with all the soldiers in the street carrying crossbows, how are we going to get a great load of pearls to the Exchange?"

Jessica broke in, "What if we . . . could disable some of those crossbows?"

Many raised eyebrows.

Steeling herself, she picked up the bead that still glowed faintly on the tiles. Immediately, it sucked warmth from her fingers. She concentrated, helped it along, feeding energy into its greedy core. A cool breeze went through the hall. The glass became hot. She resisted her body's call to siphon off that energy, instead holding onto the burning glass.

Lightning-like arcs crackled from her hand.

The bead flew from her fingers. Floated for a split second . . . and exploded into a glittering cloud that rained on the Pengali spectators, who hastily scrambled back.

Councillor Semisu swallowed, his throat working. "Impressive."

Even Daya's face showed awe.

Jessica went on, "I don't think we can destroy the weapons completely. But each of the enhanced crossbows contains a marble like this. If we destroy the glass balls and turn some enhanced crossbows into ordinary crossbows, at least for a short while, would that be enough for some people to get through to do what they need to do? I can teach Ikay and the others how to do this—"

Sheida said, his eyes shining, "We bring charged pearls from Far Atok. Then we use parade to take them to the Exchange. We tell the fighting-men that Pengali have to complete the parade or the harvest will fail."

Councillor Semisu frowned at him. "Really? I never knew that bit of Pengali mythology."

Sheida laughed, a weird neighing sound.

His cheeks red, Councillor Semisu snorted. "All right, you got me. If some of you will show me the way through those blasted drains, I'll get Merilon and bring him to the Exchange so he can start it up."

Daya said, "I will fly to Damarq."

Jessica hurried down the corridor a little while later. The food had done her good; she didn't feel quite so sick any more. Now, while they were waiting for the Pengali to bring the pearls, there was just one thing left to do. If he wasn't going to talk to her, she would talk to him, whether he liked it or not. He could not go on ignoring her. She entered the hall and stopped, staring at the empty spot amongst the councillors.

"Daya?"

"Not here," one of the councillors said. "Maybe in one of the other rooms."

The first room she tried was empty. Her footsteps echoed hollow against the high ceiling; every mattress on the floor lay abandoned.

Shit—did the councillor mention going somewhere? He was going to get the operator of the Exchange. Did Daya go with him? Was he avoiding her?

"Daya?"

A giggle sounded in the back of the second room. A light from outside cast a greenish sheen over an outline of two Pengali on a mattress, the spots on a male's back, his tail curled around a female's legs. A painful stab went through her. The same mattress where she and Daya . . . "Oh—I'm sorry."

"Anmi." The young male pushed himself off his partner and crouched on the floor, so that the light fell on the female. Maire.

She, too, scrambled up and knelt next to the male, her head bent, her shoulders still heaving with deep breaths.

"Don't be silly," Jessica said, trying to dispel memories of hungry lips on her skin, and how a small spot of warmth had flowed from his lips and caressed her in places no one had ever touched her.

Maire bent deeper.

Jessica strode across the floor and pushed up Maire's chin. "Get up. I don't like it when you treat me this way. I am not some figure of worship. You may have hope but nothing is going to change unless someone is punished. If Miran is responsible, Miran should be made to pay the price. So if you have nothing better to do than shagging each other, go and help the others bring the pearls, or help me find Daya."

They both nodded, with the same ridiculous reverence.

Where was he? Why wouldn't he talk to her?

29

THE FRONT GATES of the safe house opened with a creak, releasing many years of built-up rust. Silent figures streamed into the yard, pushing the caterpillar-like structure over the uneven pavement. Thick wooden wheels rumbled, each set of two with forked beams holding up a section of the cloth or hide that formed the tray of the vehicle. Flowers spilled over the edge of the cloth.

Ikay stood knee-deep in them, waving instructions. Her body sinewy and muscles corded, she wore nothing except a wreath of flowers on her head. Her tail waved free and snapped when things didn't go to her satisfaction.

Energy hummed from within the tray of the cart. All night, a line of porters had streamed in carrying bags. They had come in through the back door, through the Pengali-known maze of alleys, drains, walls and doors, bringing the precious load that would revive the Exchange.

Jessica stood on the porch, her gaze straying to that small part of the street visible between the foliage. Where the hell was Daya?

She, Ikay and a few others couldn't do this on their own. Yes, more females with avya had come in, and Jessica had spent most of the night teaching them how to blow up the glass beads, but

Daya was the only one with any kind of real strength and he simply had to be there for the plan to succeed. However, he and Councillor Semisu had left to get the operator of the Exchange and had not come back.

They had not come back. The thought gnawed at her like so many rats. Now it was time was to go. Soon it would be light and the reason to continue with the parade would be gone: this night would be the last of the Bachelors festival.

The caterpillar stopped. Ikay called out. "Anmi, come."

"But Daya isn't here."

"We find him . . . in street."

Jessica met Ikay's eyes. What did she mean by that?

A shout sounded from the other side of the gate. Alla, waving her hands and snapping her tail. *Hurry up.*

Damn it. After one look down the empty street, Jessica crossed the yard and climbed on a massive wheel to heave herself into the cart. Sheesh—they could have chosen less obnoxious-smelling flowers. She sank through the thin layer onto a more solid footing. The pearls were warm under her and released a scent of hot stone. Jessica lay down and Ikay shovelled flowers over her. In amongst them, it was hard to breathe.

"Anmi?" A soft female voice.

Jessica lifted her head, but saw nothing but flowers. "Who are you?"

"The merchant's daughter, Seleni." The girl she had helped at the dressmaker's shop.

Jessica reached out in her mind and sensed the girl not far from her, similarly buried under a layer of flowers.

"My servant told me what you are going to do. I think I can help."

"Thanks." Jessica could say no more. She couldn't bear if all was to fail now, if Barresh were overrun, if she fell into the hands of Miran and never saw her parents again, or if Daya was already in their hands and never got to know she expected his child.

A shout and a crack of a tail and the wagon started moving.

They rumbled along slowly. The Pengali beat their drums,

clapped and sang. People yelled out in the houses they passed. Jessica didn't dare look up, but sensed people joining them. They had to be Pengali. It was the middle of the night and everyone else would be asleep.

A harsh shout interrupted the music. The drumbeats and the singing stopped, leaving an eerie silence. Jessica pressed herself flat against the pearls, holding her breath.

Hard heels clacked on stone. "What is the point of this?" A Mirani voice, cold and disdaining.

"This is the Bachelors festival. We must finish the parade." Jessica was surprised at how well Sheida spoke Mirani.

"Do you have an authorisation for that?"

"Pengali must have the parade, or we will not have good harvests until the next festival. We must bring this offering to the spirits—"

The harsh voice cut him off. "So you don't have authorisation?"

Jessica held her breath, afraid Sheida would make some defiant comment, but he said nothing.

"Where is this parade going?"

"The harbour. We have to float the flowers in the water."

More footsteps clacked on stone. Jessica wished she could see how many soldiers there were and what they were doing. She cast out for Daya, but sensed only the weak presence of Ikay, in front of the cart.

Someone rocked the tray. "Flowers, eh? Seems pretty heavy duty for carrying flowers."

"We use these for our harvest. No—please don't get in. You will crush them."

A hand rummaged in the flowers. Jessica pressed herself more closely to the layer of pearls. "I have orders to search everyone coming past here." Footsteps moved along the other side of the cart.

"You can search us."

Jessica bit her lip, imagining Sheida standing up before the soldiers, wearing nothing but a belt.

"I think we'll pass. Stick to the main street. Go straight to the harbour. No diversions or we'll shoot. Don't think we're not watching you."

When the cart jolted back into movement, Sheida blew out a long sigh. The drumbeats started again, a sweeping five-beat rhythm. Three strong beats, two weaker ones. Females sang and clapped.

Jessica lifted her head so she could see between the flowers. The cart rumbled past buildings. A shuttered-up shopfront, a tree, empty pavement. "Are we almost there?"

"I can see the square," said Sheida, seated at the edge of the tray.

"Any sign of Daya?"

"He would wait for us here."

"Can you see anyone?"

A tense silence.

"No."

Damn, where was Daya? Without him, and without the man who could operate the Exchange, the plan would fail.

A sharp whistle from Ikay brought the cart to a stop. The drummer broke into a different rhythm while people sang and clapped. Jessica felt sick.

On the map, it hadn't looked that far from the Exchange owner's house to here. Daya had been gone most of the night.

Jessica closed her eyes and reached out in her mind. She had avoided doing this, as it would use up precious energy, and she wasn't sure Daya's mind was open to her.

Daya, where are you?

A dark tunnel, splashing footsteps, rasping breath. Men's voices calling in the distance.

Daya!

Warmth flowed over her. *I've been calling you. I've no idea where I am.*

What happened?

We came out of the drain and someone had tipped off the soldiers. Jisson's been captured, Merilon, too, I think.

Where are they now? But Jessica knew: the whole plan was

falling to pieces. Without Merilon Damaru, the Exchange wouldn't work; without Daya, she wouldn't have the strength to disarm more than a few crossbows, and no one in the Pengali party knew how to fly an aircraft anyway. She reached out. "Sheida."

The elder started. "Be careful. The soldiers are watching."

"Sheida, the Mirani have stopped the other party. They've got Jisson. Daya's running around somewhere in the drains."

Before he could reply, a Mirani voice shouted. "Move on, the lot of you. You're disturbing the citizens' sleep."

Several voices shouted protests.

"I tell you to move on. I permitted you to tow this . . . donation to the harbour, not to disturb the citizens' lives. Move, or I'll order my men to move it for you."

Creaking and groaning, the cart jumped back into motion.

There was more shouting further down the street. Jessica raised her head just above the rim of the cart. Shadows ran across the street ahead. There were shouts and people throwing things.

A tingle.

Daya?

Dark tunnels. An open trapdoor. The flash of light on metal crossbows.

Daya!

Sheida pushed her. "Get down!"

"But Daya's somewhere out there."

All around the cart, people shouted. Further away in the shadows, male voices barked orders. The air chilled; crossbows discharged.

No, no.

Jessica shouted, "Ikay!"

The old female stood amongst a group of females, all with closed eyes, focusing their energy. A long strand of crackling light snaked out to the crossbow in the nearest soldier's hands. The bead flashed and exploded. He yelled and dropped the mangled weapon, but two more soldiers took his place.

Too slow; there were too few of them.

Daya!

On her belly in the flowers, Jessica pressed her hands together, but couldn't concentrate. Her ears roared too much; her heart beat too loudly. This wasn't working. Yes, they could take out the weapons one by one, but there were too many soldiers. They needed . . .

Holy shit.

Energy, focused energy, and she was sitting on top of it.

With both hands, she grabbed an armful of pearls. About the size and weight of a billiard ball, they were perfect—for throwing.

The first one hit a soldier in the side. He yelped as the pearl fell to the ground, crackling, releasing its charge, which went straight into the bead in his crossbow. A net of blue lightning engulfed the soldier. The bead exploded into fragments like fireworks.

Pengali cheered. A couple of hands reached over the edge of the tray. Jessica gave them pearls.

Within moments, the street crackled with blue lightning. Soldiers yelled. Some stumbled about, hands and face bleeding from glass cuts. Besieged by Pengali fighters with knives, others reached for sticks. A drain cover opened, spewing a tide of small bodies like rats. Pengali knives glittered. Jessica passed pearls into questing hands, and flung them into the seething mass of street fighting, as the tide of white uniforms receded.

The soldiers were retreating. *They were winning.*

She passed more pearls over the side, and more.

Under the trees at the side of the street, a number of soldiers regrouped. A commander shouted orders. One by one, the men turned to the wall, testing their weapons. Some were so badly damaged the arrows jammed in the slide. These, the soldiers flung aside, loosing batons from their belts. Accompanied by hoarse shouts, the men charged back into the crowd, swinging batons at the Pengali, knocking knives out hands. When one soldier went down with a throwing knife in his chest, two others sprang at the Pengali knife-thrower. Jessica hurled a pearl across the heads of the crowd, but it fell short of the mark. In the noise, she didn't even hear the Pengali's death scream.

More soldiers poured in from around the corner, outside the

range of the pearl-throwers. The first shot trailed through the air like a firecracker. It hit the ground and brought down half a dozen Pengali in an explosion of blue. The second one took the drummer in the chest. Jessica screamed and turned away, but the spray of blood hit her arms.

More soldiers streamed into the street until the Pengali were hemmed in by a sea of white uniforms.

Nowhere to go.

Still, the Pengali around the cart threw their pearls and Jessica passed them, while glass knives dripped with blood and bodies littered the pavement.

Then a scream rose next to the cart.

Light flashed on the curved surface of a charge gun. A gleam of reflection on a silver mane of hair.

Iztho, aiming his gun at the cart, his face hard and emotionless. Pengali pearl-throwers pushed away from him as his hand tightened around the release.

No!

Jessica scrambled up, but trying to get out of the tray was like walking on marbles. She slipped and fell hard amongst the by now crumpled flowers.

Her hand closed around a pearl to fling at his head, but he was quicker.

He yelled, "Stand back!" And fired the gun. A flash of blue hit the wheels. The undercarriage exploded in a shower of wood. The tray listed. Pearls rolled to one side, rumbling over the top of one another. Jessica threw herself to the higher side to stop it tipping, to no avail.

The cloth tore, and Jessica slid onto the pavement in a waterfall of glowing, radioactive caviar. Bouncing, crackling, releasing their charge into strands of blue lightning, which extended from the crippled cart to cover half the street.

Jessica scrambled to her feet, grabbed mental hold of as many of the strands as she could and screamed, "Please help! Anyone!" She guided the strands to anyone who responded: Ikay, the Amazons, and a warm presence all the way behind the soldier line.

Daya?

I'm here.

A web of lightning wove over the street, as a wave of panic struck her. They were using up their chance to get the Exchange working—

You must help me. Daya's mind voice cut into her thoughts. His mind link gripped her hard and pulled her into a vortex, a maelstrom of light that was so bright her eyes watered. She wanted to close her eyes, but that made no difference because the glow was inside her mind. Still, Daya pulled, his light a powerful presence.

Where are we? Although she recognised this stream of energy. The very first time she had seen Daya, she had experienced the maelstrom, too.

I am on the corner of the Barresh town square in front of the Exchange. You are in the middle of the fight.

Even without words or shared thoughts, Jessica knew what he wanted. The Exchange network used life energy; they could both sense and use life energy—he wanted to send some sort of signal through the network. That was how she had come in contact with him before . . . but those incidences had been mostly accidental . . . hadn't they?

A window opened in her vision, and then another one, and another.

A woman sat half-dozing before an instrument panel, staring out a window into a star-speckled sky.

A group of workers dressed in blue shared a joke in a hall where screens flickered and the hum of voices provided background to their laughter.

A man typed on a touch screen, his fingers fast like dancing spiders.

When Jessica was little and visiting her grandparents in the city, her grandfather had taken her to a shop where hundreds of television screens occupied the back wall. This was bit like that, only each screen displayed a different channel, representing a node in the Exchange network, and the maelstrom of light connected all of them.

How can we talk to those people?

We can't, or I don't know how to do it. Communication requires a two-way response, a second able mind. All we can do is upset the system, and hope someone traces the signal back to Barresh. Are you ready?

Jessica was dimly aware that she still stood in the street, and that all this took perhaps a fraction of a second. The pearls still crackled around her feet. She grabbed as many strands as she could reach.

I'm ready.

The lightning twisted into a rope, shot into the sky, sucked into the vortex.

In the world where it was night, the panel flashed, lights reflected in the window. The woman jolted from her doze. On a dozen screens before her, the same image was displayed: a violent street fight.

In the large hall, the workers stopped chatting. All stared at the screen wide-eyed, as a white-uniformed soldier slashed at a small figure. The image dissolved in snow. Beeping alarms went off, and people ran past.

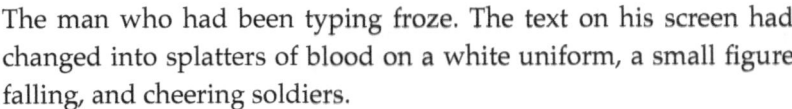

The man who had been typing froze. The text on his screen had changed into splatters of blood on a white uniform, a small figure falling, and cheering soldiers.

The world exploded in a flash of white. Men screamed. Bodies toppled. Lightning crackled. A whoosh of wind tore at hair and clothing. Jessica's consciousness returned to her body.

Then there was silence.

Jessica stumbled, black spots dancing before her eyes.

At her feet lay a body—the Pengali drummer, his face covered in blood and a hole torn through his chest. To her right, two females helped up a young male, trembling hands clutching his belly. Rivulets of blood pulsed down his fingers.

A wave of wild panic gripped her. There was no one she recognised, none of the people she had come to love. Iztho—where was Iztho?

Jessica whirled around to where she had last seen him.

He was still there; he lay on his belly, very still, his eyes closed, discharged pearls all around him, his hand draped over the gun. With sickening feeling, Jessica realised what he had done. A perfectionist, he wouldn't have carried a weapon unless he knew how to use it and if he had intended to kill her, he would never have missed at such close range.

He had known what she and the Pengali were trying to do by throwing the pearls, had seen the process was too slow and, while there was no time for words, had sped it up. He could easily have killed her had he wanted to, but instead he had saved her, and probably a lot of Pengali lives as well.

Had he paid the ultimate price?

He lay there so peacefully, as if he were asleep. Splatters of blood caked his hair and his cloak was wet. She brought a shivering hand to the soft skin of his neck. It was warm; a vein pulsed weakly. "Iztho, wake up." She stroked his cheek, and when he didn't react, pushed up his shoulder. "Iztho, please." He had to wake up; she had to get him off the ground, get someone to look after him. "Someone, please help me."

Three Mirani soldiers had come up behind her. One pointed a crossbow at her, blackened, the slide bent. Blood ran down his tunic from a gash in his cheek.

Jessica didn't think the weapon would still be effective, but he gestured with it, and she backed off.

"At least take him to a hospital," she said.

Two soldiers bent, not taking their attention from her. They grabbed Iztho under his arms and heaved him up. He mumbled some incoherent words, his eyes only half open. In this fashion, they dragged him off to where the soldiers were setting up a sick bay for the injured, who outnumbered the uninjured.

Jessica watched him disappear in the shadows. The last she saw of him was a glimpse of his silver hair. She couldn't do anything, wasn't sure she wanted to do anything. Maybe he spoke the truth, maybe he had been forced into bringing her and had fallen in love with her during the trek through the forest. Maybe he had wanted to take her somewhere else and start a new life, but on the other hand, he had lied to her about too much for too long. And she wasn't ready for what he wanted.

Maybe if times had been different . . .

30

A HUMID SQUALL of wind tore at Jessica's hair. It whipped up branches of the large trees around the square and sent a flurry of pink petals dancing between rows of soldiers. Mud or blood stained once-white uniforms. Many of the men nursed injuries, but they stood, silent as bowling pins, as the six blue-clad figures walked between them, stopping at the end of each row to type on their screens. The observers the Union had sent.

They were counting. Checking if their numbers matched those as approved by the Barresh council.

Seated on the fence, Jessica had counted them in two minutes.

There were twenty-five soldiers to a row, and there were twenty-five rows. Yet, the Union delegates scribbled their notes and conferred with each other.

Commander Nemedor Satarin, lips pressed in a thin line, stood at the gate to the airport, flanked by two high-ranking soldiers. Blue eyes staring into nothingness, he clutched a document to his chest, white-knuckled hands clenching and unclenching. His gaze avoided those of the Barresh council, the lines of council guards and the citizens of the city who had come out in their thousands.

Through the foliage of the red-flowered bushes that edged the airport Jessica could see the purple surface of Daya's aircraft. Two men in grey had taken off a side panel. He had damaged the engine by leaving from Miran without defrosting. All sorts of parts and tools lay spread out on blankets. Jessica wondered if this meant that Daya would leave soon; he was free to go after all. She wondered if he cared for the city and their kinship with the Pengali. Most of all, she wondered if he still cared for her; she missed his voice in her mind.

She couldn't believe he would give up so easily, but maybe he found her too hard to please. As a handsome and rich man, women would be throwing themselves at his feet. She already saw it each time one of Councillor Semisu's wives mentioned Daya; a dreamy, swooning look would come over her eyes, and Jessica would feel more lonely.

The place where Iztho's craft had stood was empty. Although gossip at Councillor Semisu's house told her that he had recovered enough to fly himself, Jessica had not seen him again. He had not even sent her a note of goodbye. She liked to think that he had been under strict supervision of the Mirani army and had not been allowed to contact her.

On the square, all Union observers had gathered in one spot. After some talk, the group moved towards the assembled councillors, the mediator woman from the council meeting in the lead. Her ponytail blew over her forehead as she bowed.

"I have here the results of our headcount. There are one thousand and twenty-one Mirani military personnel in Barresh. The contract you hold with Miran provides for three hundred and fifty troops. Under Union Law, you have a number of options: you could ratify the new contract and allow the men to stay. You could request that the extra troops leave. It is also your right to renegotiate your contract."

Commander Satarin inclined his head. "Miran has already ratified the contract. In addition, I would like to sit down and complete negotiations for our trade relations. Once Barresh is integrated in the Mirani agricultural cooperatives, benefits can flow into this city. But we will need to maintain our troops to protect the merchant class from the whims of the natives."

"Natives!" Sheida pushed himself through the crowd. No longer dressed in the insulting turquoise garb, he had gained in stature. Navy suited him.

"The natives are the majority of the population. We grow the things you want to sell. You negotiate with us. And we will not be mistreated."

Jisson Semisu added, "The Barresh council can't tolerate barbaric acts against any of the city's citizens. We are natives, too."

Commander Satarin eyed both men in a moment of silence. "If I'm hearing you correctly . . ." He licked his lips. "Losing the support of Miran would be very unwise. What do you think would be the viability of an entity the size of only a city, especially one dependent on us for services and export?"

The guards next to him tensed. Sweat pearling on his brow, Jisson Semisu glanced at the councillor next to him, who gave a tiny nod. "We are not part of Miran. We are independent. Some independent Traders have never deserted us, and more will come once we've upgraded the Exchange. We have people who are committed to the education of our citizens."

One of the guards reached for his crossbow, but Commander Satarin held him back with a hand gesture, directing a smile at the mediator. "Of course, Barresh has the right to decide."

"We do indeed. So here is what I do with our agreement." Councillor Semisu held the contract in front of him and ripped it in half. "I know Barresh has issues to be set straight, but when that is done, we will be applying for full Union membership. You will be welcome: as visiting foreign official." He ripped the card again and again and scattered the pieces on the wind. They fluttered through the air; one came to rest at Commander Satarin's feet.

He ignored it, his face still an unemotional mask. "Very well. It is your right. Don't expect it to solve any of your problems. Worse, we will be taking everything we have paid for." He gestured to his guards. "Evacuate." Then he turned on his heel.

Within moments, commands rang out over the square and the

population of Barresh watched, first open-mouthed, then in mounting disbelief, as line after line of soldiers marched through the gate.

They cheered and whistled, Pengali pulled out instruments and within moments, the square was awash with music.

Jessica stood amongst the councillors, the soft and squishy arm of a rotund councillor around her waist, the councillor's daughter's hand on her shoulder.

Merilon Damaru shook his head. "Do you really think they'll be gone forever?"

Councillor Semisu snorted. "Of course they won't. They'll make life as hard for us as they can."

Sunlight had turned orange and gilded the trees that half-covered the façade of the Barresh Exchange. The heaving mass of Pengali revellers had left for Far Atok and once again, the square lay deserted. For the first time in over three hundred years, no Mirani soldiers stood sentry at the airport.

Jessica sat on a bench under a tree, reluctant to go back to Councillor Semisu's house, reluctant to mingle with the crowd. She felt sick and dead tired, like she could sleep all day. Recover from all the emotions of the past few days and prepare to start studying for the Union citizenship.

A rustle of cloth sounded next to her.

Without a word, Daya came out from behind a tree and sat down on the bench. He sighed and sat in silence for a while longer. Finally, he said, "You've been busy."

That was true. In the morning, two keihu girls had come in, the first ones who wanted to be taught, but she didn't want to talk about that; she shrugged. "So have you."

He glanced at her and then looked away. "I'm sorry . . . I'm . . ."

"Sorry?"

"Well . . . I noticed . . . I heard that . . ." His gaze strayed to her stomach.

Disappointment flooded her. He knew, and she had wanted to tell him, and he didn't even seem happy. "I'm not sorry."

"But I shouldn't have treated you as I did. I hurt you, and that was never my intention. It was the smell—no, that sounds like I'm shifting the blame and I'm not . . ." He jumped up, clawing his hands at the sky. "I'm no good at this personal stuff."

"Daya, stop it. I said I'm not sorry and I mean it. A few days ago, I decided to have the baby. That was my decision. I'm happy with it." Her voice cracked as she added, "I don't want to be alone any more."

He averted his eyes, fiddled with the hem of his tunic. Jessica sent out a careful tendril of power, but it bounced.

Daya, please.

"I came for this." He pulled out a small box and pressed it in her hands. "You may have noticed I wasn't there for the counting. I would have liked to be there, but Jisson said, no he insisted, that I take time off from official things and do this first. Open it."

Jessica pulled the ribbon, wondering, dreading maybe, what she would find inside the box. She wasn't ready for another marriage proposal, and seeing the tenseness on Daya's face, it had to be something like that.

Her hands trembled. What would she say?

Was there a good way to tell him *I need more time?* A way that wouldn't hurt him and drive him away?

No, she knew. If he asked, there was only one thing she could say.

Yes. It had to be yes, because he was the father of her child, because no one else could be beside her when she wandered off to places no other person could go, but ultimately, because his smile warmed her heart.

She opened the lid . . . no wedding ring, or any piece of jewellery, just an oval device, made of gleaming metal, a few buttons on the side that faced her.

"What is this?"

Then she noticed the note tucked underneath it. Her hands

trembled when she unfolded it. "Number one, Sunset Street? What is there?"

He rose, a spring in his movements. "We will have to go and have a look then, shall we?" Puzzled, she followed him across the square, past the market stalls, and into the street that ran along the very edge of the island.

They stopped at a freshly painted gate. Jessica recognised the flower pattern in the wrought iron, even if she didn't recognise the yard. Someone had swept the path and removed all loose tiles, cleaned out the fountain, which once again twinkled with water. The old furniture had gone from the porch, including a solid wood door replacing the one that had fallen off its hinge. The old Pengali safe house.

Daya opened the gate, which no longer creaked. He took the box from her hand, passed her the device, pointing at the buttons. "Go on, press here."

Jessica pressed, and a flood of light came on. Under the porch, inside the rooms, in two lines along the path.

Jessica whispered, "Wow."

Slowly, she walked across the yard, past newly planted flowers, up the steps to the porch. The door clicked open. Late afternoon sunlight shone in through coloured glass in the ceiling, making coloured spots of light over the fountain in the hall. All cleaned-up, the place looked amazing.

Daya followed close behind. "This was all I could get done today. Most rooms are still a mess, but there's one room upstairs that's very comfortable. You should see the view. Much better than living with Councillor Semisu and his gossiping wives, I'd say. Look at the size of the hall. You could have your lessons here. There's also a perfect room for a library—"

She interrupted his nervous stream of words. "Daya."

He froze; his eyes met hers. "Go on, go inside. It's yours."

The whole house? "What about you?"

"Oh, I'll stay in town, at least for the time being. I'll live in a different part of the house, unless you don't want me here at all, which I could understand, but—"

She grabbed his hand. "Daya, stop it."

He eyed her, drops of sweat pearling on his upper lip, then he averted his gaze. *I'm no good at this.* "I can do all the arranging." He shrugged. "Buy you a house, arrange for the parts assembly to come here, talk to Union delegates, work for the council, but . . . up until I met you, I mean really met you, and we . . . I thought I knew everything. Now I realise I know nothing. I cannot expect you to share my ideals."

"But you still need me for the plan? You still want to resurrect our race?"

"Yes . . . no. Maybe there would be a keihu woman who has enough Aghyrian blood to cross with a zhadya-born man, but the other men are still in Miran and I need to think of a way to get them out . . . Yes, my plan needs you, but I'm not talking about that. I'm talking about you . . . me . . . us. I need you, too. I don't want to be alone. I had never envisaged our relationship like this —" His voice faltered. He took a deep, shuddering breath. Moisture glistening in his eyes.

You discovered you have feelings.

He looked away.

"Daya, listen. Of course you have feelings. We are to be parents. That is not something you do without having feelings. A child is not just some dot on a line in a breeding programme; it's a living being to love. This child will probably share our abilities. Do you think I'd want to cope alone with that? We don't want to abandon this child, like we've both been abandoned."

Then a silly thought struck her. *I guess I do want to be a breeding cow, with some provisos.* She did want to bring her race back, put back the pieces until they had enough genetic material for an Aghyrian settlement. A community of people who shared her ability and her looks.

Slowly, he unclenched his fists. He licked his lips.

Jessica pressed her hands together before her face and an instant later, let the light float into the air. It hovered before his face until Daya, too, made the light without even using his hands. The two lights frolicked around each other like a piece of firework.

Heat radiated from him into her, first a trickle, then a flood. Images of dark tunnels, of Jisson Semisu's face, all dirty, looking up at a drain cover from below. Then there was a bolt of jubilation *I've found her* and an image of herself, wide-eyed and frightened, emerging from a rubbish compartment, and herself staring up at him, running her hands over his back.

Whoa, stop. Not everything at the same time.

He withdrew his light and her vision cleared, but his warmth still surrounded her, caressed her like loving arms. His face was so close she could count his individual eyelashes. Then his arms were around her in soft warmth and he kissed her. She groaned softly, nestling in his arms, breathing his delicious scent. When he released her to catch his breath, she said, "Can I see the rest of our new house?"

A Word of Thanks

Thank you very much for reading *Watcher's Web*. The story is not finished here! I hope you will go on to read *Trader's Honour*, the second book in this series. (Turn the page to see a sample chapter.) Find out what deeper secret is responsible for Iztho Andrahar's betrayal and how a young Mirani woman gets horribly tangled up in this mess.

Buy Trader's Honour direct from the author, with delivery via Bookfunnel.

FROM: TRADER'S HONOUR

Chapter 1, Book 2 of *Return of the Aghyrians*

THE ENVELOPE LAY in the middle of the table, between the silver tableware and the gold-rimmed plates. A bowl with rolls of fish bread stood on one side, and a steaming terrine of bean soup on the other. Father, dressed in his Lawkeepers tunic, sat at his usual place at the head of the table, Mother on the other end and little Liseyo with her silken hair on Father's right hand side. Old Rosep stood at Mother's elbow while ladling soup into her plate and talking to her in a low voice.

All of them were looking at that envelope.

Mikandra hesitated in the doorway. Her face still glowed from having run from the hospital against the biting wind to be home in time for dinner. Father cast a Meaningful Glance at the envelope, and then met her eyes in that severe way of his that said *Young lady, I demand an explanation.*

Mother stopped talking to Rosep, and Rosep scurried out the room as fast as his sore knees and bowlegs allowed, shutting the door behind him with a soft snick. The fire popped.

"Good evening, Mother and Father." Mikandra sat down at her

regular spot at the table, facing Liseyo, who looked at her with large eyes.

Into the heavy silence, Mother said, importantly, "A Trader Guild courier brought this for you this morning."

Totally unnecessary. The envelope could have been anything if it wasn't so unforgivingly carmine red, and that colour meant only one thing: Trader Guild. And the Guild only ever used couriers to deliver these types of messages.

Mikandra licked her lips and, avoiding her father's penetrating gaze, picked the offending object off the table. The paper was heavy and smooth in her hands. It exuded a faint smell of ink, which was old-fashioned and classy all at once. A white label affixed to the front held her name, written by hand by the Guild's calligraphers in Coldi and Mirani script. Mikandra Bisumar. As if there was any doubt.

She clutched it on her knees, out of the reach of her parents' penetrating gazes, and met Liseyo's eyes, whose expression said, *Well, aren't you going to open it?*

Mikandra didn't want to, not here where her parents were watching her; not now, before she'd sorted out this part of her future, because certainly, the Trader Guild wouldn't use a courier if her application to the academy had been rejected, would they?

The thought filled her with panic. She hadn't expected a reply so quickly; she had expected a rejection, because almost everyone who didn't come from a Trading family got rejected, right? Because at night in bed, she'd been telling herself that she was full of stupid dreams to even have applied and that she should prepare herself to bandage frostbitten fingers in the hospital for the rest of her life. And if her dreams ever came true . . . well, didn't the older people say that dreams looked good when you were young, but seemed silly in a yeah-like-that-is-going-to-happen way when you were older?

Going to the academy had been such a silly dream, something she'd never seriously thought would happen, but now she had this letter and all of a sudden, the dream that had been her childhood wish became frighteningly *real*.

She didn't want to open the letter at the table while her family was watching.

But Father would never let her leave the room. He'd stop her before she could reach the door, grab her by the arm and lift her up so that her shoulder would be jammed up against her ear and then his fingers would dig into the soft flesh under her arm and he would demand that she show him the contents. She still had the bruises on her arm from last time he'd done that. That time it had been about her not wanting to audition for the boring classic theatre. This was worse. Much worse.

He said, in his hard and unforgiving voice, "Open it, daughter." In that unemotional tone that masked his worst kind of anger.

No choice then.

Mikandra turned the envelope over and prised her fingers under the seal. The waxy paper ripped. Her hands trembled and made sweat marks on the red paper.

Folded inside the envelope she found a cream-coloured sheet and some printed papers, all in the antiquated dialect of Coldi which was the official language of the Trader Guild.

She spotted the words *Registration details* at the top of one of the sheets.

Her heart thudded like crazy. The field of her vision narrowed while black spots danced in the edges. It was as she'd hoped, dreamed and feared.

The very large, looming, huge problem of course was that this response came before she'd worked up the nerve to tell her parents that she'd applied.

Trader's Honour is available on all book retailers.

ACKNOWLEDGMENTS

Before this book arrived at its finished state, many people have read and commented on it. I would especially like to thank my friends from the Online Writers Workshop for Science Fiction and Fantasy, and in particular Stelios Touchtidis, Sherry Thomas, Sue Curnow, Phill Berry and Linda Dicmanis.

ABOUT THE AUTHOR

Patty Jansen lives in Sydney, Australia, where she spends most of her time writing Science Fiction and Fantasy.

Her career started in earnest when her story *This Peaceful State of War* placed first in the second quarter of the Writers of the Future contest and was published in their 27th anthology. She has also sold fiction to genre magazines such as Analog Science Fiction and Fact, Redstone SF and Aurealis, before making the move to independent publishing.

Patty has written over fifty novels in both Science Fiction and Fantasy, including the *Icefire Trilogy* and the *Ambassador* series.

pattyjansen.com

BOOKS BY PATTY JANSEN

MORE INFORMATION:

PATTYJANSEN.COM

For a complete list of books, scan the image below with your phone.

www.ingramcontent.com/pod-product-compliance
Lightning Source LLC
Chambersburg PA
CBHW030627110726
47901CB00002B/346